The Bad Sister

Julie-Ann Corrigan was born in Mansfield, Nottingham-shire. She studied in London, completing a BA (Hons) Humanities degree, majoring in Modern History and English Literature. Travelling in Europe for several years, she taught in both Greece and Spain – countries and cultures she found fascinating. On return to the UK she gained a BSc (Physiotherapy), becoming a Chartered Physiotherapist. She lives in Berkshire with her family.

Also by J. A. Corrigan

The Nurse
The Bad Sister

*For more information about novels by J. A. Corrigan please
visit www.jacorrigan.com*

THE
BAD
SISTER

J. A. CORRIGAN

 CANELO

First published in the United Kingdom in 2022 by

Canelo
Unit 9, 5th Floor
Cargo Works, 1–2 Hatfields
London, SE1 9PG
United Kingdom

A CIP catalogue record for this book is available from the British Library.

Print ISBN 978 1 80032 377 3
Ebook ISBN 978 1 80032 376 6

Look for more great books at www.canelo.co

Printed and bound in Great Britain by Clays Ltd, Elcograf S.p.A.

1

For Rhiannon

And all the strong, vibrant, and clever women of the world

The man who lies to himself and listens to his own lie comes to such a pass that he cannot distinguish the truth within him, or around him

Fyodor Dostoevsky, *The Brothers Karamazov*

Prologue

She is able to tilt her head back; not much, but enough to catch the rustle of leaves on the old oak's thick gnarled branches. After only seconds the wind dies down, disappearing as quickly as it had vanished earlier. Her eyes move away from the tree and towards the sky, which is now a startling azure blue. Bright, and cloudless.

It is only the black shape of the bird circling above that spoils what she knows will be her end view of this world.

The scene she now inhabits, a place of serenity, is the last place she will ever be, and she admits there will only be three people who she'll truly miss. The tears on her cheeks are warm. She closes her eyes.

It had happened so quickly and taken her by surprise. The pain she'd felt in her chest, ribs and back was fleeting, almost as if it was happening to someone else. She manages to open her eyes again, looks up at the sky again, and studies the raven's outline. Ravens are... oh, so very elegant. She tracks the bird's circling movements above and it comes as a revelation that when death came, she would be so accepting of it. In the not so many years that she's been alive, she has always envisaged her own death as being painful, messy and tragic, but lying on her back and facing the beauty of the summer sky, hearing the gentle rush of the river, it isn't any of those things.

Once, she'd heard that drowning was one of the most euphoric ways to go, but she disagrees. Lying next to the old oak, the sun's rays on her skin, not being able to feel her body, takes the prize in the exhilarating death stakes. She wishes she could tell someone this.

Seventeen is too young to die, but then again she's been too young for a lot of the things she's done, and experienced.

She senses rather than sees one of those experiences standing close to her, watching her, doing nothing to help, and slowly, both confusion and incredulity fills her.

It isn't supposed to be like this.

A light pressure on her thigh as the fabric of her short skirt is smoothed, done as if with love. She isn't sure if it is the bird or a human touch.

And the young girl will never know.

1

Then
March 1991

Natalie

It was Saturday but Natalie had forgotten to turn off her alarm the night before and so awoke bang on six. Rolling out of bed, she drew the curtains, pushed the window open and a rush of cold air belted at her face. It was still dark, but because her stepfather always kept the outside security lights on, she could see the river was dangerously high. She leaned out further, the outline of Raven Island and the trees coming into a blurry focus. She shivered and banged the window closed, just as her family slammed shut any mention of the island and what had happened there.

Dom, her stepfather, planned to take them out on the motorboat later. It'd be fun, and her best friend was coming over too, so double fun. Fun was something in short supply at Raven House, and her friend's presence somehow deflected from the constant underlying strain.

Putting on a thick sweatshirt and socks, she picked up a pile of books and notepad off her desk, planning to make a start on a practice O-level English Lit essay that was due in on Monday. She was keen to do well in her exams, which kicked off in May.

Natalie tried to be quiet as she made her way downstairs so that no one would hear her. Sometimes she just needed a bit of time alone and it was only in the mornings that she could manage that.

She made some tea and sat down at the huge kitchen table.

'Natalie.'

She jumped. The tea inside the mug that she'd just put to her lips was now all over her sweatshirt. 'Bloody hell, Jess! You startled me.'

'Sorry. Can sit?'

Her youngest sister's usual staccato reply: no pronouns; it was as if she was saving superfluous words; a trait that had worsened in the last five years.

'You can sit with me if you're quiet.' She didn't know why she said that because Jess was always quiet.

Jess nodded and plonked herself down, placing the book she had tucked underneath her arm on the enormous table.

Natalie peered at it. 'That looks a bit heavy for a twelve-year-old.'

The Nurture Assumption: Why Children Turn Out the Way They Do.

Jess didn't respond but she often didn't. Natalie would have been surprised if she had. 'Jess, answer me.'

'Said keep quiet.'

'I didn't mean it literally. You have to stop taking everything literally. It's a bit wearing.'

Jess nodded.

'Honestly, you are a bit young for that stuff.' Natalie inclined her head at the book.

Jess looked up and half smiled.

Her little sister never took her the wrong way and Natalie punched her playfully on the arm. She didn't mind her being there. Jess was a bit odd, but she loved her. And with that thought, Eva appeared. Eva was their mum, but all her children called her Eva.

Natalie checked the huge designer clock ticking away on the wall, wondering if it had stopped sometime last night around seven p.m. No one ever saw Eva this early. She was definitely looking the worse for wear. Despite the fortune she spent at the exclusive beauty clinic in the next town, her jowls sagged and her hair lay limply on her over-red cheeks. She looked as if she hadn't slept at all, and she probably hadn't much, because last night Natalie had spotted Eva's dealer standing at the side door that led into the double integrated garage.

It had been her stepfather who'd gone to sort it out.

She wondered if her older sister knew about Eva and Dom's ramping up of the drug usage; Natalie suspected she didn't. Her sister was smart but things passed her by; too wrapped up in her own life at university, and ambitions. And more so since Eva had stopped getting up early.

Eva made her way straight to the sink, picked up a glass from the draining board, filled it, and slugged it back. She then turned to survey her two youngest daughters.

'Rough night?' Natalie said, and straight away wished she'd kept her mouth shut.

Ignoring Natalie's comment Eva walked over to Jess, who didn't even look up.

Look up, Jess. Please.

'What crap is this?' Eva asked.

Jess didn't take her eyes away from the book. 'Reading.'

Eva snatched it from her, turned it over and scanned the back cover. 'You looking for answers? Maybe, young lady, if you learnt to talk properly and interact with the world you wouldn't need to read this garbage.' She threw the book onto the table.

'Eva…'

'Let your sister answer for herself, Natalie.'

Jess looked up then, her expression set in a mask of… was it disdain? Fear? For moments Natalie saw both, mixed strongly with true sadness. 'Safer not to talk,' Jess said finally.

Eva was in a foul mood that morning, although she'd been in a foul mood for five years, longer. But what about them? It was as bad for them, and in many ways, worse.

'Christ.' Eva turned on her heel, picked up the water and made her way back upstairs.

'It's okay, Jess,' Natalie said, stroking her sister's head.

'Will be one day.'

'Eva doesn't mean to be horrible. You know what she's like. All growl and no bite.'

'Know.'

'Come on, let's make waffles and then go down and sit on the bench by the river.' She'd do her essay tomorrow. 'Dom's taking us all out in the boat later. You'll like that, yes?'

'Dom took me on boat yesterday. Went Raven Island.'

'You went to the island?' It was an unsaid rule that none of the sisters went to Raven Island. *Bloody Dom.* Immediately her fingers moved towards her scalp.

'Do not itch, Natalie.'

'Oh, Jess.'

Jess peered up at her; her blonde fringe really needed cutting. Eva was so useless at organising stuff for her.

'He took you after school?' she carried on.

'No. Did not go to school. Felt ill. Stomach ache.'

'Then Dom took you out on the boat? God, he's such a tool.'

Jess's forehead furrowed.

'It means stupid, Jess.' She still didn't think Jess understood. So clever but so not focused on the here and now, the small unimportant things.

Their stepfather took Jess to school most mornings when Eva couldn't be bothered to, which was most mornings. Although yesterday Eva had been up reasonably early to make the meeting she had with her accountant. Natalie had a creeping respect for Eva's accountant, who always scheduled their meetings for nine in the morning. What a man. Eva never missed those meetings, as they were connected to her inheritance money and its management.

'Came home,' Jess finally replied. 'Eva out.'

'And Dom took you to Raven Island?'

She remained silent. Jess was super-bright but Dom should not be encouraging her to skip school, although she knew her sister was bored in classes. Everything they taught her, Jess already knew.

Natalie pushed it. 'Why did he take you to the island?'

Jess shrugged.

'Why, Jess?' A horrible foreboding washed through her. So much on the TV about… although, no, Dom was many things but he wasn't a paedo. 'Tell me or I won't let you stay with me in the kitchen.' She hated doing the bribery thing but it always worked.

'To talk.'

'About what?'

'Nothing.' Jess rubbed her temples.

'Jess?' Natalie pushed.

Jess shrugged. 'Who'll be here today?' she asked instead.

'Your big sis and her new boyfriend. My mate, some others, I think.'

Natalie made the waffles. Jess had many problems but eating wasn't one of them. She looked on as Jess wolfed down four. Straight afterwards she disappeared to the toilet. Fifteen minutes later they were sitting on the bench at the bottom of the garden overlooking the river. Jess did look a bit ill. Maybe she had had an upset stomach, and that was why Dom had brought her home yesterday. God knows why he took her out on the boat, to the island. Eva would go nuts if she found out.

Jess was quiet. The oaks and willows surrounding them became animated as their branches swayed violently in a gathering storm. Natalie ripped her eyes away, rested them momentarily on Raven Island and wished – not for the first time – that every single one of the trees had been felled and burned. That had been Eva's plan, but the trees were under a conservation order. They were all stuck with the daily reminder.

She scratched at her scalp, her agitation creeping, building, and indefinable.

2

Teresa

'Sorry you have to do this,' Teresa said.

Luke turned to her at the same time he turned on the ignition. 'Do what?'

'Meet my family.'

He swerved out of their precious Primrose Hill parking space. 'I'm looking forward to finally meeting your mum and Dom. And I'm sure they're not as bad as you make out.'

'Whatever you do, don't refer to Eva as "Mum", okay?'

He rolled his eyes. 'I know.'

'I'd rather we were going to see your mum,' she said, folding her arms.

'Don't act petulantly. It doesn't become you. Anyway, we only saw her last weekend.'

'I know, but you know what I mean.'

'I don't really know what you mean. I want to meet your family, your two sisters… and it's good to get out of London. The past week at the hospital's been a bastard.'

'You work so hard.'

He put his hand on her lap. 'Chill out. You're a bit diamond shoe-ish, you know.'

'What's that supposed to mean?'

'You know what it means. You have a good life, but think you don't.'

'I do have a good life but only because you're in it.'

Teresa had known Luke for eighteen months and in that time she'd managed to totally evade the subject of her past; the most important things about her past, anyway. As was Luke's way, he waited patiently for her to open up. And maybe one day soon she would, and today might be the catalyst. Him meeting Eva and Dom, Natalie and Jessica, although she knew there would be nothing in the house that would force her hand into baring her soul. Eva had ensured there were no memories of their sister. It was weird, the way she dealt with it. But the memories were there, in nature, in the outside; sometimes Teresa felt as if the outside air was laden with them. She'd been so relieved to get to university.

She glanced at her boyfriend. She couldn't keep her family under wraps forever, although she'd tried; she hadn't wanted the hassle of them fogging up her mental space as she navigated the final term of her degree, and being with Luke.

'Shall we pick up some flowers for Eva?' he asked.

'She won't appreciate the gesture.'

'Any other ideas what we can get for her, and Dom?'

Teresa didn't share with him that the only thing Eva might appreciate would be a kilo of cannabis. 'Flowers'll be fine. Stop off at Tesco and I'll pop in to get a bunch.'

He smiled, taking the red baseball cap that she despised from the glove compartment and ramming it on his head. 'Okay.'

An hour later, Teresa and Luke pulled up to the grand drive of her childhood home.

'Wow.'

'You impressed?'

'I am a bit. Great setting. A house like this must have a name as opposed to a number...'

'Raven House. Something to do with the ravens that we never see.'

He wound down the car window, and she watched as he took in the gentle curve of the Thames. 'Are people allowed on that little island?'

'That's called Raven Island, although I've never seen any ravens on there, like I said. No one goes to the island...'

'Looks like you can easily get to it if your stepdad has a boat—'

'He does have a boat. Two, in fact, and a rowing boat. We'll be going out on the river later, I'm sure. It's a Keane family thing.'

'So we can go to the island?'

'No, Luke, we can't.'

He shrugged. 'Looks as if we have a welcome committee.'

Teresa followed his gaze. 'That's our housekeeper, Mrs A, and my youngest sister—'

'Jessica? She's not at all like you described her.'

'How did I describe her?' she asked.

'You said she was odd. Looks pretty normal to me. Healthy. She's tall for twelve. Looks very sporty.'

'She's nearly thirteen.' Teresa got out the car to greet Mrs A, who she adored. All the Keane sisters loved Mrs A. Luke quickly got out the driver's side.

The elderly woman's hand was awkwardly resting on Jessica's shoulder; Jessica was a good two inches taller. 'Lovely to see you, Teresa!' Mrs A moved her eyes to Luke. 'You must be Teresa's beau?'

'Mrs A,' Teresa said, smiling, 'I don't think that word has been used for centuries!' She noticed Mrs A had her big bag with her. It looked as if she were clocking off for the day. 'Aren't you staying?'

Mrs A took her arm away from Jessica's shoulder. 'No, I'm afraid not. I'm off to see my brother.' She looked at her watch. 'Must dash or I'll miss the bus.'

Luke stepped closer to Mrs A. 'Do you need a lift to the bus stop?'

'Very considerate of you, but no, it's only around the corner.' Mrs A offered a handshake.

'Great to meet you… Mrs A,' he said, shaking with vigour.

'And lovely to meet you too, Luke.' Mrs A turned to Jessica. 'See you tomorrow, young lady, and be a good girl for Eva.' And hitching her enormous bag onto her shoulder she left.

Teresa turned to her youngest sister, who had not yet said a word. 'Hi, Jessica.'

'Hello,' Jessica said.

'Jessica, this is Luke.'

Jessica avoided eye contact, looking at the ground instead. 'Dom says, a doctor. Do doctors wear those?' She pointed to Luke's baseball cap.

'I am a doctor. And doctors do wear baseball caps when they're not at work. Nice to meet you, Jessica.' He held out his hand, which of course Jessica didn't touch. Christ, this was going to be a long day. 'What do you want to be when you grow up, Jessica?' Luke carried on.

'Brain doctor.'

'You mean a psychologist?' he asked softly.

'No.'

'Brain surgeon?'

'No. Psychiatrist.'

'Ah. Well, I think that's a great ambition.'

Jessica didn't answer.

'Everyone in the house?' Teresa asked her sister.

Jessica nodded.

'Come on, Luke,' she said. 'Let's enter the lions' den.'

Jessica said, her voice a whisper, 'Going on boat.'

'Weather's a bit shite for the boating today.' And it was – the sky an aubergine-black canopy.

'Natalie waiting. With Juno.'

God, not Juno too, Natalie's best mate. A really long day. 'Come on, then, we'd better make an appearance,' Teresa said. 'Why don't you take Luke inside, Jessica?' To Luke she said, 'I'll sort out the flowers and booze.' She'd picked up a bottle of what she knew was Dom's favourite wine: a South African Pinot Noir – Storm Ignis. She couldn't believe it when she saw the bottle on a Tesco's shelf.

Luke went to take Jessica's hand. She flinched away.

Teresa looked at him and shrugged. 'Jessica doesn't like to be touched that much. You'll get used to it.'

'I'm sorry,' he said to Jessica.

It was Jessica's turn to shrug then. 'Wish Teresa alone.'

Jessica seemed more introverted and monosyllabic than usual, and a shimmer of older sister concern rippled through her, which she attempted to shake off. She could not become embroiled in her family's dynamics. Anyway, Natalie was around and she took care of Jessica. Natalie had to be good for something.

Teresa sighed as she watched Luke and Jessica walk into the house.

A really, really long day.

3

Teresa

The weather had done a U-turn and the dull morning had turned into a dazzling and bright afternoon. Perfect weather to go out on the river, which was fine by Teresa because Eva wouldn't be going anywhere near a boat or the river, and so she wouldn't have to put up with her. Eva was terrified of the water and she couldn't drive a boat. It was the reason why five years before it had been Jessica who'd gone to the island. No seven-year-old should have had to go through that. Teresa had always held muffled reservations about the accident that had changed her and her sisters' lives. Yes, her sister had been acting strangely in the weeks leading up to the accident, but as the years had passed she'd begun to think her memories of that summer were misplaced, or distorted. The thought of her tree-climbing twin sister, her soulmate, brought the threat of tears. Teresa swallowed the threat away.

They'd been there an hour when they sat down for lunch at just after one. Mrs A had obviously been busy before leaving: the table was laden, and included her very best triple chocolate cake. It was almost worth being there. Almost. She really wished Mrs A hadn't left.

Teresa laid her hand on Luke's lap – he was sitting on her left – and at the same time took in the people sitting at the table.

To his left was Juno, Natalie's limpet friend, who was dressed as inappropriately as ever. She wore a jumper so thin that Teresa wondered how she wasn't shivering in the chilly space. Heating the massive house they'd all grown up in had never been on Eva's list of priorities – and this was borne out when Teresa surveyed the rest of her family's attire: all of them wisely layered in ways that wouldn't be out of place in a Siberian hut. Her eyes dropped to Juno's skirt, which barely covered her crotch, and again a prick of grief shot through her. *Just no, not today. Stop thinking of her today.* But Natalie's best friend reminded her so much of her sister. When Natalie had first brought Juno to Raven House, Teresa was certain it wasn't only her who saw the similarity in both personality, and looks. Jessica saw the resemblance too and that was probably why she liked Juno so much.

Sitting next to Juno was Natalie who, as usual, was looking grumpy and unkempt. They'd hardly said a word to each other, and Natalie, hardly a word to Luke. He'd persevered though, until finally her rude sister had entered into some conversation.

Juno had been a different matter altogether. From the moment they'd walked into the sky-lit hallway, Juno was on it, and on Luke. Teresa sometimes failed to register that Juno was the same age as Natalie. So self-assured and confident. She was totally at ease with her long legs, microscopic waist and Bardot lips. Juno was classic jailbait. No one else seemed to notice her antics though, and so Teresa decided to give up and go with the flow. She trusted Luke implicitly.

Teresa carried on studying the menagerie that was her family. Next to Natalie was Jessica, who'd not said a word since meeting them outside. And next to Jessica was Eva.

Teresa couldn't work out if Eva liked Luke or not, but then she did appear a bit high. It wasn't even close to the evening. She must be starting earlier.

Perched next to Eva was Dom. *Perched* was just the right word to use when talking about her stepfather; he always looked as if he were about to up and leave, as if he weren't a permanent fixture. It surprised her that he was still around, because what man would willingly stay with Eva? But maybe she was just hard-wired in this thought.

It was the money. Dom had his own business, he made a living, but it was Eva who kept him in the way in which not only had he become accustomed, but also a way in which he wanted to remain accustomed.

Dom was both innocuous and useless, but it was in Eva's nature to not live alone and Dom was as good as any to fill the vacancy. He was harmless enough, and he took care of Jessica, after a fashion. Did her mother love the man she was married to? Teresa could never quite be sure. Did Eva still play around? Teresa wasn't quite sure about that, either. She suspected not, and anyway, Dom didn't have a brother so history couldn't repeat itself too precisely.

Finally her line of vision tracked towards Dom's best friend, and his wife. She'd never been sure about him but liked his wife, who was a primary school teacher. Luke had immediately hit it off with both.

She felt the warmth of Luke's hand on her knee. Christ, she could do with a shag to release some of the tension, and was already looking forward to getting in the car and going home, and to bed.

A shaving of guilt slid through her as her gaze rested again on Jessica. She really had worsened while she'd been at university. She should do something – talk to Eva, even

Dom, but her own life took priority. It had to. She had to get away from this crap. And intended to. Already had.

'So, Dom,' she said now, 'are we going to initiate Luke into the Keane family winter boat outing tradition?'

Dom scraped back his chair and leant backwards, lifted his arms and clasped his hands behind his head, which held a full scalp of shiny black hair, short but with a long fringe that he was always flicking away from his face. 'Yep, I got the boat ready this morning. She's fit to go.' His eyes roamed around the table, his eyelids fluttering open and closing rapidly, like an amphibian's. 'I've already instructed Juno in the finer workings of a motorboat. She's taking the helm, aren't you, Juno?' He turned to her.

'I'd love that,' Juno replied. Her voice held a hint of the teenage seductress.

Did she never stop?

Dom smiled like a schoolboy at Juno, but said to Eva, 'You coming too?'

Eva was reaching across the table to put another mound of Mrs A's wonderful and calorie-laden Russian salad onto her plate. As she did so, two protesting buttons of her over-the-top ruffled white blouse popped open, revealing a black bra and too much flesh. No one dared tell her and Teresa had to stifle a smile.

Blissfully unaware, Eva said, 'You know I won't be seen dead on a boat, or on the river.' She stared at her plate. 'The island is out of bounds.'

'Yep, we know, Eva.' Dom allowed the front two legs of the kitchen chair to touch the ground and looked at Jessica, who was staring at the untouched Russian salad on her plate. That was unusual for Jessica. Teresa had no idea where her little sister put all the food she ate – and supposed she must be happier than she looked. 'You're joining us too, Jess?' he finished.

As usual Jessica didn't reply, only nodding.

Dom leant forward and rubbed Jessica's knee, while Eva got up and began clearing the plates. For the first time since they'd all sat down, Teresa felt Jessica's eyes on her. About to smile, she turned to her, and for a slice in time her sister looked absolutely terrified. Teresa's smile didn't come. She got up too and went to stand behind Jessica's chair, catching Natalie's eye as she did so. 'You okay, Jessica?' she asked, ruffling her little sister's hair.

Jessica slowly nodded.

Natalie, who'd been remarkably quiet throughout lunch, spoke. 'Dom, was Jess ill yesterday?'

'Why you asking me?' he replied. 'Ask Jess.'

'Jess said you brought her back from school,' Natalie said.

'She did feel a bit unwell, so yes, I did bring her home,' Dom mumbled.

'What was wrong with you, Jess?' Natalie asked.

'Stomach ache, told you—'

'It's all that food you pack away,' Eva interjected, as she rattled the plates.

Ignoring Eva, Natalie said to Dom: 'Probably wasn't the best move to take her on the boat, then?'

'I didn't take Jess on the boat.' He raked back oil-slicked hair.

'I thought you said Dom took you on the river?' Natalie asked Jessica.

Teresa took a sideways glance at Natalie, who was not letting this go, and then turned and watched for Jessica's response. Jessica didn't reply to Natalie, shuffling uncomfortably in her chair instead.

'I'm going upstairs for a nap,' Eva said. 'You're all too exhausting.'

Natalie lifted her eyes upward in exasperation then, and for a fleeting moment of sisterly solidarity, Teresa had the idea that they should make up.

'Teresa is exhausting,' Natalie said. Juno giggled. And Teresa's moment of madness about making up with Natalie was short-lived.

Natalie continued, saying to Dom, 'Jess says you both went to the island?'

'Jess is getting mixed up,' he replied. 'We didn't go out on the boat... did we, Jess?'

Jessica stared at her plate and shrugged.

'Right then,' Juno interjected. 'Shall we get out of here, people? It's a gorgeous day.' She walked over to Jessica's chair and ran her hand through the younger girl's hair; finally, and for the first time since they'd sat down, Jessica smiled. 'That's more like it,' Juno finished.

–

Later, and much later than Teresa had wanted, she and Luke were sitting in the lounge with Natalie and Juno, although they were making moves to leave. Eva hadn't reappeared, whilst Dom, his mate and wife had absconded to the pub. Jessica had disappeared to her bedroom.

'I'm going to go have a word with Eva,' Teresa said.

Natalie glanced up from the magazine she and Juno were flipping through together. 'What about?'

'About Jessica.'

'Good idea,' Natalie replied.

'I think so too,' Juno said. 'Poor Jess.'

'Jess's got nothing to do with you,' Teresa retorted, taking a sideways glance at Natalie. She bet Natalie talked to Juno about the thing that the three sisters never talked about together, which had the effect of making her like Juno even less, if that were possible.

'Teresa,' Natalie said. 'Give it a break.'

Teresa glanced at Luke who was gazing at Juno. *Bloody hell*.

Natalie carried on, 'Jessica *did* tell me Dom took her to Raven Island.'

Teresa nodded but said nothing. Turning, she made her way upstairs. Lightly, she knocked on Eva and Dom's bedroom door.

'Door's open, Teresa.'

She stepped inside. The doors to the Juliet balcony were wide open; it was absolutely freezing but the influx of winter air didn't disguise the heavy, sweet smell. 'How did you know it was me?'

'Your other sisters don't bother.'

'To knock, or come to your bedroom?'

'The latter.'

'It's hardly surprising, is it? Especially Jessica. You have to take a firmer hand.'

'Don't start preaching.'

Teresa walked over to the balcony and closed the doors. When she turned around Eva was sitting propped up in bed, her carved wooden box of spliff-rolling paraphernalia next to her. 'Aren't you getting a bit old for that?' She pointed to the box. 'Dom shouldn't be encouraging you.' She fixed her gaze on Eva. 'He's younger than you, it doesn't affect him so much… although it would be good to see you both tone down the drugs… taking them doesn't make things better.'

'No, it doesn't. Taking them won't bring my daughter back, I know that. But, please, stop lecturing me, as well as preaching. I pay for your education, your life. Seems you have a nice life with Luke. I've given you everything… whilst everything's been taken from me.'

Teresa sat down on the edge of the bed, about to attempt to make physical contact with her mother, but couldn't quite manage it. Eva didn't seem to comprehend that losing her sister had changed Teresa's life forever. Or maybe she just didn't care. Instead of talking about her sister, which they never did, and which Teresa recognised was half the problem, she said instead: 'You need to do something about Jessica. She needs some help… has done since—'

Eva held up her hands, indicating she didn't want to hear more. 'She needs to join the human race.'

'She shouldn't be missing school… Dom shouldn't be encouraging her.' Teresa paused. 'Maybe she shouldn't be spending so much time with Dom.' Should she mention Jessica and Dom's supposed visit to the island?

'What's that supposed to mean?' Eva said.

'You should be encouraging her to make friends in her own age group.'

'Can you hear yourself?' Eva began rolling a joint. 'You and your sisters have ruined my life.'

'I think you should invert that statement,' she said, her voice a whisper.

'Who do you think you are?' Eva rasped. 'If you remember, it was Natalie who ruined *your* life. I made the most of the fallout from what she did.'

Teresa paced to the balcony again and opened the doors, allowing in the cold air. 'It really does stink in here. Natalie was six. She walked in on you because you're so bloody indiscreet.' She took a breath. 'I mean it, Eva, do something about Jessica… she's still traumatised from…

Dom still lets her drive the motorboat… encourages her to do things that a girl her age shouldn't be doing.'

Eva stared at her. 'Is it serious with Luke?'

'Very.'

'You're set up then.'

'I'm glad you've asked me about my course and how it's going.'

'I'm sure your life is all going fine.'

'Will you spend more time with Jessica? Please? Talk to her… take an interest in her life. Go to her sports events… don't leave it all to Dom.' Teresa swallowed. 'Be a bit more observant…' She wasn't sure what she was trying to say; she wasn't really sure what Natalie had been trying to achieve earlier in her questioning of Dom, and, for sure, she was not going to ask her sister. 'Thanks for lunch. Tell Mrs A it was great.'

And with that, she turned on her heel and left. Walking by Jessica's bedroom, she slowed and stopped. Finally, steeling herself, she knocked on her little sister's door.

–

'I'll drive,' Teresa said, getting into the driver's side.

'You sure?' Luke replied.

'Yes, it'll relax me.'

'I thought it'd gone okay.' Luke got in the passenger seat and pulled his mobile from his pocket, checking for anything urgent from the hospital. She knew he'd operated on a severely injured driver from a car crash the night before.

She flicked on the headlights as she pulled out onto the road. Luke had the capacity to be wonderfully unaware of what was going on around him in the world outside

23

the hospital. Her mind went back to Jessica. Her questioning of her little sister had been clumsy, mainly because she didn't really know what she was questioning her about. But it was strange that Dom had taken her to the island. He never normally went against Eva's 'laws' – none of them did, in reality. Not the three remaining sisters anyway. Why had he taken Jessica there? She was still none the wiser about that alleged incident, although Jessica had told her that she'd overheard the argument between her and Natalie the previous summer about their real dad.

Shit. That was not good. Jessica now knew why the father she couldn't remember had left them. It was too much for Jessica, on top of everything else.

Teresa accepted it didn't help that she never talked about their sister, but she just couldn't. Natalie did get on her nerves, although she believed her when she'd said Jessica had told her that Dom had taken her to the island. What an absolute twat he was. She should have confronted him.

'The lights are green, Teresa,' Luke said, dragging her away from places that not only did she not want to go to, she did not have time to go to. He carried on: 'Eva mentioned that she'd like to throw a party for you in the summer, August time, to celebrate you finishing your degree.'

She almost stalled the car. 'Really?'

'Yes, really. Why so surprised?'

'No reason. No reason at all.'

4

Jessica

Juno, Luke and her sisters were in the lounge warming up after being on the river. Dom, his friend and wife had gone out. Eva was still upstairs.

Jessica was in the kitchen, keeping out of everyone's way. She hovered around the table, eyeing up the leftover chocolate cake. Picking up Mrs A's special cake knife, she slid it underneath the cut piece. She managed to shovel most of it inside her mouth in one pleasing go. In the quietened kitchen she tried to put some sort of structure on the day's events. The conversation between her two sisters and Dom had made her feel odd. She couldn't tell them why Dom had taken her to the island. Ever. Not speaking was the last weapon she possessed. And she could not say a thing because if she did, Eva would blame her, just as she had blamed Natalie.

She finished off another piece of cake and, taking Eva's lead, made her way to her bedroom. Back to her head. Away from inside her own. She sat down and dragged her phrenology head across the desk towards her. She stroked the porcelain smoothness. Dom had bought it for her on her last birthday. Giving her the head was a nice thing of Dom to do. Dom did do nice things for her. He took her to the sports meets, helped with her football and rowing techniques. There were two sides to Dom. He was a little like the phrenology head.

Outside her bedroom someone was coming up the spiral staircase. She heard loud knocking, although not on her door, but on Eva's. Then Teresa's voice. She got up from her desk and opened her own door to see Teresa slipping inside Eva's bedroom, hearing their raised voices soon afterwards. Teresa had been home for less than a day and it hadn't taken long for the arguments to begin. But Eva had seemed to like Luke. Jessica didn't like him, even though he was a doctor. Teresa would never come home again now, not properly, not for good. Luke's fault. Her two older sisters would never make up, and soon Natalie would be leaving too – she was always talking about it. She would then be in the house, alone, with her secret.

She closed her door. Turned. Looked at the head, and then quietly opened her bedroom door again and padded to the bathroom. Turning the key and locking herself in she took the seven large steps to the toilet. She always counted them. She knelt beside the pan and with expertise cemented her fore and middle finger together and placed them down her throat. She completed her task quickly.

Why had she told Dom after all this time? Because she could not keep her secret in, any longer. She'd told him on the way to school. He'd stopped the car straight away, stalling it, and had turned around and taken her home, knowing Eva would be out all morning with her accountant. Then, he'd taken her to Raven Island. Said it would be good for her. And that is where they had talked.

She wiped her mouth with loo paper and threw it in the toilet and flushed.

Ten minutes later she was back in her room and sitting on her bed, her head tilted to one side, looking through her window and trying to will her stomach to settle, when she heard a knock on her door.

'Hi, Jess. It's only me.'

Her big sister walked nearer to her bed. Standing next to her, Teresa shifted her weight from one foot to the other. When had Teresa stopped talking to her? After her argument with Natalie? When she'd met the man downstairs, Luke? No, before. When Eva had changed forever. When the Keane sisters had broken. When the Keane family had broken.

Teresa carried on, glancing at her duvet. 'I can't believe you still have your Indiana Jones cover.' Teresa laughed then. She loved it when Teresa laughed. She loved Teresa.

'Like him.'

Finally Teresa sat on the edge of her bed. 'You do look a bit peaky. You did pack away a fair amount of lunch, and then the trip on the boat. My stomach was heaving a bit.' Teresa touched her thigh. 'Look, Jess, I'm sorry if I don't see much of you. I'm going to try and come home more—'

'Better without Luke.'

'I love him,' her big sister replied.

'Miss you.'

'Jess...' Teresa said. 'Did Dom bring you home yesterday because you were ill?'

'Yes.'

'And did he take you on the boat? Did you go to Raven Island?'

Teresa was waiting, and she saw the little frown that always appeared on her sister's forehead when she was trying to work something out. She could not allow Teresa to work anything out. Because it would all go wrong again. 'I heard you and Natalie arguing,' she said, finally.

'Today? We haven't argued today... only the usual.' Teresa grinned.

'Before. About Dad. Our dad. Why he left. Natalie told him about Eva... and his brother. Eva with his brother.'

'Aw, God, Jess... have you been stewing on this? That was last summer when me and Natalie argued... about the dad thing.'

'Why our dad left me. You. Natalie. All of us.' She studied her older sister. 'Cannot happen again. Do not want Dom to leave too.' She did not want Dom to leave because then Teresa and Natalie would argue again and it would all be even worse than it already was.

'Aw, Jess. Dom's not leaving... and you weren't meant to hear that... me and Natalie arguing.'

'But did.' She fixed her gaze on Teresa.

'It's all in the past now,' Teresa said, pulling Jessica into her arms. Teresa hadn't cuddled her for such a long time.

'You hate Natalie.'

'No, I don't.' Teresa got up and suddenly started acting more like Teresa. '*Did* Dom take you to Raven Island, Jess?'

'No.'

Teresa nodded. 'Okay. Okay. Look, Luke and I are going now... it's been lovely to see you... and see you soon, okay?'

'Okay.'

'Talk to Natalie if you need to talk, promise me?'

'Will.' She could not talk to Natalie, or Teresa. She could never tell them. Jessica could not talk to anyone and it was why she did not talk very much. Dom had told her not to talk, too. Said it would upset Eva. And it wouldn't change what had already happened. Said he'd have to leave if she said anything.

She carried on, feeling brave. 'Why you, Natalie and Eva not ever talk about our sister?'

'What happened wasn't your fault, Jessica.' Teresa was now standing by her bedroom door. 'She fell from the tree. It was an accident. No one could do anything, because she was alone on the island.'

It was not her fault but it felt like it was.

5

Now

Natalie

Natalie's mobile begins to vibrate and jump across her desk like a thing alive. She goes to grab it and sees her hand shaking at the anticipation that her daughter might not have pulled it off. She stares at Hope's name on the screen. A lot is riding on her degree results.

'Mum!'

'And?' she says.

'A First. I can't believe it!'

Her whole body sags in relief, remembering the car crash of her A levels in the summer of 1993 when she'd been more than grateful for the University of Humberside's offer to study English. 'Oh, Hope, and Leeds is a great university to get it from too! I knew you'd do it.'

'I'm so pleased.'

'I know—'

'Mum, Teresa and Matt are taking me out tonight, for dinner, to celebrate.'

Her daughter had called her sister first. What is it that she feels? Anger, envy, annoyance? None of these three emotions. Even these many years later, it is guilt.

'That's nice of them,' she replies.

'Teresa invited me yesterday, Mum. She said we'd either celebrate or commiserate. I haven't told her about my results yet. She's invited one of her barrister buddies who specialises in human rights law – she lives in Geneva but she's staying with Aunt Teresa for a week. Teresa said it would be good for me to talk with her, you know, because that's the area of law I want to specialise in… human rights law…' Her voice trails off.

'Hope, it's fine. I'm glad… glad you'll be with family.'

'I love you, Mum, and Dad too. I've booked my bus ticket for this Saturday so we can celebrate properly, but I'll be coming back up because of my job—'

'That's fine too.' Hope has managed to find a nice little job in a local boutique. She loves it, and gets 50 per cent off the clothes too. 'I thought you might like to go into London, the theatre, then Five Guys?'

'Mum, I miss you.'

'I know.'

'One more thing,' Hope says. Natalie waits, and something tells her to grip the edge of the desk. 'I'd really like it if the whole family could get together to celebrate my results.' She clears her throat. '*Everyone*… this once?'

What to say?

There is only one thing she can say. 'Sounds like a good idea.' Her daughter knows about what happened, and Natalie knows she's googled it too, but this is one thing that she has not talked about with Hope. She wants to ask her daughter how she really feels but can't. It's a sleeping monster.

'Would you like to have a party here, at home?' she says finally.

'I've been thinking about it and think it'd be nice to have it up here. You know, we could all get together in a

31

local hotel or something.' She pauses. 'Or will that be too expensive?'

She attempts to get a handle on what Hope's suggesting. 'I think at home would be good...'

Has Teresa offered to pay for a family get-together in a hotel? She knows Teresa can more than afford it. No kids, her lucrative job, and Matt's earning power in pharmaceutical sales is colossal too. Her gaze moves to the framed photo tucked away out of sight behind the dictionaries on her desk. Her, Teresa, Jess and Hope. It's as if it was taken in another life and, despite the tropical temperature in her attic study, icy fingers of anxiety start to curl around her.

Maybe her daughter is the catalyst for change. *Hope.* Jess was so young in the image she's staring at. Her youngest sister is hugely successful in her medical career as a psychiatrist; the satire of which isn't lost on her, or Jess, come to that. She's married, but remains fragile. She always has been and always will be. Natalie is relieved, in a way, that she found a man to share her life with, although he's much older than Jess and not a man she'd thought Jess would end up with. Like Teresa they have no children, but these days Jess is stable, most of the time. An outsider would only see her perfect life.

She remembers *the call* – seventeen years ago, 2002, Jess's final year at med school. It was Natalie's subsequent call to Teresa about Jess that finally brought her eldest sister back into the fold – for a time, anyway.

Natalie's hand automatically finds her stomach.

'Mum, you still there?' her daughter is asking.

'Sorry, darling, I think we lost the connection for a short time.'

They hadn't, but her mind had lost the connection. She has to stop raking through the past. Their family's tragic history seems to be following them all: her, inside her head; Teresa, with her obsession to bond with Hope. And Jessica, with the man she eventually married. All interwoven. In different ways and for different reasons, and in two split timelines, all three are slaves to Raven Island.

She carries on. 'No, it's not too expensive to hire a hotel, but it might be nicer to do it here, at home, or even a venue near home?'

'Maybe.'

Hope's going to run it by Teresa, she knows it, and she suppresses a sigh. 'Do you want to mention this to Teresa, and Jess?' she asks.

'It'd be good if you asked them, Mum.'

She does not want to do this, but she will – for Hope. 'Okay.'

'I mean, I'll talk to Aunt Teresa… But could you talk to Jessica?'

Hope doesn't have a problem with Jess, but she doesn't like her husband. 'I'll call her. Don't worry,' Natalie says.

'That's good… I can't wait to see you and Dad next week.'

'We can't wait, either. We love you. And big congratulations again. Your dad's going to be over the moon. I can't get in touch with him as he's on a plane on his way back from Norway.'

'I know, I spoke to him last night from his hotel room.'

'Ah, that's good.'

'Thanks, Mum.'

Hope disconnects and Natalie flops back into her chair. Hope was fourteen when she told her she wanted to be

33

a barrister, like her aunt, Teresa. They were in Frankie and Benny's, eating over-salted chips and drinking vanilla milkshakes. That day Hope had looked more like Jessica than she'd ever done before. It was on that day too when she told her daughter properly about her namesake. Hope had only listened, not said a word. Squeezed her mum's hand. Let the subject drop. That was the thing about Hope: she sensed when to talk, and when not to.

She picks up her mobile, does a search in her contacts list for Teresa's name. It's been years since she contacted her directly; she leaves any calls that have to be made to Teresa for her husband, Oli, to do.

Her fingers find her scalp and she scratches and scratches, scrapes and scrapes, and finally presses the green call button.

6

Teresa

The best day of a trial is sentence day, especially a win, and Teresa has again. Better still, it was all wrapped up by mid-afternoon.

She's forgone the usual chambers' celebration, got changed in her office, congratulated her team, and apologised profusely for dipping out of the post-sentence drinks.

She's heading for the bus stop, and the supermarket. They have a weekly delivery of essentials, but when she's cooking a special meal she likes to go choose the ingredients herself.

Sitting on the bus – luckily it's not busy so she has a seat by herself – Teresa allows herself thinking time. Normally, at the end to a trial – whether it's been a successful outcome for her and her team or not – she'd be thinking about her client, thinking about the jury, the judge, the crime; going through every day of the proceedings, mentally logging what she got right, what she got wrong. Mentally mapping how she'll approach the next case. This one has been tough and very much touch and go if she'd nail the defendant, but she had, and so another piece of absolute shit is now behind bars. It'll be a while before the bastard will be supplying drugs again to vulnerable young women.

Her closing speech was one of her finest – just enough eye contact with the jury and she'd ensured, as she'd spoken, that she glanced at the victim too. Only sixteen. She'd been working the streets since she was fourteen, and a few months shy of her fifteenth birthday, she'd become addicted to heroin. The man who has just been banged up had picked her up early, making sure she earned the money to pay for her habit but also ensuring that he took the rest.

Teresa pulls out her mobile and clicks on her diary, making a note to check on her in a few days.

She returns to her home screen and an image of Hope stares back at her. As her niece has got older she looks more and more like Jessica. And so like her other sister too.

The pain of Teresa's loss and the confusion of her twin's death still sits like an unrelenting lead weight in the pit of her stomach. It always will. Disorientated in her own grief, it had made it so that Eva hadn't allowed her other children to grieve. Such was Eva's selfishness. And because they did not grieve, the three of them never healed.

Teresa touches the screen with her forefinger. It's good she gets on well with Natalie's husband; it's due to Oli that Hope's in touch with her. She supposes she should give some credit to Natalie on this, and she tries, but any feeling of gratitude towards Natalie is hard to come by.

Taking her eyes away, she turns and stares through the window, clocking every teenage girl she sees, her mind flitting back to the teenage girl she has just been representing. What she's been through Teresa can't comprehend, and at such a young age, too. She still abhors drug taking and detests drug dealers and pimps. She thinks of what she calls her dark years. She'd been saved by her studies and then later her career. Raven Island had been the catalyst that had changed her ambition of becoming a highly paid defence barrister to pursuing a career with the Crown Prosecution Service. Yes, Raven Island and what happened there changed everything for her.

Even now, the top of her cheeks ache with unshed tears for the teenage girl. She can count on two fingers the times she has cried since being a grown woman – 1998 and the winter of 2002. She is not a crier.

The latter date had taken her by surprise. It was the day Oli drove up north with Hope, and only a few months after *the call*, the terrible incident with Natalie, and Teresa's disastrous stay with Jessica in London. Natalie hadn't accompanied her husband and daughter to Harrogate, but that she'd allowed Oli to bring their precious four-year-old daughter had been a momentous event for Teresa. She has, over the years, tried to forgive Natalie, but despite all that had happened at that time, and yes, her own guilt about Natalie, she could not. Still cannot, and purges herself of the hate she feels by emotionally embracing Hope.

–

It was a spring day in 2002 and Oli had driven up their gravel driveway and parked right outside the steps that led up to the house's impressive front door. Teresa had watched from the front window of their high-ceilinged sitting room as Oli, still inside the car, surveyed her and Matt's home. Teresa attempted to see what Oli was seeing – an expensive house set in its own grounds, just outside

Harrogate. He'd see Teresa's car parked outside the triple garage, which sat adjacent to the Georgian building – a current-year Mercedes convertible SLK.

Oli jumped out and opened the back passenger door, lifting a four-year-old Hope from the booster seat. Her hair was down, long and wavy, and platinum blonde. The Keane sisters were all varying shades of blonde – although at thirty-three her own hair had been a striking silver-grey for years. She'd lost her youthful colour early. Stress, her GP had told her. Hope's hair was just like her sister's, and just like Jessica's, too.

Hope was staring at her standing in the window. The child was a picture of utter beauty, so like her sister, and it had been then that Teresa's tears had made their unwanted appearance, like some sort of cosmic joke.

Looking at Natalie's child, her niece, she experienced every ounce of maternal feeling that she'd never felt with any other child in one concentrated tsunami-like dose. It was also the exact same feeling she'd experienced on seeing Jessica for the first time, only a few hours after Eva had given birth to her fourth daughter. Even as a baby Jessica had looked so much like her sister. And now, so did Hope. But a few years after Jessica was born their father left, and that was when Teresa decided – even at only twelve years old – she would never want kids.

She often thought that that early conclusion was why she couldn't have any. Tempting fate and all that.

Waving at Hope, she'd wiped away the tears and left her post by the window, making her way outside to greet her brother-in-law and niece. From that first day the bond with Hope was constructed – with Oli, too. Her worry about explaining to little Hope why her mum never came to Harrogate seemed unfounded. It was as if the four-year-old knew something that she could not know.

There could only be one reason why Natalie had allowed her husband to visit her and her own husband, and bring Hope: Natalie *did* know the truth, and therefore her daughter was safe.

—

Teresa jerks forward in her seat and realises the bus has arrived at its destination. She doesn't move, still thinking of her sister and Hope. Back then, when Oli first brought her, Hope would have had no understanding of the history surrounding Raven House and Raven Island. But she does now. Teresa has held nothing back, except what she needs to, to protect Hope, and Natalie. And Jessica. Because even though she is totally estranged from her two sisters, her natural instinct is still to protect. On Hope's frequent visits to Harrogate in the past three years they've touched upon the subject more than once, and she's talked more to Hope about her sister than she has with anyone, including Matt.

She gets off the bus, pulling her shopping list from her leather satchel and peering at it. She hasn't put down the prawns; she mustn't forget them. Hope loves a proper prawn cocktail. She makes her way inside the store, so glad she's not at the post-win celebrations. Glad she's going home to Matt. Glad Hope's coming over. Glad that she's in a position to help her niece to do some networking with her friend from Geneva. She loves Hope. She still loves Natalie too, she admits grudgingly, although still cannot stomach seeing her.

As she passes by the flower stand at the front of the supermarket, she admits to herself that she's on tenterhooks knowing if her niece has got the results she deserves. Moving quickly to the desserts aisle, she puts a massive chocolate cake in her basket just in case comfort is needed. For years it had been Natalie's, Jessica's, and her and Hope's favourite too. The Keane sisters, all sitting in the kitchen, munching Mrs A's famous triple chocolate creation.

She pays for everything at the checkout and hurries back outside, looks at her watch; time is moving on and so she forgoes the bus and walks to the taxi rank. Her bulging bags weigh a ton. It's the three bottles of Bollinger she's bought. Hope *will* be successful.

Luckily, there's an available taxi. She swings her shopping onto the back seat and gets in too, giving the driver her address. She takes out her mobile to check for urgent work emails. Nothing, and she sighs with relief. But she does have a missed call. The caller isn't in her contacts so there's no name, although she recognises the area code. It's Natalie and Oli's. It has to be Natalie. She stares at the device but doesn't return the call.

The taxi pulls up at her at home; she pays and makes her way inside, dropping her bags on the parquet hall floor. Her mobile rings from inside her bag. She pulls it out. Same number as the missed call. She answers.

'Teresa Keane speaking.'

'It's Natalie. I wanted to talk to you, before you see Hope later.'

'Okay.' It's as if no time has passed since they last saw each other in London seventeen years before.

Teresa listens. Natalie keeps it short. To the point.

Teresa waits, considers her response. 'Could you actually bear to be near Matt, Natalie?' she finally replies.

'What does that mean?'

'You know what I mean…' Teresa hears a crackle on the other end of the line. 'Look, Natalie, I appreciate what you've done with Hope—'

'What *have* I done with Hope, exactly?'

'Allowed her to know us. Allowed Oli to bring her all those years ago.'

'I don't hold grudges.'

Teresa has to hold back a bitter laugh.

Natalie carries on: 'Will you and your husband come to a party for Hope?'

'Are you inviting Jessica?'

'Of course I am.'

'How's Hope done?' Teresa asks.

'She's done great. She'll tell you later.'

'I love her, Natalie,' Teresa says.

'I know you do.' Natalie disconnects.

Teresa makes her way to the kitchen with her hoard of shopping. Puts the champagne in the fridge but takes out the bottle that is already in there, chilling. Opens it, enjoying the sound of the cork popping. She takes a champagne flute from the cupboard and pours herself a glass. Waits for the bubbles to settle. Picks it up and turns to face the massive mirror on the kitchen's east wall. Holds up the glass.

'Cheers, Hope.' She tips the flute back and then places the empty glass on the counter. Looks at the clock. Matt will be home in just over an hour. He's promised to change the guest beds for her. God, how she loves her husband.

After taking off her coat, she begins peeling the prawns, although she's unable to peel her thoughts away from the day her world imploded. The day she swore she would never speak to any of her family again. The day her sisters lied and broke her heart.

She thinks of Hope. Of both Hopes. The pressure builds inside her upper cheeks. Her beautiful and capricious sister had been many things, but she would not have lied intending to hurt.

She glances at the image of her niece that's attached with a magnet to the side of the fridge. She will do anything to make Hope happy.

7

Jessica

Surreptitiously, Jessica checks her watch. Her fortnightly session with her own therapist is feeling like a particularly long one. Yes, it is, she realises, still peering at her wrist. They are heading into a second hour. Her therapist has just got up to pour herself a glass of water, although Jessica is aware of what she is actually doing; giving herself time to digest what Jessica has just told her. About Dom. She told her therapist months ago about the day before she left for medical school, her stroll with Dom to the jetty. She'd told her therapist that she had confronted Dom with the secret, which he had coerced her into keeping. But she hadn't told her therapist what the secret was. Today though, she has. Jessica examines her own feelings. Does she feel better for sharing? Not really, although on many levels it's helping her to understand more about little Grace, and for this, she is grateful. It's why therapists have to undergo therapy – so the therapist is better equipped to understand their patients, and Jessica has been determined to understand seven-year-old Grace, committed to gaining the girl's trust. And finally, in the past six months, she has. Treating Grace has been a turning point for Jessica and this has been confirmed in the revelation to her therapist today.

Unwanted and with stealth, the past invades her mind. Like many of her adult clients, she is stuck in the groove of self-destruction. Her insecurity has powered her life, set her on her own personal trajectory. It was a moment of supreme assertiveness when she had challenged Dom; laid bare to him the consequences of the secret he'd asked her to keep.

Her therapist is sitting back down opposite her. She crosses her legs and leans forwards. 'Tell me how you feel about your stepfather's death, Jessica.'

Jessica contemplates her reply for long minutes and her therapist waits, oh so patiently. 'It was a relief and yet... when I knew Dom was dead – the man who had looked after me better than my own mother – deep in the sinew of me, I was, at the same time, desolate with the news.'

'Did Dom's death, perhaps, mark the end of your childhood and symbolise the finality of the already distant memory of your deceased sister?' the therapist asks quietly.

'Perhaps.'

'Going back to the night in the cocktail bar,' the therapist pushes, 'the night you were out having fun with your housemates, and you saw a man who was so connected to your past. Did it feel to you as if that past had returned?'

'Again, perhaps.'

'And you did not want to confront that past?'

'No, I didn't,' Jessica replies. 'But then, when he knocked on my door only a day after Teresa had left, it was as if I'd been saved, rescued. And he didn't want me to talk about the past, that was what he said, right from the beginning. *Do not talk of the past.*' She brushes away an imaginary piece of fluff from her skirt. 'And that suited me.'

'Jessica…' The therapist leans forward in her chair slightly more. 'Was the familiarity of the past, being with him, more important to you than the restrictions of the future?'

Jessica glances at her watch again. 'It's been a long session. Your last question, I have to think about more.'

The therapist gives her a tight smile. 'I think it would be good to formulate your response in this session, Jessica. Give me your immediate thoughts upon hearing my question. An honest answer?'

'I'm not ready.'

Her therapist sighs. 'How do you feel about your sister now, Jessica?'

'The same as I've always felt about her. I love her, loved her. Despite everything.'

'And Teresa? How do you think her sister's death affected her?'

'Teresa was affected the most. Of course she was.'

'And would you like to talk to Teresa about what you've divulged to me today, about your deceased sister?'

Jessica breaks protocol and stands. 'Actually, I think it's time to end today's session.'

The therapist, her expression neutral, stands too. 'Okay, Jessica. Let's meet next week.'

'It's normally fortnightly. I'd prefer in two weeks.' She scrutinises her therapist, for a few seconds feeling the battle of wills within the room.

'Okay. Two weeks.' Finally, the therapist smiles. 'And happy birthday for tomorrow.'

'Thank you.' And with relief, Jessica escapes.

8

Jessica glances the bathroom clock. It's early: just before seven a.m. After the session with her therapist the day before she'd been unable to sleep, her mind ablaze with what she had finally admitted – to both herself and her therapist. Despite the sleepless night, she doesn't lie in. She never does, even when she hasn't got to be in work. Impossible. It makes her feel anxious – breaking her routine and her manufactured order. What is she without her routine and order?

She's taken the day off. She has far too much annual leave to carry over. The hospital director had suggested she take the entire week off, but she can't. She's in court tomorrow as an expert witness, giving testimony for Grace.

Grace is her patient and it is a professional relationship, but in the months that she's been treating the little girl, Jessica has grown to love her. Anyway, her workload is insane and she knows it would take her weeks to catch up after too much leave. Thank God she isn't doing any private work at the moment – much to her husband's horror. They have enough money, but for her husband that is a phrase that doesn't exist inside his head. *Inside his head*.

'You can never have too much money' – one of his favourite phrases. And he will never understand that she thinks it is just wrong, private practice, and the reason she keeps her private patients to a minimum. She would end up treating people who had far too much time on their hands and too much money in their pockets. She wants to help people with genuine problems. Most of her patients are women, and a good percentage of those, young women – the ones that society has forgotten, not that society is aware that these women existed in the first place. There are many messed-up Jessicas in this world, although no one would recognise her as being one of them.

Her mind flits away from these thoughts, although it is them that bring an image of Connor O'Leary. She stares at her reflection in the bathroom mirror, and with the barrister's kind eyes imprinted inside her brain, she smiles at herself. His image is like a big mental hug. She has been seeing a lot of him over the past year; he often comes over to her office to talk about the case they are both working on – Grace's. Connor is the barrister heading the CPS's prosecution of Grace's stepfather.

Once, maybe six months ago now, Connor had come to their home, totally unannounced. A normal visit, a normal thing to do. He'd had some queries on Grace's case. Luckily, it had been her husband's golf day. She had kept Connor at the front door, told him she was getting ready to go out and was in a hurry. He had not visited her at home again uninvited, sensing rightly that it was off limits. Connor was a smart man; he probably suspected the reason why she couldn't ask him in.

She has, though, been out for coffee with him many times, although she always refuses his lunch invites. Her refusals do not come from disinterest – the absolute opposite. No, they come from fear. Fear of how spending too much time with Connor could unbalance her coping mechanisms. It is so conflicting – doing the opposite to what she wants to do. After so many years of doing it, it should come easily, but it does not. Several months ago things shifted a little with Connor. Her husband had been away and her car wouldn't start that morning. It was imperative that she got to Grace's preliminary court proceedings on time and when she'd texted Connor, he'd immediately come to pick her up. He'd used his car horn to tell her he was waiting outside and that's when she knew for sure that he understood the dynamics of her relationship with her husband. That had marked a change, a subtle quickening, in their friendship, although after their working morning was over she had still, reluctantly, refused his offer of a late lunch.

She bends over the basin to wash her face, brushes her teeth and studies herself. Despite her unease with life she likes the image that stares back. Her blonde hair has no grey in it yet, her youthful face remains unlined She does not look like either of her sisters, but even at forty she looks so much more like Hope.

She is absolutely certain that because she appeared so young it took at least an extra three years to get to where she wanted to be career-wise. Add on to that being a woman, she's done okay. She manages. She doesn't often kneel by the toilet these days – only when something trips her: a memory, a trigger. It made it easier though, when Dom died, and easier still when Eva died. After Eva's death, all three of the Keane sisters were glad to see Raven House sold. Jessica, though, had refused Eva's inheritance. But eventually, at Natalie's request, she took the money and put it in a trust fund for her niece, Hope. Her husband had been furious, but as is his way, the rage hadn't lasted long. He reins in his rage quickly. He is so very in control of his passions. But she would not like to test him. And this is another reason why she avoids Connor socially – because eventually it might lead to a meeting between him and her husband. Fear clasps her body at that thought.

She hasn't closed the bathroom door and hears their bedroom door open. It is much too early for him to be up and about. Since he retired six months before, he gets up later and later, and at the weekends, when she is home, it suits her.

'Happy birthday, Jessica,' her husband says, lingering in the bathroom doorway. He's wearing the Czech and Speake dressing gown she bought him for Christmas. It was the wrong colour when it arrived in the post, and not the shade he'd pointed out. She'd had to visit the shop to change it. The trek had been worth it, though. She couldn't bear the thought of his displeasure.

He is holding a very large envelope and two beautifully wrapped boxes – one large and one small.

'Come in,' she says, trying to inject enthusiasm into her voice.

He wavers. He's not sure. He's more than aware she needs her space in the mornings – all day, really. It is why their marriage is so stable. One of the reasons. He understands her, of course he does – he has known her a long time. He's been through everything with her. They are a Pacific Ocean apart in personality, but ultimately they are well matched, despite what Natalie thinks.

He touches her cheek and she feels a flutter of the unwanted arousal. Just as she has always done.

'You look superb on your fortieth birthday,' he says. 'You're aging like a fine wine.'

He smells good. The repellent flutter intensifies. 'Thank you.'

'You make me feel very ancient,' he says.

Her husband is fifteen years older than she is. 'You shouldn't have retired so early.'

'Perhaps you're right. I might look for consultancy work soon. Work when I want to.'

'I think that's a good idea.' She knows that he has already looked for work, because she has seen the correspondence. That was when she had discovered the missing years. She should ask him about it, but how? He will know then that she has rifled through his papers.

He sold his business at the beginning of the year. It was a business that sourced and sold display stands for exhibitions. It was a business he'd run with his best friend. A boring business. It was why he looked for a different sort of excitement, she was sure.

'Open your card and present,' he says.

'Let's go downstairs and do it.'

'Good idea. I'll put the coffee on, and you finish off in here.'

'I put the coffee machine on auto last night.' He takes his hand away from her elbow. She rubs her arm. His grip had been too tight. Like a warning. 'It'll be brewed by now.'

He grins at her. His teeth are a little too bright. His dentist has overdone the whitening. 'Of course you have, and yes, I'm sure it'll be ready.' He pauses. 'I hope you haven't overdone the amount of coffee in the filter. I don't like it strong.'

'I know all of your likes and dislikes.'

'You do, Jessica, you do.'

'I'll be down in five minutes.'

She's holding the edge of the basin and hasn't noticed the translucent skin of her knuckles. She is coiled like a spring, but then she always is. It is the only way she can function and cope with the dichotomy of both her life and her marriage. About what she has begun to think she knows. But what she still refuses to analyse.

She peers into the mirror again and moves closer to the reflection staring back. She's still lean and muscled, although her chest remains flat. Teresa and Natalie are the big-busted Keane girls. She and Hope, the opposite. Her husband never complains, though. He likes flat-chested women, very much. Always has. His ex had been flat-chested. Men never change their preferences.

She can hear him downstairs. She knows his routine so well and is able to envisage every movement he is making. It is a good thing that he does not often surprise her, and he has not surprised her, not since he turned up in the London cocktail bar all those years ago. Seeing him again is what had made her lose her fragile mental footing – she can see that now. She has been seeing it more and more over the past year and wonders if this is connected to her frequent meetings with Connor. Yes, the last twelve months have felt different for her, inside her head. Surprises send her into a paroxysm of anxiety, although no one would ever guess at her inner turmoil; only the man downstairs making coffee understands. Unless he had asked her to marry him she would be still single. She is damaged, and always will be, but glad she can use some of that damage for good in her job. Because she can, and she does.

It was soon after her discharge from hospital when he proposed. Did she love him then? She had thought she did. She has no idea what love is, and is pleased that she doesn't have to analyse herself as she analyses her patients, because she would find it incredibly difficult, if not impossible.

Natalie is the only person in the world with whom she has a proper relationship.

Her sister's initial response to her marriage was of both massive surprise and a badly concealed reaction of horror. Natalie would be even more horrified if she knew more; but she will never know more. Jessica ensures that her sister and husband rarely meet, and the price for that has been her relationship with her niece, Hope. But the price is worth paying.

She covers her face in Clarins, wraps her silk dressing gown around herself and makes her way downstairs. A big mug of coffee is awaiting her, next to a plate with a croissant sitting on it. Her card and presents are waiting too. Her husband is sitting at the breakfast counter.

'Come on, then!' he says.

She sits next to him and moves the plate and mug so they are in complete symmetrical alignment, and then opens her card. She smiles. 'Thank you. Beautiful card. So, big or small present first?'

'I think small one first.'

Jessica gently pulls at the luxurious wrapping. Carefully. It is a long slim box. It is jewellery. She opens it. A bracelet. Rubies. Some diamonds too. It looks expensive. He has something planned and she senses a weakening in her steel resilience.

He takes her hand. 'Put it on. Let me.' He places it around her wrist and deftly fastens the clasp. 'Beautiful, like you.'

'And like Hope? Like Juno?' She glances up at him, noting the hardening of his expression. He makes no reply.

She touches the large rubies and the small diamonds. *Why did I say that?*

He pushes the bigger box towards her, his facial muscles loosening, deciding not to bite.

'You've spoiled me.' He likes that. She opens her next present. It's a phrenology head, crafted from dark grey stone. So very like the one from her childhood.

'I've never been able to believe you don't have one in your office,' he says. 'You loved your head...'

She turns and inclines her own to the piece of artwork that takes pride of place in their kitchen. 'This was my replacement.'

A wire head sculpture sits in all its grandness at the far end of their island unit: six foot high and a few feet in diameter. It's the centrepiece in the airy space. The head is crafted out of chrome wire, two eyes staring into the kitchen; the eyes are the only human-like features represented on the 'face'. They are a vivid blue, with realistic flecks of grey, made of glass. Inside the wire structure sits certain parts of the human brain, these made from papier mâché and where the human emotions are labelled, just like a phrenology head. The part of the sculpture that grabs the eye is a thicker piece of wire that protrudes from the head's nose-like structure, swirling outwards, a foot-long spiral, the end spiked. It is menacing, dangerous. Literally dangerous, like a twisted knife. When the sculpture had been delivered her husband was concerned about the maverick wire. In all fairness, she could understand his worry, although it was the entire point of the sculpture – inside coming out. Like a tube, a feeding tube perhaps, or a ventilating tube. Or, the person inside trying to escape? As with all art, it symbolises what is inside the viewer's own head. She'd told him that, although she was annoyed that she had to explain, but she hid her irritation well; she's learned to do that. Art should never have to be explained, just as you should never have to explain what is inside your head – not unless you want to.

She thinks of her childhood phrenology head, the one she'd smashed on Teresa's graduation day. The wire head is her replacement. But now her husband has given her another head. It feels ominous.

'You like it?' he pushes.

'I do.'

'Good. That pleases me.'

'Do you ever think about Juno?' she asks.

'Why are you doing this today, Jessica?' he says, although looking at the wire head and not at her. His words measured. Very.

Why is she doing this, and today? She does not know why. She'd promised him she would never talk about Juno, just as she'd promised to never mention Hope. Maybe she is doing it because it is her birthday. Forty feels as if it's a time to reflect, reorganise, analyse. To make way for the second phase of life.

She shrugs but does not reply.

With no children, the second phase is looking desolate.

'I can take the head back if you don't want it. It's no problem.' His last three words are clipped and the inton-ation gives them the total opposite meaning. She is adept at combing out the real substance of his words.

'No,' she says. 'I'll take it to the office.' She gets up and makes her way to the fridge. Pulls out a bottle of champagne. 'Shall we have a Buck's Fizz, seeing as I'm forty today?'

He laughs and the brittle sound reverberates through the kitchen, bouncing off the dove-grey empty walls like unwanted sexual advances. Hers.

She still remembers the night she tried to entice him, although she does as much as she can to scrub away the memory of feeling so unwanted. So undesirable.

'Let's,' he's saying. 'I'll do it. You eat your croissant.'

Occasionally — although very rarely in their seventeen-year marriage — there is a feather touch, a brief dusting from the past, something that links; often it's tiny, and although they both acknowledge it they don't ever tackle it. It slips unseen into the fissures and they both seal it up.

Her mentioning of Juno and Hope today is not a feather, nor a dusting.

It is a sledgehammer.

They drink two glasses of Buck's Fizz and read the morning papers in faux companionable silence. Jessica stops herself from going to her study to check her work email, and instead suggests a walk in Hampstead Heath. On their return they have another glass of champagne and then get ready for the reservation he has made at her favourite restaurant in Soho. An early dinner.

9

Now

Jessica

They are on their way home in a black cab when Jessica's mobile rings. She takes it from her bag. Natalie. She suddenly realises that her sister has not sent her a birthday card. She will be calling to wish her a happy birthday.

'Hi, Natalie,' she says.

'I'm so sorry, Jess. I forgot to put your card in the post. I feel terrible.'

'It's fine. You know I'm not into that stuff. Just in the taxi home, been out for an early dinner.'

'Nice?'

She turns and smiles at her husband. He does not smile back. They have had a lovely dinner, a reasonable evening, apart from the two women at the next table. That had thrown her. Thrown him too. Especially the younger woman. 'Yes, it was.'

'Hope got a First, Jess.'

She doesn't speak for a moment. Natalie rarely talks about Hope to her – it makes everything so much easier for them both. 'That's brilliant,' she finally replies, but then pauses. 'A real Keane girl. Top of the class.'

'Like three of the Keane girls, Jess. Not this one.'

She doesn't answer immediately, taken unawares by Natalie's statement. 'Stop. You love your teaching job... most of the time. It's great news. Tell her congratulations from me. I'm really pleased for her, and you and Oli.'

'I know you are... you can tell her yourself, if you'd like to,' Natalie replies. 'Hope's asked me to invite you to a party. Her graduation party. She wants all of her family there.'

This unsettles Jess nearly as much as the physical appearance of the girl in the restaurant. 'I can't do it, Natalie.'

'You can, Jess. Please.'

'Have you spoken to Teresa?'

'I have.'

'And?'

'She said yes. Hope's over at Teresa's this evening.'

'That's nice for Teresa. Is Matt invited?'

'He is. I'd like you both to come, Jess... Hope would like you both to come.'

'Both of us?' She looks at her husband, who is staring out of the window, although she knows he's listening intently.

'Yes. Have a think. And call me tomorrow?' Natalie says.

'I will...'

'Happy birthday, Jess. Love you.'

'Love you too.' Jessica disconnects.

'Bad news?' her husband asks.

She tells him about Natalie's request.

'We've had nothing to do with Hope. Natalie's kept her away from us.'

Tension hovers between them. An odourless gas, like carbon monoxide. Insidious, but deadly.

He carries on: 'There's no love lost between you and Hope… even though you're giving her all of Eva's money.' He turns away.

She sees a flash of his anger return regarding Eva's money and in her reply she ensures her tone is calm and measured. 'I'm giving Hope *a third* of Eva's money. And I love Hope.' Immediately, she wishes she had not responded at all. He is obsessed with money, and he hates her talking about Hope. Did he marry her for Eva's money, which she subsequently didn't take? Does he hate her talking about Hope because the name brings back too many memories?

He places his hand on her thigh, moves it upwards.

She suppresses a moan and she despises herself.

It's Jessica who's staring through the window now, watching normal people going about their normal lives. It's always fascinated her. Normality. Repelled her too. Just as her husband both fascinates and repels her.

Jessica repels herself.

She cannot do another graduation day.

10

Then
August 1991

Natalie

Raven House and its gardens were heaving with people. Most were over forty and most Natalie didn't know. And most of them were drunk, and getting drunker by the hour. It was the first party the Keane family had thrown in five years and so Eva had pulled out her address book, inviting everyone and anyone to the all-day party. Luckily, Juno had agreed to come and keep her company, but, as usual, her best friend was nowhere to be found. With the sun near its highest, the temperature the same, after Dom's speech Juno had disappeared. 'Off for a wander,' she'd said, and seeming like hours ago now.

Natalie was sitting on the bench that overlooked the river, far enough away from the party's heart and therefore with no chance of being accosted by a pissed oldie. She had brought a book with her, knowing she'd no intention of returning to the party. She'd moved only once since Juno had gone, taking a walk by the water's edge, making her way along the river's bend and the inverse curve of the garden. At the periphery of their plot the river took a sharp loop to the right and that was where they moored the two small motor launches and a rowing boat; the jetty and boathouse was out of sight from the main part of Raven House, as was Raven Island. After walking for a few minutes, the island came into view. Being an inanimate object, it had no recollection of its history and looked gorgeous despite it. It was then that Natalie had seen the family's motorboat, apparently heading to Raven Island, with two people inside – one of whom she recognised as being Juno. She'd swivelled around quickly, returning to the bench. That had been two hours ago.

She really would have to have a word with Juno about her boat trip, and with that thought she got up, tucked the book underneath her arm, and walked towards the jetty to check if she'd returned. On arriving at the point where the jetty came into view, Natalie stopped and peered towards it, straining her eyes and cursing the fact she hadn't bothered to put her contact lenses in that morning. She could make out that both motorboats were now in situ.

They'd returned.

She swivelled around and made her way back to the bench.

Plonking herself down, she pulled her knees up to her stomach and surveyed the party, which was by then in full swing. It was as if they had parties like this routinely, as if everything was so completely normal; she supposed after five years it *was* normal. It wasn't, though, and never would be.

Women milled on the elevated terrace, all wearing over-bright and revealing silk dresses, all looking as if they'd been bought from the same local boutique, the one from which Eva's royal blue ensemble had been acquired too.

The men roaming around were more diverse; many wearing similar-coloured suits, although set off with an array of differing loud floral ties, which signalled their dire absence of individuality. The rest of the blokes wore casual camel-brown chinos, accompanied by regimented polo shirts – the predictable palette of colours marking out their complete lack of originality. Where did Eva know these people from? Who knew. She didn't, but they made up the numbers and that was the most important thing.

There must have been a hundred guests, and none, she was sure, were Teresa's mates. A slither of unaccustomed pity swept through her thinking of her older sister. Teresa had been dreading today, probably more than she had been, and probably even more than Jess. Eva had pulled out all the stops, because it wasn't just Teresa's graduation day party – it was her engagement celebration too. Luke had popped the question soon after their visit in March.

The trestle table on the terrace groaned with sushi and Mexican food. The sushi was Eva's choice; the Mexican was Teresa's. Eva had surpassed herself for Teresa's party; the run-up to it for the past five months had even seen her almost back to normal – apart from the drugs. She tried to remember if Eva did them before their sister's death and stumbled around in her memory. No, she didn't remember drugs, but then again, at eleven she wouldn't have known anyway. Her mind went back to the boat. She had to say something to Dom.

Why was it always her who saw what she didn't want to see?

-

Natalie reopened *The Great Gatsby* but her concentration was gone. Snapping it closed, she checked her watch –

still only 4.30 p.m. The day was going on forever. The scheduled fireworks on Raven Island were due to start after the sun had gone down, at ten p.m. – finally, Eva had lifted her Raven Island embargo. Still, ages to go yet for the fireworks, which would be the official end to the painful day.

Where *was* Juno? She was always doing this – wandering off and then forgetting to return. Doing things she shouldn't be doing. But that was why she liked her best friend so much. Juno was the exact opposite to her, and more like… more like… Her mind flitted back to the boat again, and the two people inside it. She shook her head, as if trying to shake away the image, and almost absent-mindedly she began to scratch the psoriasis plaques on her scalp, watching with both horror and satisfaction as the flakes fell onto the book. She rubbed harder, easing the irritation although knowing it was a short-term and false solace. Suddenly disgusted with herself, she sprang up from the bench and walked towards the big oak, leaned against it and allowed herself to slide down its trunk, content to sit on the grass and view the river slowly flowing past.

Her mind moved to Teresa, her clever and gorgeous sister who'd just completed the next step to becoming a barrister. It had been an expensive haul getting to where she wanted to be, and although there were many problems within the Keane family household, money wasn't one of them.

Teresa and Luke were like Greek gods. Beautiful and untouchable.

Natalie took in the late afternoon cloudless sky. The gentle wind of earlier had died down, not a rustle. Lowering her head, she stared at her jeans, picking off the dried-on toothpaste from the morning. She'd planned to put a dress on but stubbornly decided against it as soon as Eva had begun complaining about the jeans.

Christ, her family. She was on countdown to when it was her turn to go away to university. Two more years. She was starting her A levels in September. She'd flown through her O levels – not that any of her family had acknowledged her results, only Dom, who'd bought her a new TAG Heuer watch to mark the occasion. She didn't think Eva even knew he'd got it for her.

She took a sip of the champagne that had been sitting beside her, untouched. Despite it being flat, straight away her head spun. How did these middle-aged people manage to imbibe so much? Juno loved all this, though – booze and food. She had no idea how she stayed so skinny. Juno's other love was on offer at the party too, gauging by the smell as the two of them had wandered around the terrace earlier.

As the very early evening approached the music had ramped up, and oh God, the chinos and dresses had begun swaying on Eva's garden terrace dance floor to George Michael's 'Faith'. On a sudden impulse, Natalie pulled herself up off the grass and made her way back to the heart of the party, dodging through bodies and trying not to make eye contact, just in case someone she'd never set eyes on before in her life started to make conversation.

'Hi, Natalie.'

A soft clasp of her elbow. She turned and her stomach flipped at his touch. The man standing so close to her was unlike any of the other oldies, and in truth she'd never seen him as being *really* old. She'd often wondered how he and Dom had become business associates, and then such good

63

mates. He was nine years younger than her stepdad and fifteen years younger than Eva.

'You came back?' she said, the words tumbling out before she could stop them. *Such a stupid thing to say.* He had been part of the Keane family's inner circle for as long as she could remember and so had been at the house early that morning helping get things ready. But he'd left to get changed and, she'd thought, to pick up his wife.

'Of course I did. Just got back. But saw you sitting Greta Garbo-like down there.' He pointed to the bench. Smiling, he flicked a thick mop of chestnut-brown hair away from sea–green eyes.

Heat touched her face, her scalp was on fire too; she cast her eyes down and her gaze rested on the pristine terrace stone slabs, then moved to the hems of his trousers, which were creased, a little stained and crumpled. Briefly, she registered surprise. He was always so immaculately turned out.

'You know how it is,' she said.

'I like the jean and T-shirt ensemble, Nat.' He smiled.

Her face burned even more and she blurted out, 'Is your wife here?' *God, Natalie.*

'Sadly, no. Libby and I had a bit of a disagreement… another one.'

'I'm sorry.' His expression had clouded. He was angry just thinking about the disagreement.

His facial features softened. 'No need to be. We've been having problems for a while, that's the truth. We're splitting up. More female-frog touching, it'd seem, before I find my princess.' He paused as he fingered his long fringe, moving it way from his eyes.

'I'm sorry… But I think it's a kiss, and not touch…'

'Indeed it is,' he said. He was annoyed she'd picked him up on the misuse of the phrase. 'Anyway, we can't all be as lucky as Dom.'

'I suppose you could look at it like that.'

He laughed. 'Natalie, the bloke you end up with is going to be very lucky.'

She huffed. 'I don't think so.'

His expression became serious. 'You all right?'

'I'm fine… really. I'm looking for Juno. Have you seen her?'

'Is she still here?'

'Yep, that's why I'm looking for her.'

His facial muscles worked a smile that his eyes didn't capture. She'd upset him again. Men don't like to look a fool, especially twice in the same conversation.

'Razor-sharp,' he replied.

Yes, she'd ruffled his ego and therefore upset herself.

He shrugged lightly, smiled properly, and carried on: 'No, I haven't seen her but I only arrived half an hour ago.' His fringe had flopped over his eyes again and he peered at her through thick strands of blond. He'd forgiven her. 'I've met Juno only a few times, admittedly… but my advice to you is to follow the smell.' He turned and nodded towards the small marquee that had been erected for the party, which was attached to the house at the kitchen French doors. 'It's all happening over there.'

Finally, she smiled at him properly.

'That's more like it,' he carried on. 'You and Juno come and find me at firework o'clock. The three of us can share a boat to the island. I'm on firework-lighting duty.'

'You're on,' she said. She had no desire to set foot on the island, but to go with him would be nice. She liked his company because as well as fancying him, he made her laugh. A bit like how Juno did. Laughing within Raven House was a rare event these days.

'Go and put on a nice dress, Natalie. Make Eva happy.' He paused. 'It's good she agreed to this party. Give her a break?'

Natalie gave a pretend salute and watched as he made his way to the other side of the terrace, while she went to investigate the marquee. If Juno wasn't having a spliff there, she was sure she'd find her inside the house, sprawled out and asleep somewhere. That was the thing with Juno – she liked to party but didn't have the stamina for it. She was a lightweight really.

Feeling a strong prod in her back she swung around.

'Natalie! Where've you been hiding?'

It was Eva's hairdresser. Natalie tried to remember her name as she watched her swaying like a reed in the wind to another of George's songs. The name didn't come. 'Nowhere,' she said. 'I'm looking for my mate. Have you seen her? She's the same age as me.'

'Ah, the blonde wearing the luminescent green tartan mini and tight white T-shirt?'

Natalie gave the woman her empty look, the one she'd refined especially for Eva's friends. 'Yes.'

'Your little sister's been looking for Juno too. Popular girl, Juno. I saw her a few hours ago.' Then she pointed, swaying a little. 'Chatting with him.' She was gesticulating towards a group of men on the other side of the terrace, but Natalie couldn't see clearly who she was pointing at, although she was unsure how reliable the hairdresser's reporting was. She did look the worse for too much champagne – or maybe something else, going by the size of her pupils.

She couldn't remember the hairdresser's name but did remember her daughter's. Caitlin was a similar age to her. She'd seen her earlier. 'Where's Caitlin?'

The woman rocked sideways a little, looking totally unstable on her four-inch heels. 'Haven't seen her for a while.' She peered at Natalie. 'You young things, always up to no good! Getting into trouble...' Her voice suddenly trailed off. 'I'm sorry, I didn't mean—'

'It's fine, don't worry,' Natalie replied quietly. 'Honestly, it's why Eva's had the party... to try and move on.'

The hairdresser nodded, and changed the subject. 'Looking forward to the fireworks?'

'I am, thanks. And if I see Caitlin, I'll tell her you're looking for her.'

'Yes, tell her to check in with her old mum!'

It seemed everyone was going missing that evening. The thought crossed Natalie's mind that Juno was somewhere with Caitlin, and her skin prickled with teenage jealousy.

'Nice seeing you,' she said to the hairdresser automatically. Her attention had already wandered from her, and her absent daughter. She nudged past and, nearly choking on the woman's perfume, walked by the trestle tables, where she saw Teresa.

Luke was not by her side and her sister had changed her bodice, which was a shame as she'd looked amazing in the original one, Natalie now reluctantly admitted to herself. It wouldn't look good on her. She wasn't flat-chested, but no way would she fill Teresa's double D-cup.

Earlier, she'd seen Teresa and Luke having words, and an indiscernible thread of pleasure had rippled through her, suggesting that something could actually go wrong for Teresa. The tension had obviously got to them, although she had to give them credit – it had taken twenty-four hours. Good going: she'd thought they'd break before now.

Teresa caught her eye and gave her a tight smile. That smile told her everything she needed to know: Teresa was hating her own party as much as she was. They had their differences but shared one common denominator: their fucked-up family, which had become even more fucked up over the past five years. This party was a mistake; she felt it in her bones.

Natalie made her way into the house but couldn't find Juno anywhere. Luke wasn't inside either, or Caitlin. She searched every one of the nine bedrooms, apart from her little sister's. The last room she checked was Eva and Dom's, which overlooked the back garden and the party. The door to their Juliet balcony was open. She made her way towards it and stood there surveying the people outside, scouring faces for Juno – her fluorescent green tartan skirt would be easy to locate. She couldn't see her.

Turning, she closed the balcony door, her eyes settling on the fake Louis XIV bedside table, taking in the curled twenty-pound note and a small make-up mirror smudged with white powder. Next to the mirror sat a tiny dish that she knew Eva usually used for her various prescription drugs. The dish held three pink tablets and one blue. Natalie picked it up and looked closer. She knew what they were – *That's private education for you.* The pink tablets each had a star logo imprinted on one side. The blue one, a skull and crossbones imprint. Natalie was more than aware the significance of the skull and crossbones – the logo indicated the stronger, purer, and deadlier ecstasy tabs.

Christ. Eva's 'little man' – her and Dom's dealer – had visited just before the first guests had arrived earlier. His early morning visit was unprecedented. The pair must have been desperate. She put the dish back down on the table. She'd have to make herself have a talk with Teresa, who was the only one who'd be able to confront Eva and Dom about the obvious ramping up of pharmaceutical pleasures.

She left the room feeling guilty she'd been in there.

As she padded by Jess's bedroom she heard muffled sobbing inside. Stopping, she opened the door. Her thirteen-year-old sister was lying on her bed crying her eyes out.

'Jess,' she said quietly. 'I thought you might be having a sleep before the fireworks so you can stay up late.' She sat on the bed next to her. 'You haven't been in Eva and Dom's room... have you?' They really should learn to lock the door.

She shook her head.

'What's happened?' Natalie asked in a whisper, taking Jess in her arms and noticing the smell of river water. Gently, she pulled the sheet away from her. Jess was wearing the dress she'd obediently put on that morning, a long blue one. Its hem was crumpled and dotted with drying mud. Her matching blue headband was long gone.

'Have you been in the river?' she asked.

Jess shook her head again but remained silent. Natalie knew not to hassle her. Her highly strung sister didn't respond well to conflict. She stroked Jess's forehead and instead asked, 'Have you seen Juno?'

Jess's tears exploded then.

It was like history repeating itself.

11

Teresa

Graduation and engagement party day at the family home and Teresa had been awake for hours. She hadn't been able to believe it when they had turned up yesterday to discover that Eva had given her and Luke separate rooms. They were engaged, for God's sake. But she had known better than to kick back; it was only for two nights.

She swung her legs out of bed and peered at the clock. Just before six a.m. She took the few steps towards the window and twisted the handle to open it. It was a glorious day, the sky as clear as a virgin canvas, the whispery rays of an early sun trickling across the vast garden. It was already warm. Perfect day for a party – she just wished it were happening somewhere else where there were no memories. But it wasn't. Luke's mum wouldn't be coming either. She'd politely turned down her invitation, saying she wasn't feeling that well and couldn't bear the thought of having to socialise for an entire day. Teresa had been disappointed, although on the other hand relieved that she could put off for longer the inevitable meeting between Eva, Dom, and Luke's mum.

She leaned outside and inhaled. Just gorgeous; cut grass and river water. Scanning the garden, river and trees, she took in the echoing energy, and Hope. High summer had always been her sister's favourite time of year; it was she who'd loved the river the most.

Teresa disliked coming home but did like the house's location. Years ago, when they'd first moved there, before their other two sisters had been born, she'd liked her life here too.

But all that had changed – changed twice. She shook her head, flinging away both memories, of their dad, and of her sister. It didn't mean she didn't love her, she'd always love her, although long ago she'd stopped loving her dad.

Turning quickly, she pulled on knickers, joggers and a sleeveless top. She didn't bother with a bra and smiled to herself. *Be coming off soon enough.* She made her way downstairs. Time to enjoy the house before everyone else emerged and began running around like headless chickens, getting ready for her party. She didn't kid herself, though – this party was more for Eva. Perhaps her mother was finally accepting what she'd been unable to accept. Teresa hoped so. Because then they could all at least try to move on.

'You're up early, Teresa.'

Mrs A was standing by the sink in the huge south-facing, light-laden kitchen, and wearing a summer cotton jacket. She was certain Eva had told her Mrs A was off duty for the party weekend and was going to her brother's. As much as she loved Mrs A, she wished she hadn't turned up so early. It would ruin her and Luke's plan.

'Morning, Mrs A! Lovely to see you, but Eva said you were off this weekend?'

Mrs A pointed to a tray of chocolate muffins covered in cling film. 'Brought these over for you girls.'

'Aw, that's so kind… are you staying?'

'Absolutely not! I'm off to my brother's.' Mrs A walked over to her, kissing her on the cheek. 'Parties aren't my thing. You know that, Teresa. But you have a wonderful time. Must dash.'

'Have a safe trip,' Teresa said, but already talking to Mrs A's back and letting out a sigh of relief at the same time.

Teresa unpeeled the cling film from the tray and then hauled herself up onto the kitchen's massive granite island counter, stuffing a muffin into her mouth. Ten minutes after Mrs A had left she heard footfall on the stairs.

'Hey, you.' Luke appeared, his red baseball cap, the wrong way round, jammed on his head. He glanced at the oversized clock on the wall. Then at her. 'You're up early.' He rubbed his eyes.

'Waiting for you.'

'Why didn't you sneak in?' He grinned and stood in front of her, cupping her face in his hands.

'Not my style.' Gently, she pressed his groin with her knee. 'And I assumed you'd be fast asleep. Anyway, our original plan is much more exciting.' She kicked him on a well-muscled thigh, her eyes fixed on his erection that the thin towelling of his dressing gown couldn't hide. It would be good for something wonderful to happen on Raven Island.

'I'll go and put some clothes on, then.'

'And lose the cap, Luke.'

He took off the bright red and worn-looking cap and put it on what she thought was the right way. 'Better?'

'It looks ridiculous either way round, it always does.' She grinned. 'I'll meet you by the jetty.'

She made her way through the kitchen doors that led onto the terrace. Luke made her laugh, and he made her happy. But that bloody cap. She really wished he'd lose it.

12

Teresa

Fifteen minutes later, at the jetty, Teresa was untying the motorboat. 'The cap?'

'Come on, give me a break.' Luke rammed it further onto his head and then glanced at the boat. 'I thought we were taking the one with oars. Can you actually drive this thing?'

Such a city boy. 'Certainly can. We all can.' She pulled his arm. 'Hop in.'

'All?'

'Yes, me and Natalie, and Jessica, and...'

'Eva?'

'No... not Eva. She hates the water.' God knows why Eva hadn't sold the house years ago. She did know why, though. It had been their dad's choice to stay there and then when Dom came along he'd loved the riverside house too. She needed to tell Luke about her dad, and about her sister. When they got back to London she'd tell him. She was taking a risk, though – one of the party guests might say something. She'd cross that bridge when she got to it.

'Who then? Surely not Mrs A?' Luke said, laughing.

She tried to find a smile and did, momentarily. She pushed him into sitting. 'Yes, Mrs A. C'mon, let's go!'

At the island's petite shoreline Teresa jumped out and bent down to wrap the mooring rope around the wooden slip, then looked up, taking in the willow trees that skirted the island. It had been so long since she'd been there, and for a moment she froze. Shaking herself, she straightened up.

'I'm seeing another side of you,' Luke said.

She held out her hand, and he took it and climbed out. 'C'mon, city boy. I'm going to show you some more of my hidden talents.' She pulled him along and then leaned against one of the willows that overhung the mooring area.

'You all right, Teresa?' he asked.

God, he knew her moods so well, even when she tried to hide them. She pulled off her T-shirt. 'I'm fine!'

'Jesus, what are you like?' he said laughing, and appeased. 'I thought you said there was a little shack somewhere?'

'Follow me...' She took hold of his hand. 'It's a perfect love nest. And a perfect way to start the day.' She nuzzled his ear. 'Get us prepared for the onslaught later.' She put her top back on.

'It's nice of Eva and Dom to organise a party for you... us,' he said. 'Give them a break.'

Teresa sighed. Luke was just too nice... but she liked that. She stopped walking and turned to him. 'C'mon, the shack's not too far away.'

They made their way through the dense foliage in silence and reached their destination two minutes later. She averted her eyes from the trees as much as she could, keeping her line of vision focused ahead. Further inland, the willows that fringed the island's shore thinned out, to be replaced by silver birches, beeches and oaks.

'Ta da!' Teresa held her arms out towards the small log cabin, as if presenting him with a gift. It had been Dom who'd got the cabin ready for the party – put in a fridge and stocked it up. It had been his idea to have the fireworks too. At first she'd been against it, but when she knew Eva had agreed, she did too.

'Very cute. Looks as if it shrank in the wash.' Luke grinned, the dark brown of his irises dappling in the shimmer of light that flecked everything it touched.

'It has a mattress and a cupboard full of non-perishable snacks and drinks.' She glanced at him.

'Perfect. I could murder a Coke.'

She pushed him towards the narrow veranda that ran the entire way around the tiny abode.

Bending to get through the door – Luke was a good six two – he said, 'Love it.' And then immediately flopped onto the mattress. 'Does Dom come over here to sleep when Eva's getting on his nerves?'

Now would be a good time to talk to him, tell him – but no. Not now. It would spoil everything. 'That would be most of the time,' she said instead.

'They seem all right together.'

She pulled a can from the fridge and gave it to him, and then sat on the edge of the mattress. 'I suppose.'

Teresa had anticipated energetic sex but, as usual, Luke had surprised her. Despite the heavy, expectant feeling deep in her groin, she really didn't mind. They talked for half an hour, about their wedding and their future plans – hers to pursue the career she'd always wanted, and about his, which was already going so well. Luke was ten years older than she was. He had a head start. At thirty-two, Luke loved his job as much as he loved his existence. And that's what Teresa adored about him the most – his absolute immersion into his own life, as well as all those to whom he was attached, which was many.

Conversation lulled and, at last, he pulled her to him, finding her lips, teasing them with his tongue. With a gentleness which pervaded everything he did, he peeled off her T-shirt, then her joggers and finally her knickers. Listening to the light morning wind and the gentle rustle of river water outside, Teresa twisted her body so she was facing his feet, and then with agility, knees astride his torso, she took him deep into her mouth and almost simultaneously felt the warmth of his lips in the place that had been aching since the early hours. After only moments, the waves of expectation built and she heard her own gasp.

And then a scream, and not hers.

Luke pulled away at the same time she opened her eyes. She collapsed to the side of his naked body and looked towards the figure standing in the cabin's doorway. In a slice of a second she thought she was seeing a ghost, but realised quickly it was her youngest sister.

'Jesus, Jessica!' she said, over her sister's screams. 'What the hell are you doing here?' She grabbed a blanket and threw it over Luke's now flaccid penis. 'And stop screaming, Jessica… stop it!' She took a breath and tried to calm down. 'I'm sorry, I didn't mean to shout at you.' She pulled on her T-shirt and knickers and moved towards her.

Putting herself in Jessica's position, she realised how the scene she'd been confronted with would have looked to a twelve-year-old. Eva would kill her if she found out Jessica was on the island – that she and Luke were on the island. She could not at that moment think of a worse scenario than Jessica finding them there.

The island. Again. Christ, today was going to be even worse than she'd anticipated. Thank God, though, her little sister seemed to be calming down. She'd stopped screaming, but was still sobbing uncontrollably.

Teresa did something she'd stopped doing with Jessica several years ago and took her in her arms. She turned to Luke, who hadn't moved. If this wasn't such a bad situation she would have laughed: the unflappable Luke, who was known for the steadiness of his surgeon's hand under the most extreme pressure, was in total shock, his expression that of a rabbit's caught in an Olympic-sized spotlight.

Jessica let Teresa cuddle her for a few seconds but quickly pushed her away, wiping her eyes with trembling hands.

Teresa was contemplating Jessica's reaction when she felt rather than saw Luke pulling on his shorts behind her. Her eyes remained fixed on her little sister. This really wasn't good. 'Jessica, it's all right. It really is.'

Silence.

She carried on. 'What are you doing here? Who else is here?' She fired the questions and Jessica's head began to shudder in much more pronounced and jerkier movements. She gentled her tone. 'Talk, Jessica. Talk to me.'

'On boat. No one else here.' She peered at Teresa. 'Should not be here.'

'*You* shouldn't be here, Jessica. Bloody hell. Eva'll kill me if she finds out you came, and on the boat... she'll blame me. What were you thinking? You came in the rowing boat, right?' She raked her hand through her long blonde hair, squeezing the strands tight.

'Came in spare motorboat.'

'Jesus!'

'Should not be here,' Jessica said again, her gaze fixed on Luke.

Teresa turned towards Luke. His expression was now one of extreme guilt. *Fuck.* Jessica must have heard them in the kitchen and followed them. Bloody Dom. He was encouraging Jessica to use the boat. Luke was probably wondering what he was letting himself in for – although there was no chance of the Keane gene pool being shared. Not through her, anyway.

'Jessica, darling—' she carried on.

'Should not be here…'

'It's okay us being here, Jess, but it's not okay that you are here, coming on the boat alone,' Teresa said softly.

Her sister stared at her. 'Do not love me. No one loves me, only Natalie. Do not love Natalie.'

Teresa was beginning to feel tired; she could never follow Jessica's stream of consciousness. 'You *do* love Natalie, Jessica.'

'You' – Jessica pronounced the 'y' as 'ya', while the rest of the word was a total breath out: 'oooh' – 'do *not* love Natalie.'

'I do. She's my sister, like you are. And I love you too.'

'I' – finally, a pronoun – 'love Natalie. *You* do not. Are still angry with her?'

Teresa couldn't find the words to reply; she should deny it, but couldn't. It wasn't in her nature to lie. She *was* still furious with Natalie, still smarting from the argument they'd had the summer before. Looking back, she knew that what they'd argued about wasn't really what lay between them. On the surface the disagreement had been about their dad, but underneath it was about something else, the other pain they collectively held. It was about their sister and the confusion that all three of them

78

still felt about her death. Her eyes flipped around the cabin, towards the window, and the oak trees outside. Her sister had been an adept tree climber. Falling from the tree didn't add up, although it had done for the coroner. There had been talk initially, that she had taken her own life, but that added up even less well. Her sister was not depressed or unhappy, in fact the total opposite. But... Teresa did remember her sister's odd behaviour and moods the summer that she died, odd even for her wilful sister.

'C'mon,' Luke said, breaking into her thoughts and taking her arm. 'Let's get back.'

She nodded and then placed her arm around her Jessica's shoulders.

'Will not say anything,' Jessica said.

'It's best if you don't, Jess,' Teresa said. 'I'm sorry you were frightened.' She pulled her sister closer. 'C'mon, lets get back and eat the chocolate muffins Mrs A's left for us.' She ended her sentence with a smile.

'Jessica's going to have to drive the boat alone one last time,' Luke said. 'I can't do it.'

'True, city boy.' She glanced at Jessica. 'One last drive then, Jess.'

With agility Jessica climbed into her boat, as, clumsily, Luke got into the other. After untying the rope, Teresa jumped in after him and glanced at her sister. Jessica had always been... mentally fragile, but she had worsened. Maybe she needed to see someone – a child psychologist or something. Talk about what had happened. Maybe all three of the remaining Keane sisters did.

At the jetty she helped Jessica moor her boat securely, not that she needed any assistance.

'Shit, I've left my baseball cap on the island,' Luke said, suddenly.

'Good,' she replied, hearing the sound of victory in her voice. 'Let's hope a raven uses it for a nest.'

'Can we go back and get it?'

'Absolutely not. There has to be some positive outcome for this morning.'

He laughed. 'Okay. I'll pick it up tonight when I go over with Dom to oversee the firework display.'

'Just go in the house, Luke. Maybe put your dressing gown on or something, so no one's suspicious.'

'Overkill?'

'Maybe, but just do as I ask.' She turned to Jessica. 'Same for you, Jess. Go back to your room and get back in your jimjams.'

'Mrs A's chocolate muffins?'

'Later, after you've got changed. There's a good girl.'

13

Jessica

Jessica awoke to the sound of movement in the kitchen. Her bedroom was over the top of it, and noises rose easily through the old wooden floorboards. Was it Natalie down there? But remembering that today was party day her stomach lurched. The next twenty-four hours loomed. Why were her family doing this? A party. Just why? She hated that Eva had suggested it. It brought everything back and she didn't want it to come back. She didn't want to remember it, and no one talked about their sister ever, so why were they having this stupid party? It might mean the subject that was never talked about would be. And she could not. Could not talk about it ever. Because if she did her whole life would collapse, like Dom had told her. Eva would never forgive her, just as she had never forgiven Natalie for telling their dad about his brother and Eva. She would hold the secret forever.

Sometimes she thought it might kill her doing so.

She placed a pillow against her headboard, propped herself up, and watched the rods of morning sun fall like light-infused iron bars onto her Indiana Jones duvet. Her pale blue eyes fell onto her phrenology head that sat on the back left of her desk. It had been moved, she could tell. She always had the head, which was set into a square base, exactly five centimetres from the wall. Now, it was a good ten centimetres away.

Throwing off Indiana Jones, she took the few steps to her desk, repositioned the head and then sat down on her chair and stared at it. One day, when she was older, when she had been to university like Teresa, she wanted to study heads. What was inside them. She wanted to work out what went on in the core of Eva's, Dom's, her sisters', all of her sisters'. But more than anything she wanted to understand what went on inside her own brain, because she had a suspicion that it was not quite like other people's.

She placed her forefinger on the part of the phrenology head labelled *Order*, just above the left eye, around the upper part of the eyebrow. It was the place in her brain that she had to protect. Then she slid her finger to the section labelled *Secretiveness*. She had to protect that part too, to shield her world. Her family's world. Eva's world.

She stood up and slipped on a pair of shorts, a T-shirt and sweatshirt, and went to find Natalie. They could have an early breakfast together.

Halfway down the spiral staircase, she heard Luke's voice – and then Teresa's – in the kitchen. She tiptoed the rest of the way to the last step and then sat down on it. Minutes later, she heard the kitchen's French doors opening and then closing. She made her way into the kitchen, spotting the muffins on the counter. She took one and went to stand by the window, biting into it as she watched Teresa and Luke walk to the right side of the house and then disappear down the steep bank that led to the jetty where the boats were moored.

She stuffed the rest of the muffin into her mouth, slipped on a pair of shoes, and followed her sister and boyfriend.

From a position where they couldn't see her, Jessica watched as Teresa and Luke got one of the motorboats ready. Stupid Luke didn't know what he was doing. Teresa was doing all the work. He was wearing that stupid hat too.

Teresa was not wearing a bra and as she leaned over the boat, Jessica could see her sister's boobs. It was obvious that Luke could see them as well. She didn't like how Luke looked at Teresa; it was the same way Dom had looked— *Do not think about it.*

Once the couple had moored at Raven island, Jessica moved closer to the jetty and peered across the river. Teresa had taken her T-shirt off and her boobs were bouncing in the spidery dawn sun. Luke was laughing. Why did he like watching Teresa look so stupid?

She turned away and glanced at the spare motorboat. She knew how to get it ready and drive it – Dom had shown her on her seventh birthday. He'd told her not to tell Eva, although she'd had to tell Eva on that terrible day, when she returned from her secret and devastating trip to Raven Island. But usually, she would never tell on someone when they asked her not to tell. She took that very seriously.

Retrieving the fuel tank from the small boathouse located next to the jetty, she connected the fuel hose with ease and lowered the propeller into the water, just as Dom had shown her. Jessica wasn't popular at school but her saving grace was found in her aptitude at sport. Dom said it was because of her unusual intuition and being able to anticipate what people were planning to do, together with her agility and strength, that made her such a valuable member of any team. *And also why no one likes you*, Eva had retorted. *So off-putting in a child.* She was in the rowing squad, and captain of the netball and girls' football team – joining the latter to please Dom. Sometimes it felt she spent her life pleasing Dom so that indirectly she was pleasing Eva, who she'd never been able to please.

She jumped in the boat, adjusted the throttle, pulled the cord, and headed for the island. She couldn't believe Teresa had gone over with Luke. It was the reason she felt she should follow them – to take care of Teresa. She did not trust Luke.

Jessica did not trust any man.

On arriving at the shore she moored the boat and made her way to the log cabin. She stared at the wooden building; the place where she had seen and heard what she had not wanted to see and hear. With her heart feeling as if it were in her mouth, she padded up the three steps that led to the veranda and opened the door.

The scene that greeted her was all too familiar.

14

Jessica

After leaving Teresa and Luke, Jessica went straight upstairs to her bedroom. Before pulling the blue dress from the wardrobe, the one Eva had chosen and bought for her, she sat down at her desk and stared at the head again.

Order. She swivelled it around. Towards the back of the head she found the section labelled *Destructiveness* – just below *Secretiveness.*

She turned away, picked up the dress and laid it on the bed, ready for later. Then she put her pyjamas back on and her dressing gown, which she wrapped tight around her body. She would do *exactly* as Teresa had told her.

She went back downstairs to see who was around. Everyone was busy and after only ten minutes she returned to her bedroom and sat on her bed, first staring out of the window, and then staring at her phrenology head. A few minutes later she slipped out of the pyjamas and put on her blue dress. As she did so, she heard her door open. She thought it was Teresa and her heart lifted – but both of her sisters always knocked.

Her heart capsized. Dom never knocked.

'Hey, how's it going?' he said.

She stared at him. 'Fine.'

'You got a minute?'

'Getting ready, Dom,' she said.

'You look very pretty in blue, Jess.' He moved closer to her. 'Sit down, I want to have a chat.' He studied her as she sat down awkwardly on her bed. 'This is Teresa's day, and Eva's, and I don't want it spoiled. What you told me… before…' He sat down next to her on the bed and she moved away. 'In the car a few months ago when I was taking you to school… have you forgotten about it, Jess?'

'Have.'

He ruffled her hair. 'I hope so.'

'I don't want Eva to be sad or upset.'

'No. So best to be silent.' He grinned at her. 'You're good at that.' Then his smile slipped. 'Eva's been through enough.'

'Did you love her?'

'I do love Eva, no matter what you might think.'

'Do not mean Eva.'

'Jess, let's keep Eva happy.'

She stared at him in the same way as she had earlier been staring at her phrenology head. 'I'm hungry.' She didn't know what else to say.

'Me, too. Come down in a bit. I'm going to make waffles.' He left her room.

She moved to her desk, picked up her head. Looked at it closely as if she might learn something.

She had not told him what else she knew, what else she had seen – something had told her not to share that scene with him. She could do exactly what Teresa had asked, and keep quiet, but she wasn't sure she could keep silent about all of this for much longer.

She wondered if Dom knew. She did not think he did.

A knock on her bedroom door. 'Can I come in?'

Juno's voice. 'Yes, Juno,' she said, as Juno stuck her head inside the door.

'Thought I'd come and say hello. You all right, Jess? Just saw Dom as I was nipping to the loo. He looked a bit… anxious when he came out of your room. Is there a problem?'

'Nice to see you, Juno.' She always spoke better when talking to Juno.

Juno leant up against her bedroom wall. She looked like a model, Jessica thought, and she loved her skirt. Loved the colour. All bright and open, like Juno. 'No. No problem,' Jessica finished.

'I bet today is tough for you, isn't it?' Juno said. 'Too many memories. I know Natalie's struggling too. It'll be over before you know it.'

'Yes, will be.'

'Aw, Jess. Your dress looks lovely… you know, if ever you want to talk about stuff, I'm always here. Natalie is too – you know that, don't you?'

'I do want to tell you something, Juno, but it really is a secret.'

Juno sat next to her on the bed. 'What's bothering you, Jess?'

Jessica told Juno what she had not been able to tell anyone. To share a secret and half the burden was a beautiful feeling. 'Cannot tell a soul, Juno. Promise.'

The colour in Juno's beautiful face had drained away and she didn't answer straight away. Finally, she said, 'I think you do have to tell someone, Jess, and I think it should be Teresa. Then… she can talk to Eva.'

'Will, but not today.'

'I'll try and do something,' Juno said.

Jessica only nodded but then heard a noise outside her door and got up to look into the corridor. The door should have been closed but it was not. She peered at Juno.

'Who was it?' Juno asked.

'No one there. Can I finish getting ready?'

Gently, Juno touched her cheek. 'I'll sort it out.' Then she left.

She loved Juno.

Jessica waited but then pushed herself up from the bed, made her way to the bathroom, and knelt by the toilet. She should not have told Juno.

15

Teresa

It was eleven a.m. and four hours since they'd returned from Raven Island. Judging by Eva's mood – she was in quite a good one – Jessica hadn't said anything. Teresa would come clean with Eva about it after the party. She'd also mention about Jessica seeing a shrink.

Some time after nine, several of Eva and Dom's friends had turned up to help get everything ready. She'd seen Dom and his mate, minus the wife, convivially drinking a beer together by the jetty not long after. Juno had turned up early too, flouncing around, trying to be the centre of attention.

She turned to examine Luke's profile as his gaze swept around the garden, observing Eva's efforts. She tore her eyes away from his perfect profile and checked out the several guests who'd already turned up. *Unfashionably early*, Eva had mouthed. She looked again at Luke, who was now examining the sushi on the long table.

'Bad idea,' he said.

She giggled, although not at his comment but the thought of him, and her, in the cabin. It would have been better if it'd been Natalie sneaking up on them. 'The sushi, you mean?'

'That too,' Luke replied, with a wry grin.

'The party hasn't started properly yet.' Teresa did a mini eye-roll and then smoothed down the lapel of her jacket. Eva had gone nuts that she'd chosen a trouser-suit to wear.

She pulled a chair away from the table and plonked herself down, then turned and took in the impressive profile of her family's ostentatious home. She'd never come back to live there, she knew that, but she had to grant an inward nod of recognition to what had been given to her – a private school education and the financial assistance to study for the bar; because although engaged to Luke, she didn't want to be financially dependent on him. She heard her own purr of satisfaction. She really was like a cat: a loner, discerning of whom she let in – she had only been loyal to two. Now though, it was Luke. No one else. The others long gone. Her and Luke's life together was going to be perfect – he with his career caring for people, and she with hers, taking the bad ones down.

Teresa catapulted herself from the chair and took hold of Luke's arm. 'Come on, let's mingle with the early arrivals and then go and check on Eva. I think she's in the kitchen overseeing the hors d'oeuvres.'

'What, you mean she's placing them on a tray?'

'Something like that, yeah.'

Teresa glanced down and took in her silver-grey suit with its long, tailored jacket, snug-fitting tapered trousers which ended just above her ankle, her feet encased in three-inch emerald-green stilettos. Her only other compromise to a party outfit, as well as the shoes, was the glittery emerald-coloured bodice encasing her slim ribcage. It was her outfit's tour de force, fitting her like a spangly green condom. The simile made her smile.

'You look sensational,' Luke whispered into her ear. 'Let's enjoy our joint celebration. It'll all be over this time tomorrow and then we'll be back in my flat.'

'I really love you, Luke.'

'I love you too, my hard-nosed-soon-to-be barrister.'

If Teresa could giggle she would have done, but she'd long ago trained herself out of the habit. 'Have you seen Natalie?' she said, instead.

'Not since this morning.' He moved a strand of hair from her eyes.

'You mean when she was skulking about and waiting for Lolita to turn up?'

'I take it you mean Juno?'

Teresa did smile then. 'I do. Do you like her?'

'As a matter of fact I do.' He sipped some of the champagne he was holding. 'She's a bright kid.' Teresa stopped herself from snorting. 'Stop it, Teresa.' Searching her features, he carried on: 'You're twenty-two years old and it's time to rein in that streak of unmodified and undignified jealousy.'

Teresa shrugged, as she always did when he said this, and left it at that, although making sure he knew she was mad with him.

–

At exactly midday, Dom turned off the music and made his faux-father speech, firstly congratulating Teresa on her academic success and then another toast on her engagement to Luke. It was all more than a little cringeworthy and Teresa tried not to make eye-contact with any of the guests. Eva was by Dom's side and although still early in the day, she was already looking a little the worse for wear.

Teresa couldn't work out if it was too much champagne or too much dope. Probably both. Dom, though, was holding it together, but he was more seasoned than Eva, and younger too, which probably helped with both the booze and the drug consumption.

After Dom's announcement the guests loosened up more, and drank even more, and Teresa decided the best thing she could do was to connect with her own party. Dom turned the music up and she was about to make her way to the dance floor on the terrace, intending to drag Luke with her, but noticed a sudden subtle change in his mood.

'You okay?' she asked.

'Course I am, just having a moment about my mum. Hope she's feeling a bit better.'

Teresa embraced him. 'I really love your mum, Luke… let's drop in and see her tomorrow?'

He nodded, although the expression of concern didn't disappear as quickly as she'd hoped.

'We could pop over now?' she said.

He touched her cheek. 'See, you do have a heart.'

She punched him playfully on his chest. 'I mean it, put your mind at rest.'

'Nah, it's okay. We'll go tomorrow. Come on, let's dance. Enjoy yourself for once.'

'Meaning?'

'Meaning you need to relax more, Teresa.'

He was probably right. They danced, smooched and, in between, Teresa talked with as many of the guests as she could. Finally she peeled off her jacket and placed it over a chair. The music was pulsing. She picked up her glass of champagne and drank it in one and then went off again to dance. It felt like the evening already, not early afternoon. She began dancing with fervour, Luke now more watching her than actually joining her. She lifted her arms, wiggled into a twist, her right leg jutting to the left and then felt rather than heard her bodice rip.

'Shit,' she said, laughing. She contorted her arm up behind her back and felt the gaping hole. 'I've an old spare somewhere in the bottom of my weekend case.'

Luke inspected the damage. 'Go inside and get changed. Take your time. I'll have a chat with Dom.'

'You do that,' she said, 'although I haven't seen him since the big speech.'

She spun around and grabbed her jacket from the chair, flung it over her shoulders so no one would see the gaping hole, and made her way inside the house.

–

By the time Teresa returned to the party, she couldn't find Luke anywhere. She had, though, been gone a long time, because after making the bad decision to lie down on the bed for a few minutes, she'd nodded off for an hour – it had been an early start that morning. Scanning around the terrace and still hoping to catch sight of Luke, she caught sight of Natalie instead. Momentarily, their eyes met but then Natalie turned and disappeared inside the house.

Teresa made herself mix with the guests, she danced, and drank too much champagne. Less than an hour passed before she again wandered around the grounds looking for Luke, but he was nowhere to be found. She tried to find Dom instead – who she couldn't find either. Perplexed, she sat down, the beginnings of annoyance starting to wrap around her. Christ, she hoped bloody *Lolita*, aka Juno, hadn't got her claws into Luke. It was then when she saw Natalie re-emerging from the house, her face was as white as the blooms on the garden's angelica trees. She looked almost demented, as she headed in the direction of the boathouse and jetty. God, Natalie really was a bit bonkers.

Where was Luke?

16

Natalie

After five minutes of cuddling a distraught Jess on the edge of her bed, hoping her tears had nothing to do with the drugs that were on such casual, open display in Eva and Dom's room, and with the sounds of the party drifting easily through her little sister's open window, Natalie gently pulled away from Jess, unsure of what to do. She stared at the duvet that was scrunched up around her sister; it had been Natalie who'd suggested that Eva buy it for Jess. Jess had others but Mrs A always had to wash, dry and iron that particular cover because Jess insisted it was the only one she wanted to use. The Indiana Jones films were her absolute favourite and this fact had surprised all of them, because it was so out of character for Jess to have such a normal and childish trait.

Eventually, Natalie stood and walked over to Jess's desk. She'd taken her shoes off to come inside. Slipping your shoes off to come indoors was one of Eva's insistences, and one that none of the sisters would go against – only perhaps the sister who was not there any more.

'Shit!' A lacerating pain in the sole of her foot. Bits of china covered the wooden floor. She bent down to see the damage: a piece of Jess's smashed phrenology head was stuck in the ball of her right foot. She pulled it out and watched her blood drip on the wood. Spotting a box of tissues on her desk, she pulled out a handful and mopped it up, and then using the Freud book that was sitting on the desk too, she scraped the hundreds of pieces together into one pile.

Natalie hobbled back to the bed and sat down again next to her younger sister. A warm gust of summer wind blew in from the open window, as did the thumping sound of Tina Turner. Natalie wasn't that worried about Juno: she'd already figured out that she was up to a bit of no good. She was also beginning to think that Juno had hooked up with Caitlin and again a flash of jealousy sparked through her. Juno was *her* friend. She glanced at Jess. Perhaps somehow Jess – who had a knack of some-times being in the wrong place at the wrong time – had seen something too, and being Jess, that was why she was so worked up. Her little sister was, though, much more hysterical than she'd be normally when something flipped her. It would only have to be something that others would see as inconsequential to massively affect Jess.

With her foot pulsing with pain, she was determined to find out what it was. She'd find Juno, and maybe Caitlin, later.

'Jess,' she said, 'how did your head get all smashed on the floor?' She turned and looked at the open window. 'Was it the wind? It's gorgeous outside... you should be outside.'

Silence.

'What happened to your phrenology head?' she carried on.

'Smashed it.'

'Why on earth did you do that? You love your head.'

Jess shook her own.

'Your dress is muddy too... have you been near the river?' She waited patiently for her reply.

'Juno.'

It was the way she said her friend's name. Natalie backtracked. 'Why did you smash the head? It's one of your favourite things.' She tried to smile. 'Along with your duvet cover, of course.' She stroked Indiana's hat.

'Because do not want to know what is inside people's heads.'

'Jess, tell me what's happened.'

'Took motorboat to Raven Island. Did not want to be at party. You down end of garden. You do not want to be at party either. I wanted to come to you—'

'You shouldn't be taking the motorboat out, or the rowing boat, come to that. You shouldn't be going to Raven Island... I need to tell Dom not to encourage you—'

'Do not tell Dom anything!' Jess almost screeched.

'What's happened, Jess?' By now, fingers of darkness were wrapping around Natalie and the throbbing in her foot became nothing compared to the building feeling of foreboding.

Jess began to cry again, shaking too.

'Jess. Tell me what's happened.'

'Juno dead.'

The sense of foreboding was now consuming her. 'Stop being silly, Jess.' Yet as she said it, she questioned if it was she who was being silly for telling Jess to stop being silly. 'What do you mean?' she carried on. Suddenly, the air coming in from the window, the noise from the garden below, the hint of river smell percolating through the room, the image of Juno on the motorboat – or was it

Caitlin, she was beginning to wonder – all made her want to throw up.

'Dead. No breath. I know. No pulse. No breath. I know. Again. Happened again.'

Natalie swallowed to hold back the sick she could taste in her throat. 'Where?'

'Took boat, already told you. To Raven Island.' Her sister stopped talking and with her cheeks red and awash with tears she stared out of the window. 'I saw a raven too. Dom said never ravens on island. But one today.' She looked at her. 'Why is it called Raven Island if ravens never go there?'

'Are you sure you're talking about Juno, Jess?' Her sister was mixed up, the party had disorientated her. Her sister was remembering before. But something *had* happened.

Jess began to cry again. 'Alone. I found her alone.'

'I'm going to get Dom—'

'No! Not Dom!' Jess said, her voice hoarse.

'Why not Dom?'

'Nothing to do with Dom.'

'I didn't say it was. But he can go to the island. Go and look.' She needed to speak to Eva. But she would be half off her head.

It never crossed her mind to go and find Teresa. That would be the second mistake she was to make that day.

'I'll come and get you when I've found Eva and Dom,' Natalie continued, as calmly as she could. 'Everything's going to be all right.'

'Was Luke. Juno went to island with Luke.'

'What?'

'I saw.'

'Are you sure? And are you sure it was Juno?'

Had it been Luke? Had it been Juno? Natalie wasn't sure then. She'd thought it was Dom in the boat, with Juno. Although she admitted inside the mess that was her mind that it could have been any of the men from the party. It might not have been Juno. Could have been Caitlin.

It *was* Dom; she'd seen Dom. And she was sure she'd seen Juno's fluorescent tartan, but then again Caitlin could have been wearing a similar colour.

Her brain felt as if it were frying. If only she'd had her contacts in.

17

Natalie

Natalie stumbled from Jess's bedroom and made her way back outside. She had to dodge around people, as the place had filled up with yet more bodies getting drunk and dancing around the terrace. As if nothing was wrong, when something was obviously very wrong. The same feeling began to seep in that had soaked through her five years before, when she had come home to a hysterical Eva in the kitchen and then gone outside and found a traumatised seven-year-old Jess sitting by the jetty, after returning from Raven Island. The thudding sensation that something terrible had happened again became real, the unnerving realisation that she'd seen the beginning of the incident earlier – and yet not seen – thanks to her bad eyesight. All the male party guests did look similar. Even Luke was dressed like the other blokes, which had surprised her. Eva must have had a word with him to conform, and he would have done so to please Teresa.

Lucky Teresa, who had everything, while she left Jess and her to rot.

A few of the revellers were plucking at her arm, trying to engage her in conversation. She asked a few incoherent people if they'd seen Dom, Juno, Luke, Caitlin. No one had seen any of them. But then at the side of the house, near the path that led to the boathouse and jetty, she spotted Eva. Thank God. She was leaning forwards over the wall that ran alongside the path. A rolled up bank note shoved up her nostril. *Jesus Christ, Eva.*

'Mum!' she said. The word came easily to her lips despite the years of doing as she was told and calling her Eva.

Natalie wanted a mother at that moment. The three of them had everything they could possibly need, apart from love and guidance. And a proper mother. A proper father.

Quickly, Eva pulled the note from her nose and turned to her. Natalie immediately saw the telltale signs: massive pupils, and her mother's relief at feeling completely omnipotent and unfazed by life. She knew what Eva was feeling, not because she'd ever felt that way, but because she'd spoken to Juno, who had.

'Natalie.' She didn't have a go at her for calling her Mum. But her cocaine-happy expression had fallen and it was then that Natalie saw what Eva would see – her looking distraught. 'What's happened?' Eva said, stepping closer.

She smelt sweat and garlic. 'It's Jess—'

In seconds Eva snapped back to reality. 'Where is she? What's she done now… is she all right?'

'I've left her in the room. You should be taking care of her…' She'd never before made an accusation towards Eva, even though she'd wanted to in the past, had wanted to five years ago when Eva had not responded to Jess's trauma in the way any normal mother would. 'Jess's distraught,' she carried on, taking a breath, thinking of what she'd seen earlier. Or what she thought she'd seen earlier. She had to tell Eva. And again she'd be ruining her mother's life, just as she had when she'd told Dad about Eva and his brother.

'Natalie, spit it out,' Eva was saying.

'Jess took the boat to Raven Island earlier. She says…'

'What?' Eva said.

'She says that Juno is dead.'

'What are you talking about, Natalie?'

Natalie thought of the stained hem of Jess's dress. 'We need to find Dom or someone to go and look. Find Juno. Juno's not at the party. Your hairdresser's daughter too – her mum can't find her. I don't know what's going on, but something is.'

'What was Jessica doing at the island? *What?*'

'She thought she'd seen Luke going over there… with Juno… that's why she went. But I'm certain I saw Dom in the boat… and it could have been another girl. It could have been Caitlin.'

'Don't be ridiculous. Dom's been at the party all afternoon. He has not been over to the island with Juno, or Caitlin. It must be Luke.'

'Eva.' She flipped back to using her name. 'Jess says Juno is dead. *Dead*, Eva.' It was all too surreal. She was in the midst of a nightmare.

Eva's jowls sagged further as the shock of her words sank in. 'Don't be ridiculous. I want to talk to Jessica.'

'*I* want to go to the island to find out what's happening.'

'Natalie, neither Juno nor my hairdresser's daughter is on the island. No one is dead. Juno's probably half-comatose somewhere, or shagging one of the guests.'

'Juno is *not* like that. You just don't like her because she's young and beautiful. You're jealous.'

Eva's whole countenance changed in a split second. It was the angriest Natalie had seen her for a very long time. 'I'm telling you now, young lady, we go to talk to Jessica and take it from there.' She shoved her drug paraphernalia into a little hole in the wall's brickwork, grabbed hold of Natalie's arm and began to practically march her back to the house.

'No! I'm going to the island. I'm going to find Juno, or whoever Jess saw.' She ripped Eva's hand off her arm. 'What *is* wrong with you?' she shouted, and so loudly a few party guests standing metres away turned around, smiling nervously.

It was then that she saw Dom walking towards them. She never thought she'd be so glad to see her stepfather.

'What's going on?' he said, whilst grinning at the guests and lightly shrugging in pretend exasperation.

Turning to him, she noticed the grin that he was directing at his guests was fake. Dom appeared to be nearly as fraught as she was.

'Did you go to Raven Island earlier?' she said to him. 'With Juno, or… Caitlin?'

'What are you talking about, Nat? Course I didn't.' He flicked a look towards his wife but then his line of vision moved to the wall where Eva had hastily pushed her stash. He then looked at her. 'What's happened, Natalie?' he finished.

'Juno's missing. I thought she might be with the Caitlin, but her mum says she can't find Caitlin either… Jess says Juno's on the island.'

She moved closer to him, so no one could hear her next words. 'Dom, Jess says that Juno is… dead. A girl, on the island, *dead.*' She peered at him hard. 'I don't know if Jess is going nuts or if I am.'

She watched for his reaction. What reaction did she expect? She wasn't sure. She wasn't sure of anything at that moment. He still hadn't replied and she carried on, 'Please take the boat over, now. Go and check—'

'Nat, don't be silly,' he replied. 'Juno isn't dead and she's not on the island. Neither is Caitlin. Maybe Juno's gone home… was feeling the worst for wear… You know what she's like – she's probably overdone it.'

'*I'm* going over to the island then.' She pushed past him.

He grabbed her arm. 'I'll go. Is Jess in the house?'

'Yes, her bedroom. She's really upset. Something isn't right…'

Dom turned to Eva. 'Take Nat inside with you and go and talk to Jess. I'll take the boat to the island.' He said to Natalie: 'Go with Eva.'

'I'll meet you in the snug, Natalie,' Eva said. 'Bring Jessica there.' She turned and started making her way to the house.

Natalie looked at Dom. 'You sure it wasn't you on the boat?'

'For fuck's sake, Nat, drop it. No, it wasn't me. I think you were seeing things that weren't there. It probably wasn't even our boat.'

'Just go to the island and find out what's going on,' she said. 'This is all too weird…' It *was* all weird, but by then she'd convinced herself that Jess's proclamation that Juno, or another girl, was dead on Raven Island was not true. Poor Jess was having one of her moments, and moments that had been increasing in their frequency since their sister's death. The party had not been a good idea.

Dom nodded, understanding what she meant, her reference to when Jess had found their sister. He turned and left.

She was about to follow Eva, but then felt a tug at her arm and turned. Eva's hairdresser, looking worried. 'You all right?' she said to her. Why could she not remember anyone's names today?

'I can't find Caitlin anywhere,' the woman replied. 'Have you seen her? I know she's fine…' She looked at Natalie. 'But you know…'

'I understand,' Natalie replied, trying to reassure the woman. She understood what she was saying: everyone here would be talking about the tragedy of five years before. 'Caitlin's probably with my mate. Dom's gone to look. Honestly, don't worry.'

The woman nodded and touched her elbow. 'Thanks. I'll be over by the food table.'

Natalie pasted a smile on her face. 'Yes, good idea.' She then made her way to the house and, doing as she was told, she went to get Jess.

Jess was sitting bolt upright on her bed, propped up by pillows, staring straight ahead, although the floor was clear of the head debris, and the mud on the hem of her dress had dried hard in the stifling warmth of the room.

'Jess,' she said softly. She could barely hear her own voice. 'Eva's waiting in the snug. She wants to talk to you… Dom's gone to the island…' She peered at her sister. 'Jess, you've got mixed up… the party, all the people here, it's disorientated you.'

Jess didn't move for what felt like ages but then finally tilted her head and looked at her, her blue eyes both vacant and soulful. 'Natalie. Need to go get Juno. All alone. Like before.'

Dom would be at the island by now. This could not be happening, again. 'Come on, we'll talk to Eva.'

Jess took her hand and together they made their way to the snug, and to Eva.

–

When they walked into the snug, Eva was pacing up and down the long rug that crossed the room. She was agitated and jittery, the coke – or whatever it was that she'd been shoving up her nose – wasn't reacting too well with the situation she was in. Eva was barely holding it together, and acting in a similar way to when she'd discovered that Dad had found out about her and their uncle. The same reaction too, as the day of their sister's death.

A few steps into the room and Jess stopped dead.

'Jessica, come in,' Eva barked, and looking at her, said: 'Close the door, Natalie. Both of you sit down.'

Eva didn't sit but carried on pacing, full of false energy that she didn't know what to do with and flashbacks pummelled through Natalie's mind.

'Eva,' Natalie said, swallowing hard, glancing at her watch and making ready to go back outside. 'I'm going to take the boat to the island—'

'Stay here. Leave it to Dom.' To Jess Eva said, 'Tell me what's happened. And talk, Jessica. Properly.'

The muscles in Jess's long neck contracted as she swallowed. 'Saw Luke on boat with Juno going to Raven Island. Did not want to join in party. Wanted to talk to Juno. So waited for them to come back. Could not find Juno so took boat to island to go swimming. Found Juno. Dead.'

'Juno is *not* dead, Jessica. And what were you thinking of, going to the island, on the boat – to swim?' Eva's voice was raspy. She coughed. 'You should *not* be going to the island.'

'Having fireworks there, thought was all right to go.'

'I don't think it was Luke on the boat, Eva.' Natalie's right hand found her scalp and she couldn't stop herself.

'Stop it. Stop scratching, and stop lying,' Eva screeched and turned again to Jess. 'Jessica, you saw Luke taking Juno to the island?'

Jess nodded. 'Yes.'

Eva's voice was tight and controlled as she directed her next words to Natalie. 'Dom's been at the party all afternoon. If anyone was on the boat with Juno, it was Luke. Jessica has said it was Luke. And I'm sure Juno is fine. Dom'll find her, and probably not on Raven Island.' She turned back to Jess. 'It was *not* Dom you saw on the boat, okay?'

Jess nodded.

To Natalie Eva said, 'And you did *not* see Dom – if you saw anyone, it was Luke. Do as I tell you, both of you.' She glared at her. 'Do not ruin my life again, Natalie. Do as I have asked.'

It was the first time Eva had openly admitted knowing it was she who'd told Dad about her and his brother. And now Eva was asking her to lie. But it wouldn't be a lie, would it? It could have been Luke. In fact, thinking back, she thought it probably *had* been Luke – the fiancé of her sister, whose life was going to be stellar with a man who adored her.

To say what Eva had instructed her to say, she knew, would be at the expense of Teresa's happiness, but Natalie hoped that by obeying Eva she would ensure that Dom did not leave Eva, and in a prison van. Eva was many things but she didn't deserve another desertion. Not after losing her favourite daughter.

'Your hairdresser can't find Caitlin, Eva,' she said. 'It might have been Caitlin on the boat.'

Eva ignored her, focusing on Jess. 'Jessica, *who* did you see on the boat?'

'Luke and Juno.'

To Natalie she said, 'Who did *you* see?'

It took her a few seconds to reply. 'Luke. It was Luke and I thought it was Juno, but like I said, it could have been Caitlin.' She stepped closer to Eva and she swore her mother recoiled a little. Sweat covered Eva's brow and the apex of her cheekbones; her pupils were wider than ever. She carried on, saying quietly, 'I'm going to find Dom—'

'You stay here with Jessica,' Eva replied. 'I'll go and find Dom, and find out what's happening.' She made her way out of the snug.

By then Natalie didn't really think there was a problem – only perhaps the problem of Juno, or Caitlin, being with Dom.

'Was it Juno, not another girl, Jess?' she asked her little sister.

'Was Juno. And Luke.'

She and Jess stared at each other. Both of them knowing and understanding, although Natalie wouldn't truly understand for years to come. That day, with her choices and decisions, her deep-seated guilt about what she'd done to Eva years before, the underlying grief for her sister, together with her desperate need for her mother's love, she set the course of all their lives. Hers, Teresa's and Jessica's. And probably Eva's too.

But it could have been Luke. Luke hadn't been with Teresa earlier in the afternoon.

It *had* been Luke in the boat.

Natalie stood, although her legs felt as if they were unable to take her weight. She glanced at her hands, which were trembling. She'd go to the island now.

18

Teresa

Still waiting for Luke to reappear, Teresa used the time to think about her family, deciding that perhaps today was the day to clear the air and make a patched peace with Natalie. To finally talk about their sister. Make up. One of the reasons she decided this was because they owed it to Jessica. And themselves. They had all been through so much. Life was too short, and Eva too broken. The three remaining Keane sisters needed each other. Today was as good a day as any. Perhaps the best day.

Teresa picked up a full glass of champagne and took a gulp, and another. She'd talk to Natalie later, after the fireworks. Sipping more bubbly, she rehearsed in her head her opening conciliatory lines to her sister.

'Teresa, darling, you've changed your top. I just loved the emerald-green. So suits your colouring.'

Teresa jumped at the interruption to her thought processes. 'Hi… Maureen.' Eva's hairdresser was wearing a cerise pink dress with a neckline a little too low and a face a little too red. Her vacant expression yelled of recent dope smoking.

Maureen was looking at her as if trying to figure something out, although Teresa couldn't be absolutely sure that was Maureen's true expression, because she herself had drunk more champagne than she would normally. Boredom, the enemy of restraint.

Maureen carried on: 'I'm looking for my daughter, have you seen her?'

'So sorry,' Teresa replied. 'I don't think I'd recognise who your daughter is…'

'Ah, okay.' Maureen wobbled a little. 'I'm sure Caitlin's around somewhere.'

'Of course she is.'

'Anyway, congratulations, Teresa, on both counts – passing your course and a catch of a husband-to-be.'

'Thanks,' she said. 'That's kind of you, and thanks for coming today.'

'I've been looking for your man, to congratulate him. Do you know where he is?'

'I think he must be in the house… Listen, I'll search him out and send him straight over to you. And if I find out where Caitlin is, I'll send her over too.'

Maureen tottered back to the dance floor and Teresa swore she'd never turn into a Maureen, or an Eva, come to that. She moved her half-full champagne glass to the other end of the table in a gesture of future abstinence.

It was then she caught sight of Eva emerging onto the terrace from the kitchen's French doors, looking as demented as Natalie had done earlier.

Maybe Luke *was* inside the house. He'd probably fallen asleep or something. She'd go and look. Once inside, she checked the dining room, both lounges, Dom's down-stairs study, the games room, even the garage. No one anywhere. She thought about looking upstairs, although a part of her had no desire to find some middle-aged, married-to-other-people couple shagging in one of the spare bedrooms. It's where she and Luke should have gone, and then the unfortunate incident on Raven Island wouldn't have happened. Teresa's faux-ice heart softened thinking of Jessica. Her little sister wouldn't rat on her and Luke. God, when had she last used that word? As a child, and at a similar age to Jessica.

Suddenly, Teresa remembered the under-used family snug, which was tucked away on the ground floor in the east wing of the house. Luke had mentioned on a few occasions that despite its dilapidation, it was his favourite room. She walked down the long, low-lit hallway towards the snug. Luke could well be in there.

She pushed open the door and the aroma of mould hit her nostrils. It took a few seconds for her eyes to adjust to the snug's subdued lighting – it was the darkest space in the house with little natural light, but when she focused she saw Natalie standing in front of her, obviously about to leave. She hadn't seen her sister come back to the house, but she'd been preoccupied in her conversation with the hairdresser, Maureen. The champagne had dulled her observations too. Her eyes darted towards the sofa, where Jessica was sitting, her knees pulled up to her chest. She'd obviously been crying.

'What you both doing tucked away in here?' she asked.

Neither sister replied.

She took a few more steps inside and carried on: 'What's going on?' She directed her question to Natalie, who was standing directly in front of her, and looking as if she'd been about to leave.

'Teresa,' Natalie said. 'Have you seen Juno, or Luke?'

'What do you mean?' Immediately, her hackles rose and she was instantly on the alert, on the defensive. After all, why had Natalie felt the need to invite Juno to *her* party?

Natalie walked to the sofa and sat down next to Jessica. It was then that Teresa noticed Jessica trembling. What had happened now? Déjà vu slipped through her like ice-cold water running along a ravine.

'Jess's been to Raven Island on the motorboat...' Natalie was saying.

'Jessica?' Teresa said in a whisper. Her little sister *had* said something about the log cabin incident. Oh, well, she'd deal with the fallout; it wasn't the end of the world.

'This afternoon, Teresa,' Jessica replied softly.

Inwardly, Teresa sighed relief. Of course Jessica wouldn't say anything about the unfortunate incident. But Jessica *had* taken the boat out again, thereby completely ignoring her advice.

She jerked her head back to look at Natalie. 'What *is* going on?'

'Earlier, Jess saw Luke and – she thinks – Juno in the boat... heading over to Raven Island.'

'I don't think so.' Teresa's words were measured. 'A, because Luke's been with me all day and B, he cannot drive a motorboat... But it could have been someone called Caitlin – she's gone missing too, it seems. With some other bloke, of course.' She turned to Jessica. 'Are you sure it was Luke, and whoever in the boat? It could have been anyone on the river today. So many boats out, as it's such a gorgeous day.'

Jessica nodded. 'Was Luke.'

'Luke wasn't with you earlier... when I saw you, Teresa,' Natalie said.

'Luke has *not* been out on the boat with Juno, or any other girl from this party.'

'Where *is* he, then?' Natalie asked.

'I don't know,' Teresa snapped. There was no way he'd do that. Not with Juno, or any girl. But, where was he? 'Jessica, are you absolutely certain it was Luke on the boat?' she asked.

Natalie coughed and then began scratching her head. 'I saw Luke on the boat too.'

'*What?* Natalie, do *not* do this to me.' *Why are they doing this?* 'It was probably Dom,' Teresa said. 'You've both got mixed up and daren't tell Eva that Dom was with some teenage floozy.' She found Natalie's eyes. 'How and where did you see them?'

'I was sitting by the river's edge earlier this afternoon. Then took a walk to the boathouse. That's where I saw them, on the river,' Natalie replied. 'I thought they'd come back, so I've been looking for Juno and I can't find her… and you can't find Luke.'

'I couldn't find Dom either, earlier,' Teresa retorted.

'Teresa,' Natalie said, her voice barely audible. 'Jess went to Raven Island in the boat. She says…' Natalie viciously clawed at her head, 'she says that Juno is there… and she's dead.'

'For God's sake, what is wrong with you two today? Of course Juno isn't dead.' Teresa looked at both her sisters, open-mouthed. To Jessica she said, 'Is it because I told you not to tell?'

'Tell *what*, Teresa?' Natalie asked, standing up.

'Jessica followed Luke and me over to Raven Island early this morning,' Teresa replied. 'Really early. Before anyone was up. We went to the cabin… Jess came in and found us…'

'Having sex?' Natalie rolled her eyes.

'Sort of.' She glanced at Jessica. 'I'm sorry you had to see that. And I'm sorry I told you to keep quiet about it.'

'I did not go to Raven Island this morning,' Jessica replied, her gaze fixed on the rug.

'Yes, you did, Jessica… it's okay,' Teresa said. 'You don't have to keep the secret any more.' What was it with Jessica? She really did have a problem. Eva really did have to do something about it.

'Did *not* go to island this morning,' her little sister was saying. 'Did not see you and Luke. Saw you when I got up and was in kitchen.'

'Jessica, *please* stop this. Stop lying.' The effects of the champagne had long ago worn off. Was her youngest sister saying she'd seen Luke with some girl, either Juno or Caitlin, because she resented Luke? And Natalie, why was she adamant she'd seen Luke on the boat? Luke had not been anywhere with Juno. And the thing about Juno being dead. It was all some sort of sick wind-up.

'Did you have your glasses on or contacts in when you saw the boat?' she asked Natalie.

It took her sister a second to reply. 'Of course I did.' Natalie pushed past her. 'I'm going to the island myself now—'

It was then that Eva flung open the door. Her blue dress had split down the side, and her face was bright red. 'Dom's found a girl… on the island…'

Natalie raked her nails through her hair. Jessica burst into tears, her body collapsing into a paroxysm of shaking, so like she had done before.

Before.

Teresa could not speak.

Her life would never be the same again.

19

Jessica

In the end Dom didn't make the promised waffles, as preparations for Teresa's party were already in full swing. Jessica worried about what she had told Juno. Worried about everything. Party day stretched ahead but then again, every day did.

When the guests began to turn up, none of her family noticed that she wasn't there. When eventually she did venture outside into the rising heat of the day to go and look for Natalie and Juno, she saw Natalie sitting by the river on the bench reading a book and Juno wasn't with her. She didn't want to bother Natalie and decided to find Juno instead.

As she walked in the direction of the jetty and boat-house, she had to dodge between the partygoers. A few asked her how she was, complimented her on her dress, told her what a handsome girl she was turning out to be, just in time stopping themselves from remarking on the physical similarity to her sister.

The narrow path that led to the jetty sprouted an even narrower path, which looped around, eventually ending up at the front of the house. That path was never used; it was overgrown, dark, never saw sunlight. Taking the detour, she pushed away the overhanging bushes and began walking up the slight incline. She'd only taken a few steps when she heard a man's voice. 'Juno, c'mon. Let's go back.'

'Why did you come, if you want to go back?' Juno's reply.

'I wanted to tell you, persuade you, to cut out the drug-taking. You have such a future ahead of you. Don't waste it.'

Jessica heard Juno's distinctive laugh then, and just as clearly she could hear the man's voice.

'It's just for a bit of fun,' Juno said. 'But okay, if you say so. After today.'

'Good,' he replied.

'One more kiss?' she heard Juno say after a few moments.

'This is a mistake. I'm sorry. Time to go back to the party.'

Jessica, as quietly as she was able, made her way back to the main path. Today was just too much. She really should not have told Juno. She would forget she had heard what she had heard. She would forget about the whole of today. Juno obviously had not believed her, had forgotten already.

Her shoulders hunched, she walked back to the house and back to her bedroom, to have a think.

When she saw Juno again, she would tell her it was all a huge mistake.

—

An hour later Jessica left her room, intending to make her way to the river. At the far end of the terrace she spotted Maureen and asked her if she had seen Juno. She had not, and then Maureen asked her if she'd seen Caitlin. 'No,' Jessica replied, and carried on towards the jetty.

Sitting on the wall she looked out on to the Thames. Away from the party, it was such a peaceful day. The water looked inviting. She would like to go swimming but the best swimming was in the middle of the river, so going in the water was better done from the island. She had not been swimming from the island since *it* had happened, but did it matter now, her going? No, it did not. She would take the motorboat. Teresa would be cross, but that didn't matter either.

Glancing at the jetty she saw that one of the boats was missing. She looked up, her eyes skimming the river: who had taken it? It was then that she saw their boat, heading for the island. It couldn't be missed. *Dominic* was painted on the side. It had been Eva's present to him. Eva, always trying to please Dom, to keep him around, and then Dom at the same time trying to please Eva, to be able to stay around. It was a parasitic relationship, on both sides.

Jessica saw a girl on the boat. She was certain it was Juno but then remembered Maureen and her missing daughter. She squinted into the bright summer light, trying to work out who the girl was with. She couldn't be sure. Was it Dom or was it Luke? Maybe another man from the party. But then she thought about the conversation that she had overheard on the unused path and decided that it was Juno, and it *was* Luke.

Luke was going to the island with Juno just like he had gone to the island with Teresa. She stood there, thinking what to do. Luke was like all the other men. She would go back to the house and think about what to do – if she were to do anything. She would wait for them to return, and then she would talk to Juno, who obviously had not taken her seriously.

–

When half an hour later Jessica returned to the jetty to see if they were back she was relieved to see the boat was in its mooring place.

She untied the spare motorboat and glanced around. No one was watching. She really wanted to swim, get away.

Ten minutes later she was standing on Raven Island. She made her way to the cabin, planning to get a cola from the fridge before going into the water. Peering through the trees, she suddenly saw, a few metres to the left of the cabin, a big ice bucket and an upside-down bottle of champagne inside, indicating it had been drunk. Near to the bucket was a baseball cap. The one Luke had been wearing early that morning.

She heard a rustle and looked up at a nearby willow. A raven was perched precariously on one of the lower branches but then it spread its wings and descended to the ground behind the tree.

She followed the bird and as she pushed through the screen of willow branches, she saw that it had taken position on Juno's left thigh, sitting just above the hem of her fluorescent green skirt. The raven flew away as she approached.

She took a few steps towards beautiful Juno.

This was all her fault.

Juno was alone.

Just as her sister had been.

20

Now

Natalie

Her husband had returned from his trip very early that morning. Oli had been quiet opening the front door because he hadn't wanted to wake her. Natalie, however, had been awake all night fretting about Hope's request for a Keane family reunion. She'd said yes, but now knew she couldn't go through with it. How, though, is she going to tell her daughter? The only way she can tell her 'no' is by telling Hope the reason why, the real reason – that she can't face seeing Teresa, or her husband.

It is Oli who's kept her up to date with Teresa, even when she didn't want to be kept up to date, but Oli sensed she wanted him to, and so he did. Thank God for Oli. They'd met in her second year at university, in Spiders nightclub. He was six years older and already working. She'd asked him what he was doing in Spiders, he'd replied that he was looking for her. It was love at first sight. She couldn't believe her luck because Luck and she are not close friends.

Oli and Hope are the best things in her life. She doesn't deserve them, she knows that, but they are both so separate from who she was back then. But not now

– it's all catching up with her. She knew it would. One day. She'd allowed Teresa access to Hope to make some sort of payback – that is Jess's analysis of the situation, her professional analysis.

It's so strange how she and Jess can muddle through without ever digging into the core of their past.

Her husband walks into their bedroom and she pretends to be asleep. She hears him get undressed, hears his trousers and belt thump lightly on the floor. He'd leave them in a heap. He's worse than a teenager. But she forgives him many habits. She forgives him because he forgives her, has exonerated her for things he doesn't even know about, but she suspects suspected. He understands the mechanics of her brain better than anyone. *The inside*, as Jessica still calls it.

Sometimes she trawls through her memory banks trying to pinpoint a time when they'd first met, when she might have said *something* to Oli; something she couldn't remember saying, something that had wiggled its way out of her subconscious after too much alcohol. Because back then she did drink, a lot. It was a problem but she kept it hidden, and under control. She was good at hiding things; better than Jess – that's the truth. She worried the words would come out of her lips, unbidden, and it would take away the man who she would die without, and so she stopped drinking altogether. She hasn't touched a drop since she was twenty-two.

Oli's taking some things out of his small suitcase. Leaving the dirty washing on the floor too, she bets. He gets into bed and enfolds her. He hasn't had a shower and smells of mild sweat and travel. She loves it. She loves him. She doesn't open her eyes but rubs his forearm.

He touches her head, her scalp, which is on fire. 'You're worried,' he says.

'We'll talk later,' she replies.

'Hope's told me. I know.'

He doesn't know. But he should.

What is going to happen? It's all up to her and the outcome is crushing her. The awful serendipity of their daughter's graduation day.

'I can't do it, I can't have us all together,' she says.

'Hope's close to Teresa. You know that. It's what I love about you the most, that you allowed me to take Hope all those years ago to connect with Teresa... I mean, I love that characteristic you have.' He rubs her back. 'Nearly the most,' he says, nuzzling her neck; despite the fatigue of travel, his hardness is apparent in her lower back. 'It's good our daughter sees her aunt—'

They've been in the spoon position but now she turns around. Another time she'd take hold of him and they would make love, as they have always done. But not this morning. 'It's never bothered you, has it? Hope being in close proximity to Matt... Why is that, Oli?'

'Nat, let's not talk about this now.'

'Teresa never wanted kids, you know,' she pushes.

'What we say we don't want at twenty-odd doesn't mean we don't want it later.'

'What are *you* saying?' She sits up. Trails of frail morning light are seeping through the curtains.

'Nothing, Natalie. Nothing.'

'Oli, talk to me.'

'I'm really knackered, Nat. Can we do this later?'

His erection has vanished. 'I need to do it now.' She swings her legs out of bed and sits there, leaning forwards, her hands enveloping her skull, allowing herself to gently rub the ferocious itch at her right temple. She feels Oli's hand covering hers. He's sitting up now too, and she feels so guilty. He's been travelling around northern Europe for two weeks. All he wants is to come home and sleep. Come home and enjoy his daughter's success. Be home and make love to his wife.

'You've never wanted to talk about Teresa before, so why now?' he says.

'Because our daughter wants me to throw a party for my family.'

'Teresa did want kids… a child,' he says.

'What?'

'She had three miscarriages when she was younger.'

She thinks of Teresa, her beautiful and ambitious sister. How she'd envied her. How she'd wanted to be her.

He carries on, 'It couldn't have been easy for her.'

'No.' She turns to look at him. 'I tried back then, to reconnect with Teresa. And then I lost… our baby—'

'Oh, Nat. It was an accident.'

She ignores his statement. 'Teresa never forgave Jess… and then when in London Jess needed her the most, Teresa abandoned her. Again.'

She doesn't mention her own miscarriage a second time, it's still too painful. It's a Keane family trait, not talking about people they've lost. It took her many years to get over the loss of her baby, but she had eventually, and had eventually admitted to herself too, if only secretly, that the cause of her miscarriage was no one's fault. There had been an underlying problem that wasn't picked up on with her baby. She'd been aware from early on that Oli had told Teresa the terrible outcome of her miscarriage – she was unable to have more children, and that had been the only time Teresa had tried to contact her. She'd ignored the calls and not even Oli could persuade her to take them. Although none of what had happened stopped her from allowing Oli to take Hope to meet her aunt, Teresa.

'She regrets everything that happened at that time,' Oli is saying. 'And not just about Jessica.'

'You know that for certain?'

'I do.'

She stands, pulls her dressing gown from the back of the door. 'I'm going to make coffee. And I'm going to call Teresa, and Jess, and tell them both that I can't do it.' She turns to him. He's flopped back into a supine position. 'Then I'll call Hope and tell her.'

'Don't. Not on the phone. She'll be home next weekend. We'll tell her then, together.'

'I can't wait that long.'

'That's my opinion.'

She scratches at her temple, doesn't reply and makes her way to the kitchen. She brews some coffee and then plods back upstairs, bypassing their bedroom, where she can hear Oli snoring. Why had she insisted on talking about Hope and her grad day celebrations this morning? Why? She carries on up the second set of stairs that leads up to the loft room. She sits on the sofa and drinks the coffee and then lies down. The sun is bright now, the day proper has begun. She closes her eyes. Oli is right. She'll wait until next week when Hope's home to tell her. But she'll call Teresa and Jess.

It's not only Teresa and her husband who she can't bear to see, but Jess's husband too. It's so odd that Hope took an immediate dislike to him as a child and, in truth, she'd never have left her with him. It's the reason why Hope isn't close to Jess.

Her eyes flicker and fill behind her lids, replaying Teresa's graduation day party, trying to find clues. She lost her other older sister that day; and Jess too, eventually, to the man who picked up the sharp pieces of her.

As the years have progressed, she's questioned if he is the reason why there are so many pieces of Jess that are still missing.

21

Teresa

Teresa hears the rattle of the front door knocker and turns, accidentally flinging flour on the floor at the same time. She thinks it's Matt, home early, but it's the late afternoon post. Her eyes dart around the kitchen counter and then at the floor and the fine mist of flour covering it. Christ, what had possessed her to make Mrs A's chocolate cake, especially as she's already bought one at the supermarket. Sentimentality, she supposes. Trying to recreate the nicer parts of her childhood, which had been mainly supplied by Mrs A.

She must remember to call Mrs A in the morning while Hope's still here – the two of them can have a chat. Alongside Oli, Mrs A is Teresa's umbilical cord to her family – to Natalie, and Jessica – because Natalie keeps in touch with Mrs A too, as does Jessica, although much more sporadically than her or Natalie, Mrs A tells her.

Mrs A is a piece of invisible silk thread, holding something broken but still viable together.

Thank God she's still alive and thank God she'd outlasted Eva. Like all the Keane sisters, Teresa loved their housekeeper more than she'd ever loved her mother. Somewhat bewilderingly, Mrs A had adored Eva and had been inconsolable in the weeks after her death.

It is Mrs A's ninety-fifth birthday in a few weeks and Teresa has been collaborating with the nursing home's manager for a special tea. She and Matt plan to stay in a hotel nearby, which happens to be near to Natalie and Oli too. Mrs A would love it if they all went together. Teresa doesn't think she can manage that... although after Natalie's phone call she is having second thoughts.

She finishes making the cake and then goes upstairs to have a shower. Looking at the clock, she works out she has another hour before Matt's due home. He works just as hard now as he's always done. When not working, he's exercising, and when he's not doing either of those things, he's writing, although recently the writing has taken priority. With his pharmaceutical knowledge, late in life he's found a way to help society. It was one of her solicitor friends who suggested he write a book about drug addiction, targeting young people. All the money he makes is donated to shelters for young women who have major problems with addiction – something that causes many of these women, mostly girls, to turn to prostitution.

She and Matt both work on this campaign, but separately. It keeps them both focused, and sane. It's like a children substitute, she sometimes thinks, or perhaps some sort of parent filler for them both, as both of them are parentless, only having each other.

As far as she is concerned, she does not have a father. It had been a surprise, her father's letter, coming soon after Raven Island. Absolutely no contact from him before then, the bastard – although he'd quickly disappeared back to the black crevice from which he'd crawled.

No matter what Eva had done, the Keane sisters did not deserve his desertion.

She takes off her suit and underwear and steps into the shower, luxuriating in the semi-cool water. Her eyes are closed and she feels a small rush of air. She opens them. Matt.

'You went to the supermarket, didn't you?' he says, smiling.

'I did.' She switches off the water and reaches for a towel. He picks it up from the radiator and holds it open for her. She steps into it and he pulls the towel and her towards him, and she leans into him. 'I've missed you.' She loves him more today than she'd loved him the first time they'd met. She has no regrets about marrying Matt – has never had any, not one.

'And you went on the bus, I'm betting.'

'I did. You know me. Like to take the bus after a big case. Bring myself back to real life!' She looks up at him. 'I've missed you,' she repeats.

'I only saw you this morning, Teresa,' he says, grinning. 'So…?'

'So, what?'

'Verdict?'

She grins back. 'The bastard got six years for living off immoral earnings, six years for supplying drugs to a minor, and four years for statutory rape.'

'Another win! Excellent news. I'm hoping it'll be a double celebration tonight.'

'I think Hope's done well.' She moves to the mirror.

'You've spoken to her?'

'I haven't spoken to her, no…'

'What's the matter?'

'I don't…'

'What, Teresa?'

'Natalie called.'

128

'Wow.'

'Hope wants a big family get-together for her gradu-ation.'

'Hope is a remarkable girl,' he says.

'She is. But she doesn't know what she's doing.' She's looking in the mirror, rubbing cream into her face.

'Is Natalie up for it?' he asks.

'Indeed she is. She'll do it for Hope. I envy her Hope.'

He is standing behind her, like a guardian angel. 'As they say, it is what it is. Let's talk to Hope tonight. What time's Greta planning to arrive?' he asks.

Teresa's friend and ex-work colleague had flown in from Geneva earlier that morning. 'She's in the UK, hired a car at the airport, has stopped off to see her mum and dad in Nottingham.' She looks at the bathroom clock. 'She's due here at eight. Hope should be here around six-thirty.'

'Time to chat with Hope then.'

Teresa paces to the bedroom. 'I need to get a move on. And you need to change the beds.'

He gives her a mock salute.

'How was work today?' she asks.

'Good.' He rakes a hand through grey hair. 'I've got a date for the next book publication. My editor wants me to do an event, something to "increase my profile"…'

'You can't. They know you can't.'

'It doesn't stop them from asking.'

Teresa puts a slim-fitting black silk dress on. She turns so he can zip her up.

'Bit overdressed?' he says, but with both amusement and pride embedded in his eyes.

'Tonight's special… and I feel it's going to be special in more ways than one.'

'I'm off to change the beds,' he says. 'And then a shower, then I'll come and help you in the kitchen.'

'It's all under control.'

'Of course it is. I take it that Natalie's been in contact with Jessica too?'

Teresa nods. 'I don't think I can bear being within three feet of her husband.'

'And Jessica?'

She's standing in front of the full-length mirror, viciously twisting her hair into a tight bun at the nape of her neck. From the vanity table sitting next to the mirror she picks up a wooden hairpin and jabs it like a spear into the bundle of hair. She replies to his reflection. 'I'm okay about Jessica.' She swivels around, pulls at the hem of her dress.

'It's time – time to let things go,' he says. 'It was years ago, when you went to see Jessica in London.' He smiles. 'And Hope... is your second Hope.'

She nods. 'It's all so complicated, isn't it?'

'Hope'll be here soon, so let's lighten up.'

She lifts her hand and caresses his cheek, smiles back at him. He turns and leaves their bedroom.

As soon as he's gone the smile slips from her face and she turns around to survey herself in the mirror again.

Why hadn't Natalie told the truth back then, or *wanted* to hear it? Or did Natalie genuinely believe she *was* being honest? Teresa is as convinced today as she was then that Natalie had lied. But why after so many years hasn't Natalie ever admitted to those long ago untruths? Why has Natalie stuck to her version of the story?

Teresa shook her head, brushing imaginary wrinkles from her dress as she did so.

Dom's death had meant that Eva was finally alone in her big, freezing-cold house. By then, she was well past her prime. Too many drugs, too much booze. Teresa hadn't seen Eva since the party that she'd thrown for her and Luke, and her graduation, and so when Oli called to tell her Eva had 'passed away', she'd felt absolutely nothing. Eva died a year after Dom. A drug overdose – accidental, the coroner had said. Teresa had, though, never been sure it was an accident.

She hadn't gone to her mother's funeral. It was Matt who attended. This said much about Matt, a lot about her, and a considerable amount regarding their relationship.

Teresa tilts the mirror so she can see her feet, which has the effect of chopping off her head, so she takes a few steps backwards to give her perspective. Perspective gives a much fuller picture. Jessica had just started her second year at med school when Eva died. Through Oli, Teresa knew that Jessica had never been home in her first year. In her holidays she went to stay with Natalie and Oli. Teresa had nearly folded when Eva died and had been close to calling Jessica. But she hadn't.

A few years had then passed, each of the Keane girls getting on with their own lives, but then came the day when she dropped everything to drive down to London to be with Jessica.

But Teresa can't think of that day now. It had all started so well and ended so badly.

She stares at her reflection and at the tender dusk light infusing her room, as if by doing so she will, all these years later, find something within the image reflected back – answers and explanations to all the tragedies of her life, and her sisters'.

22

Jessica

Jessica and her husband had flagged down a taxi outside the Soho restaurant where they'd celebrated her birthday and are now home. He leans forward to pay the driver and, knowing he won't tip, Jessica opens her clutch bag to take out her purse. Her husband shakes his head. She always gives a tip. She should just hand the driver a fiver. But she dare not. She still feels like the young Jessica in many ways. Acquiescent. Vulnerable. Her colleagues and peer group at work would not believe who the real Jessica is; she can't believe who the real Jessica is, although in many other ways she is a long way from the girl she once was. Her speech is fluid and comprehensible, and she has worked hard on hiding her flaws, because she understands the world sees people like her as a threat, someone to be scared of; people are frightened of something they do not understand. Her brain is not wired the same as most of the population. Teresa never understood her, and that is why her eldest sister is always wary of her. As a grown adult she often wonders if Teresa subconsciously blames her for their sister's death; after all, it is she who found her. And then after Juno, Teresa's wariness turned to anger, and then, hatred.

Is she that far from the girl she was? She stares at the back of her husband's head as he clambers out of the taxi. She isn't.

She is in exactly the same place.

All the patients she sees, all of the sickening stories she hears – and there are many – her own story in many ways is still one of the worst. Her life is a hologram, laser lights crossing and penetrating, half-truths and lies, mirages and misconceptions. And if a hologram, does she exist at all?

'Are you staying in the taxi all night?' he is saying.

She looks up, almost startled that she is here with him. He's holding the door open for her. She turns and catches the driver's grumpy expression in his rear-view mirror. She also catches the sheen of sweat on her forehead, feels the quickening of her pulse. She is unsure if it's the pleasurable anticipation of the night ahead, or terrible expectation of the night ahead. She is so split, like the two sides of the brain. She has not yet discussed with her therapist this part of her life. Her marital sexual life. And she may never do so. 'Sorry,' she says to both the driver and her husband.

She steps out and she and he are standing on the pavement outside their shared home.

'You like my presents?' he asks.

'I do.'

He smiles. Like a smile a father would give to his child. 'I'll always take care of you. You know that, don't you? You know I love you?'

'I know you love me.'

'And you love me?'

It is a full moon tonight and the reflected rays bathe the features of his face, making it seem like a shiny, grey mask.

Tonight he looks old. It's not the alcohol either, because he watches what he drinks. She has never seen him drunk.

'Jessica?' he pushes.

'Yes, I love you.' So easy to lie. Perhaps before today it might have been true, but after Natalie's phone call an intangible hesitance has taken hold. The possibility of all the Keane girls being together again, and with one added to the trio, making it a quartet once again. Something is shifting within the depths of her. Memories are pushing to the surface.

'You don't sound very convincing,' he replies.

'Don't I?' She searches his face and now that a big cloud has blotted out the moon, he appears as he always appears. 'I love my bracelet.'

He pulls her towards him. 'I wish you hadn't taken Natalie's call. It's ruined everything.'

'Let's go inside.'

'Why are you doing this?'

'What?' she says.

'Even thinking about a reunion with sisters who hate you?'

That stings. She doesn't reply.

'Why are you ruining your own birthday?' His voice is as flat as his expression.

She turns to him. She is sabotaging the evening and isn't entirely sure why she is doing it. It *is* Natalie's call about a reunion. That is why she is doing it. She is beginning to think she *can* do another graduation day. Be there for Hope. Confront who she is and what she has done. And what has been done to her, because something terrible has been done to her, in so many ways.

He is wearing an underlying anger tonight; it is palpable. She senses something more too, a sexual urgency

134

within him that she has not felt, in this way, before. Not in seventeen years. It's a potent mix of anger, fear and sexual urgency.

They make their way inside the house and straight to the bedroom.

He is desperate; she can see it in his unusually quick and jerky movements. For years she has been desperate for a different kind of intimate contact and yet tonight, as she somehow knew it would happen, suddenly, she is repulsed by him, and herself.

Her mind travels back in time again, to when she had been a patient at the hospital in which she currently works. But she is not the Jessica she was then. She is not. She now inhabits both parts of the phrenology head. She is left and right and she can be whole, a complete person.

She slips off her dress and he stares at her slender body. Her small breasts, her pubis, shaved prepubescent smooth. He can't take off his trousers, shirt and underpants quickly enough. His penis is engorged. He pushes her onto the bed and her ruby bracelet gets caught up in a loose thread from the duvet. His finger enters her but not too far. He takes his time as he always does, and she despises herself for the roll of pleasure that he elicits. He moves above her and holds himself near her mouth, as he has always done. But after only minutes, he does what he has never done and yanks her head away, pushes her hard down onto the bed. Tonight is going to be different, as she sensed it would be. He holds her wrists, her arms above her head, and enters with force. The pain inside is excruciating but as she lets out a stifled scream, he finds his release and at the same time mouths a name, and not hers.

Hope.

His body drops to her side and he's lying next to her. She does not think he even knows he's said the name. The sickness in the pit of her stomach is rolling and all-consuming but then a sense of violation and rage overcomes her, filling her, engulfing her, a tsunami that is picking up everything she should have felt about the horrific entanglements of her life, but which she has buried.

She places her fingers in between her legs and feels wetness – not of arousal but of blood.

Sometimes, she has wondered what it would be like to experience normal intercourse. This, though, is not normal. Nothing about her relationship with this man is normal.

By refusing to have intercourse with her for seventeen years he has controlled her, every part of her.

Why did he marry her?

In the cavernous and secret part of her, she knows why.

Jessica Keane is forty and up until the last ten minutes her hymen has been intact.

Jessica is forty and has just awoken, as have her memories.

23

Then
August 1991

Natalie

When Eva said those words inside the snug: *Dom's found a girl… on the island…* in a split second Natalie's life changed forever; these were the words that would change all of the Keane girls' lives forever.

Natalie thought the universe was playing a hellish joke on the Keane family, that their home really was cursed, and the women inside it, or visiting it, were cursed too.

Eva moved away from the doorway and further into the room. 'Dom's called the ambulance. And the police.'

'Caitlin?' Natalie whispered.

Eva turned to her, her eyes glazed, her dress torn. She had looked like Rochester's mad wife, Natalie remembered thinking, years later. 'Juno. She's dead.'

Her throat was so incredibly dry and her tears came then. She loved Juno. Like a sister. She looked towards Teresa and the memory of their other sister, found dead and cold on Raven Island too, scorched into her mind. 'I can't believe it.'

Teresa nodded and as she did so her mane of blonde hair fell across her face, like a curtain, blotting out her features and the pain that lived within them. Teresa was twenty-two and in that moment looked ancient, and as she'd appeared five years before. Their sister's death had hit Teresa the most. All three of them were devastated, but for Teresa, the death of their sister had been cataclysmic.

But Teresa was always Teresa and she got herself together in only seconds. She turned to Jess. 'Did you tell Eva you saw Luke on the boat with Juno, going over to the island?'

Jess picked up a cushion and pushed it up against her face.

'Jessica, stop it.' Teresa carried on, her voice laced with frustration and anger and not knowing who she should aim it at. 'Take the cushion away. *Was* it Luke you saw?'

Jess moved the cushion sideways. Her expression set in terror, her body shaking uncontrollably.

'Natalie?' Teresa said to her.

'It was Luke,' she replied quietly.

Eva was standing by the fireplace and completely sober, any signs of her earlier drug use long gone. 'Teresa,' Eva said, coughing and clearing her throat, 'I believe Luke might have some explaining to do... to the police.'

'This is such crap!' Teresa shouted. 'It was Dom, wasn't it, on the boat with Juno? He took her to the island.' She raked her hair away from her face with her hand, staring at Eva. 'What is going *on* here?'

'I've asked around, already,' Eva said. 'Luke hasn't been seen for a while. Where is he, Teresa?'

Teresa shook her head. 'He's around somewhere. I left him to go inside and change my top. When I came back out from the house, I couldn't find him. But he's somewhere.' She gave Eva a stony stare. 'Maybe he just couldn't stand being around your fake mates... I know for sure if given a choice, I'd have disappeared for as long as possible too.'

'Stop it!' Natalie suddenly shouted. '*Stop* it! My friend… is… d—' She couldn't say the word. 'Why are we all arguing?'

'Because of *you*,' Teresa hissed at her. 'Jessica and Eva are saying that somehow Luke is involved, and we all know it's Dom. What's this all about?'

'It was *not* Dom who went to the island with Juno,' Eva said, evenly. 'It was Luke.' She stepped closer to Teresa. 'I know… because I saw them on the boat too.'

'You really have to be joking,' Teresa said, her face white. '*Why* are you doing this?'

'I'm not *doing* anything. I'm telling the truth,' Eva replied, quietly.

Teresa turned to Jess and Natalie. 'Tell the truth now, both of you, and stop fucking around.'

'Teresa. Watch your language,' Eva whispered.

'Watch my language? Are you even on this planet?' Teresa stared at her. 'How much have you smoked today?'

Natalie was staring at Eva too. She could not go against her mother. Not after being the reason of her parents' divorce, especially now it was clear that Eva knew it was she who'd told Dad about Eva's affair. But she still wanted to say something to Teresa, about Dom, the drugs, the dealer's visit that morning. The coke she'd seen Eva shoving up her nose. The ecstasy tabs in Eva and Dom's room. But she could not. She pretended to be a rebel, she pretended she was her own person, she pretended to be like Teresa, and Juno, but she was not.

Juno. Dead.

She could not look at her older sister. Could not bear to see the reignited pain in her eyes.

'This is not about what I do,' Eva finally replied to Teresa. 'It's about what your fiancé has done.'

Teresa turned away. 'I'm going to find Luke. This is all just too ridiculous.' She shot a look at Natalie.

'Teresa,' Natalie whispered. 'Juno's dead. It's happened again.'

Teresa's face crumpled then. 'I'm so sorry about Juno. But you are *all* lying, and I will *never* forgive you.'

Teresa disappeared from the snug, and would never return, not to the snug, the house, or their lives.

Natalie turned to Jess, whose eyes were closed, although the shaking had stopped. Her face as white as the paint of the snug's wall. Her breathing laboured.

'Mum, Jess's unwell,' she said.

Quickly, Eva moved towards the sofa and pulled Jess into her arms. 'She's okay, aren't you, Jessica? Just worked up. Take some deep breaths and you'll be fine.' Looking at Natalie, she said, 'Who did you see on the boat with Juno, Natalie?'

She didn't answer, couldn't answer. Who had she seen? She'd thought, assumed even, it was Dom. Jess told her it was Luke. Did she want to hurt Teresa? Hurt Luke? Hurt herself?

'Luke,' she said.

At that point Natalie believed that whatever Jess or she said wouldn't matter, wouldn't impact anything. She didn't believe Luke had anything to do with Juno's death. At that point, she didn't really believe Juno was dead. She thought it was all some horrendous mistake or misunderstanding.

So strange how a mind can refute what it doesn't want to acknowledge.

She'd had to acknowledge it, though, because soon after Eva left the snug, a tall woman dressed in casual black trousers, a T-shirt and wearing sensible black Doc Martens entered the room with a man who wore plain clothes too, accompanied by Dom, not Eva.

As Dom walked in, followed by the police, he threw a look towards her that said everything: *Do as Eva has asked.*

The detectives introduced themselves, but it was the female detective who did most of the talking. She asked her colleague to take Jess to sit with another policewoman who was waiting in the kitchen.

The female detective's name was Rebecca. Natalie didn't find out her surname for a while, until afterwards. To children, she was Rebecca. It made it less formal. It was only many years later she remembered Dom's mate coming in with coffee. He'd nodded at Natalie, given her a comforting smile.

Rebecca's questions were gentle but precise.

She told the policewoman exactly what she'd seen. A man with Juno on their motorboat heading towards Raven Island.

Rebecca looked at her notes written in a tiny little notebook. 'Were you wearing your glasses, or contact lenses at the time you saw this, Natalie?' the detective asked.

How did the policewoman know she was short-sighted? She'd obviously already spoken to Eva. 'I was.'

'Contacts or glasses?'

'My lenses.'

'And who did you see with Juno, in the boat?'

'Luke.'

'Luke Harris?'

'Yes.'

'You saw Luke Harris accompanying Juno Morrison on your stepfather's motorboat... maybe heading towards Raven Island at around one to two o'clock this afternoon. Is that correct?'

'I'm not sure of the time.'

The male detective coughed and stared at his colleague, shaking his head slightly. She threw him a *be quiet* look and carried on. 'The guests seem to have sobered up now.' Rebecca turned and looked at Dom, who didn't say a word.

Dom was perched on the sofa next to Natalie. He didn't look like the Dom she'd known all those years. He'd lost any semblance of his every-single-day-laid-back demeanour. He actually looked terrified, and she wondered if the detective saw that too.

Rebecca carried on. 'Natalie, do you think there is any possibility it could have been another man from the party in the boat with Juno?'

'Should you be questioning now, Detective?' Dom intervened.

A flicker of what Natalie thought was anxiety passed over the policewoman's features. 'Mr Keane, these are preliminary questions I need to ask but... we've questioned Natalie enough at this stage. Further questioning will take place at the station.'

'It was Luke... on the boat,' Natalie blurted out.

'It's okay, Natalie,' Rebecca said to her. 'We'll talk more in a different place. Really, it's okay.'

She started crying then. 'Juno is... was my best friend. I wish she hadn't come...'

'I'd like to have a very brief word with Jessica now, Mr Keane.' Rebecca said to Dom. To Natalie she said, her voice infused with softness, 'You can go now.'

Dom got up from the sofa.

'Natalie and Jessica are minors,' Rebecca said. 'So we will be pursuing our questioning at the police station, Mr Keane, with appropriate measures taken to safeguard their well-being. Your children will not be interviewed in your presence, or your wife's. The utmost care will be taken.'

'I see,' he said, hovering by the door.

'However, I do need to see Jessica for a few brief questions.' Her eyes seemed to bore into Dom's. 'Questions I'd like to ask now, to get a feel for the scene here today. Perhaps you can go and get Jessica?'

Natalie dipped her head and got up to leave with Dom. If she'd been able to stay there after Dom left, she could have said something to Rebecca the detective; that she hadn't been wearing her contacts, that it could have been Dom on the boat. It was her moment. But it was not to be.

Natalie left the room with Dom.

In her bedroom, five minutes later, she was standing by the window surveying the carnage below. And then her eyes moved to Raven Island, which instead of being lit by fireworks, was illuminated by sterile white police lights; the entire small parcel of land ablaze. So like the day Jess found their sister's body, only it had not been at night, but broad daylight. She turned and went to sit on the bed, her shoulders jolting, unable to stop the tears. She was sixteen but for all of her bravado, she still felt like a child.

She lay down on the bed and closed her eyes, shut it all out; all, which would cause her so many problems in the years ahead.

Later that evening, and around the time that they should have been watching the fireworks, Luke was taken to the police station to be questioned, along with Teresa, Eva and Dom.

Eva had told the police that she'd seen Luke on the boat with Juno, and her timescale of events was the same as Natalie's – because Eva had ensured it was – and the same as Jessica's too. Dom, of course, denied being on the boat with Juno.

But from the first untruth that she'd unleashed in the snug, there was no turning back – or so Natalie had thought then. Of course it wasn't true. The days she spent in interview rooms chaperoned by an approved independent adult, she'd kept telling herself that she'd say what she wanted to say, finally.

What Eva had instructed her and Jess to recite to the police hung over her like a dark cloud but when, for a moment, she would decide to go against Eva, she would also remember what she'd told Dad all those years before: walking in on Eva having sex with his brother, while her dad had been away. Dad left them all pretty much immediately afterwards. And Eva had all but left, emotionally.

She hadn't wanted to lose more of her mum and so she hadn't wanted to say it was Dom on the boat with Juno. Because then Eva would lose another husband too.

And anyway, it could have well been Luke.

By the time of the trial she'd convinced herself it was. It was Luke who she'd seen with Juno. That is what she had seen.

It was Luke.

Natalie had no idea of the implications. Not really. And she didn't know then that there was a big question mark over Juno's death. She didn't know then that Luke would be arrested on the charge of *manslaughter due to gross negligence*. He'd known Juno was in distress, left her on the island, told no one, least of all the emergency services. But, ultimately, the evidence was all wrapped around Jess's, Eva's, and her testimony. Luke's baseball cap had been found very near to Juno's body and he didn't have an alibi for the time he'd been missing at the party.

The domino effect of her actions would stay with Natalie for the rest of her life. They would shape her life.

24

Teresa

After leaving Eva and her two sisters in the snug Teresa made her way back outside, and into the chaos. The police had arrived and gathered the guests on the terrace. As she passed by, keeping her head down, she heard snaps of conversation, slowing when she caught the distinct hoarse voice of Eva's hairdresser, Maureen, talking to another guest. *The police want to find Luke, the fiancé.*

Ignoring all of her instincts she turned towards the woman. 'Maureen,' she said. 'Have you found your daughter?'

Maureen jumped and her face immediately reddened. 'Yes, I've found Caitlin, thank God.'

Teresa nodded. 'What have you heard?' she asked.

'The detective, a woman, has already spoken to some of the guests… me included… and Caitlin. She was wanting to talk to your fiancé,' Maureen said, her eyes darting around and finding anywhere to rest as long as they didn't rest on Teresa. 'I told her I haven't seen him around all afternoon. Remember, I asked you where I could find him… *Did* you find him?' she finished, finally looking at her.

'Luke's here,' she snapped, and turning away without waiting for a reply, she carried on walking to the end of the garden to the bench by the river.

She sat down and watched the police boat that was moored at the island. Luke had not been on the boat with Juno. Christ, poor Juno. She had no idea how she'd died but she'd died alone on the island – whoever had gone over there with her had returned without her. Left her there.

But had Juno been dead when that person had left? Had Juno been murdered? How had she died?

Where *was* Luke? She'd searched the entire house after leaving the snug and still couldn't find him.

Agitated and unable to sit, she sprang up from the bench. She should go back to the house – the police would want to talk to her. But instead she walked to the west side of the garden, following the river's edge, and took the unused and overgrown path at the side of the house, which brought her to a small gate that opened up onto their driveway. Two police cars were parked there, although both were empty. She wondered why there wasn't an ambulance present, but then remembered the police boat at the island. Like before.

She peered at the road where they'd parked the car. Luke's car wasn't there. Where had he gone? *When* had he gone? A curdle of acidic liquid was pushing up her gullet. She swallowed, rooted to the spot. Why hadn't he told her he was taking the car somewhere? Standing with him earlier on the terrace dance floor already seemed like an age ago. But if he'd taken the car soon after she'd gone inside to change her bodice, then he couldn't have been on the boat with Juno.

Leaning against the gate, she wasn't sure what to do. And it was then that she heard the rumble of a car engine. She peered down the road. *Thank God*. Of course he hadn't been in the boat with Juno.

She ran from the gate and some way down the road, flagging him down. He didn't see her straight away as he was staring at the police cars. But then he pulled over. She rushed around to the driver's door and flung it open.

'Christ, what's going on?' he said.

'You've been gone for ages. Why didn't you tell me you were going somewhere in the car, Luke? You just vanished.' The tears came then, in floods. She had never before felt as she did that day. Confused, disorientated, bewildered. Out of control.

He got out and pulled her to him. 'What's happened?' He inclined his head to the police cars.

'Something terrible. Juno—'

'What about Juno?'

Did she see a shadow of guilt cross his features? 'She's dead, Luke.'

'What are you talking about?'

'Juno is dead, that's why the police are here. Jessica took the boat to Raven Island. She told us that she saw you on the boat with Juno earlier, going over there. She took the spare motorboat over… she found Juno there… alone and not breathing. Luke, tell me it wasn't you! You'd been gone so long… Where've you been?' But then a sort of calmness enveloped her. He'd been somewhere. Of course it wasn't him on the boat with Juno. What the fuck were Natalie and Jessica, and Eva, playing at? Momentarily, her anguish evaporated, until she thought of Juno.

'I went over to my mum's, took the opportunity when you went to get changed. It's such a short drive from here. I was worried about her.'

'You've been gone a long time, Luke.'

'I know, I'm sorry.'

Despite everything that was happening, she said, 'Is she all right?'

'She wasn't home.'

She took hold of his arm. 'You need to tell the police this, Luke. I don't know what happened to Juno, no one does yet. But Jess and Natalie said it was you with her... and it couldn't have been, could it?'

He shook his head. 'Jesus. This is a nightmare.'

'It really is. C'mon. Let's go back to the house. You need to talk to the police. We both do.'

25

Jessica

The policewoman called Rebecca was sitting next to Jessica. Dom sat on the sofa opposite. A policeman was standing by the door.

Jessica couldn't understand why they weren't in uniforms. Uniforms would give the police lady and man a place, a role. She took in the police lady's black trousers, T-shirt and kind smile and was thrown because it shook the order of how she saw the world. And today, after finding beautiful Juno's dead body, she was more desperate than ever for the order that she had painstakingly built around herself over the past five years.

'Jessica, would you like a drink?' the police lady asked.

She shook her head.

'We only want to ask you a few questions today, Jessica, because we know how upsetting this is for you. Perhaps tomorrow, after you've had a good night's sleep, you'll be able to come to the police station where there will be a nice lady who will help you tell us more about... what's happened today.'

'Juno dead,' Jessica said.

'She is, Jessica. I am so sorry—'

'Detective, maybe this is better done another day?' Dom interrupted.

Dom was protecting her. He said that he always would. He'd said that he would stay with Eva as long as she stayed quiet.

'Mr Keane,' Rebecca said. 'A teenage girl has been found dead. I need to ask Jessica just a few questions.'

'Guv?' the man detective said, pulling at his tie. 'Better doing this tomorrow? At the station…?'

It was so very hot in the room.

The policewoman nodded, but the movement was jerky and the muscles around her jaw flickered. 'It's fine, Sergeant. Give me a few minutes.'

'On your shoulders, guv,' the sergeant almost whispered.

Rebecca carried on. 'Jessica, was it you who found Juno on Raven Island?'

Jessica nodded.

'Is that a yes, Jessica?'

'Guv…' the policeman said.

Rebecca held up her hand and he shrugged heavily.

'Did,' Jessica said.

'And Juno was alone? No one else there?'

'Yes, Juno alone.'

'And you went over to the island on your stepfather's motorboat?' Rebecca asked.

'Did.'

Rebecca turned to Dom. 'Can Jessica drive a motorboat?'

'She can,' he replied.

Rebecca turned back to Jessica. 'We are going to leave now. Please try to get some sleep, Jessica. I'll send your mum in.'

'No.'

'Then we'll leave you with Dom?'

'No.' Jessica got up. 'I need to go to my bedroom.'

'That's fine,' Rebecca said. 'See you soon, Jessica.'

As she walked from the room she didn't look at Dom. Couldn't, and for many reasons.

Their kitchen was filled with sobered guests all milling around, and several police people in uniforms. Jessica walked straight to the walk-in store cupboard and picked up the Tupperware box that held Mrs A's triple chocolate cake. She wished Mrs A hadn't taken the weekend off. None of this would have happened if she hadn't.

Mrs A had been away the weekend her sister died.

She disappeared upstairs to her bedroom with the box. Sat on Indiana's hat and ate all of it with her fingers. Thought about Juno. Thought about her sister.

She slid off the bed and checked the hundred broken pieces of her phrenology head that she had put in an empty shoebox on the top of her desk, and then made her way to the toilet.

26

Teresa

It had been three weeks and five days since the love of Teresa's life had been arrested. Juno's post-mortem showed that she had died of a heart attack, which had been caused by the ecstasy tablet she'd taken on the day of her party. Juno had an underlying genetic heart disorder, making her heart weaker. If she had received immediate medical attention, the coroner reported, she would likely not have died. Luke had been taken to the police station late that Saturday night, had appeared at the local magistrates' court two days later, and just over three weeks after that – in early September, and in the midst of a blast of an Indian summer – he had appeared at the Old Bailey in London, where the judge granted him bail and set a date for his trial: 10 January 1992. Teresa asked Luke's mum for the bail money; she had absolutely no intention of asking Eva. His mum wasn't loaded, but she'd always been careful with what little she did have.

The situation with Luke and his mum was unbearable, but at least the three of them had been able to talk about it. She'd found out in only the past week that his mum had been taken to the police station the morning after Juno's death, where she told them that she had not seen Luke that day. She was not at home when he allegedly went to see her. She could have given him an alibi.

All he was going through, but all he was concerned about was protecting his mum, and her.

She and Luke were sitting at their dining room table. For something to do, Teresa had made a mound of grated cheese and ham sandwiches and a huge pot of tea, although she knew the sandwiches would remain untouched. Luke's mum was supposed to be coming around, but had called to say that she'd gone back to bed to rest. She really wasn't well. Teresa was beginning to suspect there might be something seriously wrong with his mum and she knew Luke would be worrying about this too.

Of course she hadn't expected Luke's mum to lie, although she'd be lying herself if she hadn't entertained the thought, if only for a second, that it would have solved Luke's devastating problem. Eva would have had no problem at all lying for one of her daughters, but it was something Luke's mum could not do. By refusing to lie, did it make Luke's mum a bad mother? No, it made her a worthwhile human being. And would lying have made Eva a good mother? No. It would show her for what she was – a total and utter excuse for a human being.

Her eyes settled on Luke.

He had absolutely no wish for his mum to provide an alibi for him and this was something on which he and his mum were adamant and united. Consolidated. Teresa would have lied for Luke. She would have given up on her legal career for him before it had even started. A senior barrister at the chambers where she had completed two mini pupillages had already told her it would be career suicide to take the stand with her true version of events –

that she and Luke went over to Raven Island at six a.m. on the day of the party.

That Luke had left his red baseball cap there.

It's your word against your sister's, Teresa. Jessica said she did not go over to the island very early that morning and therefore, she did not see you and Luke there, so he could not have left his red baseball cap there. And Eva and Dom's statement too. They say that Jessica, you and Luke all got up much later. Natalie affirms that too. It's just too risky.

'I'm willing to take the risk,' Teresa had said.

But Luke wouldn't allow her to take the risk, and his mum had warned her against doing so too. Teresa had got angry with her then; it had been the first time since meeting her she'd felt any hint of antagonism towards her future mother-in-law. Teresa had asked her outright why she wouldn't lie for her son.

I can't, Teresa. Deep down, you know I can't. And Luke doesn't want me to.

And his mum was right, to change her mind would be madness, the prosecution would be all over it.

Teresa took hold of Luke's hand. She was sure even his hand had lost weight. 'You okay?'

He nodded but his facial expression told another story.

'You *will* be acquitted,' she said, picking up a sandwich, staring at it for a second and then placing it back on the plate. 'You have numerous character witnesses. Why would a trained doctor leave a young girl in distress? Where is the reasoning, the logic?'

'They'll say I gave Juno the ecstasy tablet. They'll say I took her to the island to… seduce her.'

Teresa had to repress a giggle. It was a totally inappropriate response, and a response that would come from

Natalie when nervous. *Bloody Natalie.* 'Sorry… It's the thought of you *seducing*.'

Luke smiled, only faint but it was there. She would be forever grateful to her flatmate for inadvertently fracturing her wrist in a game of squash and her subsequent visit to A&E. She'd loved Luke from the moment she'd set eyes on him, but now she loved him even more, if that were possible.

'Are you saying I'm not a seducer?' he asked, although the smile had slipped away.

Just as a career had slid away.

'You only ever seduced me…' Teresa fixed her gaze firmly on him. 'You didn't go to the island with Juno,' she said. 'The jury will believe you.'

'We'll see.'

She'd promised herself that she would not bring up again what could have been Luke's alibi, and which *was* his alibi. But she did.

'The only way to guarantee an acquittal is for your mum to say that you went to her house that day… Because you *did*.'

Luke sighed. 'We've gone through this Teresa. Mum wasn't home—'

'But she hardly ever goes out—'

'Well, that day she did. Mum's made her statement. She could not lie, and I don't want her to. It's done, Teresa,' Luke said. 'Mum didn't see me. If I hadn't hung around so long at her house, things would be different. I would have got back to the party sooner and then it couldn't possibly have been me on the boat with Juno, because I would have been with you. I let myself in and when I knew Mum wasn't home, I didn't think she'd be long. I stayed longer than I thought I would. It was so calm inside the house… Mum didn't come, and then I left. Too late, I left.'

'Let's leave it,' Teresa said with weariness.

He pushed back his chair, stretched out his legs, turned towards the window, and then back at her. 'I'm afraid I've more bad news.'

Teresa's insides felt as if they were contorting. What more bad news could there be?

'The prosecution has come up with something from my past,' he carried on.

'What?'

'In my first year as a junior doctor, I prescribed myself Valium.'

'You are kidding me, right? You, Valium?'

'It wasn't for me. It was for my friend. He was having a bad time. I wanted to help him.'

'Jesus, Luke! Why haven't you told me about this before?'

'Never the right time.' Luke got up and went to stand behind her, resting his hand on the top of her shoulder.

She turned to look up at him. 'What happened?'

'I was cautioned. It's not illegal to self-prescribe, as you probably know.'

'But you weren't self-prescribing, Luke. You just told me that.'

'I lied to the board. I only did it once. It was a stupid thing to do.'

'I hope your friend appreciated it.'

'I'll never know. He committed suicide before I was able to give it to him.'

'Oh God. I'm so sorry,' she said. But then Teresa's legal brain kicked in. 'The prosecution will drag this up to show that you're a drug taker and that you supplied Juno with the ecstasy tablet that essentially killed her.'

'I think that's how it goes,' he replied. 'But I've got three character witnesses from the hospital. It'll be fine.'

'It'll cast doubt within the jury, Luke,' she said, her voice so quiet she could barely hear herself.

'It will. But I did *not* take Juno to Raven Island and I did *not* give her drugs.'

Teresa squeezed her eyes closed. 'It was Dom. And probably Dom who gave Juno the tablet.'

'We don't know that,' he said. 'It could have been anyone at the party... Juno could have brought it to the party...' He smiled a sad smile.

'It could have been anyone. And yes, Juno could have brought it with her...' She found his eyes. 'Oh, Luke.'

27

Natalie

It was Mrs A who stayed with Jess and Natalie when the trial began, because even though Eva and Dom were in the house, they might as well not have been. Natalie couldn't concentrate on anything, least of all her A levels, which she'd started the previous September. She knew then that she was going to flunk them spectacularly. Every time she sat down to work or read, she thought of Juno. It was what they had done together – have a laugh and do their schoolwork. It's what their whole friendship had been based on; because the truth was, despite her friend's outer persona of being a good-time girl, Juno was a born academic. Great things had awaited her, and everything had been taken from her.

Just as everything had been taken from her sister, in one fatal accident.

She had been to see Juno's parents twice since her friend's funeral; her second visit was when she'd found out that Juno's mum had had a small stroke. The death of her daughter was just too much for her to handle, Juno's dad had said. Natalie hated herself for not having visited the couple again. She couldn't face it.

Earlier in the morning she and Mrs A had visited a local boutique and chosen a black trouser suit and white blouse to wear at the trial. They'd gone to McDonald's afterwards and she'd wished they'd brought Jess, because as well as loving Indiana Jones, she loved a Big Mac too. They'd returned home around three. Jess was still in her room, as was Eva. Dom had disappeared off somewhere, something he was doing more and more.

She knocked on Eva's bedroom door. She knew she'd still be in bed. Juno's death had raked everything up for her. It had raked everything up for Natalie. 'Mum, you awake?'

No answer and she knocked again, louder.

'Come in.'

She was lying on her side, facing the curtains, not the door. 'You all right?' she said.

No answer.

Natalie stepped further inside the room. 'Eva, Teresa won't speak to me—'

'What you and Jessica told the police was true, Natalie. You'll be fine in court. There's nothing to worry about.' She turned over, peered at her. God, she looked terrible. 'Luke left Juno to die on the island. *Not* Dom.'

'But you didn't see it,' she said. 'The boat, with Luke inside, with Juno.' She stepped nearer. 'I know you didn't.'

'You know nothing.'

'This has ruined Luke's life, and Teresa's. Don't you care?'

'You were always jealous of your sister.' Eva peered up at her. 'Your other sister too.'

In the pit of her stomach something vaulted at that last comment. 'That's not true.' Why was she doing this? But she *was* jealous of Teresa.

And, if she were truthful, of both her older sisters.

'You've always wanted to ruin everything.' Eva pulled a pillow from where Dom would normally be sleeping, sat up and pushed it behind her head, carrying on in a much quieter voice: 'You didn't have to tell your dad.'

'I was six.'

Eva yanked the pillow away and threw it on the floor, then slid back down. 'Don't worry about tomorrow. Just say—'

'The truth?'

'Jessica told the truth in court, and so will you. It'll be fine.' Eva caught her eye and then sat up. 'When you saw *Luke* on the boat, with Juno,' she said, fixing her eyes on Natalie's and emphasising Luke's name. 'He was wearing his red baseball cap, wasn't he?'

Natalie stared at her mother. 'I'm not sure.'

Eva leaned forward. 'Yes, he was, and you *are* sure. Remember that. He went to Raven Island, with Juno, wearing it. He left it there, when he left Juno.'

Natalie didn't reply but felt herself dipping her head in a nod.

'Good.' Eva peered at the bag that Natalie was clutching in her right hand. 'Mrs A's chosen something for you to wear in court?'

Pulling out her outfit, she held it up.

'Nice. Shame it's taken a court appearance to get you to wear something decent.'

Natalie decided to let that one go. 'How's things with Dom?' she dared to ask, even though she knew how things were with Dom.

'I'm not sure.'

'It'll be okay,' she said.

'I don't think so.'

'You've lied for him. What else does he want from you?'

'For the last time, I *did not* lie, and neither did you… I'm sorry about Juno, Natalie, but she died because of her own actions.'

'That's not true. Juno did nothing wrong. And what about Luke, and Teresa?'

'If I know my daughter at all, she'll distance herself from him because it'll ruin her career before it's even started if she doesn't. Teresa will get over him. She's fickle, won't take her long to find someone else.' She slid down the bed. 'Please go, Natalie.'

—

'Natalie,' Mrs A was saying, knocking on her bedroom door. 'Time, Natalie.'

It was Mrs A who was accompanying Natalie to the Crown Court.

Before leaving, Natalie poked her head through Jess's door. She was sitting at her desk, her head stuck in a book. 'Jess,' she said. 'I'm going.'

'You scared? I was, a bit.' Jess's speaking had improved since Raven Island.

'I am,' she said. 'A little.'

'What will happen to Luke?' Jess asked.

'We don't know yet.'

'Will Teresa come and visit ever again?'

'I'm sure she will, Jess.' She wouldn't. Ever.

Natalie didn't know what *had* happened very early in the morning of Teresa's party, because it had been one morning when she hadn't got up early. It was recorded in Teresa's statement that she and Luke had gone over to

Raven Island together, very early, on the morning of the day that Juno died.

Jess denied going to the island early that morning, despite Teresa and Luke saying she had.

Did she believe Jess? She did. Why would she have lied about that?

—

Mrs A and Natalie took a taxi to the Old Bailey in London. Natalie hadn't expected Eva to take her but she'd thought that Dom might have volunteered. He hadn't; instead, he'd disappeared outside on the pretext of cleaning the boats. They didn't need cleaning; no one had used them since the party.

The taxi dropped them off. The building was impressive and daunting. Natalie swallowed, her mouth dry, and already she could feel the silk of her blouse wet underneath her armpits and along the bumps of her spine.

After their bags had been searched, a short, round woman made her way towards them. 'My name is Patricia, I'm part of the Witness Support Service. I'll be taking care of you.' She smiled at Mrs A. 'I'll take Natalie from here,' she said.

'I'm going to do some shopping,' Mrs A said. 'What time shall I return to pick up Natalie?' she asked, directing her question to the woman.

The woman looked at her watch. 'It's nine now, so I'd say no later than three.'

'That long?' Natalie said. *God, what an ordeal.* But then she thought of Juno. The reason she was there was because Juno wasn't. The tears stung. At that moment she felt Juno's presence, as if her friend was unable to rest.

Mrs A had told her that Juno's dad would be at court and a part of her hoped she didn't see him. She really wasn't a very nice person. As it turned out, Mr Morrison didn't attend that day.

'Just to be on the safe side, Natalie,' the woman was saying. 'Please don't worry, and don't cry. We aim to make this as easy as possible for you.' She smiled, and it seemed genuine.

Mrs A took Natalie's hand and squeezed it. 'See you later, Nat. You'll be fine. Jessica was.'

She wanted to cry more then. Instead, Natalie kissed Mrs A on the cheek.

Mrs A calling her Nat. Only Teresa called her by that name, but then had stopped after the argument.

Why did Teresa always blame her for everything?

28

Natalie

Natalie was summoned at 10.30 a.m. Patricia led her into court, just as she'd explained. She entered, thankful for the screen that blocked everyone from seeing her, apart from the jurors, barristers and judge. She sat behind it. Luke couldn't see her, and the gallery had been cleared of the public. Once she was settled – helped along by a few reassuring smiles from the judge – Patricia sat on the chair next to her. Natalie's scalp was itching like mad and although she tried to keep her fingers from her hair and the skin beneath, it proved to be impossible. She dug into her right temple with her nails.

'Are you okay, Natalie?' Patricia whispered.

She snatched her hands away, pulling out a handful of hair at the same time. Patricia's expression fell into one of dismay and Natalie felt a bit sorry for her. 'I'm sorry,' she whispered back.

'It'll be over soon.'

The judge began talking and she only half listened, staring instead at the screen, imagining Luke, but then imagining Juno.

After the judge had finished speaking, a man, who Patricia had told her would be the prosecutor – *the barrister who wants to ensure that if Luke is guilty, he will go to prison* – began to talk.

'Hello, Natalie,' he said. His voice was deep and gruff and didn't sound like she thought he'd sound from the way he looked. 'I hope you are well this morning and are being well cared for.' He nodded at Patricia. 'I'm sure Mrs Dewsbury is doing a fine job.' He smiled at Patricia, and at her, but the smile was uneven; the left side of his lip lifted higher than his right. 'I'd like to begin this morning by asking you if you know the defendant, Luke Harris?'

Patricia had told her to just answer the questions and to tell the truth – *that's all you need to do.* That was what she would do.

'Yes… sir.'

'There's no need to call me sir.'

'Okay.' She looked at the judge. He smiled. Juno would have said he smiled magnanimously. *Oh, Juno.*

'Okay.' The barrister was still smiling unevenly. He had crooked teeth and a very thin face. She wondered if she liked him. She wasn't sure.

'How do you know Luke Harris, Natalie?'

'He's my sister's boyfriend… fiancé.'

'Ah. This all must be very upsetting for you, and your sister.'

'I think it is… for my sister.'

'And Juno, she was your best friend?'

'She was.' Natalie swallowed. She couldn't allow herself to cry.

'You are keen then, I'd think, to find out exactly what happened to your friend, on the day she died?'

She caught her breath.

The judge said, 'Please be mindful of your questioning, Mr Benson.'

'Of course, Your Honour' Mr Benson replied, looking contrite. He carried on, 'Natalie, are you fond of Luke Harris, your sister's fiancé?'

Was she? She did like Luke, if truth were told. And she always told the truth. 'I was… am, yes.'

He nodded but it was an over-the-top and exaggerated movement. 'Could you tell me, the judge and the jury, the sequence of events on the day when Juno Morrison lost her life, Natalie?'

Natalie took a deep breath. 'It was my sister Teresa's big day. Her graduation and engagement celebration. We were having a party at home to… celebrate.'

'How did the day begin?'

'We got up reasonably early to get the house ready for the party.'

'Did Luke sleep at your house the night before the party?'

'He did, yes. He and Teresa came to the house the day before.'

'Who was up first on that day?' he asked.

'Eva… I mean my mother, I think.'

'Ah, your mother was up to do her chores?'

She stared at him. 'Chores?'

'Helping to get everything prepared for her eldest daughter's celebrations?'

'Ah, yes.' She didn't think Eva knew the meaning of the word 'chore'.

'Who awoke after your mother, Natalie?'

'I think I came down next… then Teresa and Luke, and then… some friends turned up.'

'Who turned up early, Natalie? Can you remember?'

'Eva's… I mean my mother's hairdresser, and Dom's – that is, my stepfather's – friend, who he's in business with.

A few other oldies… I mean, a few more of my mother and stepfather's friends.'

'Busy morning,' he stated, with a grin.

'It was, yes.'

'Amongst the friends who turned up, was Juno amongst them?'

'Yes, she was. The caterers turned up pretty early too.'

He smiled again. His face seemed to be in a permanent smile. Patricia had explained that the prosecuting barrister would probably be nicer to her than the defence barrister. 'And your younger sister, Jessica. What time did Jessica come downstairs?'

'Jessica was the last one to come down, as I remember.'

'Did Jessica come down in her nightwear?'

'Yes, she did.'

'And Luke and Teresa. Were they dressed or still in their night clothes?'

'In dressing gowns.'

'Did Teresa or Luke tell you, or anyone, that they'd been out very early that morning and taken a motor launch to Raven Island?'

'No. I don't think so.'

'Try to remember, Natalie.'

'No. They didn't tell me that.' Patricia had allowed her to read her statement. She *had* said that. And it was true. 'We don't go to the island these days…'

'Why is that, Natalie?'

'We… since my sister's death… we just don't.' Furtively, she looked at the judge. Would they all know about that? These people probably knew everything.

'Mr Benson,' the judge intervened. 'Please stay with the relevant facts and questioning.'

Mr Benson nodded. 'Were you aware that your sister, Jessica, had been to the island very early that morning, before seven a.m., in the motor launch?'

'No, I wasn't and she didn't tell me that.' And Jess hadn't.

'Later in the day, around four p.m., you went inside the house to find Juno but instead found Jessica. In what emotional state did you find Jessica, your sister?'

'She was crying.'

'Jessica was very upset?'

'I think so.'

'Yes or no, Natalie.'

'Yes.'

'What did she tell you?'

She looked hard at him, then at the judge. At the people who were the jurors. 'Jess told me she'd been over to Raven Island, but later in the afternoon, after the party had started... and had found Juno. She said that Juno was dead... At that point I didn't believe her, Jess. I thought... I thought... it couldn't be true.'

'And what did you do then?'

'I went to find Eva to tell her.'

'Your mother, Eva?'

'Yes, my mum. We all call her Eva.'

For a second, the barrister appeared confused but quickly bounced back. 'Thank you, Natalie. We're nearly done. The time between your stepfather's speech at approximately midday, which lasted around twenty minutes, I believe, to around four p.m....' He scratched his head as if thinking, but she knew he wasn't. He had all the facts. He'd read her statement. 'Did you see Luke at the party?'

'I saw Luke during the speech, and I saw him with Teresa a short time afterwards.'

'How long afterwards?'

'About a quarter of an hour afterwards.'

'Tell the court what you did then, Natalie.'

'I went to sit by the river for a lot of the afternoon, after Dom's speech. I was waiting for Juno.'

'Where had Juno gone?'

'Just off for a wander… as… she called it. It's what she does… did.'

Mr Benson turned to the judge then. 'I'd like to show Your Honour and the jury a photograph of the house and grounds, the river and Raven Island, to put into perspective the size and expanse of the building and its surrounding.'

'You may do so. Carry on,' the judge said.

'Could the usher please present exhibit number four to the judge and jury?'

A man made his way to the jury and presented the exhibit. He gave Natalie the photographs to look at too. The size of their property was obscene. Easy for people to get lost, and not be seen. So many rooms, nooks and crannies, both inside and outside.

'So, Juno went off to mingle while you stayed sitting by the river?' Mr Benson ploughed on.

'Yes, that's right. I don't really like big gatherings… it was why I asked Juno to come to the party – Teresa's party… To keep me company.'

'I understand,' he said. She really didn't think he did. 'Did you go back and join in with the party?'

'I did.'

'What time would that be?'

'I'm not sure, but around two or three p.m.'

'And when you went back, did you see either Teresa or Luke?'

'I saw Teresa but I couldn't see Luke.'

'And when you found Jessica in her bedroom, you'd actually been looking for Juno, is that right?' he pushed.

'Yes. She'd been gone a long time.'

'And Natalie, going back to when you were sitting by the river and before you went back to the party, did you stay sitting on the bench the entire time?'

'No, I didn't. I got up a few times to walk along the river's edge, away from the house, towards the jetty where the boats are moored, and where I had a clearer view of Raven Island.'

'And did you see anything?'

'The first time I went, I did, yes.'

'And what did you see?'

'I saw one of Dom's motorboats heading towards Raven Island.'

'And could you see who was in the boat?'

'Yes.'

'Do you wear glasses or contact lenses, Natalie?'

'Yes.'

'You are short or long-sighted?' he asked.

'Short-sighted.'

'Were you wearing your glasses or contact lenses on the day of the party?'

Natalie looked at the judge, turned to Patricia. Then stared at the man asking questions. 'I was, yes.'

'Glasses or contacts?'

'My lenses.'

'Who did you see inside the boat?'

'Juno… and Luke.'

'What made you certain it was Juno, Natalie?'

'Her skirt, the colour. A vivid green, and I'd recognise Juno anywhere.'

He nodded. 'And Luke, how could you be so sure it was Luke? Did anything distinguish him for you?'

Natalie shook her head, although remembering what Eva had said. 'No, I don't think so, but I could see it was Luke.'

'That's fine, Natalie, but if you do remember anything, please do let the court know.'

'I will.' She should have said something about the red baseball cap.

'Did you later return to the jetty area to check if the boat had returned?'

'I did, yes. That was why I went to find Juno… because… because I thought she'd returned. I didn't know, then, that she hadn't.' She blinked back rising tears. 'I had no idea she was still on the island…'

'Please take your time, Natalie. You are doing very well.' Mr Benson took a breath. 'So, you didn't know that Juno had *not* returned until you spoke to your younger sister, Jessica, in her bedroom?'

'No, I didn't.'

'And what did Jessica say to you?'

'She told me she'd taken the motorboat to the island… she told me she'd found Juno, that she wasn't breathing… that she was dead.'

She cried then. Couldn't help it, and felt Patricia's hand on her knee.

'Thank you, Natalie. I appreciate your responses.' Mr Benson nodded towards the judge.

'Thank you, Mr Benson.' The judge turned to Natalie. 'Would you like to take a short break, Natalie, to gather yourself? It really is not a problem.'

She wanted to get this over with. 'No, sir… Your Honour…'

The judge addressed the other barrister. 'Do you have any questions for the witness, Mr Hamilton?'

'I do, Your Honour.'

'Natalie,' the judge said. 'Mr Hamilton will be cross-examining you. Are you absolutely certain you don't want a break first?'

'No thank you, Your Honour,' she said.

The judge moved his head a fraction and inclined it to Mr Hamilton, the barrister who Patricia had told her was the defence counsel. The person defending Luke.

She knew this would be much more horrendous than Mr Benson's questioning and in that moment she thought of Teresa. She would be so good at this job.

'Good morning, Natalie,' Luke's barrister said.

Mr Hamilton was the exact opposite to the other man. Young and full-faced. Hungry-looking. Her stomach lurched.

'Good morning,' she said.

'Natalie, are you aware of the cause of Juno Morrison's death? Your friend… Juno.'

'Yes, I am.' Natalie had always known about Juno's heart condition, but had never known its name. It had been Mrs A who had filled her on the details, given her its official name. 'She had Wolff-Parkinson syndrome.'

'Wolff-Parkinson-White syndrome, yes, which made Juno particularly vulnerable to the effects of some drugs, especially the much stronger form of MDMA. Natalie, were you aware of Juno's propensity for taking drugs?'

'She had the odd spliff sometimes, that's all.'

'That is all Juno took?'

173

'I think so, yes.' Natalie's mind travelled back to that long ago day when she found the ecstasy in Eva and Dom's room; the image of the blue tablet, the skull and crossbones imprinted on it, burned inside her brain. The skull and crossbones were there for a reason.

'Were you aware of the drugs that were available at your parents' home the day that Juno died?'

That took her unawares.

'Mr Hamilton,' the judge said, 'I think we can leave that question for another witness, seeing as you are asking Natalie's opinion on something that is conflictive for Natalie.'

'On the day of Juno's death, Natalie,' Mr Hamilton continued, 'were you aware that Juno had taken something other than cannabis?'

'No, I wasn't aware she had taken anything.'

The party had been awash with cannabis. It was why Juno had gone off, to find some.

That had been her chance to tell the court about the ecstasy tablets she'd found in Eva and Dom's room. But she said nothing. She also didn't tell the court about finding Eva with a note stuck up her nose by the jetty wall.

Her scalp was on fire and she had to stop herself from scraping it with her nails. She clutched at the wood of the witness stand, claustrophobia beginning to strangle her. Fear grabbing her at the thought of what would happen to Eva if Dom were arrested, or worse, if Dom left Eva due to Natalie's potential testimony. History repeating itself. Eva losing her husband again. She had no desire to save Dom – the Keane sisters would all be better off without him – but still, she wanted to save Eva. Felt she owed Eva.

The barrister carried on, a Rottweiler. 'Going back to when you saw the motorboat, when you took your walk along the river. Are you certain it was Juno you saw in the boat, and not another young girl from the party?'

'I did think it could have been another girl, afterwards…'

'So, you weren't sure?' he pushed.

Heat pricked at her. 'My mother's hairdresser had told me that she couldn't find her daughter – she's about my age. I thought it could have been her in the boat, but I only thought that afterwards, when I knew her mum couldn't find her.'

He nodded. 'Are you certain it was Luke in the boat? Could you see clearly?'

'I could, and it was Luke.'

'It couldn't have been another man from the party?'

'I don't think so.'

'I'm afraid you have to be clearer than that, Natalie. A young man's career, his life, is at stake here. A doctor. A man who has spent his life saving people.'

'I understand.'

'Are you sure it was Luke?'

'I am.' She *was*. It *was*.

'How can you be so sure?'

She took a mouthful of air – and changed her life. 'I've just remembered something… and Mr Benson did say to mention anything that came back to me… Luke was wearing his baseball cap. It was bright red. You couldn't miss it.'

The man's face twitched a little. 'Are you certain, Natalie?'

'Absolutely certain.'

Luke's defence barrister glanced at the judge. 'That will be all, Your Honour.'

The judge nodded. 'You may leave the courtroom now, Natalie. Thank you for coming today.' He then turned his head away from her and addressed the court. 'We will convene for an early lunch and reconvene at one-thirty p.m.'

—

Mrs A was waiting for her when she emerged. She didn't say a thing, only gave her a hug. They got in the taxi to go home, but London was busy and it took a while.

'Eva loves us, doesn't she, Mrs A?' Natalie said, as they finally made their way away from the city's centre.

'Of course she does… in her own way.' Mrs A patted her hand. 'But you know, she hasn't been the same since…' Even Mrs A had a problem saying her sister's name.

'Teresa will never forgive me.'

'As long as you tell the truth that is all that matters. You and Jessica.'

'How was Jess, here, at court?'

'She was calm. Calmer than I'd thought she'd be.'

'Have you seen Teresa?'

Mrs A now took her hand. 'I have.'

'Did she… did she say anything?'

'She said that whatever the outcome, she'll stick by Luke.'

Natalie thought about asking the taxi driver to stop so she could get out and throw up. She waited, though, and the wave of nausea passed.

If she waited long enough, this whole thing would pass.

Staring through the window she thought about the red baseball cap she hadn't seen. She also thought about the dealer who'd turned up later in the morning of Teresa's party. He never came in the day, always at night. She was so glad they didn't ask her anything about that in court.

It would turn out that the jury, led gently by the judge, believed that Juno had come to the party with the ecstasy tablet that had killed her. The judge and jury were convinced by the statement given by Caitlin, the hairdresser's daughter, who told the court that Juno had offered her a tablet at the party. Juno's reputation had been obliterated by Luke's defence.

29

Then
December 1998

Natalie

Natalie had woken up full of relief on the first day of the school holidays. She didn't absolutely love her job – she liked it – but she absolutely loved Oli, and the baby growing inside her. She'd been counting down to the Christmas holidays for weeks – pregnancy was taking it out of her. She was three months in, having conceived on a Greek island where they'd been celebrating their first wedding anniversary.

Their wedding had been low key and taken place inside a register office. After four glorious years up in Humberside doing her degree, where she had done her teacher training too, Oli, ironically, had been offered a job very near her birthplace. So they'd moved back down south. She didn't see Eva or Dom often, and since Jessica had left the family home a few months earlier for med school, she foresaw she'd be seeing even less of them, which suited her perfectly. Mrs A still worked for them, and she made sure she and Mrs A met up as often as they could, although never at Raven House.

Oli had left earlier that morning for work. Although December, the weather was unseasonably warm and she was just about to go outside to hang out the laundry in the minuscule garden. They were renting a two-up, two-down cottage; it was tiny, and suffered from rising damp, but it was home. It was also miles away from the river.

That had been her only stipulation to the letting agent: *Nowhere near the river.*

She slipped on her coat and picked up the washing basket, thinking about how much she loved being a housewife and a soon-to-be mother. Eva had said she was far too young to be 'trapped in domesticity'. She wasn't. She wanted to be everything Eva wasn't. She had a job too, which was more than Eva had ever had.

She made her way outside and, as she pegged out the washing, she allowed herself to think about the past, and her family. The last time she'd visited Raven House was a month after Jess's departure, in October. She was never sure if she avoided Raven House because she couldn't stomach Dom, or if it was because she couldn't stomach Eva. Both. She'd made sure that Mrs A would be around, as her presence made things more manageable.

Dom had been home and she'd been really shocked at his appearance. He'd lost weight and aged a lot, during and after the trial. Also, since the trial, the deeper and further-away memories had become more painful. These had been the memories she'd been able to share with her husband. On their holiday where their baby had been conceived, she had told him everything about her other older sister. It was if a dam had been opened.

She was pegging up the last pillowcase when she heard the telephone ringing inside. Thinking it might be Oli, she rushed in to answer it. Kicking off her shoes, she grabbed the phone.

'Natalie, it's Mrs A.'

'Is everything okay?' It wasn't, she could tell by the tone of her voice. A hundred reasons flitted through her head, the main one being that Mrs A was in her early seventies. 'Are *you* okay, Mrs A?'

'Natalie, you need to come over to the house. As soon as possible.'

'Is it Eva?'

'No. It's Dom.'

Relief swept through her. Whatever Eva was, she was her mum and the grandmother to her child. Family really was a strange paradigm.

Mrs A carried on, 'We heard a noise on Raven Island. Eva went over in the boat—'

'Eva can't drive the boat, Mrs A, are you sure? She hates the water.'

'Natalie, she went because it was a gunshot sound and Dom had disappeared earlier this morning. Dom… he's shot himself. He's committed suicide.'

She should have been surprised but wasn't. Was she upset? No, she wasn't. But her overriding thought was that Eva could not drive the boat. 'I'll come over now, Mrs A.'

'I've called the police.'

'Can you put Eva on the line?'

'She can't talk. She's in shock, Natalie.'

'I'll be as quick as I can.'

After putting down the phone she called a taxi and was at Raven House within half an hour.

-

By the time Natalie arrived, so had the police. Eva was sitting inside her enormous kitchen, dishevelled, her skin the colour of the pale grey granite work surfaces surrounding them. Mrs A was holding her hand.

'Eva,' she said softly. 'I'm so sorry.' Eva didn't answer – just stared ahead at nothing and no one in particular. 'You went to the island, Eva,' she carried on. 'In the boat? You went in the rowing boat—'

'No, she went in the motorboat, Natalie,' Mrs A interrupted.

Natalie scrutinised Eva. Something was not ringing true, yet… what ever did ring true in her family?

Unbidden, the scene inside that very kitchen from twelve years previously, five years before Juno's death, came into her mind. The day when Eva tried to find Dom at work to insist he come home to check Raven Island; she'd had a strange feeling something had happened, and it was connected to the island and her daughter. If anything would have motivated Eva to face her fear, it would have been the driving need to check her favourite daughter had come to no harm. In the end, though, Eva hadn't been able to contact Dom, and it was a seven-year-old Jess who had taken it upon herself to drive the boat to the island, in an attempt to put Eva's mind at rest. In the darker corners of her mind, Natalie had questioned if Eva had asked Jess to go.

She was just about to quiz her traumatised mother more when a policeman came in, entering through the kitchen French doors.

'Are you Eva's daughter?' he asked.

'I am yes.' To Mrs A, she said, 'Take Eva upstairs, if you don't mind.'

'Of course. Come on, Eva.'

Natalie waited for them to disappear. 'Could you tell me what's happened?'

'Mr Keane has taken his own life, using an unlicensed and highly illegal handgun.'

'Ah. Please, sit down.' She strongly suspected the gun had come from a similar place as the drugs.

'I'm fine standing, but thank you.'

'Has he left a note… or anything?'

'No, no suicide note.'

'How did he—'

'It would have been very distressing for Mrs Keane. He shot himself in the mouth… I'm so sorry… are you all right doing this?'

'I am, yes. He was my stepfather, not my real dad.'

The policeman nodded. He knew. The Luke Harris trial was pretty famous locally.

'What happens now?' she asked.

'The body will go to the coroner. Post-mortem. There are no suspicious circumstances, but it's protocol with a suicide.'

'Yes. Thank you.'

'I'll leave you in peace.'

She nodded but he'd already slipped back through the French doors.

Why had Dom killed himself? She'd have said it was totally out of character, but since the trial, and more recently since Jess had left, perhaps it wasn't. He'd been going downhill for years.

The guilt, the quiet whisper inside her head told her. Guilt that it was he who'd left Juno to die, not Luke. These words inside her head were words that she tried to repress on a daily basis. And more than that these days. Every few hours. Her mind cut across to Jess. Her sister had severed, completely, her ties with Eva and Dom, which she completely understood, but she'd also been a little surprised. After Luke's trial, Jess, Eva and Dom had seemed to have fallen into a way of living together that suited all three.

Jess had obviously just been biding her time. As she herself had done.

Without a suicide note they would never know why Dom killed himself, why he blew his head off. In the deeper parts of her mind though, she knew. But why now, so many years later? She wondered too if Luke's recent release from prison had anything at all to do with Dom's decision.

She got up and walked to the phone that sat on the wall in Eva's kitchen. Eva never called Teresa but her number was in the list of contacts. An internal alarm buzzed. Something about today's date. And she suddenly realised: it was Teresa's birthday. She'd call her tomorrow. There really wasn't anything spoiling. Teresa wouldn't be coming down from Harrogate to comfort Eva.

She speed-dialled Jess instead who didn't seem surprised at the news, but often she never knew what Jess was really feeling or thinking. She told Natalie that she wouldn't be coming to Raven House. She said she had too much university work on.

Jess added that last line at the very end of their conversation, as if to reiterate how inconsequential it was to her – Dom spreading his brains over Raven Island.

30

Teresa

Teresa had spent the first part of her twenty-ninth birthday at work, in court, to be exact. There was no way she could have taken the day off, and hadn't wanted to. This case was the biggest of her career as a prosecuting barrister. Her defining moment. It was also a case that together with her team she had won.

She threw her leather satchel onto the floor in the hallway and then closed the door. The Leeds semi-detached Victorian house felt empty. Felt cold too. She hated renting and relying on someone else to get things fixed. It was a nice house though, and Matt was in it. Maybe he'd gone out to get something from the shops. It was then that she smelt the aroma of freshly baked bread mingled with a sweeter smell of chocolate.

Without taking her shoes off she walked to the galley kitchen at the back end of the property. Two fresh loaves sat on the left countertop. She touched one. Still warm. She turned to the right countertop and saw a chocolate cake, cooling, on the opposite counter. Teresa smiled and checked her watch. Three p.m. She said she'd be home at five.

Matt had probably nipped out to get supplies. She'd pretend she hadn't been in the kitchen and seen the home-made bread and birthday cake in the making.

She heard the front door open, walked out into the hall and looked in the mirror as she pushed a smile onto her face. She turned and, as Matt walked in, her fake smile turned authentic. He'd been to the barber's.

'Looks good,' she said, touching his dark brown hair.

'Have you been in the kitchen?' he asked.

She was about to say no, but then looked into his eyes. She could not lie. She could not lie to anyone. 'Sorry, I have.'

He grinned. 'It's an important birthday, the last one of your thirties… I wanted to make you a cake.' He pulled her to him. 'I wanted to take you out to dinner, but you said you didn't want to, so I'm cooking for you instead.'

'The bread's a nice touch.'

'I thought so.'

'You all right?' she asked.

'I'm fine. Tell me, how did the big day go?'

'We won.'

'You mean *you* won?'

'It's a team effort. It's always a team effort.'

He moved a strand of silver hair away from her eyes. 'It always is.' He turned and began making his way to the kitchen. She followed him. 'You have to leave while I decorate your cake…' He winked at her. 'And I went to the library this morning. I took my notebook and wrote some stuff. I also applied for a sales job.'

'That's great, about both.' She placed her hand on his, which was resting on the kitchen counter.

She left him to finish making her birthday cake, went upstairs with her satchel, sat on the bed with a pile of papers for a while, and then had a shower.

Matt's birthday dinner for her was fabulous. She must remember to call Mrs A in the morning to let her know that now there was another person in the world who could make her triple chocolate cake.

They went to bed that night happy, and made love for most of it.

–

It was Teresa who got up the next morning to pick up the ringing landline. She was concerned it was work, something she'd forgotten to finish.

'Hello, Teresa Keane speaking,' she said, tying up her dressing gown. Christ, it really was freezing.

'Teresa, it's Natalie.'

She held the phone away from her ear. She could really do without this this morning. Any morning.

'Teresa, are you there?' Natalie said.

She put the phone near her ear. 'I'm here. Why are you calling?'

'It's Dom… he's… he's killed himself.'

What did Teresa feel? She felt glad, that's what she felt, although it wasn't a good feeling. 'How?'

'Handgun. Mouth.'

'They're illegal.'

'Handguns or mouths?' Natalie said.

Teresa stifled a laugh. 'Suicide note, admitting everything?'

'No note, Teresa.'

'Eva's got rid of it then.'

'There was no note.'

'It was Dom, Natalie, on the boat,' Teresa said quietly. 'It wasn't Luke… you *know* that.'

'I do *not* know that. I saw Luke.'

'You saw a man, and you didn't know who it was. I know you, Natalie. I know when you're unsure. And I

186

knew you were unsure that day when I asked you. I *know* you didn't have your contacts in.'

'How do you *know*?'

'Because, Natalie, I know you.' She took a breath. 'Have you any idea what it's like to see an entire career, life, being flushed down the toilet?'

'It was Luke on the boat,' Natalie said quietly.

Teresa changed the phone to her other ear. 'I'm sorry you have to deal with this alone. But I won't be coming anywhere near Raven House.'

'I have Mrs A.'

'Yes. Give her my love.'

'I will.'

'And don't make up anything to say to Eva. Don't say I send my love or anything like that, because I send her *no* love.'

'Okay… Belated happy birthday, Teresa.'

'Thanks, and tell Oli thanks for the card.'

'I will.' There was an awkward silence and Teresa thought Natalie had put the phone down. Then: 'Teresa, I'm pregnant.'

'That didn't take long.'

'I wanted to tell you. I wasn't sure if Mrs A had…'

'No. She stays neutral. I'm happy for you, Natalie. Oli's a nice bloke… I hope you treat him well.'

'What the fuck is that supposed to mean?'

'I just hope you don't, in some way, ruin his life. You seem to make a habit of it,' Teresa said, her voice barely audible.

'I told the truth… just like Jess did.'

There was a long silence.

'Are you still on the line, Teresa?' Natalie was saying.

'I am. Does Jessica know, about Dom?'

'Yes, I've called her.'

'Right then,' Teresa said. 'I have to go. One thing, though, Natalie. Do not bother calling me when Eva dies. I don't want to know.'

'I won't. I won't call you again, don't worry about that,' her sister said.

And with that the line went dead.

Teresa sat down, as if she'd been winded, but then she felt a hint of a smile forming. Natalie sounded just as she had as a kid. Petulant and bolshie. It had always annoyed her, that tone, even back then. She always had so little patience for Natalie. Hope told her she was mean, mean and opinionated. *Oh, Hope.*

She shook herself away from any nostalgia, or love, for her sister. Both sisters. But she did admit to herself that a call telling her that either Natalie or Jess had died would send her into a spiral of grief, despite everything.

But just… no. Natalie and Jessica had both *lied.*

She sprang up again, as if flinging off any danger of forgiveness. She stood, motionless for a moment, thinking of Dom. What a way to go. Your brains blown out. She wondered if a raven had sat and watched him do it. Jessica's telling of the day she found Juno still haunted her, and on so many levels. Although Dom's messy death wouldn't torment her.

The *bastard.*

31

Jessica

'Jess!' It was her housemate, Caro, calling up the stairs. 'Phone for you. It's your sister, Natalie.'

Jessica sighed, cross she'd been interrupted. She snapped closed the textbook. She was full of anatomy: bones, nerves and joints. Year one of medical school was both brilliant and boring. Brilliant because she was learning, boring because she had to interact with people every day, although she did like both of her housemates, as different as they were to her.

She got up and made her way down the stairs to the phone.

'Hi, Jess,' Natalie said.

'You sound upset. Is everything all right?'

'Not really,' her sister said. 'Dom's dead.'

The news was not a surprise. On her very last evening at her childhood home she had laid the seed. Not planted it, but cautiously left it on fertile ground. A tiny part of her was sad – the part of her that still existed from before she knew what she knew about her stepfather. The part of her that had loved the Dom who took her to sports days, football practice, netball matches and athletics meetings. Taught her to drive the boat when he knew it was pretty much illegal.

But.

There was the other part of her that hated him because of his ultimate betrayal. Of her, her sisters and her family. It had shaped everything about her.

'Jess, are you still there?' Natalie was saying.

'I am,' she replied. 'How?'

'Suicide.'

'Right.'

'You don't sound surprised.'

'How did he do it?'

'That's something that I'd imagine Teresa asking,' Natalie replied.

'You've spoken to her?'

'No, I thought I'd wait until after her birthday.'

Jess didn't reply.

'Are you okay?' Natalie asked.

'I'm fine. So, how did he do it?'

'He shot himself.'

'In the mouth?' she said.

'Yes... Jess... how did you know that...?' Natalie asked.

'Just a guess.'

Natalie didn't reply straight away and Jess knew her sister was thinking hard about her response. Finally, Natalie carried on, 'Eva says that he'd been acting strange since you left in October.'

Jess sat down on the floor, the phone held tight in her right hand. 'Sorry you're having to be there, at Raven House. Dealing with it alone.'

'It's fine.'

'How are you? The pregnancy? How's Oli?' Jessica asked. Her voice was calm but the inside of her – every muscle, every bit of sinew, every nerve pathway – felt as if it were contracting and releasing, sending rolls of diffuse spasms throughout her entire body.

'Everything's good.'

'The job?'

'That's good too… Stop it, Jess.'

'What?'

'Changing the subject. What's wrong?'

'You mean what's wrong apart from our stepdad blowing his brains out?'

'You're upset, aren't you?'

Jessica didn't answer.

'Jess… it *was* Luke on the boat.'

'I think about Juno every day,' she replied, her voice a whisper. 'I think about our sister every day, too.'

'I know. I do too,' Natalie said. Jessica could hear tears in her sister's voice. She waited for more. She knew there was going to be more. Natalie carried on. 'Juno didn't bring any drugs to the party.'

'It must have been Dom who gave it to her,' Jessica said. This was the most they had talked about Juno and Raven Island for years. 'But it was Luke who left her, Natalie. When Juno had the bad reaction to the ecstasy, Luke didn't come back to get help. He didn't tell anyone. He left Juno to die…' She stopped talking.

All the talking was exhausting.

'Jess, you still there?'

She finally spoke. 'Maybe Dom topped himself because it was him who gave Juno the tablet… and it *was* Dom on the boat with Juno.'

'Do you actually *really* think that?' Natalie said. 'Think about what you're saying, Jess.'

'I don't know what I think any more.'

'If it *was* Dom…' Natalie said, her voice small. 'Then everything, everything… we made a mistake.'

Jessica could not do this to Natalie. She did not know when the crossover had been made, but these days it was as if she, Jessica, were the older of the two, despite Natalie being married, having a job, being pregnant. Recently she had felt that it was she who should be looking after Natalie. She felt like that now.

'It's in the past, Natalie,' she said. 'We can't change the past… And listen, it's best not to even talk about it… not now… you're having a baby.'

'When the body's released there will be a funeral,' Natalie said. She seemed to have gathered herself. Either that, or buried it all again, like Jessica did. 'Will you be coming?'

'I have too much university work on.'

'Okay. I understand,' Natalie replied.

Jessica knew she didn't understand. How could she?

The two sisters hung up simultaneously.

Jessica wanted to go make a cup of tea in the kitchen to take back to her room, but she could hear Caro and Kat in there and so decided against it. She made her way upstairs, to her clean and tidy room.

She sat down at her desk. It was the first time since she'd smashed the phrenology head that she wished she'd replaced it. She still hadn't. She wanted to look at the head. Imagine inside it. She'd promised herself she would buy a new one when she completed her medical degree. It would be a landmark. Only four and half years to go. Not long. And now Dom was dead she would be able to concentrate even more effectively.

Jessica would never know if what she had confronted Dom with on the night before she left for med school a few months before had pushed him to suicide, but she guessed it had. Had he left a suicide note? She was certain he would have done. He was that sort of man. Messy, pathetic and, unfortunately for him, he possessed a conscience. It wasn't within him to just top himself and die with no explanation. No, Dom was the sort of man who'd have to spill his guts, about everything, and not just about Juno. Dom would have easily admitted to it if Eva hadn't intervened. Where did that leave her, and Natalie? She tried not to think about it. They had both been children, and Natalie had never been as mature as she thought she was. Natalie had been able to convince herself that it *was* Luke on the boat with Juno, and Jessica was more than aware that Natalie had lied because she didn't want to hurt Eva again. An insecure Natalie still cannot admit to herself that Eva manipulated her into lying. Manipulated them both. Even as an adult, Natalie can't admit that it wasn't Luke on the boat. And Jessica knew it was destroying her sister.

She couldn't undo things and go back in time, but she could do something.

She had done something. And now Dom was dead.

She stared at the wall behind her desk, her mind going back to October; and the last night she would ever spend under Eva and Dom's roof. She tapped the inside of her desk with the heel of her foot rhythmically. She'd had a long time to construct her speech and knew exactly where, and how, she was going to deliver it.

Dom had lasted for longer than she'd thought. At the time, she'd given him less than a month.

She just wished that he hadn't done it so close to Christmas.

That night in October and her last night in Raven House, Mrs A had prepared a gorgeous dinner. The last ever in Jessica's childhood home. She was sitting at the table with Eva and Dom, and had hoped that that night Mrs A would stay and eat with them; but she'd had a meeting at the local church that she didn't want to miss.

'Of course you can miss it. It's only a church meeting,' Eva had said to Mrs A. Mrs A hadn't raised an eyebrow – she never had at Eva's insensitive outbursts. Jessica could not understand why Mrs A still worked for Eva and could understand even less why the lovely, dependable and churchgoing Mrs A genuinely adored Eva. One day she would ask her.

'So, Jessica, everything you've worked for has come to fruition,' Dom said, shoving a piece of fillet steak and salad into his mouth. One of Dom's less endearing habits, although the least dangerous, was talking with food in his mouth.

'Yes, indeed it has,' she replied. She turned to Eva. 'Food's fabulous. I'll miss Mrs A's cooking.'

'I've set up a direct debit for both your accommodation and living expenses, Jessica,' Eva said.

Jessica scooped a heap of salad onto her fork. 'That's good of you.'

'A thank-you is fine, Jessica.'

Dom coughed. 'Thing is, you're on your way, Jess. Everything you've wanted.' He pushed his chair back from the table, bent down to pick something up from under the table, and then leant forward, holding a large box wrapped in silver paper. 'Eva and I bought you this.'

She glanced at Eva, who nodded.

Jessica pulled off the wrapping and opened the box. Inside was a phrenology head. The exact same one that she'd smashed in her bedroom all those years before.

She wanted to put it back in the box and return it to Dom. But she did not. She would quietly dump it when she had a chance.

'Finally, a replacement.' She engineered a smile for her mother and stepfather.

'Thought it was time,' Dom replied, picking up the box and wrapping and putting it on the sideboard.

'Yes, it is time.' She paused, momentarily. 'And talking of time, Dom,' she said, 'I thought we could take a walk by the river. Go and sit on the jetty and chew the cud?' She was banking on Eva declining. 'Before we lose the light.'

Dom's eyes lit up. She supposed because he thought they were going to have a nice little chat. She was still in total awe of the ability he possessed to wipe out everything, as if it had never happened.

'Good idea,' Eva said. 'I'll leave you two to it.' She poured herself another glass of wine. 'You two go. I'll load the dishwasher.'

'C'mon, Dom. Put your coat on, it's quite fresh outside,' Jess said, standing, her voice silky with a camaraderie-like tone.

They made their way through the kitchen French doors and onto the terrace.

Jess shivered; she had not put her own coat on. She had wanted to feel the slicing October wind that was belting its way across the river; she wanted to feel the slight pain of coldness on the bare skin of her arms.

As they walked around the corner of the house, Raven Island came into view. In her mind's eye she saw Juno's fluorescent green skirt, her beautiful and laughing face. She saw too her sister's image.

They arrived at the boathouse and jetty and Jessica sat on the wall, watching the moored boats dipping like huge ducks in the rippling water of the Thames.

Dom remained standing, watching her, smiling.

As if nothing had ever happened.

'You ruined my life, Dom.'

He opened his mouth to speak. She placed a finger to her lips. *Shush*. 'You should have come clean, Dom. You should not have asked me to lie.'

'I'm…'

'Sorry?' she said quietly.

'For everything, Jess.'

'Tell me, Dom, was it you on the boat with Juno? Was it you who left her to die?'

He shook his head.

Something broke in Jessica. 'You're *scum*. And you'll never know if or when I'll tell Eva.' Her heart beat like a wild thing inside her chest. 'How could you do what you did?'

He opened his mouth to speak but nothing came out.

And he cried then. He actually cried.

'Think about it all, Dom. Think hard, and if you can still live with yourself after all that thinking, it will be a sad day.' She paused, rubbed at her bare arms. 'Juno knew your secret because I told her. But you know that, don't you, because you heard me telling her. Is that why you let Juno die?'

'I'm sorry…'

Jessica turned away from him and looked towards the island. A raven was flying high overhead, its form casting

196

a long shadow on the water. She made her way back to the house.

Opening the French doors, she found the kitchen empty. Eva had already gone to bed. She made her way to the table and picked up the dish of beef salad, picked up a fork, and took it upstairs with her. She'd polish it off whilst she finished packing.

32

Then
January 2002

Jessica

Standing in the bathroom of her shared student house Jessica was peering in the mirror and carefully applying eye shadow. It was taking her longer than she remembered: it had been an age since she'd worn make-up. But tonight she was going out, to a bar, with her housemates, to have some fun. She had stipulated the bar. She liked to go to the same place. Needed to go to the same place. It was the only way she felt safe. The routine.

They were celebrating because, only a few days before, the three of them had finished their respective clinical placements. This was the final but one term of her medical degree. The five years had flown by. Caro had hated her placement in obs and gynae, Kat was neutral about hers in orthopaedics. Jess had completed her psychiatric clinical placement at the Royal Free. Yes, psychiatry was definitely where she wanted to specialise.

This last year of her course was going well, she was seeing a counsellor (at Natalie's suggestion) and, although she was finding some solace from talking, she was managing, with practised and already professional deftness, not to talk about what she would never talk about to anyone.

She had not made herself sick for months, she'd felt calmer than she'd felt since Eva's death, and she was even interacting more naturally with her housemates, Kat and Caro, hence the night out. She almost felt normal; she almost felt how Kat and Caro always acted. Things would never change for her but she was, at last, learning to deal with how she was. She felt, and she felt it strongly, that her own problems, her own personality flaws – if she were able to control them, and she knew she could – were issues and traits that would make her not only an effective psychiatrist, but a truly empathetic one too.

'You ready, Jess?' Caro shouted up the stairs.

'Five minutes,' she replied.

True to her word, because if Jessica said five minutes it would be exactly five minutes, she was standing in the hallway five minutes later.

'Wow,' Kat said. 'You scrub up well!'

–

Two hours later, the three young women were propping up the bar. Jessica was just about to order another round – three more Cosmos – when from the corner of her eye, sitting at the very end of the bar, she caught the profile of someone who she thought she would never see again.

The noise in the wine bar dimmed, the people disappeared, her friends were non-existent, her heart forgot to beat. Her past had come knocking at her door just as she'd been learning to deal with it.

'Money, love?' the bartender was asking.

'Oh, sorry.' She got out her purse and handed him a twenty-pound note, at the same time leaning forward, peering past the people at the crowded bar.

It was him. She was absolutely certain.

'Change, you want your change?' the bartender was saying.

'Yes, of course.'

He handed it to her, huffing at the same time.

'You all right, Jess?' Caro asked. Caro, she had decided very soon after moving in, was the more intuitive of her housemates.

'Yes…'

But as she said it, she glanced at him again. How old would he be now? Mid-thirties, maybe a few years older. He was still a good-looking man. His physical presence seemed to bring everything back. She could not stop staring at him. *Stop it, Jess. Ignore him.*

The weeks and months of stability disappeared in a shaving of a second.

She felt Caro's hand on her arm. 'Jess, let's go and sit in a booth. You don't look that well.'

She glanced at her friend, whose dark brown eyes were full of concern. 'Okay.'

'Is it to do with the bloke over at the far end of the bar?' Kat asked. 'The one who's looking over here now? Do you know him?'

'Someone I once knew… I'm just going over. I'll only be five minutes.' She took another note out of her purse. 'Get another round in,' she said, giving the money to Caro. 'Get some crisps too, peanuts, whatever they have.'

'Well, they do great bar nachos here,' Caro said, with a grin.

'Get the nachos then,' she said, managing a smile. Caro loved food as much as she did, although Caro did not empty it all down the toilet afterwards.

She got up and made her way through the crowded bar. She knew he was watching her as she did so.

'Hi there,' she said, as she approached.

He grinned at her. 'Hello, Jessica. You've barely changed at all. But you do look more like your sister than ever, now you've grown up.'

The remark threw her. Did he know about Dom? No. No one had known about Dom, only her. *That isn't true, though*, a voice whispered inside her head. The voice she silenced.

He inclined his head to the booth where she'd left Caro and Kat. 'Out with friends?'

'Yes. Fellow med students.'

'Ah, so glad you pursued your dream.'

'Yes.'

'It's good to see you,' he said. His tone was soft, concerned. 'Really is.'

'The odds are phenomenal.' She studied his response.

'They are. It was meant to be… I'm sorry about Eva…' he said.

'And Dom?'

'Yes, of course, Dom too.'

'You managed then, afterwards?'

'I did.' He opened his jacket and from the inside pocket he pulled out a card and handed it to her. 'Take it, my number and address are on there… if ever you need to talk.' He grinned again. 'Or need someone to take you out for cocktails.'

She did take it and wasn't sure why. But in the moment from spotting him to now, her entire mood had changed.

The connection to the past had reopened the closed vaults of her mind.

After he left, she walked back over to the booth to Caro and Kat – the two most normal girls in the world. A huge plate of nachos rested on the table in front of them. She sat down.

'Who was the bloke?' Kat asked.

'Leave it, Kat,' Caro said, in her soon-to-be doctor voice.

Kat shrugged.

Jessica tried to smile at Caro. She wanted to go home but stayed and ate the nachos, and even ordered another plate. Caro and Kat watched in ill-disguised surprise as she polished it all off.

'I think I have a headache coming on,' she said, as she'd finished the last tortilla. 'Do you two mind if I get an early taxi home?'

'No probs,' Caro said. 'Go home and chill, Jess.'

Kat nodded in unison.

Jessica made her way home, unsettled and disorientated.

Once inside the house she made her way to the kitchen to get a glass of water, and sitting down at the table she texted him her address. Hating herself for doing so. He didn't respond.

–

A week later, Jessica was sitting on the edge of her bed, knowing her entire life was in front of her but that it was a life she could not face. It was a similar feeling she'd had at twelve when she'd told Dom in the car on the way to school that she could hold his secret no longer; a similar feeling to the day she found Juno; a similar feeling to when she had found her sister. It was all so inextricably linked. The desolation of her life was overtaking her.

Seeing *him* had brought it all back, and she'd had to let it in.

She'd missed all of her lectures since the cocktail bar. Had hardly moved from her room. Had hardly eaten and when she had, she'd brought it all back up again. Her counsellor would call the chance meeting in the wine bar a trigger event – and she could see that, understood it on an objective level too, and yet she still did not acknowledge the scene she held hidden in a black corner of her mind.

She was totally unable to admit that final truth about her sister. It was easier to bury it, and so therefore bury herself.

She took out the bottle of barbiturates from the bottom of the wardrobe. There were more than enough to do the job. She swallowed them down with a can of Coke and lay on her bed. In those minutes as she waited, her mind was so beautifully clear, her body so wonderfully relaxed.

33

Natalie

It was nine p.m. on a Saturday night and at last the house had fallen quiet. Oli was out at the pub with a mate. Hope was fast asleep. At four years old, their daughter had long ago refused her afternoon nap; the upside being that she did at least go to bed on time.

Natalie had been made deputy head of the English department a year before, which was great for her salary, but wreaking havoc with her life. The increase in paperwork was phenomenal and so, although a Saturday night, she was in the dining room, sitting at the table and catching up on marking. She had insisted on keeping all her teaching classes, even though it was only six weeks until the start of her maternity leave.

She rubbed her ample stomach. *Not long, my little boy.* With this pregnancy, she and Oli had decided to find out the baby's sex. She had been desperate for a boy to enter the Keane family.

She stood up awkwardly from the chair and stretched her back, at the same time cradling her small lump. That was when the landline rang. She thought about ignoring it, but it might be Oli. Maybe he'd decided a night in front of the TV instead of the pub was a better idea after all.

'Hello?' she answered.

'Am I speaking with Mrs Mitchell?'

'Yes, you are.' A cold caller. She was just about to put the phone down.

'Jessica Keane's sister?'

'Yes, I am.' Guilt tripped through her at the same time a cold chill blasted through her entire body. She hadn't spoken to Jess for over three weeks. Her little sister had been sounding so fine, had even told her that she was going out with her housemates. 'Is Jess… okay?' she asked.

'I'm a doctor on ICU at the Royal Free, Mrs Mitchell. Jessica was brought into the hospital an hour ago. Her housemate found her unconscious in her bedroom. She's taken barbiturates. A lot of them, and for which she has a prescription. I don't think she meant to fail, but luckily she has failed. It's good her friends got her to hospital so speedily.'

'Oh my God…! Is she okay? I mean…'

'We think Jessica – although it's early days – is going to be okay. Her housemate gave us your number. I'm so sorry to startle you, but I thought you'd want to know.'

'Yes… of course. Yes, I do want to know. I need to sort a few things out but I'll be at the hospital as soon as I can. Thank you for letting me know.'

She put the phone down, her hand shaking. She made her way to Hope's room. She was fast asleep. She went back downstairs and called Oli's mobile, telling him to get a taxi home as soon as he could.

Then she called Teresa. The first time she'd contacted her since Dom's death. Despite Teresa's explicit instruction about not wanting to be informed when their mother left the world, she'd been compelled to let her know, although choosing to do so through Oli.

Teresa answered after only three rings. 'Natalie,' she said.

She didn't reply immediately: suddenly, her throat was as dry as desert sand and her head was pounding. Her scalp itched.

'Natalie, you still there? Is Hope all right?' Teresa carried on. 'Are *you* all right?'

That last question took her by surprise. Oli had obviously told Teresa about her pregnancy. 'Yes, I'm fine and Hope's fine. It's Jess.'

'What's happened?'

'She's in ICU at the Royal Free.' The irony wasn't lost on her and certainly wouldn't be on Teresa. It was the hospital where Luke had been during his impressive but short-lived medical career. 'She's taken pills. A lot, the doctor said. She meant it.' She paused and took a gulp of water. 'Do you care?'

'Of course I fucking care. I'll get some stuff together and drive down tonight.'

'Okay.'

'You sound surprised.'

'I am.'

'Why?' Teresa asked.

'I don't think I need to spell it out, do I?'

'Jessica lied, but she was young, and she had Eva on her back.'

What Teresa was actually implying was that Natalie was *not* young, although she had had Eva on her back too.

Teresa continued: 'She's my baby sister. I'll be at the hospital in four or five hours. I'm sure I'll see you there.'

'Does it have to take our baby sister trying to kill herself to come to see her?'

'No. It doesn't. I've been in contact with Jessica. Soon after Eva died. She wouldn't speak to me, or see me,' Teresa carried on. 'You didn't know, did you?'

'No.'

'See you later, Natalie.'

With that, Teresa hung up.

Natalie turned and, as she did so, caught sight of a photo of Jess, Hope, Teresa and her. She swallowed down the lump in her throat. If anything happened to Jess she didn't know what she would do. She suspected that Teresa felt pretty much the same, despite everything.

She heard the taxi dropping Oli off outside, him opening the front door. 'What's happened, Nat?' he shouted from the hallway.

'Jess – she's taken an overdose. She's in ICU at the Royal Free. I need to go.' She looked at him, really trying not to cry because if she cried, if she looked at all out of control, he'd be reluctant to let her drive into London. He might even suggest that he went instead of her. They couldn't both go because of Hope. 'I've been dreading a call like this for years.'

'Jessica's a strong girl. She'll be okay... But are you happy to take the car into London... when you're this upset?'

'Yes, traffic'll be light. I'm fine. I really am.' She was already putting her coat on, checking she had everything in her handbag.

'She'll be okay, Nat.'

'If Hope wakes up, tell her I've gone to see a friend.'

He nodded. 'Just drive safe.'

She left.

She managed to find a parking spot near the hospital, although it was only for an hour. She didn't care. She'd take the chance on a ticket, or a clamp.

Half an hour later she was in the relatives' room on the ICU.

'Mrs Mitchell?'

She nodded.

'I'm the doctor who spoke to you on the phone. My name is Emily Friel. I'm the ICU's consultant anaesthetist.'

'How is Jessica? Is she going to die?'

'Please, sit down. Would you like tea or coffee, water?'

'Thank you, but I'm fine. Jessica…?' She sat down on an overused blue sofa and the doctor perched next to her. She smelt nice. A perfume that she didn't recognise, but she found it calming.

'We've had to intubate Jessica. The large amount of barbiturates she has taken has depressed her respiratory muscles and so she needs help ventilating… breathing.'

Natalie leaned forward and held her head in her hands. 'Poor, poor Jess.'

'We hope to take her off the ventilator in a few days.' The doctor paused. 'When she's stable we will ensure she's seen by the hospital's psychiatrist.'

'You know that she's a med student?'

'I do. And I know Jessica. She's completed a module placement on this unit recently. The psychiatrist who'll be assessing her is a locum. We thought it best it isn't a member of staff she knows.'

'Yes, that's a good idea. Thank you.'

'Would you like to see her?'

'I would.'

Inside, the unit was dark, only low lighting around each bed, of which there were six, although only three were occupied. From the doorway, Natalie saw the tube that was invading her sister's throat and heard the low buzz of the ventilator.

'I'll be in the office.' Mrs Friel pointed to the far end of the unit. 'If you need me. You're more than welcome to kip on the sofa in the relatives' lounge. It's not that comfortable but better than sleeping in a chair.'

She nodded.

The doctor carried on, 'Will there be someone coming to relieve you?'

She looked up at her, at her kind face. 'Yes, our sister. Her name is Teresa Harris – Keane, if she's using her work name. I think she'll be here sometime in the middle of the night. She driving down from Harrogate.'

'Good. Be good for Jessica to know her sisters are here.'

'But she's unconscious?'

'Some medics believe the patient knows.'

She stared at her, a woman she didn't know, but to whom she wanted to unload her heart, and Jessica's heart, maybe even Teresa's. 'I'll talk to her.'

The doctor smiled and left and she walked to Jess's bed and looked down at the beautiful face of her sister. She looked so much like Hope that her heart cramped: for the past, for everything and everyone. Her hair was lank and greasy, but a nurse had combed it through, and tucked it behind her ears. Her eyes were also swollen in their false sleep, as if she'd been crying for days before this.

Natalie hadn't spoken to her for over three weeks. She'd been busy at work, and Hope had had a bad ear infection and so she couldn't take her to the childminder and so then had worked at home instead, catching up on everything. Her weekly call to Jessica had taken a back seat.

She took hold of Jess's flaccid hand. It was warm and sweaty. She peered up at the monitor that sat above the bed, informing her of Jess's heart and oxygen saturation. The numbers appeared normal. She leaned towards her and kissed her forehead 'I love you, Jess.' Of course she didn't answer. The artery in her left temple was pulsing at the rate the monitor indicated. 'Teresa will be here soon,' she said. Her temple pulse increased and she glanced up at the monitor; her heartbeat had increased from 78 to 110. She stroked her forehead. 'Shush, Jess. I love you. We all love you. It's all going to be good after today. I promise.'

She really did think it would be good after today. It really was time she spoke to Teresa properly and although never in a million years would she have wished this to happen, for Jess to feel so hopeless that she'd tried to kill herself, there might after all be a positive outcome.

She had to hope for that, and so it was what she did hope for.

She sat down on the hard hospital chair, closed her eyes and the subdued lights and monitors of the unit lulled her towards sleep. It had been a long, long day – but then she thought of her car parked in a one-hour parking slot. She should move it, but it was as if she'd been given the same drug as Jess.

Her head dropped to one side, and then the blackness of sleep.

–

'Natalie, wake up.'

She opened her eyes, although it felt like pieces of lead were glued to her lids. She lifted her chin, utterly disorientated, and saw Teresa crouching down next to her. 'You came,' she said.

'Course I did.'

'What time is it?'

'Just after three in the morning.'

'I left my car in a one-hour spot. Christ, they'll clamp it,' she mumbled.

'Give me your keys and I'll go and move it to where I've parked mine,' Teresa said softly. 'Looks like you can barely move with that bump.'

Natalie smiled and rubbed her belly but, looking at Teresa, saw some emotion pass over her sister's features: sorrow, regret? She picked up her handbag and handed her keys to Teresa. 'It's parked on Rosslyn Hill, near Hampstead High Street. A Ford Fiesta. Silver. Last three letters "FCU".'

Teresa grinned. 'Personalised?'

Natalie bit back a laugh. 'No, came that way.'

'Be back soon.'

Natalie looked sideways at Jess.

'I already said hello, while you were asleep,' Teresa said, turning to leave.

Natalie watched her walk through the unit, her premature white but still thick hair swishing as she strode away.

Everything was going to be okay. Jess would pull through, Teresa was there. The three of them could finally talk… when Jess woke up. She *would* wake up.

It was almost as if the past hadn't happened: she had not been consumed with guilt about being the catalyst that had made their dad leave; she and Jess hadn't obeyed Eva; she had not betrayed Teresa; Juno was still alive; her sister was still alive.

Sitting waiting for Teresa to return in the quietness of the unit, she started to question Dom's suicide. Another man had gone to prison, not him. Dom had got away with it. She couldn't imagine Dom being eaten by guilt after so much time had elapsed. It wasn't in Dom's nature.

What did all those thoughts make her? A woman who did not deserve anything she had. Her hands found her stomach, her mind travelled back home and to her daughter in bed asleep, Oli looking after her.

She pulled herself up from the chair and stood looking down on Jess. Her heart rate was steady. What had caused her to try to take her own life? Since *the call*, and all the way on the drive to the hospital, she tried to frame their lives, Hope and Raven Island, Juno's death, Dom's suicide.

Had Jess reached her tolerance for feeling guilty for so long, like her? Like Dom?

34

Teresa

Teresa woke up more exhausted than she'd felt for years. The drive from Harrogate and then spending most of the night at the hospital, seeing and talking to Natalie for the first time in so long, had taken it out of her. She got up and grabbed her weekend bag that she still hadn't unpacked properly, trying to find the paracetamol that she was sure she'd put in the side pocket. No, she'd forgotten them.

She rubbed her temples, thinking of the night before, about Natalie. They hadn't talked that much about anything other than Jessica's current predicament, Natalie's job, her job a little, and about Hope. The most important exchange had come just before they parted ways.

Her mobile began jumping around on her bed. She picked it up.

Matt.

'Hi, darling.'

'How's Jessica?'

'She's intubated but hopefully it'll only be for a short time. I'll spend the day here tomorrow, and drive back first thing the following morning.'

'Stay as long as you need to.'

'I have to be in court. I can always come back down.'

'How's it going with Natalie?' he asked, although she sensed tentativeness in his tone.

'Sort of okay, as long as we don't talk about certain things.'

'Jessica has tried to take her own life. It's time you three sisters made up… You're not as much of a bitch as you like to make out.'

Teresa felt herself smiling despite everything. 'Perhaps I'm more of a bitch than I make out?'

'I'm going to ignore that… do we know what prompted Jessica to do this?'

'No. Her housemates say she's coping well with the final year at med school. On top of her work. It's not stress connected with her course. Natalie's in touch with her regularly but hasn't been the last few weeks. Jessica has big downs, but Natalie doesn't know what's happened to cause this.'

'It's a culmination, I'd imagine. Jessica's fragile,' Matt said.

'Jess's housemates did say that she's been more introverted than usual recently. But they don't know why, as they did say that up until the last few weeks she's actually been much more sociable than normal. Even went out to a bar with them a while back, which as Natalie pointed out, is unusual for Jessica. And Natalie also said she thought Jessica has seemed much more together, less anxious recently, which is why she didn't feel compelled to call her all the time. Caro, one of Jess's housemates, did say something, though. The night they went out to a bar together, Jessica saw someone she knew, and, according to Caro, the evening went a bit pear-shaped after that.'

'In what way? Who did she see?'

'Apparently the night had started well. But then she saw a man who she seemed to recognise. Jessica left her friends to go talk to him. Came back, and soon afterwards left the bar. She was upset. And she hasn't been the same since… and now this…'

'It sounds as if there's a connection there,' Matt said.

'Maybe. But there's something else. Natalie's been trying to get Jessica to see a counsellor. Apparently, she started seeing one a few months ago. Natalie thinks it's brought everything out…'

'Maybe. And what about Natalie?'

'What about her, Matt? She won't ever admit that she was lying.'

'That's because she didn't think she *was* lying.'

Teresa shrugged. Her sisters, and Eva, had lied. End of.

'Jessica's planning to specialise in psychiatry,' she said instead.

'Often the best mind reapers are the most damaged.'

'Maybe all three of the Keane sisters should have gone into psychiatry.'

He laughed down the phone but then stopped abruptly. 'Something's tripped Jessica, and maybe it's what's coming out with her counsellor.'

'Maybe.'

'Think about what I've said – about making up with your sisters.'

It is something she has been thinking about a lot already. 'I'll see you in a few days.'

'Love you,' he said, and disconnected.

She *did* listen to Matt. She took on board what he said. She took on board what he didn't say too, because often it's what someone doesn't say that speaks the loudest.

Teresa brought her thoughts back to the current situation and her and Natalie's parting conversation as they went their separate ways on a London street in the early morning of the next day.

'I'd like Hope to know you, Teresa,' Natalie had said, and so quietly, she could barely hear the words.

'I'd like to know Hope too,' she'd replied, and just as softly.

The abyss of Teresa's sorrow about being unable to conceive was always with her. And time was moving on, a relentless progression. She suspected motherhood was never going to happen to her.

Before getting into their respective cars, Natalie had offered her bed and breakfast. Teresa knew the offer was genuine. She declined. It was a step she wasn't yet ready to take.

–

In the end Teresa did stay in London for longer than she'd planned. She handed the case she was representing to a colleague and worked from her hotel room. The day after she'd arrived Jessica was taken off the ventilator, having made a remarkable recovery, the doctor had said. Jessica was a tough cookie, her body healthy and strong. But her mind, not as much so.

After Matt's words and in subsequent conversations with him, Teresa came to her conclusion, and a decision. She had to tackle what she believed was causing Jessica so much pain, which she believed was her little sister's guilt. She would, though, leave Natalie out of it – that was a completely different story and one she would tackle another time. Jessica was her pressing concern.

A week after being admitted to hospital, Jessica was discharged. With Natalie's job and Hope to deal with – Oli was away on a business trip that he hadn't been able to postpone – Teresa insisted she took Jessica back to the house she shared with Caro and Kat.

Kat gave up her bed for her and went to stay at a nearby aunt's house. Teresa was touched at the gesture and grateful for the empathy that was being shown to Jessica.

It was at the end of the first week, when Caro had gone to the pub, that Teresa steeled herself to say something, and she knew where she was going to start. Natalie had told her about Jessica's bulimia. It was a revelation that had shocked her; she had no idea, but why would she? She and Jessica had been estranged for so long.

In the tiny kitchen she set a tray, then poured tinned tomato soup from the pan to a bowl, cut up some fresh bread she'd picked up from the local deli, placed it on a plate and took them upstairs. She put the tray down on the floor and knocked. 'Can I come in, Jessica?'

'Sure,' Jessica replied.

She picked up the food and entered the clean and tidy bedroom. 'Thought you might be hungry.'

'I am, as a matter of fact.'

Teresa put the tray on Jessica's bed and stood by the window looking onto a busy London street while she ate in silence. When she turned around, the bowl and plate were empty.

It was then that Teresa clocked the duvet cover. 'I can't believe you still have that!' she said, gesturing to the old Indiana Jones cover.

Her sister didn't smile. 'I do.'

She pulled a chair away from Jessica's desk and sat down. 'We need to talk.'

'Thanks for everything you've done, Teresa.'

'I haven't done anything.'

'You came, and you stayed,' Jessica replied.

'You're my sister... Look, Jessica, Natalie's told me about your... your bulimia...'

'It's no big secret.' Jess looked at her. 'No one ever noticed. To be honest, I thought everyone knew but didn't say anything. Sometimes I even thought it was normal... if you live with something for long enough, you think it's normal.'

Teresa was able to take so much from that statement. Poor Jessica. Neither she nor Natalie, nor Eva, had supported her as they should have done after Hope's, and then Juno's, death. 'I'm so sorry you've had to deal with this alone... all of what you've had to deal with. I really and truly am.' She gently took hold of her sister's chin, tilted her head upwards and found her clear blue eyes. 'The way Eva was, Jessica, was not normal. Our lives were not normal. None of us grieved properly for—'

'None of us even talked about her.'

Teresa leaned towards her. 'I know. It's time we did.'

'Not now.'

'Okay.' Inwardly she sighed with relief and hated herself for it. It was part of the problem, how the three of them could never talk about their sister. 'But we have to talk about other things, Jess. And maybe this isn't the right time to say this, but I'm going to say it anyway.' She leaned closer to Jessica. 'I want to talk about why you tried to take your own life. I know it's all so complicated, but I think... the way you feel, why you did this, is connected to everything that's happened. And I know you don't want to talk about it... but I think you should try.'

'What are you trying to say?' Jessica pulled away, and turned to look out of the window.

Anywhere, Teresa thought, Jessica wanted to look anywhere, as long as she wasn't looking at her.

'I'm trying to say… trying to ask… is it an underlying guilt you feel about doing what Eva asked you to do, asking you to lie, that is making life so unbearable for you?'

The words had come out totally wrong. In a court situation this line of questioning would be a disaster.

'I saw Luke on the boat with Juno,' Jessica said.

'Okay… and that morning, the morning you came over to the island…'

Jessica threw off the cover and swung her legs from the bed, sat on its edge, her head in her hands.

She shouldn't be doing this. It was too soon, and it would make no difference to her life, not now. But it was eating Jessica, and if she could say it, admit it, then Jessica would heal, and her sister wouldn't attempt to kill herself again – because the next time she might not be as lucky.

'I *did not go* to the island that morning,' Jessica finally replied.

Teresa studied the fine features of her sister's face; her expression was resolute and… genuine. 'But you *did*. Don't you remember? I told you not to tell Eva, and you didn't tell Eva. And I appreciated that.'

Staring again at the window, Jessica replied: 'I didn't tell her because I didn't go.'

'Okay, okay. Is that what you really believe?'

'It's what happened! Or rather, what *didn't* happen, Teresa.'

'I want to help you…' She swallowed, hoping it would help the next words come out properly. 'You don't have to admit to anything. You just have to tell me why you feel your life is this worthless? You have a career ahead of you. Everything you ever wanted.' She swallowed again. 'Talk to me, Jessica. Why?'

'There is nothing to say.' Jessica stood up. 'I'm not admitting to anything because there is nothing to admit to. I DID NOT LIE. I think maybe it's best if you went back home. You've appeased *your* guilt, so you can go now.'

'Jessica—'

'I can't tell you what you want to hear. You're blind, Teresa, to everything that's going on around you. You always were. Blind and selfish… you asked me to lie… Luke wasn't who you thought he was.'

'Go on,' Teresa said softly, cajolingly. 'You *do* remember.'

Jessica walked to the window. Stared through it, her back to Teresa. 'Go home.'

'I can't help you if you can't tell me the truth.'

'You don't want to know the truth.'

Why was Jessica blaming *her* for her own inability to accept the truth and, finally, admit to that truth? Matt's words disintegrated in a moment. She wished he were here. He'd handle this so much better than she was doing. Christ, her sister had tried to commit suicide – but perhaps the reason she'd done so wasn't connected to Raven Island at all.

Teresa shook her head in puzzlement. It *was* connected. It *had* to be.

'I do want to know the truth, I always have,' Teresa replied. 'Our childhoods are a long way away now. It was what it was, I accept that, and so should you. We need to move on.'

Suddenly, Jessica whipped round. 'Go home, Teresa. Thank you for coming, but please, just go home.'

Why had she thought she could make a difference? Because she wanted to help Jessica. She stared at the duvet, at her sister. She couldn't do this any more. *I should not have come.*

Teresa walked to the doorway. 'I'll call Natalie and ask her to come over as soon as she can.'

Jessica nodded, her gaze fixed on the floor.

'Are you going to be okay?' she pushed.

'You mean, will I try again?' She didn't wait for her reply. 'No, I won't. You can go home with peace of mind.'

Teresa slipped from the room and gently closed the door behind her. As she headed to collect her things, she decided not to call Natalie but to drive over there instead. She needed to talk to her in person.

She could do no more with Jessica. She had tried. But had she tried hard enough? No, she hadn't. And they still hadn't talked about their sister.

35

Teresa

After quickly packing her bag, Teresa called Matt explaining she'd be home later that evening, just telling him it was a change of plan. She'd explain when she got back home. He would be disappointed with her – that she'd messed it up with Jessica. Because she had. Big time.

She took her small case down the narrow stairs of Jessica's student house, her handbag slung over her shoulder, half expecting Jessica to emerge from her room, but she didn't. In the narrow hallway she could feel the icy flow of air seeping through the bottom of the front door. It was a freezing day, below zero. She hoped her car would start. She flung on her coat, turned and looked up the stairs. She should go back and try to talk to Jessica again.

She stood for a moment but then turned, opened the door, picked up her case, and left.

The path was icy and she nearly slipped over. As she got to the gate, she put her case down to open it and it was then that she saw Natalie across the street, getting out of her car. What was she doing there? They'd agreed Natalie shouldn't be coming. She was having a few problems with her pregnancy – nothing serious, but the doctors had told her to take it easy.

'Natalie!' she shouted. 'You shouldn't have come.'

Natalie closed her car door, checked there were no cars coming and tentatively crossed the road. A few moments later she was standing next to her, looking at her case. 'You leaving? I thought you were here for another week.'

'Yes… but no, I'm leaving,' she replied, pulling at the collar of her coat. 'You really shouldn't have come, Natalie. It's bloody freezing, and the roads must be treacherous.'

'I could say the same.' Natalie searched her features. 'What's happened? Something has, I can see it.' She moved closer to her. 'Tell me.'

'Just go inside, Natalie. Warm up. I'm surprised Oli let you come.'

'He didn't want me to, but I need to see Jess. I'm so worried about her.'

'Look, we've had a bit of an argument. It's best I leave.'

'About what?'

'It's freezing, Natalie, I'll tell you another time.'

'Tell me now.'

She looked at her sister. She didn't look that well and appeared half frozen too. 'Let's get in your car and talk.'

'Just tell me, Teresa.'

'I asked Jessica about the day Juno died, about who she saw in the boat. I thought it might help her, if she could talk about it, get it out in the open.'

Natalie stared at her. 'Our sister has recently tried to kill herself. Couldn't that question wait, Teresa? God, you're so selfish.'

Fatigue as well as the cold was overwhelming Teresa; she had the deepest desire to just get in the car and go home. She had fucked it up with Jessica, but she could do nothing about that today. She turned to look at the tiny frontage of Jessica's terraced house and saw her sister standing at the bedroom window, watching.

Anger and frustration folded through her.

Natalie was standing in front of her car, next to the driver's door.

'Please move, Natalie. I'm going to get in my car and drive home. You go inside and warm up.' She looked at her. 'You shouldn't have come.' She bent down to pick up her case, slipped and caught Natalie's arm to stop herself from falling. 'Sorry,' she said.

Natalie didn't reply, her expression set like stone and as white as marble.

Teresa made her way to the boot, flipped it open and threw her case inside, then turned to get into her car.

Natalie was still standing by her driver's door. Losing her patience, Teresa pulled gently at her sister's arm to move her. Natalie, always so bloody stubborn.

'Get your hands off me,' Natalie hissed. 'You're not going, Teresa, and leaving Jess like this. You can't.' Natalie grabbed hold of her coat sleeve and pulled.

Now totally frustrated, Teresa pushed her sister, and harder than she had wanted. It all happened so quickly and yet in slow motion as Natalie skidded on the icy pavement and went down. Teresa couldn't seem to move and was only catapulted into action when Natalie began moaning, and then screaming in pain.

She crouched down. 'Oh my God, Natalie, I'm so sorry.' With shaking hands, she pulled out her phone from her bag and called 999, then took off her coat and put it over her sister. 'Don't move. The ambulance will be here soon.'

'Something is very wrong,' Natalie rasped.

Teresa was about to reply when she sensed someone standing behind her.

Jessica.

'What have you done?' Jessica said, kneeling beside Natalie. 'I saw you pushing her, Teresa.'

The condensation coming from Jessica's breath surrounded her, engulfed her.

What had she done?

She was still asking that question when the ambulance arrived to take Natalie to hospital. Jessica went with her.

Teresa waited inside the student house for news. Unable to keep away, however, instead of driving back to Harrogate, she took a taxi to the hospital.

Natalie's baby boy had died inside his mother's womb.

36

Now

Teresa

Teresa is inspecting Matt's bed-changing as he finishes off in the guest room that Hope always sleeps in.

'Thanks,' she says, standing in the doorway.

'No problem. Greta's room's ready too.'

'Food's all prepared and table set.'

'I just got a text from Hope,' he says. 'The taxi'll be dropping her in the next ten minutes.'

'Perfect,' she says.

They both make their way downstairs and five minutes later they hear the taxi pull up on the gravelled drive. It's Teresa who rushes to open the front door just as Hope, rather clumsily, emerges from the back of the taxi. The sun is still out; it's been a warm if not a boiling summer's day. Feathers of lengthening light caress Hope's sun-freckled and open face; she's wearing her long blonde hair down and it isn't properly brushed. She looks both magnificent and happy.

She looks so like Jessica, and so like Hope.

She turns around to haul her weekend bag from the back seat. Her niece won't be aware she's spoken to Natalie earlier so Teresa pretends she doesn't know about her results.

Matt goes to help her. Hope hugs him and then looks towards Teresa, a smile as big as the overhanging late day sun covering her face. She takes in Hope's features, her sublime joy and innocence. It really is time for movement in the Keane girls' lives. She feels it, knows it, and yet is still stuck in the quicksand of the past. Matt wants her to move on, but she's never managed to do so. As Natalie and Jessica haven't either.

Yes, it is time.

'I take it you did okay?' Teresa says, her own smile real and genuine.

'I did! A First. I can't believe it!'

'Fantastic news, Hope... I bet your mum and dad are pleased?'

'Yes, they are!'

Teresa pulls her niece towards her, enfolds her. Hope smells of apricot soap, youth and optimism, and she questions if she had ever smelt this way. Once, she had. Once, they both had. Her and her sister.

'You look fantastic,' Teresa says, taking in Hope's long boho-style dress.

'Thanks. Got the dress off eBay. Luckily it was delivered this morning.'

'Looks lovely,' Matt says. 'Come on, girls, let's go and drink champagne!'

Matt takes Hope's bag upstairs while she and Hope make their way to the kitchen. She retrieves a special bottle of Bollinger from the fridge.

'Shouldn't we wait for Greta?' Hope asks.

'We'll open another one when Greta arrives. She'll be here around eight so there's time for us to catch up.' She pours the bubbly into glasses, waits for it to settle and for Matt to take a seat when he comes back into the room.

'Here's to you, Hope,' Matt says, lifting his glass.

'Congratulations, Hope,' Teresa says. 'You've done so well. The world is your oyster.'

'Thank you, and thanks for inviting me.'

They clink and drink. Teresa places the hors d'oeuvres on a plate. 'Your favourites.'

'You're a star, Aunt Teresa.' Hope takes one and pops it in her mouth. She takes another. Hope possesses the same appetite as Jessica, looks like Jessica, but is as different to Jessica in personality as Teresa is to Natalie, and as different as she herself was to Hope.

The young Hope wipes her mouth and sits on a kitchen stool, eyeing the plate of hors d'oeuvres.

'Go for it,' Teresa says, grinning. 'Do as you'd do at home. I've always told you that.'

Hope grins back and takes another. Eats it slowly and fixes her gaze on Teresa. 'I've asked Mum to organise a family get-together for my graduation. Spoke to her this morning when I called her about my results.'

'I know. She's called me.'

'Wow. I didn't think she would,' Hope says.

Teresa studies her niece. A child, but not a child any more. A young woman. 'Does Natalie talk about the past to you?'

'She did, when she *had* to tell me something, but it's one of those things that we don't talk about. I know she doesn't want to.'

Teresa turns to Matt and nods. 'We want to talk to you about it.'

'I'm all ears,' Hope says, but her expression has settled into one of absolute seriousness.

'Matt didn't do what he was put in prison for doing,' she says.

'I think I know that,' Hope replies.

'Does your mum know you think that?' Teresa asks, so very quietly.

'Yes, I believe she does.'

'And?' Teresa says gently.

'And, I don't know.' Hope pauses, rolls a thick strand of hair around her finger, just like her sister used to do. 'My mum is a great mum, not perfect, but perfect enough for me.'

'Oh God, Hope, I know that,' Teresa says, realising that it sounds as if she's attacking Natalie to Natalie's own daughter. Hope smiles and at the same time takes hold of her hand. Teresa continues: 'I've told your mum I'm up for it, the party, as is Matt. I hope Jessica and her husband will be too. It's a shame Eva's not still alive...'

'Or Dom?' Hope asks quietly.

Hope will go far in her chosen field, but Teresa feels her own happy expression disappear thinking about Dom.

Hope doesn't wait for her to answer and turns to Matt, who is munching on the last hors d'oeuvres. 'Are you okay about it, coming to my party?'

'Course I am,' he says. Talking with his mouth full.

'Do you mind if I ask you a question, Matt?' Hopes says.

'Go ahead.'

'Why did you change your name?'

'New start. And Matthew *is* my middle name.'

'I like Luke.'

'I liked Luke too,' he says.

Teresa's heart pitches. Hope is looking at her, but has the emotional intelligence to let the subject drop. 'How's the new book coming along?' Hope continues.

He grins in that lazy sort of way that she's always loved. 'I'm a survivor, Hope. Book's coming along fine.' He moves his stool closer to her. 'It might not be the time to talk about this but I'm going to anyway.' He glances at his watch, conscious that Greta will be here soon. 'Do you believe I'm innocent?'

'I do,' Hope says.

The breath catches in Teresa's throat. *No, Matt, don't do this.*

Hope carries on, 'My dad and mum have never stopped me from spending time with you. And because of that, and as I've grown older, I've always… sensed… that neither of them thought, think, Matt did what they say you did.' Hope glances at Teresa.

'This isn't the time, Matt…' Teresa says.

'It—'

'I think it *is* the time,' Hope interrupts him quietly. 'I've read old newspaper reports, of course I have. Mum and Dad know I have. It was all down to Aunt Jessica's testimony, and Gran Eva's.' She is looking at Teresa intently.

'Your mum's too,' Teresa says quietly.

'Yes. I know… what happened ruined the relationship between the three of you, and so… my life has been impacted too. I just want the family to come together, you, my mum, Jessica… and me.'

'Hope's so right,' Matt says.

'Are you ready for the fallout?' Teresa says quietly.

Hope inclines her head. She stares at Teresa. 'Mum's told me about—'

The doorbell rings through the house. Thank God for Greta. She can't talk about who her niece is on the verge of mentioning.

'Greta's arrived,' she says, and Hope squeezes her hand, then lets go.

–

The next day Hope doesn't mention her namesake, instead she talks exuberantly about how great it has been to meet and talk to Greta about law, human rights, and saving the world. But Teresa is now absolutely certain that Natalie has at some point lowered her guard with both Oli and their daughter and admitted to Eva's influence on both her and Jessica's testimony.

As Teresa waves off Hope in the taxi, her mobile begins to wriggle in her trouser pocket. She pulls it out and swipes the green button.

'Hi, Teresa, Natalie here again.'

'We've just waved off your amazing daughter,' she says.

'I'm glad she was with you two last night, and… thanks for introducing her to your barrister friend.'

'No sweat.' Teresa waits but the line is silent. 'You still there?' she says.

Natalie's next words come out all in a rush. 'I can't do it, Teresa. I love Hope but I can't organise this get-together for her. It's too much.'

'It will be a good thing to do,' Teresa replies slowly. 'And Jessica. I want to see Jessica.'

'There's been nothing stopping you keeping in touch with her,' Natalie says. 'You're so bloody stubborn and… self-righteous.'

'I'm asking you to come together with me, Natalie. For Hope,' she says.

'I can't.'

'Matt forgives you,' she carries on. 'And he forgives Jessica.' Teresa hears her sister's light sobs but ploughs on, as if she's in court, or in the witness prep beforehand. 'We need to help Jessica.'

'I can't do it. I can't do a party for Hope.'

'Hope will be devastated.'

'*Stop it*, Teresa. She's *my* daughter, not yours.'

'I know that.' She's gripping the edge of the hall table.

'You had the chance,' Natalie is saying, 'to make amends with Jess… back then, in her final year at med school. You walked away. It was *your* choice.'

'As it was *yours*, at my graduation party. *Our* engagement party. Mine and Luke's, Natalie.'

'My mind's made up, Teresa,' Natalie says, and disconnects.

Teresa stares at the device. Part of her is stunned, but there is another, larger part of her, that is relieved Natalie didn't bring up her miscarriage.

37

Jessica

It is the night of her birthday but Jessica has been wide awake for all of it, although the man lying next to her had fallen asleep almost immediately. As if what had happened, and not that many hours before, was totally normal.

The name he'd uttered when he had found his release is still echoing inside her head. Her relationship with him, and his with her, is more complex, more fucked up than even she could imagine, and the sickness rolls through her again.

Finally, she gets up and pads across the deep-pile grey carpet, tripping over her shoes from the night before. 'Damn,' she mutters under her breath, and turns to look at him. Still fast asleep.

She makes her way to the bathroom at the end of the hallway rather than using the en-suite and waking him. Once safely inside she uses a flannel to wipe away the dried blood on her thighs and then kneels beside the toilet.

Ten minutes later she opens the door and contemplates the spare room to sleep in. No, she must not. She must not act any differently. But things are different. Last night was a seismic shift; not because of what had happened – but because of why it *had* happened.

It's always about the whys, and suddenly it has become so blindingly obvious to her. In the early hours of the first morning of being forty, the flash of understanding is acute and clear.

She tries to work out what has caused his change. Her mind travels back through the previous day, her birthday, her mention of both Juno and Hope, then the early evening dinner in her favourite restaurant, and the two women sitting at the table next to them.

She slips back into bed and shivers as the heat emanating from his body consumes her. She lies on her back and stares at the ceiling, thinking.

Why had she said Juno's name? Actually said it aloud. It's a name he avoids. Not in seventeen years of marriage has it ever been mentioned. He had forbidden it. A stipulation on their marriage. *We need to put your past behind you, Jessica.* And she had agreed, because was it not the past that was destroying her? He has prohibited any mention of Hope too. She has never allowed herself to question why.

But now the memory emerges, uninvited.

It was not only Dom.

Seventeen years with this man snoring in her bed. She's been sleepwalking and it's time to wake up the part of her brain that has been dormant for so long. Her love – if she could ever call what she felt for him *love* – is not love. It is dependence, the fear of loss, of the consequences of being part of the world proper. It's a place where she feels… not safe… but secure. He has controlled her, through the past, through subterfuge and through sex: impersonal and non-penetrative sex.

Last night had not been his desire for her, far from it. Last night, on her fortieth birthday, she was both violated, and liberated.

Trying to mentally remove herself from lying next to him, she thinks of seven-year-old Grace. She will be in court that afternoon in her role as expert witness, she will be fighting for the little girl. This is the second week of her stepfather's trial. Today is a big day for Jessica, and although Grace doesn't fully comprehend it, it is an important day for her too.

She acknowledges to herself it has been her sessions with Grace that have allowed her own mind to open up. By encouraging Grace to talk, and realising how Grace's stepfather not only abused her, but manipulated the little girl too, she can finally admit to her own abuse.

And also, she can now see clearly who was on the boat on the afternoon of Teresa's graduation party.

It was not Luke.

She can also see distinctly, now, another scene. Inside the cabin.

Why had she married him? It will take her the rest of her life in therapy to work that one out.

For the first time since he walked back into her life, she accepts the deviant nature of their relationship, and the catastrophe of it for her. He has manipulated her, and has done from the night in the cocktail bar.

He saved her, and then destroyed her.

Last night, when two women had come into the restaurant, taking the table next to theirs, he had been unable to keep his eyes off them, to the point where it became embarrassing. She had her back to the women but after half an hour of watching her husband's captivation, she had to turn to look.

235

The startling appearance of the youngest woman had momentarily floored her. They were undoubtedly mother and daughter. Both attractive and blonde. But it was the younger woman on whom she became transfixed – she looked so much as she herself had looked at that age. And she looked so much as her sister had looked at that age, too.

It was then she accepted that there was something so very wrong.

She has to say something. And that is when she knows things are changing. That they have changed.

All the teenage girls from Jessica's youth crowd her brain. Caitlin, who'd survived the Keane party, has three kids, a husband and is living a quiet life working in her mum's salon.

Juno.

And her sister who, even now, she has a problem allowing into her mind – Jessica has always despised herself for this.

Perhaps she has always known who was on the boat that day when Juno died, but it's only now that she is able to admit it. As if looking through someone else's notes, she cannot believe she has missed this. Allowed herself to miss this.

Deaths. Girls. One common denominator.

Carefully, she gets up from the bed. She looks at the clock on the bedside table. Seven. As quietly as she can, she picks up the clothes she wore last night – dress, jacket, scarf, even the knickers – from the floor and takes them downstairs.

In the kitchen, as she drops the scarf and the other clothes onto a kitchen stool, she touches the wire head whose eyes always follow her. She then walks to the expansive kitchen counter where the coffee machine lives. As she goes to pick up the jug, she notices the ruby bracelet hanging like a beautiful manacle from her wrist. She attempts to take it off, but can't. It's a piece of jewellery that demands a second person in either putting it on or taking it off. She does not need the second person in her life any more and waves of frustration, impatience and anger swamp her. She cannot get it off her wrist. She stops trying and yanks it hard. The fragile creation breaks easily, and Jessica is free.

She hears a tinkle on the hard wooden floor and looks down, seeing a glinting ruby, and she thinks a small diamond too, disappearing underneath the dishwasher. She turns and pours her coffee, takes a sip and savours the taste. She places the mug on to the counter, bends down again and opens a drawer, takes out a bin liner. She picks up the scarf from the stool that sits next to the wire head, but a corner of the fabric snags on the long, knife-like wire protruding from the nose, slitting through the material easily. Pulling at it gently, she examines the scarf and then puts it in the black plastic liner, together with the other clothes. She wants no reminder of last night. Holding the bag, she walks back to her mug, picks it up and takes another sip. Puts it down again and shoves her hand underneath the dishwasher, sweeping her palm over the floor, feels the hardness of the diamond.

She picks up the broken bracelet, its gems sparkling like oversized Christmas glitter, and throws it into the bin liner, together with the ruby and diamond, and the gift of the phrenology head. She ties it up. Wrapping her dressing gown tightly around herself, she grabs her car keys, goes outside and places the bin liner in the back of her car.

Once back in the house she showers and gets dressed. She pokes her head into their bedroom. He's still fast asleep, still snoring. He's not a drinker, almost teetotal, but last night he'd drunk more than he normally would. He likes to be in control, and alcohol takes that away. Last night he had lost control.

The image of the young woman in the restaurant flares inside her mind.

She goes back downstairs and checks herself in the full-length hallway mirror. As she does so it hits her again: her likeness to both the girl in the restaurant and her sister. She attempts to work through the puzzle that has been sitting inside her head since he'd said Hope's name.

She examines herself more closely. There are the beginnings of dark circles around her eyes. She steps back a little so she can see more of herself. She's wearing a chocolate brown suit, a yellow silk blouse, and mid-height square heels in leather that matches the fabric of her suit. Her hair in a tight chignon.

She so wants to like the person peering back at her. It is time to finally like Jessica.

Picking up her briefcase and handbag, she leaves.

38

Jessica

Less than an hour later – the London traffic is light for once – Jessica arrives at the court building. She had intended to get here earlier to touch base with Connor before the day's proceedings began, but her morning has not quite turned out as planned. She looks at her watch. The prosecution's medical expert witness is in court now, his slot was the first of the morning. Connor will be in the courtroom doing his utmost, she knows, to ensure that Grace's stepfather is found guilty. She's holding her briefcase close to her chest and thinks of checking her notes, although she has no need to. All the information, everything she knows, is inside her head. From what Grace has gradually revealed to her over the past eighteen months there is no doubt in Jessica's mind that she is telling the truth. The little girl has described sexual acts she would have no way of knowing about, not without experiencing them herself.

At eleven a.m. the usher takes her into the courtroom. She has provided expert witness testimony many times over the years but has never been so heavily invested in the outcome of the one she is providing for Grace's case. She tries not to look at the defendant and instead her eyes find Connor. He nods his head almost imperceptibly as she takes the stand. It is Connor, the prosecution barrister, who questions her first. His voice is clear and concise, although today in court the lilt of his Irish accent is stronger than she has noticed before – perhaps an indicator of the intensity of emotion connected to Grace's case.

This is the easy part of her court appearance. The real work begins with the cross examination by the defence counsel – because the stepfather has pleaded not guilty to all the charges made against him. Connor, though, has briefed her on the tactics the defence may well use – warned her. She is ready, and in many ways more ready because of her own home life situation.

She and Connor had gone through the areas that she is likely to be questioned about, and it all goes smoothly. Her answers to Connor's questions leave no room for doubt – Grace has been systematically abused by her stepfather since the age of three, and at the age of five, the stepfather's friend began abusing Grace too, and with the stepfather's knowledge. Jessica tries to ensure that the judge and jury are convinced of Grace's ability to tell the truth.

'Dr Keane,' the judge says to her. 'Thank you.' He then addresses the defence barrister. 'Mr Wayne, do you wish to cross examine the prosecution's expert witness?'

'I would, Your Honour. Thank you.'

The barrister stands, looks fleetingly at his lectern, then turns his head a quarter of a circle and fixes his gaze on Jessica. She senses immediately his hunger to win, the way he rotated his head so purposefully, the way he smiled. She takes a deep breath, stares at him, not returning his smile.

'Dr Keane,' he says. 'Thank you for coming to court today.' His pseudo-affable demeanour disappearing quickly. 'How long have you been treating Grace?'

'Eighteen months.'

'And why was Grace referred to you?'

'Two years ago her mother had noticed that Grace was very withdrawn, and her teacher had also registered her own concern regarding Grace.'

'So it was Grace's mother who brought Grace to see you?'

'Yes, although on the first and subsequent second visit, Grace's father came to the hospital too.'

'So the defendant, Grace's stepfather, was happy for Grace to see a psychiatrist?'

Connor had flagged this line. 'Yes, he didn't seem to be concerned. In fact… he appeared to take Grace's treatment with me… as inconsequential. It was clear to me after talking with him that Grace's problems, including attempting to harm herself, was not something he worried overly about. He felt she would grow out of it.'

'But the defendant made no comment, he did not indicate, Dr Keane, that he was unhappy for his step-daughter to be your patient? Put more concisely, for his stepdaughter to undergo a treatment programme with yourself, a psychiatrist?'

'No, no direct comment.'

Mr Wayne appears to let that go. 'When did Grace first mention that her stepfather was, allegedly, engaging in sexual acts with her, Dr Keane?'

'Grace finally told me six months ago. It has taken a year for her to trust me enough to tell me.' She stares at him.

'And what did Grace tell you?'

'Grace described her stepfather's penis and ejaculate. She told me in the first session in which she properly opened up to me – and may I add after months of sessions when Grace said hardly anything at all – that the defendant

241

forced Grace to take his penis into her mouth. That was when she first described ejaculate. In my following sessions with Grace, she described penetrative intercourse, and again with accurate descriptions of ejaculate... and the defendant's reaction to orgasm. A seven-year-old girl would not be able to fabricate such vivid and authentic descriptions.' She stares at him harder. 'And her testimony is authenticated by the physical examination, which Grace underwent. Bruising around her vulva and damage inside her vagina, which is consistent with penetrative sex in a child so young.'

The barrister does not take his gaze away from her, although she suspects strongly he would very much like to do so. He continues. 'During your sessions, Dr Keane, did Grace admit to watching her mother's extensive library of porn, which Grace was easily able to access and view on her mother's phone and other devices, as the mother did not use passwords for these devices?'

'The defendant's wife has informed me that she is aware that Grace may well have been exposed to some erotica. However, the vital word here is erotica. Grace was not exposed to images of either oral or penetrative sex.' She allows her gaze to bore into his. 'And certainly, Grace was not exposed to images of ejaculate. And, Grace sustained severe physical injuries, Mr Wayne.'

'Indeed, Grace did, and this is so very unfortunate and heartbreaking. However, the medical examiner has made it clear that the injuries Grace sustained may well have been caused by Grace herself, by an object such as a pencil, or some other object that was easily accessible.' He looks away from Jessica, first at the judge and then at the jury, his expression one of pain, as if he has no wish to mention what he's just mentioned. He carries on, 'Could it not be that Grace is a fantasist, and has made all of this up to satisfy a deeper need for attention, which is, according to social workers' reports, severely lacking at home?'

'I agree with Dr Vanessa Land, who examined Grace and whose professional opinion states that Grace did not cause her own injuries, including vaginal lacerations and bruising, which, and Dr Land states too, were caused by penetrative sex. It is *my* professional opinion that Grace's account of her abuse, and events leading up to that abuse, as well as her behaviour, is consistent with a child who has been subjected to such abuse.' She pauses, lifts her hand to move a strand of hair away from her cheek. 'This situation is not *unfortunate*, Mr Wayne, it is devastating.'

'Indeed, Grace's allegations against the defendant are devastating.' He maintains eye contact with her for a few seconds, glances at the jury, and then moves his gaze back to her. 'How do you know that, Dr Keane?'

'Sorry?' she says.

'How do you know, definitively, that Grace did not inflict those injuries on herself?'

For the first time since taking the stand, Jessica moves her feet. She places her hands on the wooden ledge in front of her, and leans forwards a little. 'Because Grace is not a liar, or a fantasist, as you suggest, Mr Wayne. She is a very bright little girl. She tells the truth. And thank God for girls such as Grace, who come forward with their truth so that the men who abuse children in their care are brought to account.'

Mr Wayne has the courtesy to redden very slightly. 'Thank you again for coming today, Dr Keane.'

'Mr Wayne, have you completed your cross examination of Dr Keane?' the judge asks.

'I have, Your Honour.'

'I am glad to hear that. There are no more witnesses to be called. We will reconvene tomorrow at ten a.m. for the speeches and summary and then the jury will retire to consider their verdict.'

Jessica looks towards the judge, whose expression remains neutral.

Half an hour later a London cab drops her and Connor off at his chambers.

Grace has made all of her testimony via a video link but today she is waiting, with her social worker and solicitor, at Connor's chambers. On entering, Grace jumps up and goes to hug Jessica. It has taken a long time for the little girl to manage any sort of physical show of affection. Jessica's thoughts move briefly to Grace's mother; the only crime she had committed was neglecting to notice the signs sooner. The woman's propensity towards erotica was not a significant issue. Connor, together with his assistant, had watched all of the mother's downloaded films. Connor had described the films as mild. Erotic yes, hardcore, no. If Grace had watched these films, she would not have seen what had happened to her. She had not made anything up. She had not fantasised.

Jessica, her arm around Grace, says, 'How are you?'

'Will he go to prison?'

'We don't know yet, Grace, but whatever happens, you're safe now.'

The social worker stands. 'I'm taking Grace to McDonald's where she's meeting her mum for an hour. We're a little late.'

'No problem,' Connor says.

The solicitor stands too, saying his goodbyes to Grace, the social worker, Connor, her, and leaves.

'Thanks to both of you,' the social worker says, taking in both her and Connor.

'I hope it won't be too long waiting for the verdict,' Connor replies. He then crouches down so that he is at eye level with the child, although Jessica notes how he does not touch her, also ensuring that he is not too close. Grace remains very hesitant with men, even Connor. 'See you soon, Grace.'

The child waves at him and then at Jessica, and she even manages a smile.

Grace has come such a long way.

Jessica turns to Connor and studies him. She observes a speck of what looks like morning coffee on his bands. It is something else that endeared him to her from the very beginning – his disregard for perfection. So different to her husband. She has known Connor properly for eight years, meeting him for the first time on a case her colleague had been working on. They had kept in touch and often compared notes. She'd been so pleased when he'd been assigned Grace's case.

'Jessica,' he says sitting down at his desk. 'It went very well. Well done. I'm optimistic of a guilty verdict.'

'Are you? I'm not so sure.'

He looks directly into her eyes, his own vibrant and sparkling. A deep and dark grey. He's forty-four but appears much younger. 'You did great. You could do no more, but you look tired.'

'Does that mean I look like shit?' she replies.

He laughs. 'Not at all. The opposite. The judge is on our side, Grace's side.'

'How can you tell?' she asks. 'The judge's expression seemed pretty inscrutable to me.'

He laughs again. Connor laughs a lot. 'I've been in his court numerous times and I know what to look for.'

'And that would be…'

'How often he blinks.'

'Go on.'

'The more he blinks during an expert witness appearance at a trial, the more amenable he is to what the expert witness is saying.'

'Grace is telling the truth, Connor. She's not a fantasist. She's damaged but she is not mad, or untruthful, or a fabulist.'

'We *will* win this case. For Grace.'

'I know you will. But then she may well be taken into care, or put in the care of foster parents. There's going to be no hope for her.'

'There is hope. She's a strong little girl… as you know.'

'She is, but she'll carry this with her forever, one way or another.' As she'd driven there today it had crossed her mind to foster Grace herself, but of course she cannot, given that she is the little girl's psychiatrist, and would not, given the way things are at her own home – and the same reason she has no relationship with Hope.

'You seem adamant that she'll shoulder her past forever.'

'She will,' she says, simply. 'That fact is not in any doubt.'

He is staring at her, trying to work her out. His expression is troubled. She has no wish to trouble Connor.

She carries on, 'How many times did the judge blink during the defence's expert witness appearance?' She grins.

'Hardly any blinking. But the defence agrees with you, Jessica, in that Grace is of stable mind, that she isn't mentally incapacitated to give evidence. They are saying that she is lying, and not "traumatised".'

'Yes, I'm aware that's been their stance. But it's utter crap.'

'Eloquently put.'

She grins despite feeling so empty.

His eyes sweep over her face. 'Do you want to grab a bit of late lunch?'

She stares back at him.

Today is different, because after what happened last night, she is different. To fill her stomach in Connor's company will nourish her emotionally too.

'Okay. Yes. I'd like to eat. Very much.'

He doesn't answer.

'Did I surprise you? You can retract the offer, Connor. Have I caught you on the hop?'

'I do like your directness.' He grinned. 'You fancy a burger?'

'In fact I do.'

'Best burger bar a few streets from here.'

Fifteen minutes later Jessica is eating what definitely is the best burger in London, washed down with a milk-shake.

Their conversation is engaging, bright and easy. She hasn't had such a good afternoon for… since when? She comes to the conclusion that she's never had an afternoon as wonderful as this one.

Connor walks her to her car. 'Great to talk, and not about work.'

'It is,' she says.

'You have my mobile. If you fancy a burger anytime, let me know.' He pauses. 'Jessica… I'm always around to talk, you know.'

Connor is one of the few people with whom she has spoken to about Hope. And he's the only person she's ever spoken to about the day of Juno's death. Apart from her therapist. 'I know you are, Connor, and I've always appreciated you listening to me.'

'I'm always here for you.' He turns and begins walking down the street.

The night before jabs into a part of her brain that is waking up, and in the taxi, which is dropping her to where she parked her car, she wonders what it would be like to be with Connor.

Once inside, she checks the dash clock. Plenty of time to drop by the tip before returning home. She should go back to the hospital, really, and finish up the pile of work on her desk. But he is cooking this evening and making his famous *moules marinières*. It is the dish he always does for the few dinner parties they throw. Good thing she's remembered. If he cooked and she wasn't home in time to eat it, his quiet wrath would be unbearable.

She drives to Kentish Town and the tip. It's not too busy. She parks and gets out of the car, opens the boot and takes out the bin liner, makes her way to the relevant skip and throws it in. Someone, somewhere, will hopefully find the broken ruby and diamond bracelet, the phrenology head, maybe even the dress and jacket. It would be nice if someone were able to enjoy something of her life.

Jessica returns to her car and drives home.

39

Jessica

'How did court go?' he asks as she walks into the kitchen. He's peeling garlic cloves and listening to classical music. She's not sure which composer as she's not interested in classical music. He's placed a tea towel over her wire head, although the wire spike is jutting out. Today Jessica sees a different meaning to the spike. A symbol of phallicism. She sees something else, too, in the art piece, that she hasn't seen before. The head is a woman's head. Why has she always seen it as a man's head?

'Went well, I think.' She has only ever shared the bare minimum about her work life with him. She's never mentioned Grace.

'Long one,' he says, glancing at the clock.

'Yes, it was.'

'You hungry?'

She isn't: the burger she'd shared with Connor not that long ago is still filling her, just as the memory of his pleasant, open features and the smell of his exquisite aftershave is packing her heart. 'Ravenous.'

Will he say anything about last night? No, of course he won't. They never talk about what happens in the bedroom. Or what didn't happen… until last night.

He stops peeling and glances at her. 'I was tidying up earlier and couldn't find the dress you wore last night.'

'I've taken it to the dry cleaners.'

He reaches for her hand, lifts it and she smells the garlic, sees too from the corner of her eye the bowl of cream he'll be using to make the French dish's sauce. Her stomach heaves. She hates mussels and dislikes French cuisine – the heavy cream and butter – much preferring the Mediterranean way of cooking, with tomatoes and olive oil. She'd prefer another burger. With Connor.

'Not wearing your bracelet?'

'No, I like to look sparse and unadorned in court. I don't think a ruby and diamond bracelet would set the right tone.'

He nods, his expression set in displeasure. 'It's not in your jewellery box or your dressing table tray, either.'

'It's in my handbag.'

He picks up a tea towel and wipes his hands. He would never normally do this – use a tea towel to wipe his hands. His order is breaking, as is hers. He grabs her arm. 'C'mon. Let's go and find it.'

He knows she always leaves her bag on the silver hook in the hallway.

She's incredibly calm and doesn't know why. She has no idea where this is going to end. He takes the bag from the hook and hands it to her. She pretends to look inside and then looks at him.

'I saw you this morning putting a bin liner in the back of your car,' he says.

'The clothes I wore last night, and the bracelet, the phrenology head, are gone,' she says.

His face contorts; his expression reminds her of the gargoyle that sits on the highest arch of the local church.

She turns away and places her handbag back on the hook and then feels his hands grabbing at her shoulders from behind, pulling her towards him; he swings her around so she's facing him. Her heart is pounding but for a moment she wills her body to relax, as if it's not her body, as if it is not her. He pushes her hard and her spine bangs with force against the substantial wooden front door, her head hitting the glass so ferociously she can't believe it hasn't smashed. She knows what's coming and she knows she cannot fight it.

This is not the time, but the time will be soon.

He rips at the front of her blouse, and she hears the silk fabric tearing. He grabs at her hips, pushing her downwards onto the hall floor. In a frenzy that is unusual for him, until last night, he pushes up her skirt and rips off her tights.

Jessica tries to take herself away from her body, and away from inside her head. If she resists he will kill her, she is sure of this. In this moment, now, she understands, allows herself to remember.

It was not only Dom. It was him too. Dom's business associate and friend.

And with her head rammed up against the front door, she hears the movement in the hallway outside her bedroom all those years ago on the morning of Teresa's party, when she had told Juno her secret. Her husband's livelihood had depended on the success of Dom's business, and therefore her husband too, relied on Dom's marriage to Eva. It was *him* listening. Mason. Mason who had known that Juno knew.

The man she has been married to for seventeen numb, futile, and infertile, years. It's all so clear now.

He's inside her and it's a violation that finally she cognises. She's hurting but the pain is something that she will use.

He finishes and lumbers up. Her neck is at a strange angle, her head still up hard up against the door. She hasn't moved and her eyes are closed but she senses him there, nearby. Then a loud noise and the pinprick of glass shards on the skin of her face. She carefully opens her eyes and he is standing there, his fist dripping blood. The front door's stained glass panes are no more.

He looks down at her. 'Be careful, Jessica. I own you, and your family, and always have, and no one can change that.' He zips up his trousers and kicks her hard in her ribs. 'Juno couldn't, and neither can you.' He pulls out a perfectly folded handkerchief from his pocket and wraps it around his hand. 'Make sure you call someone to fix the glass.' He turns and makes his way back to the kitchen.

She doesn't move and within minutes she hears him using the blender, making the creamy garlic sauce.

She finally moves her head away from the door, turns onto her side and curls her body into the foetal position. She allows her mind to go back in time, to Raven Island, her sister, to Teresa's party, and when she and Natalie waited inside the snug for Eva to return, the trial, and then finally, to the day when she could cope no longer.

And when, afterwards, *he* rescued her. Mason.

Dom's best friend.

40

Natalie

It's Tuesday and Oli's been home for four days. He's taken some time off work and has been researching where they can have a party for Hope, surreptitiously going around venues and checking them out. Natalie has pretended not to notice and he's pretended he's not doing it. It's quite funny really. He's being a good dad, like he's always been a good husband. But she won't change her mind. She can't do what Hope has asked her to do, as much as she knows it'll make her daughter happy.

He left on one of his research trips an hour ago, just before eleven. She's been up since five preparing lessons for the next academic year. She likes to be ahead of schedule, and she's also doing some private tutoring for A-level students. She does much of the tutoring for free, and is able to root out the families who can't afford her fees, operating her own means-tested benefit system. With some things she trusts her instincts.

She puts her work to one side and picks up her mobile to call Jess, who takes Tuesday afternoons off work. She also knows that Tuesday is Mason's golf day.

Jess answers straight away. 'Hi, Natalie. How's it going?'

'Okay. You at work?'

'No, I'm at home. Day off.'

'How was your birthday?'

'Oh, you know.'

She can hear a new level of flatness in her sister's tone and doesn't know if to question her more. She decides against it. 'Did you go anywhere after the restaurant?'

'Just home.'

'How's things with—'

'Changing.'

'What does that mean, Jess?' she asks.

'I'm not sure.' She hears a rustle: Jess is moving the phone to her other ear. In the background the coffee machine is rumbling. 'Can you come over?'

'That's what I'm calling about. I wanted to see you. Is it golf day?' she replies.

'It is.'

'You're not ill, are you?' she asks.

'No, I'm not ill…'

'I'm driving over now. Won't take me more than an hour.'

'I'll be here,' Jess says.

Natalie had heard the trepidation in her own voice at the end of the conversation. Jessica still has her moments, but nothing ever as bad as the crisis in 2002. More recent depressions never seem to link to the anniversary of Raven Island; either of the anniversaries.

She writes on a Post-it: *Driven over to see Jess, be back this eve. Nat X*

She stares at the fluorescent green paper of the Post-it, the colour, and momentarily Juno's image seizes at her mind.

She peels off the sticky note, takes it down to the kitchen and leaves it on the table. Picking up her handbag and jacket, she makes her way outside to the car. Her sister needs her.

For just a moment she thinks of calling Teresa. But she does not.

41

Natalie

Natalie is standing inside Jess's Victorian tiled entrance porch staring at the couple's ornate front door. Whenever she visits, which isn't often, and always on golf days, she admires the impressive-looking stained glass. Today though, she notices the panes have been broken and it's covered in hardboard. It's unusual for Jess not to fix a problem like this immediately and she assumes it's because it happened very recently. They must have had a break-in, or an attempted one. Hopefully the bastards will be caught. She pulls on the old-fashioned iron rod and hears the sound of the Mozart door chime sound inside the house. It always throws her. Jess isn't a classical music fan, and, thinking back, she'd never have taken Mason as being one either. But what did she know as a teenager? Nothing. She was so naive, so stupid, so suggestible.

Jess opens the door to her amazing home. Her postcode howls wealth. NW3, and very near to Hampstead Heath.

'It's good to see you, Natalie.' Jess looks at her watch. 'You made it in good time.' Her lips lift into a smile. 'I hope you didn't speed.'

'As if I would.' She takes a step into the light and airy hallway of Jess's home. Everything is so in order and maybe that's what attracted Jess to the man she married. Once

Natalie had thought Jess had married him for his money but she had that wrong, because like Teresa and her, Jess doesn't want Eva's inheritance, either.

Hope will be a very wealthy woman on her thirtieth birthday.

'I don't break the law,' she says, with a grin.

Jess glances at her. 'Only once.'

Natalie hears the intake of her own breath. The reverberations from those two simple words cause her entire body to stiffen. She stares at her sister thinking her gaze will drop away, as it always does, but today Jess holds eye contact and it is she who averts her gaze.

This is a marker. Jess's marker. A subtle transposition of their relationship, which has been symbiotic, constant, but static since Juno and Raven Island. They never speak about it, as they never talk about their sister, even when they should have done. Inside Jess's home, and as she'd felt inside her own since Hope's request, Natalie intuits a shift in her own internal emotional and historical walls.

In the physical vicinity of her sister and with those two words, *Only once*, this feeling is reflected back at her: a dark and shining light of change. She and Jess each possess their walls, although they are more like dams, curved and strong and fortified. Today, though, both of their dams are displaying hairline fractures, maybe more than that – significant cracks – and cracks that will not be fixable. She questions if either of them want to mend them, although she is getting an unsettled, disruptive and anxious feeling that the time is very close for Jess's metamorphoses.

She's not ready for it, and it's why she's here – to tell Jess not to worry, that there will be no reunion in which all three remaining Keane sisters are present.

'I hate it when you look frightened, Natalie,' Jess is saying.

When did their roles reverse? When did the younger sister become stronger than the older? After Jess's suicide attempt? When Jess married? Before? When their shining sister died?

She's not even sure if she'd recognised a reversal before today.

'I'm not frightened,' she replies.

'You are, Nat.'

She hasn't called her Nat for a very long time.

All the pain her sister carries inside her is more apparent in this moment than it's ever been. Jess is allowing it to become visible, and Natalie wonders why. What has changed? Is it the thought of a reunion that has ignited something within Jess as it's done in the depths of her too? She sees in the set of her jaw, the piercing gaze of her blue eyes, that Jess is embracing what she has unwittingly unleashed. Jess is stronger than she is. She always has been, and she wonders from where Jess acquired this quiet force.

Natalie is like neither of her sisters, none of the Keane sisters. She is the weak link. Jess was so young, so damaged, even then. Damaged even before Juno. She should have been stronger. She's let Jess down and for the past twenty-eight years, which equates to roughly three-quarters of Jess's life, she's wanted to make up for it.

Gently, Jess slips her bag off her shoulder for her and hangs it up on one of the smooth silver hooks next to the front door.

And then she turns and hugs her.

Jess allows no one to embrace or touch her unless it is absolutely necessary, which of course it never is. *Absoluteness and necessity are such relative terms* Natalie has heard her say. And for a moment, in the midst of a rare display of affection, she imagines her sister in bed with her Mozart-loving husband. It's an image she'd rather not seek out but it's an image that's always troubled her. It is so wrong and always has been. Her gorgeous and genius sister, her irreparably damaged sister. Her youthful and in many ways childlike sister.

She stops dead in her thoughts then. *Stop*.

If she felt strongly enough about the situation to stop her own daughter's close proximity to her sister's husband – then why has she never attempted to examine more deeply this unequivocal decision? Why?

Jess draws her close, and she nestles her head into her younger sister's shoulder. She's now very disorientated. Jess hasn't touched her like this, held her, allowed her to hold her, since that terrible day when she was so very young. The very first time Jess had been to Raven Island alone in the motorboat. The day Jess found her sister dead. It had been yet another thing that she held against Eva; not stopping Jess going to the island, although in all fairness, Eva could never have known what tragedy Jess would find.

They remain in that position for what seems like a true eternity. It is Natalie who moves away.

'What's happened to your front door?' she asks.

'I've got coffee brewing,' Jess says. 'And I've made smoked salmon, cream cheese and caper bagels. Come through to the kitchen, Natalie.'

Her name has elongated again but she still sees the alteration in Jess and she really is questioning what *has* changed. It's as if the air is crackling with potential energy, as if atoms are splitting inside the internal world that Jess and she both inhabit, a world unseen by others, although it's a world that Teresa occupies by proxy: a world only felt and experienced by the Keane girls. The nuclear fusion and fallout of their childhood, the double tragedy of that childhood, is coming closer. The catalyst that is her daughter's graduation is turning out to be the stimulus of… what? Retribution, forgiveness, discovery, the unreeling of secrets. Revenge? Or is it hope?

Hope.

The real secret lies between Jess and her. That is not true, though – the secret is corporeal and nestles like a thorn inside Jess, and Jess alone.

The broken glass is bothering Natalie. She follows Jess through to the enormous kitchen, which reminds her of the one from their childhood house on the river, as if Jess has tried to recreate it. This space though, is more chic, more modern, and dotted with pieces of abstract art.

She doesn't come here often but when she does she always spots something she missed on a previous visit. Jess isn't into classical music but she loves to collect beautiful art. The business that her husband has recently sold – as boring and unexciting as it was – must have been very successful: Jess's salary is not up to what she sees surrounding her.

Natalie is always drawn to the artwork that takes pride of place in the huge kitchen. Jess had once said that she thought the protruding wire from the head signified a pathway for all the human emotions to pass through. Natalie didn't get it and Jess knew she didn't. *But art is to be interpreted by the viewer*, Jess had explained.

The head is grotesque but mesmerising. A bit like their early life.

She turns and looks at her sister as she pours the coffee. The bagels are sitting on a large platter on the counter top, with two plates next to them, a napkin folded neatly on each.

'I came,' she says, 'because I wanted to talk to you properly about Hope and my call the other day, about Hope's graduation, about a reunion—'

'I didn't think I could do it,' Jessica says. 'But I can. I want to.'

'But *I* can't do it, Jess.'

Jess looks at her. 'You have to… we have to.' She takes a huge bite of her bagel and Natalie, on reflex, glances in the direction of the downstairs toilet. 'I'm fine at the moment,' Jess says, knowing exactly what she's thinking. Natalie searches her sister's features and then stares at the wire head.

Jess carries on, 'Natalie, I'm sorry I haven't been there for Hope.'

'She would love you if she got to know you properly.' She lays her hand on Jess's knee and she doesn't flinch away. 'You could have visited us more. You stayed with us way back in the eons of time when you didn't want to go back home to Eva…'

'We both know why I could never go back to Raven House after leaving for med school. I should have talked about it.'

Natalie nods. 'Yes, you should. But why are you talking about it now?' Natalie gives her sister's knee a light affectionate rub. 'It might be time to talk about why, Jess?'

'Front door.'

Natalie's heart dips inside her chest. Jess's staccato sentences again. She only reverts to her childhood way of speaking when agitated, anxious or worried, although all three states are ones she suspects Jess is constantly living with. But there are levels of severity. 'What happened to the front door? Have you had a break-in?'

'Argument,' she says, pushing a porcelain mug of delicious-smelling coffee towards her.

Natalie turns so she can clearly see her sister's expression. 'I didn't know he had a temper... I'm sorry...' She'd suspected, though.

'No need to be. It's been for the best.'

Those five words say so much of what has been unsaid. Perhaps this is why she wanted her to come over.

'But from what I do know,' Natalie says, trying to choose her words carefully, 'it's not his style... is it... violence?'

'It simmers. Fear. Fear turns to violence. Eventually.'

Natalie pulls a sliver of smoked salmon from the bagel and puts it in her mouth.

'Natalie, just eat the whole thing.' Jess's words and cadences are suddenly back to normal.

She picks up the bagel and takes a bite. Chews and swallows. It tastes as good as the coffee. 'Why is he... fearful, scared?'

'I never mention anything about the past, it was something I promised the day I married him. He always said it was bad for me... to talk about it.' She looks at Natalie. 'And *we* never talk about it, Natalie, you and I.'

'What happened with the door?'

'He was agitated.'

'Why was he agitated?'

Jess let out a long and laboured sigh. 'I'd mentioned Raven Island... Juno, Hope, on the morning of my birthday...'

'I think I see.'

'No, I don't think you do.'

'He punched the glass of the door instead of you?' she asks.

'Maybe.'

'*Does* he hit you, Jess?'

'No, he doesn't hit me,' she says.

But he does something to her sister. As clear as the day is outside she now sees the oddness of their marriage. Why *had* Jess married him? And although Jess was beautiful, why had he married Jess? It didn't gel. It never had. 'Can we talk?' she says. Jess is so close to doing so.

'I think you should go ahead with your preparations for Hope.'

Natalie is thrown by Jess's reply, and tries to quickly think of her own, but is only able to come up with a weak: 'I can't, Jess. I can't do it.'

'Think about it.' Her sister begins clearing up. Natalie glances at the wire head; its eyes seem to follow her sister to the sink. 'I haven't been around for Hope,' Jess carries on. 'I want to make amends.'

'I'm worried about you,' she says.

'Don't worry about me.' Jess looks at her watch. 'I have work to do, I'm so sorry. I'm behind on a report for a case I was an expert witness for in court.'

'It's no problem, I need to get back home. What's the case?' she asks. She finds Jess's work fascinating, and more so in many ways because of the demons she knows Jess battles every day.

'My professional opinion on a seven-year-old girl's mental capacity regarding testimony about her stepfather, and his friend, who have both been abusing her. We – the prosecution barrister, Connor O'Leary, me, and the rest of the prosecution team – are currently awaiting the jury's verdict.' Jessica wrings her hands together. 'The child's name is Grace.'

'Jess—'

'Drive home safely, and don't speed.' She gathers Natalie to her. 'And stop blaming yourself. If there's anyone to blame, it's Dom.' She releases her, gently pushes her away and then finishes, 'Dom was a bastard. I'm glad he is dead.'

—

The vitriol of Jess's parting words stay with Natalie all the way home.

She thinks of her Hope. She has to tell her daughter that she can't do what she wants her to do.

42

Teresa

Teresa is late into the office that morning, which is highly unusual, although what is even more unusual is the missed call she's just picked up. It's Jessica's mobile number. It was Oli who'd given her her youngest sister's number, and at least ten years ago now. She's never called it and Jessica has never called her, although she knows about Jessica's life trajectory through Mrs A, who knows about it through Natalie. That invisible thread of family still at work.

Hope's request to her mum about a graduation party, a Keane family reunion, is beginning to infiltrate the sleeping dog of their lives. She is experiencing a change within herself, and she's sensed it in Matt too. For the first time in twenty-three years, last night she called him Luke; it was a mistake, and she never makes mistakes. He hadn't called her out on it. He'd just kissed her. Moments later they were making love. And after that they talked about Raven Island in detail for the first time since the day he'd been released from prison.

She turns and catches her reflection in the mirror behind her desk. It had belonged to Luke's mum. One of the saddest days of her life had been the day she went to Luke's mum's funeral, watching Luke sandwiched between two prison officers. On that day the hatred for her two sisters and her mother hit a peak.

She touches her geometric hairstyle. Her hair had changed colour almost overnight. By the time she visited Matt in prison the first time, she was completely white.

Is it the zephyr of change, or is it obliterating gale force winds? She's as yet unsure, but in the days that have followed Natalie's call, it's felt like she's been sitting in the eye of a storm.

Hope is doing something indefinable to all of them. Staring at the missed call number, she is even doing something to Jessica too, it would seem. And Natalie's call suggesting a reunion for Hope… despite the clumsiness of her middle sister's words, she'd heard the indicator of change in Natalie's voice too.

For a moment, just a moment, and as she catches sight of the photo that sits at the back of her desk, she lets herself think about Hope. Her Hope. Jessica does look so very much like her.

She's just about to close the door of her office and return Jess's call when her mobile rings. It's Mrs A. Teresa smiles and takes it straight away.

'Hi, Mrs A,' Teresa shouts into the phone. Mrs A is still all there, but very deaf, even with her hearing aid in.

'Hello, Teresa. It's Mrs A.'

Teresa smiles. 'I know. Your name comes up on my phone.'

'Are you busy? Are you at work, putting away all of those nasty people?'

'I hope so… putting the bad people away, I mean. I'm definitely at work. How are you? Looking forward to your birthday?'

'I am. It's what I'm calling—'

The line disconnects. Mrs A has only had her mobile for a few months. She was still getting to grips with it, Oli had told her. Teresa calls her back.

Mrs A answers after only a second. 'Darned technology. Anyway, Teresa. I'm calling about my birthday. And Hope's magnificent news. I have never interfered and I'm too old to change the edict of a lifetime, which is not to interfere in the lives of my employers—'

Teresa interrupts. 'Mrs A, you aren't anyone's employee any more.' She stops herself from mentioning that in fact she is heading for her ninety-fifth birthday. 'And you can interfere as much as you like.'

'I want all of you at my birthday get-together... you, Natalie, Jessica and Hope. Together.'

'What's brought this on?'

'Hope's news, and what she wants. It will be much less traumatic for Hope, and you three sisters, if you meet and reconcile before Hope's big day.'

'It hasn't been decided yet... about a graduation day reunion, Mrs A.'

'Will you arrange that all three of you are at my birthday?'

'I can't promise anything,' she says. 'You know that... Have you spoken to Jessica?'

'No. I thought you could do that.'

Teresa smiles. Mrs A has never interfered; she's only been there in the background, seeing each sister separately. 'You know we don't talk.'

'It's time you did.'

'Leave it with me.' The ball has already begun to roll down a very steep hill, and it is as if Mrs A knows this. Natalie must have told Mrs A that she'd called her.

'How's that gorgeous and talented husband of yours?' Mrs A carries on.

'He's fine.'

'Eva was a vain and misguided woman, Teresa. Lost. But I loved her. I think I'm the only one who did love her.'

Mrs A never does this. Never brings up the past. And this is so... out of the blue. 'Our dad loved her. Once,' she replies cautiously.

'No, he didn't. He married her for the money. I'm sorry, Teresa.'

'I guessed as much.' Teresa has never told Mrs A about the letter she'd received from her father after the trial, postmarked Canada. 'But thank you for making me see that, now. Admit to it.'

'I couldn't help you. I couldn't interfere. I couldn't say that Eva was lying about seeing Luke, because it would only have been my subjective opinion. I wasn't there, Teresa.'

'Yes,' Teresa says.

She would have lied for Luke. She would have done anything for him. She'd been prepared to give up her career for him. He had forbidden it.

'So you three girls'll think about coming to my birthday tea,' Mrs A carried on. 'All on the same day?'

'I will... we will. See you soon.' And Teresa ends the call.

She stares at her mobile, just about to call Jessica back, but then hears knocking on her office door. It opens and Irene, her PA, dips her head inside.

'You have a visitor, Teresa.'

Teresa glances at the diary that's open in front of her. 'But I've a free morning.'

God, has she forgotten something? As if she has and as if she needs to be somewhere now, she jumps up, nearly knocking the photo frame off her desk.

'Calm down. It's your sister.'

'Natalie?' Teresa isn't sure how she feels but hotness envelops her instantly. She doesn't like to be unprepared and she's surprised Oli hasn't warned her. Or maybe Oli doesn't know his wife has travelled to see her.

'No. Jessica.'

Teresa gathers herself. Irene's been with them for more than two decades and is aware of her past. The start of her career. The trial. She knows who Matt is. Everyone does within the chambers, of course they do. 'Send her in.'

Irene looks at her. 'Shall I bring coffee?'

'Please, if you don't mind. A double espresso for me.'

'You okay?'

Teresa nods.

Irene leaves and a few minutes later returns with her baby sister, who she hasn't seen for seventeen years.

Jessica walks into her office and gently closes the door. She holds herself well. A casual observer would look at her and see a confident, self-assured woman in her late twenties, or early thirties at most; but Teresa is aware that it has been Jessica's fortieth recently. In all these years she's hardly aged at all and, to her eye, she seems taller. Her waved hair is a shining dark blonde still, just like their sister's, and she wears it quite long, an inch or two below her shoulders. Exactly as her sister had worn hers.

Teresa experiences the most incredible feeling of relief, liberation and spark of sisterly love. Why have they all left it so long? Why has she been so stubborn? Because she's been so hurt, so devastated, so traumatised. So lost.

'Hello, Jessica.' Her sister looks good but, as she takes the several steps towards her desk and the chair that sits in front of it, Teresa sees beyond how Jessica appears physically and registers the sorrow that is entrenched within her sister's pale blue eyes.

Jessica smiles at her, pulls out the chair and sits down. 'Thanks for seeing me. I'm sure you're busy.'

'No, I've a free morning. Do you want me to ask Irene to get you a coffee? She's about to go and get me one.'

'No, but thank you. I won't stay long… don't worry.' Jessica is looking at the photo on the desk. 'Hope.'

Teresa nods. 'I'm not worried, Jess—ica… about you coming. It's good to see you. It really is.'

'Hope's request and Natalie's call has rocked the boat, hasn't it?' Jessica says.

'It has, although I think Natalie's changed her mind.'

'Yes, she has. I think it's a good idea, though. Do you?'

'I do.' Teresa gets up and walks around her desk, stands next to Jessica's chair. Slowly, she sits on the desk. Jessica is still looking straight in front of her – at Teresa's vacant seat. 'Jessica, I'm sorry. Look at me, please.'

She's saying sorry for what happened in 2002, when she left Jessica in her student bedroom. Perhaps the worst decision of her life. The day she left Jessica. The day Natalie lost her baby boy.

'It's me who should be apologising,' Jessica says, finally turning to her. 'For Luke, and what I did, what I caused.'

Teresa places her hand on her arm. 'It's in the past… *I'm* sorry for not understanding back then in London. That was when we could have cleared this up… but I was too impatient, too brutal. Maybe if I'd have tried harder, understood you better, we wouldn't be where we

270

are today. And maybe too, what happened with Natalie wouldn't have happened either.'

'What happened with Natalie was an accident,' Jessica says. 'She knows that… now. But it's why I've come. About what happened afterwards… after I…'

'What else happened afterwards? What do you mean?'

'I got married.'

'It *was* a surprise,' Teresa states. 'Your choice of husband.'

Jessica nods. 'I have to tell you something and then I want to ask you something and then I will leave.'

Teresa tilts her head. 'Have you spoken to Natalie about… this?'

'No. She's not strong like you are.'

'She's stronger than you think. What's brought this on? Hope's request?'

'Perhaps.'

'Tell me,' Teresa says, 'and then ask your question.'

Jessica begins to talk, beginning by telling her about her patient, a seven-year-old girl, who has been abused by her stepfather, and his friend. She tells Teresa about the trial, how she and the prosecuting barrister – Connor O'Leary, who is also Jessica's friend – have been working on the case together. She tells Teresa how listening to Grace, and Grace opening up to her, has allowed her to open up to herself.

Teresa listens and hates herself for not taking care of her sister, although the depth of her self-hatred is nothing compared to the loathing she feels for her sister's husband. For years she has attempted to *not* think about Juno because she's always known that whoever caused her death had got away with it.

'Why did you marry him, Jessica?' she finally asks.

'I don't think I would have finished my medical degree if it weren't for him. He came to see me soon after you left me… back in that January of 2002—'

'Oh, Jess.' Teresa's voice wobbles. 'I'm so sorry, for leaving. For everything.'

'He came a few days after you left, and after Natalie was released from hospital… Stayed with me all day. He went home that night. He returned in the morning and repeated the routine for three days. I can't remember what we talked about, but by the third day I was ready to pick up my studies again. On that third day too, he asked me to marry him. The deal was that I would never talk about Raven House, Raven Island, Juno, or Hope. About anything, or anyone, connected with my family. He said it would upset me. He said we had to live in the present… I had to live in the present.' She looks at her. 'I signed a deal with mammon, Teresa.'

Teresa has never understood why her sister married him, but has never questioned it too deeply. Until today. There is something so wrong about all of this, and she feels very strongly that Jessica still isn't giving her the entire story.

Teresa's eyes flick towards the photo, then she stands and crouches down in front of her sister, taking her hands. 'Jess… I am so, so sorry.' She needs to get in touch with Natalie. They have to lay down their arms and, together, dig as deep as they need to. She suspects, she *knows*, the core will be as murky as the surrounding crust.

Finally, Jessica asks her question and Teresa answers, giving as much advice as she's able. The two sisters put together their plan.

Over an hour later, Teresa is standing by the window and watches as Jessica climbs into her car, which she's parked on double yellow lines in the street below. Luckily she's got away with it. She turns and picks up the photograph and feels wetness on her cheeks. She has not cried for a long time.

A knock on her door and gently she places the photo frame back down on her desk. Irene enters, pretending not to notice her tears. She puts another espresso on the low-level bookshelf near the door's entrance and leaves.

Teresa picks up the drink and sits down, still thinking about Jessica. Initially, she'd made negative noises about her sister's dangerous plan but knew instantly her protest-ations had fallen on deaf ears. Jessica is the strongest of the three. Looking back, she always was. In the end Teresa hadn't even tried to change her mind, there was no point. Jessica's complicated and rare brain was made up. Inside her office Teresa did everything she could to support her sister – to help her execute her strategy.

Jessica had shared with her the most intimate details of her marriage. She's heard many stories in her capacity as a barrister, but this one is sitting in the category of *worst*. There is something wrong with Mason's mind.

She thinks about herself, Luke and her two sisters. As she does so she realises that, for the first time in nearly thirty years, her rage has dissipated; it's blown away and vaporised.

Teresa has spent her entire career nailing the dregs of society who ruin the lives of young women. But if their plan culminates in the end of her career, so be it.

She walks to the window again, stares at the street below. A traffic warden is putting a ticket on the car that's parked where Jessica's had been. She sees this as an auspicious sign.

For once, luck is on the side of the Keane sisters.

Her intuition is telling her that she will dig up something in Jessica's husband's past, because from her professional experience, she knows there will be something. And if she finds nothing, she'll think of something else.

Yes, together the three of them will think of something else.

She picks up her car keys, planning to call Natalie when she's arrived.

43

Natalie

Natalie is in the middle of the cereal aisle at Tesco when she hears her mobile inside her bag. She doesn't bother pulling it out to check who it is. It can wait. If it's important they'll call back. She picks up a box of cornflakes, and then makes her way to the coffee aisle. She's been putting off the fridge section as it's always so bloody cold, but finally she walks to the cheese counter and finishes off her shop. As she makes her way to the checkout, her trolley heaving nearly as much as their credit card bill will be when she gets the total for her not inconsiderable haul, her mobile rings again. She stops, drags it from her handbag and hears someone huffing behind her. She moves to the side of the aisle, next to the chocolate bars.

It's Teresa. She presses the accept button quickly and sticks her finger in her other ear so she can hear. Her voice is soft but clear – the cadence of Teresa's speech is quite beautiful. She can imagine her in court. She can imagine her being amazing and clever and wise.

'Hello, Teresa,' she says.

'Hi... Nat.'

'It's a long time since you called me Nat.'

'Where are you?'

'What, now, this moment?' Natalie replies.

'Yes.'

'At the supermarket.'

'I spoke to Jessica earlier,' Teresa continues. 'She came up to see me at my office to Leeds.'

'Wow. Hope really has started something.'

'I need to see you, Natalie.'

Tears prick her eyes. 'I can come up. I can get Oli to bring me.'

'I'm nearly at your house now. I've driven down,' Teresa is saying. 'I told myself it was on the pretext of seeing Mrs A, and I am seeing her, but I came to see you... Will you see me?'

'I'll be home in half an hour. Oli's taken Hope out for the day. If you get there before me, the key is in the pot outside the house.'

'Original.'

Natalie laughs. But she knows somehow this call is not about Hope's get-together.

'I'll see you in a bit,' Teresa finishes, her tone now serious.

She can't wait to see her sister. She gulps back the tears she knows are coming but they appear anyway.

'Bad news, love?' a man says to her, as he grabs a chocolate bar from the shelf.

She smiles at him. 'No. Good.'

He gives her a thumbs-up sign and hurries off.

–

Half an hour later, she sees a smart car parked at the front of their modest semi-detached house. She parks behind it and gets out. She sees a woman sitting in the driver's seat;

she knows it's Teresa, her hair as white as it had been when she'd last seen her: that terrible afternoon outside Jess's student house. She calculates Teresa's age. Fifty. Matt… Luke, sixty. She doesn't know if she's going to cope with this.

The two sisters emerge from their cars simultaneously. Teresa is immaculately dressed and looks fresh, despite a four-hour drive.

'I don't know what to say,' Natalie says. 'Only I'm sorry and I know it's too late.'

Teresa smiles at her, and it's genuine. 'It's never too late.'

They walk up the path to the front door.

'Come in, Teresa.' She opens the door, so pleased she'd spring-cleaned in the week before Hope's arrival. 'You go in. Kitchen's at the end of the hallway. I've just got to retrieve the shopping from the back of the car.'

'Need any help?'

'No, but thanks. Kettle on the right worktop, flick it on.'

Ten minutes later, the bags still on the floor – she's only put away the frozen stuff – she's sitting at their tiny kitchen table talking to her sister. It's been nearly thirty years – seventeen since London. Whatever reason she gave herself all those years ago for allowing Oli to take Hope up to connect with her aunt, that real reason is now staring her in the face. Teresa is her sister and a sister to whom she's done a terrible wrong. When had she begun finally admitting the truth to herself? On Eva's death? Meeting Oli? Hope's birth? And where did this leave her with Juno? That had always been her demon. By lying, not only had she ruined a man's life, she'd also made it so that her best friend never found justice; Juno's parents had never found justice.

'Your home feels lovely, Natalie.'

'Hope says your house is awesome.' She's not sure that's come out the way she wanted it to come out. 'She loves staying with you… and Matt.'

'We love having her. You've done a great job with her.'

There is so much she wants to say to Teresa but maybe she will have time to say these things another day. She hopes so. 'Thanks. I have to be good at something.'

'Oli tells me you're a great teacher.' Teresa's eyes light up then, in the mischievous way they had when they were young. 'He says that you do a lot of private teaching, for underprivileged girls… for free.'

'God, how did he get to know about that?'

'Just did.' Teresa laughs. 'Jessica often waives her private fees too, she told me.'

'I know,' she says.

'Of course you do. Do you know any details about the case she recently attended court for, as an expert witness for the prosecution counsel?'

'Yes, I do know about it but she didn't discuss anything in detail. She has with you? Why… why did Jess go all the way up north to see you?' She touches her sister's arm and it's such a good feeling. The best. 'What's happened?'

Teresa takes a sip of tea. 'She's told me some things. I think the case she's working on – the little girl is called Grace – has been a significant factor for Jessica… in facing the past… remembering the past, and not just about the day Juno died, but perhaps before too.'

'Things she hasn't told me?'

'She wants to protect you.' Teresa tucks short white hair behind her ears and studies her face. There is a thin film of sweat covering her forehead. 'Her husband raped her, Natalie.'

Instantly, Natalie's scalp begins to warm. She scratches her temple. Mason. The crush she had on him years ago feels like another life.

'It still bothers you?' Teresa carries on, pointing to her head.

She nods. 'When? How long has this been going on?' *How could she have missed this?*

'He's been controlling Jessica for years. It's the most sinister kind of relationship.' Teresa fixes her gaze on her. 'They have never had sex… his decision. Jessica was still a virgin, until recently, her birthday… Jessica says it wasn't rape, although unexpected. But the day after her birthday *was* rape—'

'The broken window on her front door? Mason did it? Broke the window—'

'Yes, and he raped his own wife.' There is a long pause, and then Teresa looks at her. 'You need to tell me the truth about what happened on Raven Island that day, Natalie. It doesn't matter now why you and Jessica did what you did. It wasn't Luke on the boat with Juno – it was *him*. Jessica has finally admitted it to herself. But what matters now is that we save Jessica, and perhaps find out more about what really *did* happen that day. I, we – Jessica and I – have a plan, and I've already put the start of it in motion.'

Natalie nods, but her mind is rewinding twenty-eight years to the party; her talking to Mason, his argument with Libby, hence Libby wasn't with him, the hems of his trousers, crumpled and creased with dried river water. 'Jess needs to leave him,' she says in a cracked voice. 'She's not safe there.'

'If we follow my – Jessica's – plan, then she can't leave him. Not yet. If anything, she needs to play the game. A game I suspect he's been playing for years.'

'Tell me.'

When Teresa finishes talking the light has long gone and it's nearing eight p.m. Natalie opens a bottle of wine. 'We have a spare room,' she says, with a shadow of a smile.

'And I have a need of it – both the wine and the room.'

Natalie hears herself laugh. It's the laugh that only usually comes out with her husband and daughter.

She watches Teresa polish off more than half the bottle; she's still a non-drinker, although today she's tempted. They carry on talking and she is about to pour another glass for Teresa when she hears a car in the road – Oli and Hope returning from their day out.

Hope blunders into the lounge like a young colt. She's wearing some new multicoloured dungarees Natalie'd bought for her the day before. Hope stops dead at the sight of Teresa.

'Wow!'

'Hi, Hope. You're looking lovely,' Teresa says.

Hope rushes towards her, practically plonking herself in her lap. 'Thanks, so are you.'

A prick of envy bites and Natalie berates herself. She reproaches herself too for never questioning Jess more deeply about her marriage. Because she's always known something wasn't right. It is why Hope doesn't have a proper relationship with Jessica. Christ, she's still reeling at Teresa's revelations.

They have both decided not to mention anything to Oli, although this goes against everything within her. She never keeps anything from him. Only those two things. About her not wearing her contact lenses that day, and the red baseball cap.

Teresa knows now, though. She's told her; and she's also told Teresa that Jess was completely blameless. *It was never Jessica's fault.*

Natalie sits back and watches her daughter. Thankfully, any sense of jealousy towards Teresa has evaporated. Hope is absolutely overwhelmed that her aunt has come to visit, but because Hope is Hope, she asks no questions – and even if she had, neither she, nor Teresa, would have said anything.

There is no awkwardness.

'Where's your dad?' she asks.

'Taking a call in the car,' Hope replies, looking at the nearly empty bottle of wine. 'I take it you're staying tonight?' she asks Teresa.

'I am.'

'Cool. I'll cook, Mum,' she says to her. 'Did you get all the ingredients I put on the list?'

'I did.'

She disappears to the kitchen, as if Teresa being there is the most natural thing in the world.

Natalie turns to Teresa. 'We've wasted so much time.' She has to say something about Luke… Matt. It's so huge. 'Hope knows everything, doesn't she?'

'Matt and I only ever talk about it if she asks.'

'What other Keane family secrets have you talked about with Hope?' she asks.

'I've touched on all of them…'

Natalie stands and walks to the window, looks out onto a dark street. With her back to Teresa, because she's not sure she can bear to watch her expression, she says, 'You've spoken to her about Hope?'

'Yes, but she already knew a fair amount.'

'Hope and I have talked about her. It's the part of the past that I *can* talk about with her. In fact… I think it's helped me accept more what happened, by talking about it to my daughter.' She pauses, then turns to face her sister. 'It was much harder for you…'

'It never really made sense did it, her death?'

'Tragedy never makes sense.'

'Eva never got over it,' Teresa says, quietly.

'She made our lives hell because of it,' she says. 'Especially Jess's. She didn't have to do that. Not Jess. Poor Jess.'

Teresa is shaking her head.

Natalie takes a deep breath, about to say more, when she hears Oli in the hallway. He passes by the lounge door and she hears him go straight to the kitchen, to join Hope. 'How is… Matt?' she finally asks, changing the subject.

Teresa gives her a wry smile. She understands Natalie's tactic. 'He's absolutely fine. He's into his writing and although he doesn't do it for the money, he makes a fair amount, and he enjoys it.' She looks at her. 'He's still doing some work for the pharmaceutical company, keeping his hand in. He's lucky that eventually he found something he loves doing nearly as much as he loved medicine. I mean the writing – not pharmaceutical sales.'

Natalie smiles but tears come too, and she isn't sure if they are for her dead sister, Juno, or the long, lost years.

They are for all of those things.

Teresa continues, calm, measured but kind. 'He's never blamed you, or Jessica. Never. That was me. But Juno, and what happened to her, has shaped him. What he does, what he writes about, who he tries to help… in many ways, it's shaped what I do too.' She looks at Natalie. 'And what you do, Natalie… and Jessica.'

Their familial bond, and what all three have made their aim to achieve – helping young girls and women – has reconnected and interconnected their lives' paths: Natalie by teaching them, Jessica by understanding their minds, and her in her role as a barrister.

Natalie inclines her head but doesn't reply.

'About Dom,' Teresa carries on. 'It *could* well have been him who gave Juno the ecstasy… or… it could have been Mason. Or both deciding together. But whoever gave Juno the tab understood its potency. The tablet that Juno took was absolute pure stuff. The toxicology report indicated it would be lethal to anyone with any kind of underlying health condition. We all knew about Juno's syndrome. Did Dom… did Mason?'

'I think Dom did,' Natalie says. 'I'm sure we discussed it, and so I'd imagine Mason knew too.' She peers at her sister and then holds her head in her hands, eventually looking up. 'The day of your party, when I was looking for Juno, I found ecstasy tablets on Eva's bedside table. Their dealer had been around earlier that morning… maybe Juno found them too—'

'Jesus, I'd no idea Eva and Dom had ramped up that much.' Teresa takes a sip of wine. 'Maybe Dom gave Juno the tablet… and maybe at the suggestion of a third party, Mason. That's what Jessica was driving at in my office.' Teresa takes hold of her hand. 'You understand that?'

'I do,' she says.

'And Dom's suicide,' Teresa carries on. 'Did you ever find a suicide note?'

'He didn't leave one, you know that.'

'Did you keep Eva's stuff?'

Natalie nods.

'You ever looked at it?'

'No.'

'Bloody hell, Nat. Where is it?'

'It's all at Oli's parents' house. Boxed up.'

'Oli's parents live in France, don't they?'

She smiles thinly. 'Yup.'

'We need to get it. Eva had no idea she was going to pop her clogs. Knowing her, she wouldn't have left her affairs in order.'

It *had* been very sudden. No warnings, nothing. Eva had had a massive and fatal heart attack due to too much drug use nearly a year after Dom's suicide. There had been murmurs of an overdose, but the evidence was inconclusive and in the end her death certificate had stated 'Heart attack' as cause of death.

'Oli's driving over to France,' she says. 'He's planned it for September.'

'We need to look through it all before then,' Teresa replies.

'I could ask his mum to send the box?'

'That's a better idea. And, talking about dads, I have something I want to tell you, and it's my turn to say sorry now. I should have told you before... at least, I should have told Oli—'

The door to the lounge opens. It's Oli, clutching a bottle of champagne and two glasses. 'Hi, Teresa, lovely to see you here.' It's as if this is the most normal situation in the world. He looks at Natalie. 'I've raided the celebration rack. Thought you could break your habit, and have a tipple? Thought this occasion deserved it.' He places the glasses on the mantelpiece and opens the bottle, pours, and then hands one to Teresa. One to her. She takes it and smiles.

'Enjoy, girls.' He leaves.

'I love your husband. You're very lucky,' Teresa says.

They clink and drink.

Natalie wants to mention about her sister's miscarriages but this isn't the time. She doesn't want to spoil the moment of their closeness because bringing them up will only bring back the fateful afternoon outside Jessica's digs. Thinking of her own miscarriage, she experiences a deep-seated, real empathy for her sister and what she's gone through. But she has Hope.

Finally, she replies, 'I do, too. And in many ways, yes, I am… lucky,' she says. 'What should you have told me before?'

Teresa breathes in, and begins: 'A few weeks before the trial, our dad wrote to me.' She takes another sip of champagne. 'Did he ever contact you or Jessica?'

'Nope.' Natalie shakes her head, wonderingly. 'I've never heard from him. I wanted to contact him when Eva died but I had no address, no phone number.' She looks at Teresa and manages a hint of a smile. 'I still think he's a shit… although I accept I should not have told him about Eva.'

'You were seven.'

'Six,' she says, and grinning properly now. 'The argument we had that day, Teresa – I often think if we hadn't had it and Jess hadn't overheard it, that somehow things would have been different. Juno and the island would never have happened. I don't know why I think that, but I do.' She takes a gulp of champagne and it goes straight to her head. 'I just think that if the two of us hadn't been at loggerheads… it would have changed everything. The aftermath.' She puts her glass down on the coffee table and stands. 'I was so jealous of you—'

'Stop, Nat—'

'I should have thought of Jess. Happening twice to her. First Hope, and then Juno. I mean, Christ, what are the odds?'.

'We owe Jessica. I'm here because it's time to end this thing. I want to tell you what our bastard dad said in his letter. You were right about him. He was – is – a shit. What we argued about – about him leaving, and never contacting us – no matter what Eva did, it was not *our* fault. It wasn't your fault. I think now, he was just looking for an excuse to piss off, to be honest.'

She wants to laugh at that. She hasn't seen Teresa for seventeen years but in her role, her job, she just cannot imagine her saying this. Although the young Teresa would have.

It hits her then; Teresa hasn't changed at all.

'What did he say?'

'He heard about Juno's death, what happened. God knows how, in Canada—'

'Canada?'

'Yep.'

'But he never got in touch before... even after Hope.'

'I know. A massive shit.' She takes a sip from her glass. 'He went there about a year after leaving Eva, when the divorce went through. He never returned. Eva gave him a substantial amount of money, Mrs A told me... after I asked her directly. Only way you can get anything out of Mrs A, bless her—'

'Eva gave him money?'

'She did. Apparently she asked that he stay in touch with his daughters, but it would seem that his damaged ego couldn't take that. He took the money and fucked off to Canada.'

'How much did Eva give him? *Why* did she give him money?'

'Mrs A says Eva gave him money because she felt guilty… and she loved him. And as an enticer for him to stay in touch with us, his kids. Obviously, that bit didn't work. Eva gave him a quarter of a million. She didn't have to give him any of her money, as her inheritance was airtight in any divorce from him.'

'Wow,' she breathes. 'So Eva did try and look after us, in a fashion.'

'I suppose you could say that.'

'Did you keep the letter?' she asks.

Teresa picks up her handbag from the floor and pulls out a brown-looking envelope. She hands it to her. 'I did. Nearly thrown it out many times.'

The English teacher in her notices immediately the poor grammar and atrocious spelling. Eva had her faults but she was literate. Mrs A told her that a long time ago, before Eva had them, before she was married, Eva was a reader, and she wrote poetry. She'd only just remembered this. *Bright and clever, just like her daughters.* What had happened to Eva? She really was the poor little rich girl and maybe that was why none of her three daughters wanted the family money. Teresa and Matt had made their own money. Jessica too, although in a way she had some of Eva's money, by being married to whom she was married. When Dom had died, a big percentage of the business had gone to his partner, Mason. Momentarily, this thought stops her in her tracks. He and Dom had been so close, their interests so interwoven. She makes a mental note of it and then reads their dad's letter.

Dear Teresa,

I'm sure this letter comes as a surprise and I can only apolagise for not being in touch before. I know that I should have been, but it was a very hard time. I don't really do death very well. Cant cope. I hope you understand why I kept away from the funeral. Anyway, a lot of water as gone under the bridge. Has you'll have seen from the postmark, Im sending this from Canada. I moved here as soon as you're mum and I divorsed. I got remarried a few years after settling here, things just got so busy. I have two boys with my new wife. Yes, you have two half brothers. Things are busy.

I came to the conclusion soon after arriving in Canada that it was best if I started life anew. You, Natalie and Jess would be better off without me. I knew that Jess would never remember me. It just felt like the best thing to do. Its funny how things work out, but you girls really are better off without me in your life.

I saw a newspaper article about whats happened Teresa. I'm so sorry. You must be devastated. I take it that you've dropped him, the Luke bloke.

This time I planned to be with you but its impossible.

This must be a tough time for the three of you. But despite everything I hope you girls manage to get through this together. Tell Natalie Im so sorry about her mate. Must have hit her hard.

I did want to write to you. Show some solid-araty to my girls.

Maybe one day you all can come to Canada and meet you're brothers.

Love Dad

Their dad really was a piece of work, and yet Natalie recalled him as being lovely. Over the years Teresa and Hope, being the older Keane sisters, could bad-mouth him but no one else could.

'Did you reply?' she asks.

'Nope, of course I didn't.'

Natalie looks at the letter again. 'No mention of the money Eva gave him. No mention of anything important.'

'Such an arse.'

There's a long moment of silence during which both sisters just look at one another. 'Let's go in the kitchen and watch Hope cook,' Natalie eventually says, brightening.

'Good idea.'

Natalie is just about to walk through the door, but turns to Teresa. 'I'm going to get in touch with Jess. Is it okay if I mention we've talked?'

'I told her I was coming to see you. We need to be together on this.'

They spend the rest of the evening in the kitchen, talking, eating and drinking. It's a strange but wonderful situation. She and Teresa decide that the first coming together of the three Keane sisters will indeed be at Mrs A's birthday celebration, which is planned for next week.

Natalie thinks of Jess's husband, of Jess, and instinctively knows there is more to this. She'll call Oli's mum in the morning and ask her to send the box that contains Eva's personal belongings. She can't believe she's never looked at them before.

Perhaps she didn't want to find what might be inside.

44

Natalie

Oli's mum has always been efficient and only a few days after calling her and asking her to send Eva's box, Natalie is signing for a delivery.

Within the packaging is a letter addressed to Oli and her, from his mum. As she pulls it out Oli pokes his head around the living room door. 'From Mum?'

She hands him the letter. 'Yes, from your mum, bless her. She's brilliant for doing this so quickly.'

He's standing next to her looking at the box. 'I can't believe you never looked inside.'

She glances at him. 'No, I can't, either. But I had no interest. I still don't, to be honest. I knew enough – more than enough – just by living with her for eighteen years.'

'Was it really that bad?'

'No, it wasn't that bad for me, or Teresa. We dealt with it. But Jess was a different matter altogether. She needed some specialist help, and before Juno, after Hope—'

He kisses her on the cheek. 'Jess's done all right for herself, though, Nat.'

'It seems so, yes.' She's revealed nothing to her husband relating to what Teresa has told her about Mason. It's not the right time, and this is between the three remaining Keane sisters. For now, anyway.

He takes the box from her arms. 'Shall I put it on the kitchen table?'

'Yes, thanks.' She follows him and watches him plonk it down.

He looks at his watch. 'Gotta go. Said I'd pick Hope up from her mate's.' He kisses her on the cheek and leaves.

Inside, the contents appear much as they had the last time she'd briefly looked, a month after Eva's funeral.

Sitting down, she begins to go through her mother's life. She pulls out an album, looks inside and sees photos she's never seen before. Her grandparents, Eva's mum and dad, taken at some location that obviously isn't the UK. She turns one of the photos over. *1935, Estoril, Portugal. Mother and Father.* My God, they were standing in the foyer of a hotel that looked so expensive, she guesses a year of her salary wouldn't cover a weekend there. She looks through a few more. A photo of a baby being held by what looks like a professional nanny. She flips it over; again, it's dated. *Home with Nanny Graham. 1950.* It's taken in the grounds of a house she's seen a picture of before – her grandparents' estate. She puts the photos to one side and rummages further. Several old magazines. Old birthday cards – she looks at those. Cards sent to Eva, but she'd kept only cards from her eldest daughter, and a few from Teresa. Her heart pitches. Still.

She picks up a notebook and flips through. Mrs A had been right. Eva did write poetry. The notebook is filled with poems. She reads a few and she sees her mother's talent. What a waste of a life. She puts the book back inside the box and, as she does so, she spots a moderate-sized wooden box with tiny starfish carved into the lid. She's never seen it before but assumes it's one of Eva's many boxes that she used for stashing her weed or resin. It's a beautiful creation. She takes it out and pulls off the lid. Inside is a piece of paper, folded four times so it fits snugly inside. She stares at it.

Taking it out slowly, she opens it up. And then lays it down on the kitchen table, her eye drawn immediately to Dom's familiar signature at the bottom, in his curled but small and secretive handwriting. Like Dom. Secretive and twisted.

She had never known the true Dom. And, reading his confession to Eva, neither had she.

Oh, Jessica.

Pushing her chair away from the table, tidal waves of sickness sweep through her. She makes it to the downstairs loo just in time, and there she stays, sitting inside the small space, her back up against the wall, her knees tucked tightly up to her stomach.

Oh, Jess. Oh, Juno. Oh, Hope.

She stands but doesn't move. Looks at the toilet bowl. Jess's bulimia. Why has it taken her so long to *know*? She should have known something was amiss. And then five years later for it to be Jess again at the island, finding Juno… She thinks back to the day when Jess told her about Dom bringing her back home from school, taking her to Raven Island, *to talk*.

She stops in her tracks, turns and rushes back to the toilet. Throws up again.

Jess had probably told Dom she was going to tell Eva. And then Jess had told Juno.

Juno knew.

–

An hour later, Natalie has composed herself enough to call Teresa. She picks up almost immediately.

She tells her on the phone. Teresa doesn't answer straight away. In fact, she's beginning to think her sister has put the phone down.

'Teresa, you still there?'

'I am. We've both let down Jessica. What a complete and utter bastard.'

'We have. He was,' she says.

'Oh, Natalie.'

'We have to talk to Jess together,' she says. 'Mason would have known. He and Dom shared everything.'

'Eva knew too, after reading the note, she would have known. And she said nothing. Kept it to herself,' Teresa says. 'I think I hate her even more. She lied for Dom, about the boat, and who was on it. She saw no boat. And then she kept this to herself too.'

'It was *not* Dom on the boat with Juno,' Natalie says. 'We know that for certain now, from the note. It was Mason who took Juno to Raven Island.' She pauses, unsure if to share with Teresa the other revelation in the note.

But as if Teresa knows there's more, she asks: 'Did Dom spill anything else?'

Natalie's staring at Dom's written words. She is so unsure if to deliver the bombshell, but makes a snap decision and tells Teresa.

Her sister doesn't respond for what seems like minutes but then finally says, 'It explains so much.'

'Are you all right, Teresa?'

'I am… I have to go, Nat. Talk soon,' Teresa says and hangs up.

Did she make the right decision in telling Teresa over the phone? It would have been better in person. She dumps everything back in the box, ignoring other stuff sitting at the bottom, and puts it in the garage, out of the way.

She's sitting in the lounge when Oli and Hope return. It's Oli who finds her staring into space. She hears Hope in the kitchen. She gets up and closes the door.

'You okay?' he asks.

'I'll tell you another time.'

'You look terrible.'

'I'm fine, honestly.' He knows not to pursue it – he's known her long enough.

'We popped in to see Mrs A. Hope wanted to see her,' he says.

'Ah, that's good. And good Hope wanted to go see her too. Not on the top of the list of things a twenty-one-year-old wants to do!' She's trying so hard to sound upbeat.

'Mrs A has cancelled her birthday tea, by the way.'

'What? I thought she was looking forward to it?'

'She's looking forward more to Hope's graduation day celebrations. Says she'll be there, wherever we have it, and with you three sisters and respective spouses present.' He looks at her. 'She said that will be the best birthday present.'

The feeling that she is going to be sick again overwhelms her, but this time accompanied by the rabid soreness of her scalp. Her fingers find her temple.

'What's wrong, Nat? What did you find in your mother's stuff?'

She doesn't answer.

'You found something, and it's upset you. Tell me,' he urges.

She checks to ensure the door is closed, even though she knows it is. 'Dom wrote a suicide note. It's written to Eva. He…' She can't say it.

'What, Nat?'

She tells him. 'Dom, or Mason, or both, gave Juno the ecstasy tablet. Mason took Juno to the island… and left her there.'

'Christ almighty.' He leans forward on the sofa where he'd sat down.

She is about to tell him about the second revelation, but stops herself. It's enough for the time being. She needs to assimilate it herself before she can talk about it to Oli.

45

Teresa

Teresa is sitting in her office when a call comes through from Natalie. Eva's box has arrived. What Natalie's found out is devastating. Juno's death wasn't manslaughter due to gross negligence, but murder.

It was not Luke who'd left Juno on the island to die – but she's always known that. And after Natalie had told her the second devastating revelation, there is motive too – because it's obvious that Juno knew. Juno knew and intended to tell Eva. And if Eva had found out, Mason's livelihood, and Dom's life, would have been destroyed. Both men needed Juno to be disposed of. *Oh, God, Juno. I'm so sorry.* She tries not to think about her sister; she will think of her later. Get it all into perspective later.

She gets up from her office chair, grabs her coat, car keys and handbag and makes her way to Leeds Central police station. Sitting outside in the car, she calls her PA.

'Irene, I need you to do some research for me, on my sister's husband. I need you to try and find someone for me.' She gave Irene Mason's ex-wife's name and some vague details, including that Libby had been a primary school teacher.

'I'm on it. I'll check out all the relevant primary schools.'

'Thanks.' Teresa disconnects and makes her way inside the station.

She's known the chief inspector for years, as they are friends, although she hasn't seen Amanda for six months in their friend capacity; last time was at theirs for dinner. Matt had cooked. It had been a good evening. They always were with Amanda. But today is business. Sort of, anyway, because this isn't about an official case. She's taking a chance coming to Amanda, but it is a chance she has to take.

The on-duty sergeant calls through and, a minute later, Amanda comes to collect her.

'Hi, Teresa, great to see you. Come through.'

Teresa follows her to her small but immaculately organised office. Amanda undoes the top button of a sky-blue silk blouse and sits down, gesticulating that Teresa does the same. 'How's Matt?' she asks.

'He's good, thanks. Been meaning to get you round again for one of his curries.'

'God, yes please. Can you make it soon? They really are the best.'

Teresa grins. 'I'll look at the diary when I get home and ping over a date.'

'You okay? You look upset under that perfect veneer of imperviousness.'

Teresa pulls a wry face at her. 'I'm okay. Sort of. I have a favour to ask. I have a name and I need to know if the person has a past record. Arrests, conviction, prison time, or just if the person has ever been questioned and released. Can you do that for me?'

'You know I can't. I could only do it if that person was under investigation.' Amanda looks with frustration at her friend. 'You know that, Teresa. Is this connected with a case you're working on?'

'Not an official case.'

'Teresa. You have a stellar career. What the fuck are you doing?'

'It's personal.'

'I have to have more than that... to put my own career on the line.'

'I know. It's connected with my sister.'

'Which sister? And you haven't seen either of them for years.'

'My youngest.'

'Jessica?'

'Yes.'

'Go on.'

'Jessica's husband quite recently retired, but applied for a part-time post at a local college, to teach business studies. Business was his thing. He didn't get the job, although he was perfectly qualified for it. He told my sister that he was probably overqualified. She wanted to help him.' Teresa smiles. 'Wanted him out the house, I'd imagine. She went through his stuff in his office, looking for his application. She didn't find the application, but did discover he has a criminal record; one she didn't know about. He's done time.'

'Wow. The crime?'

'We don't know. That's what I need to find out. I need to know everything.'

'Can't Jessica just ask him?'

Teresa looks at her friend and knows that the position she's putting Amanda in is unfair and untenable; she also knows that the position she's putting herself in is a dangerous one. She should tell Amanda the truth. About the rape, his behaviour, about what Jessica has shared with her regarding the chain of events at Raven Island. She and Jessica should go to the police officially. But she cannot do that; the outcome needs to be something very different if they are to nail Mason for more than rape.

For Juno's murder.

'No, she can't,' Teresa finally answers.

'Do you believe he's committed another crime, subsequently? Because if you do, then you and Jessica should go to the police. You know this.'

He *has* committed more than one crime. For a moment, Teresa questions the road she's taking with this. She should have insisted Jessica press charges and that she should leave him. But, they'd both decided against this, because they may never ever find out the entire truth, and they need the bastard to admit to Juno's murder. 'I know this,' she says, finally.

'I can't do it,' Amanda says, picking up a pen and writing on a Post-it note as she's talking. She hands it to Teresa. 'Ex cop. Do not mention me. It's been good talking about the girl's case you've been working, Teresa.'

Teresa nods and puts the note in her jacket pocket. 'It has. Thanks for listening. I'll send over a dinner date as soon as I get home.'

'I'm glad you're talking to your sister.' Amanda scrutinises her. 'Perhaps time to make up with Natalie, too. And finally accept Hope's influence on your life?'

'I do accept Hope's influence on my life, without question.'

'I don't mean your niece.'

Teresa nods again and then gets up and makes her way out of the police station.

Sitting in her car, Teresa's mobile alerts her to a text from Irene, about Libby Thomas, Mason's ex. Irene has come up trumps. Contact details, address, lots of info. Libby has never moved from the area. She still lives very close to Raven House and the river. She contemplates driving south to see Libby in person, but decides against it. She calls her mobile number. Straight to answerphone. She waits five minutes and tries again. Still no joy. She repeats four more times. Still no answer, and she throws her phone onto the passenger seat in frustration.

As she does so, Libby's number flashes at her. She's returning her call.

Teresa answers. 'Hi, Teresa Keane speaking.'

'Libby here... How are you, Teresa?'

'I'm good. Thank you for calling me back... I have some questions about Mason... is that okay? I wanted to see you in person, but I need answers quickly, Libby.'

'I'm happy to help you, because I feel I know what you're going to ask me.'

Teresa takes a breath and begins her questioning and as Libby opens up, she gets the impression that it's a massive relief for the teacher. And they spend the next fifteen minutes talking. Libby tells Teresa three pertinent facts: a fact that Teresa already knows from what Natalie told her was in Dom's suicide note, and one fact she doesn't know – a fact that floors her more than the other revelations. Jessica's husband really is off the scale in the morality stakes. The third piece of information from Libby confirms Mason's violent tendencies.

'Why have you kept all of this to yourself, Libby?' Teresa asks at the end of their conversation. 'You must have been aware of Jessica's marriage to your ex-husband. The danger she might have been in, which she was, is.'

'I'm sure you have an idea about my reasons,' Libby replies.

'Domestic violence is one of the largest proportions of unreported crimes,' Teresa says quietly.

'It is, and trust me, people don't always have much choice,' Libby replies.

The answer Libby gave as to why she'd kept quiet about his violence towards her was that she'd needed his maintenance, but the overriding fact was that she was terrified of him.

It isn't Teresa's place to judge Libby, and she tries not to. But the fact was – if Libby had intervened all those years ago, done something, said something, then perhaps Juno might not have died, and… Hope too.

Because as far as Teresa is concerned now, somehow, the two deaths are linked.

46

Teresa

Teresa checks the address that Amanda has scribbled on the note. The ex-policeman doesn't do mobile calls or emails, obviously. Passing a service station that she knows has a cash point, she stops off. She has no idea how much this sort of 'service' costs and takes out £300. She already has £100 tucked away inside her purse. After getting back in her car, fifteen minutes later she finds the block of flats easily.

Parking in the communal parking area, located at the front of the building, she gets out and looks at the address again to check the number. Fifth floor. The flats have a lift but the strong stink of urine inside the foyer encourages her to take the stairs; at least inside the stairwell there's more air circulating to dilute the smell. She holds her breath on and off for almost the whole five flights.

With relief she gets to the fifth floor and follows the small balcony path until she arrives at the right number. She knocks and almost immediately a tall man with receding grey hair, although slim and athletic-looking, opens the door.

He smiles. He looks completely normal.

'I've been given your address. I'm sorry, though, not your name.'

'Who sent you?'

Teresa thinks quickly. 'I'm here. I have your address, I know what you're offering. You don't need to know who sent me.'

He smiles again and shrugs at the same time. He's not bad-looking and she wonders fleetingly about his background and history. 'Tell me what you need to know. And let's say no names for either of us.' He steps backwards. 'Come in, stand in the hallway. Don't want anyone overhearing our conversation, do we?'

Teresa follows him into the small space and closes the door behind her. She takes an envelope from her pocket and gives it to him.

He opens and reads it. 'You need to know his past convictions?'

'Yes, and anything you can tell me about him.'

'It's quite straightforward PNC stuff.'

'PNC?'

'Police national computer.'

'Ah, yes, of course.'

'Two hundred and fifty pounds. Cash.'

Teresa opens her satchel and takes out the money. Gives it to him without any questions.

'Write down your mobile number… and your name.' He hands her a pen and a scrap of paper. 'Just in case.'

'You said you didn't want any names.'

'Change of protocol.' He stares at her. 'Trust me.'

Teresa does not trust this man and thinks about writing down a fake name but doesn't, although uses her married name.

He takes the piece of paper and looks at it. 'Give me forty-eight hours, Ms Harris. Same time. Just knock on the door.'

Teresa turns and makes her way back to her car.

–

Teresa had revisited the ex-cop's flat exactly forty-eight hours later. He had delivered on the information she'd asked for, although by then she hadn't been surprised to hear it, not after her conversation with Libby.

Her sister's husband is violent, and probably a psycho-path, and it's confirmed that he has definitely done time in prison.

Sitting at their dining room table, she's going through all the information she has. She should be at the office but it feels so wrong doing this there. She's told Irene she'll be in a bit later.

The ex-policeman had thrown in some 'freebie' advice, telling her there was a high probability that the police would have kept clothing from the time of his arrest. The ex-policeman had also revealed other pertinent info regarding Jessica's husband. She'd felt slightly uncom-fortable with these 'freebies',, paranoid he might know why she was doing this. Although it had also made her a smile a little too, because it indicated that she'd paid far too much for what she'd asked for. But the bonus information is important, and something that she hadn't been banking on.

All she and Jessica would need to do would be to manufacture an incident that would lead the police to put his DNA profile through a national database.

Trying to manage her anxiety about what she is doing – what she and Jessica are doing – Teresa tells herself that she'll worry about the implications for Jessica at a later date. Jessica was thirteen at the time of the trial. Children misremember traumatic incidents; this is common knowledge in the world of law. She knows from her own vast experience that most judges would throw it out before it even got to court. A bid by the CPS to prosecute Jessica retrospectively, for perverting the course of justice, is something on which she is willing to take a gamble. It won't happen.

The means – the fallout, if there is one, for her and her sisters – will justify the end.

She picks up her mobile to call Jessica, using the number to the new phone she'd told her sister to purchase. Jessica picks up instantly.

'Hi, Jessica. It's me.'

'I know it's you – either you or Natalie. No one else has this number.'

Teresa grins. 'Keep it that way too.'

'I've got everything – the cameras and the audio. I'm ready to go.'

'Good girl.' She pauses. 'Are you sure about this, Jess? I've found things out about him.' She tells Jess what she knows. 'We can pull out. You don't have to do this,' she finishes.

'I'm going through with it... Have you told Luke... Matt?'

'No. He doesn't need to know. Not yet.'

'I'm so sorry,' Jessica says. 'So sorry, Teresa.'

'Stop it. Please,' she says gently. The line goes quiet. 'Are you okay?' she asks.

'I'm fine.'

She's not fine, Teresa can hear her visceral pain. 'We'll nail him, but this is a risk, Jessica, for you. I *am* having second thoughts, but only for you. It's a dangerous plan.' She tells Jessica what Libby has told her about his violence.

But she doesn't tell her about Libby's other revelation, the revelation that was not recorded in Dom's suicide note.

About Hope.

Jessica doesn't need to know, as Natalie doesn't. Not now. Not yet. Maybe never.

'I'm not having second thoughts,' Jessica says. 'I know exactly what to do to rile him. He's gone away for a few days and is due home the day after tomorrow, late evening.'

'I'll be on the other end of the phone. I'll be nearby too – I'm driving down to Natalie's tomorrow night. I could stop by London to see you?'

'No. Thanks, but no.'

Teresa nods and lets out a slow breath. 'This is the right thing to do, Jessica. Securing a rape conviction on a husband is a difficult one in court, especially when there's no history of violence.'

'I know. And that's what I hoped you would say. I need to do this. I need to make him attack me.'

'Jesus, Jess… I'm not sure—'

'I *am* sure. I'll see you on the other side,' Jessica replies.

'Okay… I love you, Jess.'

'I know you do.'

Jessica disconnects.

Teresa rings Irene. 'I'm out of the office for a few days. Can you clear my calendar? Sorry it's such late notice.'

'As of tomorrow?' Irene replies.

'No, as of now.' With her mobile lodged under her chin, Teresa gets up and pulls a small holdall from underneath the dining table.

'Where you off to?' Irene is asking.

'Just a little break. I'll be staying with my sister Natalie if anything urgent comes up.'

47

Jessica

After having put the phone down to Teresa five hours before, Jessica has just returned from an impromptu meeting with Connor. He'd called saying he was having a coffee in a nearby Costa. There was no reason for him to be in a Costa in Hampstead.

Well, only two reasons. The verdict on Grace's case, or to see her. It could be both.

She'd gone to meet him immediately. He told her that he was still awaiting the verdict. *We're expecting the jury to come to a decision very soon.* He was one hundred per cent optimistic they would win. She has no idea how she will tell Grace if they don't. But despite what was playing out in the underbelly of her life, their meeting had been calm, easy and fun.

She's been home just over an hour and is sitting on a stool at the kitchen counter, drinking a glass of sparkling water, mulling over recent events. Since making the decision to go and see Teresa at her office she feels much calmer – even Connor had remarked on it. And Teresa has made it clear what she has to do. The stuff is in the boot of the car. He left last night and isn't due back until tomorrow night. She hadn't asked him where he was going, generally she never does. It's only now that she can admit why she has never asked; because she doesn't care where he goes. She acknowledges now, though, that his departure had been rushed, unplanned, which is unlike him, but she'd been so glad to see the back of him that she hadn't questioned his unscheduled trip.

She picks up the instruction manuals, which she's already gone through twice. She's technical-minded and at the shop where she bought the equipment – Teresa had told her where to go – the assistant had been very helpful. She'd told the assistant that the equipment was so she could keep an eye on her new puppy when she was out. *I need visual images as well as audio*, she'd said.

She leans both elbows on the countertop, not relishing having to recreate an incident like the evening when he'd smashed the glass of the front door, although as she'd told Teresa, she knows exactly how to instigate it.

Talk of Juno and the day she died.

Talk of Hope too, although she hadn't told Teresa the latter. When she visited Teresa at her office she kept this from her, needing time to work out how she'll break it to Teresa. About their sister.

If what she is finally admitting to herself is true – and she knows it is – then it is a gossamer thread of diplomacy she has to navigate, to get him to talk. She thinks she can achieve this because he possesses all the characteristics of the typical narcissist. He thinks he is special, better and more deserving than others; he has a fragile self-esteem, relying on others, her, to recognise his worth, and needs. He resents other people's successes, especially hers. His needs are paramount. He is arrogant. She is also aware that with this profile, especially the last characteristic, he'll be desperate to share something he thinks he's got away with. She gets the feeling that in the past week her husband has

308

been bubbling with the need to share. It's as if he can't hold it in any longer.

Things have changed.

She stands and makes her way outside to her car and retrieves her stash from the boot, looking around at the same time. Her heart feels as if it is sitting somewhere in between her sternum and throat, as if it's dislodged. It feels as if it's been dislodged for so long. Her forehead is damp with perspiration and underneath her shirt her armpits are prickling. He won't be back until tomorrow. *Stop worrying.*

She has her head inside the boot when she hears a booming voice: 'Good afternoon, Jessica.'

She bumps her head on the boot lid as she looks up. 'Shit.' Her neighbour is staring at her. She suspects he's more concerned about her swearing than about the fact she just banged her head. 'Hello,' she says cautiously.

He's peering inside the boot. 'Ah, good idea. I noticed that your front-door glass had been smashed. An attempted break-in?'

'Yes… it was. All fixed now though, as you can see.' She slams the boot shut. 'Off for your morning walk…?' She's forgotten his name.

'Terence.'

'So sorry, terrible with names.'

'Unusual in your profession?'

She's sure she's never talked about her job to her new neighbour. She leans on her car. 'Most of us possess a split personality where work and home life is concerned, don't you think?'

'Indeed, yes.' He inclines his head and then glances at the newly glazed front door again. 'If you ever need any assistance, at all, I'm only next door.'

'That's very kind.'

'This is the first attempted break-in I've ever seen on this street.' He looks at her. 'Very rare.'

He doesn't believe her. He knows. Is she that readable? 'I'll mention it to my husband. Perhaps we were being targeted, or something,' she says.

'Yes, your husband. I'd mention it to him. Give him my best. Quite an uncommunicative man.'

She's startled at his openness. He's telling her everything she needs to know and she's not sure if she's happy about this, or fearful. She is even wondering now if he knows why she has internal surveillance cameras inside the boot of her car.

'Have a good day, Jessica.' And off he trots down the road as if they've just had the most normal conversation in the world. Maybe they had.

She waits until he's out of sight and reopens the boot, pulling out the two bags containing the equipment. One box has fallen from the bag. The box that Terence saw.

She's bought so many. She wants every room covered and at every angle.

It takes her a good three hours to set up all the cameras. Two in each room, including the bathrooms, although she installs three in the hallway, and three in the bedroom. Thinking of her husband's propensity for cooking and violence, she puts three in the kitchen too. Once they are all set up, she tries them out, making sure there is a clear view of all areas of the house. There is. The only blind spot she can find is in the downstairs loo. She puts one in there too.

It's six p.m. by the time Jess has finished. She opens a bottle of wine and pours herself a glass and as she walks past the wire sculpture, she touches it, thinking of Teresa and her total acceptance of what she'd told her inside her office.

What she told Teresa had rocked her sister. Of course it had. A seventeen-year marriage that had gone unconsummated, and Juno's real killer was not the person Teresa had thought it had been for the past twenty-eight years. She hadn't been able to bear telling Teresa more. And Teresa hadn't needed to know.

She takes a sip of wine, lost in thought. Why hadn't she told Teresa and Natalie back then, the day Juno died, that she had never been sure it was Luke on the boat? She delves deep into her memories of that day, and plucks out the overheard conversation on the unused path at Raven House, the day of the party. It was that incident which had wired her brain into believing it was Luke on the boat with Juno, although knowing deep-down it was not.

She had wanted to believe it was Luke. After seeing him with Teresa in the cabin, it had brought so much back – when five years before she had come across exactly the same scene – two people having sex who should not have been having sex. Seeing Luke and Teresa had switched something off within her. It had been a huge shock seeing the scene the first time around, especially so soon after finding out about her sister and Dom.

But now she acknowledges, as a child, she did not like Luke. She felt he was taking Teresa away from her, from the family. In this moment Jessica tries to untangle her motivations. Teresa had told her to say nothing about seeing her and Luke in the cabin, and as Jessica was then – obsessed with carrying out instructions – it suited her to obey Teresa's. Telling the truth to the police would have saved Luke, but she did not want to save him. Not then. And she had been so desperate to please Eva.

By the time the police questioned her she didn't even believe she was lying.

Inside her head it had become the truth.

Her thoughts move to Grace. It's Grace who has given her the strength to confront her life and her past. And her future. By admitting to her abuse by her stepfather, by talking and telling Jessica, by agreeing to give her testimony, the little girl has done what she herself has been unable to do.

Her mobile pings a text alert. She thinks it will be her husband. It's Connor. He's asking if they can meet again soon. She texts back saying tomorrow early afternoon would be good. Just saying she will meet him makes her heart pick up in pace.

She decides to have a bath. Mason's not due back until tomorrow evening and so she will use this time to prepare herself, calm herself. Walking out of the kitchen, she passes by the head sculpture, lightly touching the wire that protrudes from its nose. She stops. Takes a step back. The wire is too sharp. Lethal really. On more than one occasion her husband has said how dangerous it is. That was the entire point of the sculpture, though – the menace of the protrusion, in an otherwise completely benign piece of art. Two sides, two emotions, two psyches. Two personalities.

The danger of it.

She drops her old mobile phone inside the sculpture. 'Thank you, Mr Head.' She touches the nose and allows the pads of her fingers to slide down the protuberance: a caress. 'Ms Head.'

The sensation of utter liberation is already beginning to enfold her. She feels Teresa's love, and Natalie's. She feels Connor's concern for her. These many years later, she discerns the love that Juno had for her too, by checking on her in her bedroom, and encouraging Jessica to unburden to her.

—

Jessica dips her hand in the bath water. It is boiling hot but she makes herself keep it in there. So painful. So blissfully painful. She keeps it there for a few more seconds and then pulls it out. Her hand is bright red. It burns and tingles, but as pain and sensation always does, it subsides, as if it's never been there. Like an addiction, the pain. Some people will always return for it. It's as if the section of the head's map marked *Pleasure* pulsates inside her own head. Her relationship with Mason, a relationship in which he had forbidden intercourse.

A jab of understanding, a needle of a discovery enters her mind, something that has been living on the borders of her consciousness. She thinks back to the one and only time she attempted to initiate full sex with him. It was the night she had received the results on her core psychiatry exams. She'd been so happy with her distinction. It was the first night she had properly seen his wrath, and now she allows herself to remember what he had said. *You are not Hope, and you never will be.* She'd questioned him immediately about his statement but he'd closed up, and then she had done what she always did, and buried it.

It was after that incident that she had stopped seeing her niece, Hope, and begun always making excuses why she didn't want her at their home in Hampstead. And Natalie had made it easy for her, because the truth was that Natalie didn't want her daughter anywhere near Mason either.

But he had not been referring to her niece.

She sits on the toilet lid, waiting for her skin to stop tingling.

The new mobile rings but she doesn't answer, and a few seconds later the landline rings too. She decides to leave it; if it's urgent they will call back.

–

The sun has long ago disappeared. She's been lying in the bath for what feels like hours, so long that the water is cooling. She has lit candles – they encircle the Victorian-style tub that sits, slightly elevated on six claw feet, in the middle of their main bathroom. Her new phone is resting on the outside ledge of the bath. Teresa has instructed that she keep it close to her at all times. *All the time, Jess – you need to be able to activate the cameras and audio quickly.*

She's left the door slightly ajar to allow the light from the upstairs hallway to cascade through, as the candles don't give quite enough brightness. Her eyes are closed and her mind is serene and tranquil.

From behind closed lids she is aware of the sudden dance of the shadows as the candles flicker, and she smells smoke as at least one of the wax pillars is extinguished. A faint rush of air wafts across her face. Immediately, she senses a change within the house and as she opens her eyes and hears the reason for the draught, the front door bangs shut downstairs.

Eyes now wide open, her entire body on high alert, she takes a deep breath.

He is home early, a whole twenty-four hours early. She sits up and water swills over the bath's curved side. She grabs the mobile, the missed call was Teresa, but she has no time to call her back or text because she needs to activate all the cameras. She had practised activating all the cameras and audio, of course, but it still takes her longer than she'd thought it would, probably because she's panicking. Her hands are shaking, as is her entire body, but she ensures that all the cameras and audio are initiated.

She hears him dropping his suitcase in the hallway; just hearing this, the thump of the case on the wooden floor below, tells her so much. He's normally careful. Not today. He's upset, agitated. Angry. He's been angry since the restaurant and taxi, and even more angry when he found out about the bracelet.

In her mind's eye, she sees him hanging his coat on the silver hook, and envisages him checking the new pane of stained glass in the front door. The glazier has done a great job, but she knows he will still find fault. Quickly, she checks again that everything is set up on her mobile and then slips the device underneath the tub, not too far that she cannot retrieve it, although far enough that he will be unable to see it.

He's making his way up the stairs. She lies back. Closes her eyes.

A stronger waft of cool air as Mason opens the bathroom door wide.

48

Natalie

'Mum, I don't want to go out. I want to see Teresa.'

'I have things I want to discuss with her, alone, Hope. You'll see her when you get home.'

Natalie's daughter huffs and flounces out the kitchen, although returning in minutes with her coat and bag. Hope looks at her dad. 'Will you drop me off? It's getting dark.'

'Course I will,' Oli replies. 'C'mon.'

Natalie watches them leave. She doesn't want Hope around when she discusses Dom's suicide note with Teresa. Or when Teresa discusses with her what she's found out about Jess's bastard husband.

She's sitting in the lounge with Eva's box at her feet when she hears a car pull up outside. Getting up, she walks over to the window. It's Teresa. Her phone pings then, twice. One text message from Oli saying he's going to the pub so she has some time alone with Teresa and he'll be picking Hope up on his way back: *Don't worry, I'm on the orange juice. I'm watching the football.* And then one from Hope: *Sorry for being grumpy. See you later X*

It's dark outside but a street lamp is situated to the right of their house, and as she watches Teresa get out of her car she sees the fatigue in not only her fine features, but in the way her body moves too. She's as tired and as fraught as she herself feels. It's a long drive from the north and Natalie is aware of the risk Teresa has taken to find out more about Jessica's husband. All of this will be taking its toll.

She allows herself to think about Mason for a moment. Such a crush she'd had on him all those years ago and she cringes, physically shivers too. The Keane sisters hadn't had much of a chance: a capricious biological father, an emotionally inept mother, and a stepfather who she's finding hard to allow into her mind. But she has to allow him in, she cannot be selfish. She has to face it all, as Teresa is doing, for Jessica. She wants all of their lives to find some peace. She wants justice for Juno. She wants justice too for Luke... Matt. Will Luke ever forgive her?

Teresa says he already has.

Teresa's also told her that in the future, if everything goes to plan, she is to say nothing about her testimony at that long-ago trial. *You don't have to say anything, Natalie. But we have to protect Jessica, and keep her away from another trial.* Teresa's confident it won't go that far. Natalie isn't so sure. Eva's dead, and so she can't change her testimony. But she can. Teresa has told her that she must not. *Think about Hope, Natalie.* Her mind makes a complete loop back to Dom. Back to the day her sister died. Five years before Juno.

She cannot help but feel, knowing all the facts now, that there is a connection between Dom, Mason, and her sister's death.

But what?

The psoriasis in her scalp is taking on a whole new dimension; the last few days have seen her hair coming out in clumps. Hope has noticed, and senses something is afoot. Hope is not stupid, nor naive – so unlike her mother at her age.

As Natalie goes to open the front door to welcome Teresa, her heart swells with pride thinking of her daughter. Teresa and Jess's niece. Hope. *Oh, Hope.*

Teresa is pulling a weekend case from the boot of her car.

'Good journey?' Natalie calls, as she walks towards her.

'Absolute shit journey. Two crashes on the M1. I would've been here an hour ago.'

Natalie looks at her watch. 'You've made good time though, considering.' It's eight p.m. She takes the case from Teresa and walks back inside. Teresa follows her and she closes the door. 'Shall I open a bottle of wine?' she asks.

'I'd love to but I'm so bloody knackered, it'll finish me off.' She looks at Natalie. 'I feel we need to stay lucid and sober.'

'Yes, you're right. I'll put the kettle on.'

Teresa follows Natalie into the kitchen. 'Hope and Oli here?'

'No. We have a few hours to talk.'

'Good. We really need to.'

'Sit, Teresa. I've chocolate cake – you want some?'

'Like Mrs A's?' She grins.

'I like to think so.'

Five minutes later they are sitting together, teapot, mugs and cake untouched in front in front of them, discussing the contents of their stepfather's suicide note.

'Great cake,' Teresa says, but her expression is both serious and sad. 'I feel so guilty. That I didn't know… we didn't know. That Jessica didn't tell us this… felt she couldn't tell us this… to hold that secret all of this time, knowing that Hope was having a relationship with Dom. *Fucking* Dom.'

Natalie holds her head in her hands. After a minute she looks up. 'Jess didn't tell us about Dom because she was protecting us. The suicide note tells us this. Dom asked her to keep the secret.'

Teresa nods. 'It explains so much. But it doesn't explain why she married Mason. He's manipulated her right from the beginning.' She pauses. 'Jessica knows exactly what to do, to encourage him to admit it was him on the boat with Juno, that it was he who left Juno on the island to die – so that it's all recorded and on record... But it's just too dangerous.' She shakes her head. 'I must be insane to have agreed with her that this is a good idea.'

'No, not insane. Focused.' Natalie tries to smile but it's difficult because Teresa's right. It is insane. But it really is the only way, and all three of them have agreed to it. She studies Teresa's face. 'How do you feel about Hope? Are you okay with it... I mean, are *you* okay?'

'I am. Our sister. Only her, eh?' But Teresa says it with no smile.

Natalie nods. 'Dom was a complete bastard. Hope was so young.' She catches Teresa's eye. 'Self-destructive in many ways, yes. And she was Eva's favourite, so she got away with a lot...'

'Yes...' Teresa sighs, then looks at her sister. 'Natalie, there's something else...' Her voice trails off.

'What?' Natalie asks.

'Nothing... nothing. It's not important.'

Natalie purposefully moves away from talk of Dom and their sister. 'You mentioned you'd found out what Mason was convicted for?'

'Indeed I have. In late 1994 Mason was in a bar, getting over-friendly with a young girl, just turned seventeen. She wasn't liking it, witnesses reported, including a friend the girl was with. Another man in the bar intervened. A person of colour. Things escalated quickly. Witnesses say the flare in Mason's temper was horrendous. Foul and racist language… he beat the guy up, and when the poor man was lying on the floor – two other men in the bar had got Mason off his victim at least – Mason picked up an ice pick and went for him again. The man lost sight in his right eye. Mason was given a four-year sentence.'

'Christ,' Natalie whispers.

'Was released after three years. I've managed to find an image of the girl. Jess bears a remarkable resemblance to her.' Teresa looks at her. 'A remarkable resemblance to Hope too.'

'This is making me feel ill, Teresa.'

'I know. Me too,' Teresa says, giving her sister a watery smile. Then she continues: 'There's something else, Nat. That I haven't told you.' She blows out a breath. 'It wasn't just Dom.'

'With Hope?'

'Yes.'

'It's something that had crossed my mind.'

Teresa nods. 'The thing is, back then, DNA testing and forensics was in its infancy. But the police will have kept items of clothing.' Teresa tucks a stray hair behind her ear. 'They will have kept Juno's too. This is the extra info I got, courtesy of the ex-policeman. He gave me another titbit regarding Mason as well – although I'd have never taken the ex-policeman as being the altruistic sort.' Pushing her chair back, she stands. 'In prison, Mason was involved in an altercation with another inmate about contraband goods. Mason walked away from that one, but a day later in the showers, Mason took the guy out, as well as another prisoner who intervened to help. Both were taken to hospital. Mason, our little sister's husband, is a very violent man.'

Natalie sits back in her chair. 'We need to call this off. I'm getting a really bad feeling.'

'I tried to call Jessica in the car,' Teresa says, 'just after I pulled up here. Nothing. I tried the landline too.' She takes Natalie's hand. 'Calm down, it's all going to be okay. Jessica is far from stupid, and we're probably overreacting.'

She searches Teresa's face. 'When Jess told me how they'd met... again... I honestly didn't think anything of it. I thought it was a coincidence, but now I'm not so sure. The bar where she saw Mason was very local to her digs in London. When Jess did go out, that was where she went. You know how obsessive she can be about going to the same places, the routine.'

'Go on,' Teresa says.

'So, Mason might have done some investigating, ensured he went to the bar frequently, in the hope he'd "bump" into Jess? Who knows? He's a control freak, I can see him doing something like that...'

'Has Jessica told you how it happened, exactly how she met him?'

'She was with her housemates at the bar. Jess spotted him, I think, or maybe he saw her. I'm not sure, I never went into that detail with her. Anyway, Mason gave Jess his card with his number on it, then she texted him later and gave him her address... I found this out much later...'

'She *gave* him her address?'

'Yes. And thinking about the time frame... soon after that, Jess tried to take her own life.'

Teresa sits back down. 'When did they make contact again?'

'Not long after you returned home, after... my fall.'

She's sure she sees Teresa wince. 'I should never have left... I have to call her, Natalie.' Teresa goes to grab her mobile, but then it rings. Teresa answers it, mouthing to Natalie: 'His ex-wife.'

49

Jessica

Mason is standing in the doorway, his tall form throwing long and fragmented shadows across the candlelit bathroom. He says nothing, just watches her. She turns her head as if she's surprised to see him, although she's aware she doesn't appear surprised enough. He takes another step inside, blows out the candles, one by one, the smell of burnt candle smoke permeating the space, and for a moment they are in darkness, save for the glow of light from the hallway. He waits a few seconds and then switches on the two bathroom lamps. The brightness takes her by surprise, as does his appearance. He looks unkempt, and he also looks... what? Drunk, not in control; the order that he carries around with him like an internal package of security has abandoned him, as it had done in the bedroom on her birthday night, in the hallway when he violated her and then smashed the window.

Finally, he speaks. 'Haven't seen you take a bath for a while. Enjoying the tranquillity of me being away?'

'You scared me.'

'Did I?'

'Yes, I wasn't expecting you back until tomorrow.'

'I know you weren't.' He's staring at her. 'I've missed you.'

'You normally let me know when you're coming home early.'

'Change of plan. I'm a little concerned. I found out that your sister – you know, the one you haven't supposedly spoken to for years – has been talking to my ex-wife.' He stares at her. 'Why is that, Jessica?'

She pushes herself up the bath a little. She's trying as hard as she can to look relaxed. 'I didn't know you were still in touch with Libby.'

'I'm not, but I found out about Teresa contacting her.'

She's wondering how to play this. 'How did you find out?'

'Once a bent policeman, always a bent policeman. All info can be bought, especially if it's been offered to you on a plate.'

She doesn't know what he means but whatever he is getting at, this is not good. She does not reply, and silence hangs inside the room.

He's staring at her body, his eyes travelling to her breasts. Finally, she leans forward and pushes herself up into standing. He hands her a towel, which she pulls tightly across her body.

'They've done a good job on the window,' he says.

'Yes, he did.' Eggshells.

'Have you been talking to the neighbour?' he asks, taking a seat on the closed toilet lid.

'Why?'

'I just saw him outside.' He searches her face.

She steels herself for what is to come.

Because she will ensure it does come.

He carries on: 'He seemed concerned. About you. About us. What have you been saying to him, Jessica? What have you been telling Teresa?'

'I've said nothing… to either.'

'He asked me about the broken glass.'

'Our neighbour? He's concerned about the neighbour-hood.'

'Is he?'

'Yes, he is… he's nice man.'

'He thinks you're a nice woman. Terence doesn't know that you're not a nice woman, does he?'

She is not a nice woman. Because of her, an innocent man went to prison. Juno's real killer was never brought to justice. She's thinking of Connor too. She suspects she won't be meeting him now, and even if she did, she doesn't deserve a man like Connor. She wonders if she will ever see him again.

She stops her eyes darting to the bathtub's rim, down-wards, to where she has hidden her phone: Mason sees everything. She knows Teresa can access the cameras and audio via her own phone, and in the event anything happens to her. She must play her part in getting the evidence they need, but feels a moment's uncertainty that her sister is expecting all this to happen the next night. She pushes the thought away. It has to be now, while Mason is in this state.

It's time to face everything, so she can be the Jessica she wants to be.

Finally she replies, 'No, Mason, I don't think I'm a very nice woman.' She stares up at him. 'But you married me. I think that you are attracted to "not very nice women"… to the "bad" girls. Were you attracted to Juno, Mason? You were attracted to my sister Hope, weren't you?' She watches for his reaction, hoping she has not overstepped the mark. But he is inebriated and he's not used to booze, and he's not a big man either. Alcohol will have affected him a lot, his reactions, his thought processes.

'What did you just say?'

'Can't you hear me? I said were you attracted to Juno, and Hope... were you? Tell me, Mason, because I'd really like to know.' She smiles at him. 'I am so bad, aren't I? I like that you wanted me as well as wanting them... that *is* bad, isn't it? Will you forgive me?' She watches as he appears to loosen up a little.

'You liked it, didn't you, the other night?' he says, although his words are staccato and the tone is wrong. He is unravelling. She is in control. Not him.

'No, I did not. You raped me, Mason.'

His features revert back to just minutes before. He's very angry now; and his anger, once ignited, becomes like a separate entity, a standalone character. This though, is what both she and Teresa have gambled on. She thinks about the positioning of the cameras. She has two in the bathroom – as if she'd known.

'Why are you doing this?' he is saying. 'Why are you ruining everything?'

It's as if the front door incident never happened.

'I saw you in the restaurant,' she says, her voice no more than a whisper. 'Looking at the girl who looked like Hope, like me. I *saw*, Mason.'

He doesn't answer, his expression a mask. Not a flicker of emotion.

'It was you in the boat with Juno, wasn't it? It was you who took her to Raven Island. It was you who left her there. To die.'

Now his expression registers his anger, but it is mixed with another emotion. *Arousal.* This is something she had relied on. This reaction.

She continues: 'Juno knew. And you knew she knew. Was it you, or was it Dom who overheard me telling Juno about Dom and my sister?' She's staring at him. 'It would have ruined everything for you and Dom, wouldn't it, if Eva had found out? The money would have dried up. As pathetic as Eva was, she would have kicked Dom out, and by default, kicked you out too.'

She steps out of the bath. He's facing her. Only inches away. She is repulsed by him. 'Who gave Juno the ecstasy tablet? Whose idea was it?'

He grabs hold of her shoulders, yanking her to him, looking her right in the eye, holds the contact for a second and then violently pushes her away. Her head crashes onto the side of the bath and the world seems to stop for a moment. She waits. Touches her forehead and feels wetness, knows it's blood. She stays in that position for seconds but the bathroom space is quiet. She manages to sit up. He's standing there, just watching her.

'*You* lied, Jessica. And you lied for me. Of course it was me in the boat, and you knew it.'

She pushes her back against the porcelain bath. 'Yes. I did. It was you who I saw on the boat with Juno.' A little voice, the remainder of her true self, reassures her that she did not. As a twelve-year-old Jessica, she *had* thought it was Luke. After hearing the conversation between Juno and Luke on the overgrown path, her brain had made wrong connections.

'Tell me why you lied, Jessica.'

'Tell *me* that it was you who left her to die, Mason. Was it all about the money from Eva?'

His expression is unfathomable and he doesn't answer. He waits just a second and then, taking hold of both her arms, he pulls her up roughly from the floor. Grabbing her midriff, he turns her around, slamming her face against the ceramic tiles on the bathroom wall. His hand is grasping at the soft place in between her legs, his penis pressing against her back. Jessica feels absolutely nothing as his finger enters. Nothing.

She feels nothing. No pleasure. She is free. Her body, at last, is her own.

She hears his moan, just as she had once heard Dom's with her sister.

Together, he and Dom have taken her life. But, more tragically, so much more tragically, they had taken Juno's, and perhaps Hope's too.

Her cheek pressed hard into tile, she says, 'It was you who gave Juno the tablet that you knew would kill her. And then you left her.' She needs him to say it. He has to say it. Admit it.

In a swift movement he snatches his hand away, takes hold of her hair and pulls her head backwards. She is looking directly at his face and smells the strong scent of alcohol on his breath.

'I told Dom to give the bitch the tablet. Interfering Juno,' he says, and despite the pain pulsing through her neck and shoulders she prays his voice will carry to the recording equipment. 'It was strong stuff. The strongest. Eva's supplier pushed the boat out.' He grabs at her hair again.

She gasps, but she's able to pull her head back slightly, the better to focus on his face.

It's like looking at a stranger. She's married to a stranger. She's married to a psychopath. If he pulls her head much further he will break her neck.

It hits her then: the likely conclusion. Death. Her muscles flutter to life. She needs her phone and she needs to contact Teresa. It will be impossible though, without him seeing her do this. She has to get him out of the bathroom.

It's then that she hears the doorbell chime of Mozart permeate through the house. She thinks he will leave the person at the door waiting, but being who he is, he's unable to leave anything. He goes to see who is at the door.

As soon as he's gone, she feels for the mobile underneath the bath. Texts Teresa. *Call the police.* Fuck, no signal. At all. She tries again, whilst listening to Mason talking to Terence at the front door. She should scream, let her neighbour know she's in trouble. She has him admitting to being on the boat with Juno. That is all she needs. The camera footage will also show his violence towards her. But something stops her from calling out to Terence. She can't be responsible for what the mad man downstairs would do to her gentle neighbour. She attempts to send the text again. Still no signal. And she hears Mason making his way back upstairs. She needs to get to a part of the house with a reliable signal. Too paranoid to put the mobile in her bathrobe pocket, she pushes it back underneath the bath.

She has to change tack, she decides, as he re-enters the bathroom. She doesn't mention the door, or the neighbour. 'I'm cold,' she says. He was about to either break her neck or rape her, but she knows that by saying she is cold he will reconsider.

It has always been such a depraved relationship.

He's studying her. The whites of his eyes are pink, his skin dull and grey. He takes her bathrobe from the hook on the back of the door and hands it to her.

She puts it on. 'I'll go and make some coffee. I think you need some coffee.' She smiles at him. 'Could you let out the bath water for me, and put the towels over the radiator to dry?' Yes, it's always been like this: the ordinary and extraordinary living side by side every day of their relationship.

He nods and allows her to leave. Her old mobile is sitting inside the wire head in the kitchen, lodged in the part of the brain that says *Order*, waiting for her.

She makes her way downstairs quickly, hoping he takes his time placing the towels symmetrically on the rail.

50

Natalie

Natalie waits with an impatience she's never experienced before, as Teresa listens to Libby talking on the other end of the phone. She takes a sip of tea; her throat is so dry, as if all the fluid in her body is draining away. She's so worried about Jess, and what she will be doing – provoking Mason to admitting to his part in Juno's death, inciting him to violence towards herself. Because it *is* rape, married or not – she believes Teresa when she told her that nailing a rape conviction in these circumstances is notoriously hard. With this plan they'd kill two birds, although with one very dangerous stone.

She glances up at Teresa's face, which is now grey.

Teresa disconnects the call and lays the mobile on the table. 'Mason's been to see Libby. She's distraught.'

Natalie pushes back her chair and stands, a terrible feeling leaching through her. 'What?'

'He knows, *knows* I've been investigating.'

'How does he know?'

'The cop I went to see, who gave me the info. He must have contacted Mason, probably for money, who knows, the bastard. I told him my name. Obviously, he had Mason's name. Libby admitted to Mason that she's spoken to me.'

'Is Libby all right?'

'She is. But we have to let Jess know.' Teresa is calling Jess again. Natalie knows there's no reply when Teresa throws the mobile onto the table and then springs up and pulls her coat from the back of the chair. 'I'm going over there.'

'I'm coming with you,' she says.

Teresa's mobile suddenly pings with a text. Both women go to grab the phone.

> M home early. He's spoken to his ex. He knows we know. I have everything we need.

'That's it,' Natalie says. 'I'm calling the police.'

Teresa puts her hand on her arm. 'No. Not yet.'

'Fucking hell, Teresa. We have to.'

'We've come this far. We have to hold our nerve.'

'Jess is in danger, Teresa. *In danger.*'

'I'll go over now. You stay here.'

Natalie is staring at her sister. Unsure what to do, and as she has always done, she leaves the decision to someone else.

51

Jessica

In the kitchen, her hands trembling, her neck hurting – everything hurting – Jessica quickly makes her way over to the female wire head. She is watching Jessica; she is smiling; she is enjoying the knowledge that, inside her depths is Jessica's old mobile, and a camera.

Jessica pulls out the phone and texts Teresa and then turns it to silent so any incoming texts don't alert him. She makes coffee, the ground granules spilling all over the counter. She doesn't clear up the mess, but instead swivels around.

The wire head is watching her, still smiling.

She feels Mason in the kitchen rather than hears him. She turns away from the head and watches as, leisurely, he pours himself a coffee, as if everything is perfectly normal. This is the way it has always been. The veneer of normality managing to cover the thick crust of abnormality.

'What happened to Juno?' she says.

'*What happened to Juno?* Good question, Jessica.' He takes a sip of coffee. 'Yes, what indeed happened to Juno? She took the tablet that Dom gave her. Stupid, pleasure-seeking Juno. She couldn't resist. I asked Dom to give her the strongest tablet. I don't think she even noticed the skull and crossbones imprinted on it, Jessica. She thought she was clever, but she wasn't, was she? Not at all. It had begun to take effect by the time I persuaded her to go to Raven Island with me, and was probably the only reason she came with me.' He gives a mirthless smile. 'She asked me on the boat about what you had told her – Dom and Hope. She planned to tell Teresa and Eva. But by then she was having problems. We got to the island. She collapsed before we made it to the cabin. I told her to sit up against the tree. I watched her, Jessica, I watched her die. It was amazingly quick. Heart attacks often are. The fatal ones, anyway.'

He's walking towards her. She is standing near to the wire head, and feels the protrusion of the wire poking gently into her upper back, as if encouraging her. He carries on, 'It was the very place where your sister died, Jessica, but you know that, don't you? Because you found your sister, Hope, just like you found Juno.'

She's staring at him. A horrendous foreboding lies as mercury inside her stomach.

Him and Hope.

It's only since the restaurant incident that she's allowed herself to retrieve that memory – seeing Mason and Hope inside the cabin having sex. They had never known she'd seen them and she had tried so hard to forget. It was only weeks before Hope died.

She has, though, enough on audio for the police to reconsider Juno's case, Luke's conviction. More than enough. But if there is not enough then… what? If he isn't prosecuted for Juno's death and he's not nailed for raping his wife, Mason will get away with everything. He thinks he's going to get away with everything. His arrogance and narcissism demands it.

And if he gets away with it? She cannot bear that thought. She would never be free.

'Why are you talking about my sister?' she hears herself saying.

'She still visits me in my dreams, you know. Sweet, beautiful Hope. She torments me… You could never be her, even though you look so much like her.'

A terrible sense of horror pleats through. Suddenly Hope's death has become as mysterious as Juno's.

'It wasn't only Dom fucking your sister, Jessica,' he is saying. 'It's why I married you, because you look so much like Hope—'

It's as if someone has just kicked her in the stomach.

He carries on, a juggernaut. 'But I couldn't fuck you like I fucked Hope because it's as if she is watching. It's always felt as if she is watching.'

Him and Hope. Dom and Hope. Juno's death. Two girls' deaths.

Inside her head she finds a connection.

She thinks back to when she found her sister's body. Was he somehow involved in her death too? Had Hope fallen from the tree? Was it an accident? It has bothered her, the unanswered questions surrounding Hope's death, as it has always bothered her other sisters too, especially Teresa.

'You really are a piece of work, Mason,' she says. From the corner of her eye she sees the set of knives sitting on the kitchen counter. She feels a shift within her. She could do it. She could kill him. But then she will go to prison, and she won't see her sisters again, she won't have the life she sees with her sisters. And Connor? She can't think of him, she cannot think of happiness or normality. Perhaps her life was never meant

335

to be normal. Because of Dom, and because of Mason. When did she realise that it was Mason in the boat with Juno? Not until the day he violated her beside the front door in their home. No, it was before that – when Grace, finally, told her everything about her stepfather and her stepfather's friend. It had been like looking and listening to a distorted mirror-image of her own life. It was the moment she acknowledged the terrible thing she had done. She told a judge and a jury it was Luke. An innocent man.

Whatever the outcome today, it will be the right outcome. If she dies today, then it is something she deserves.

She's staring at him, the comfort of the nose spike caressing the upper part of her back, urging her to be brave.

He turns away and makes his way over to the cupboard, pulls out a container of rice. 'I'm making a mushroom risotto tonight.' He takes a few steps to the fridge, opens the door and takes out a bag of mushrooms and a tub of cream. He places them on the counter, and then pulls the long filleting knife from the rack, and begins to chop the mushrooms. He hasn't cleaned the mushrooms and he's using the wrong knife. There is no order in his work. The muscles in his neck appear corded, like wires in an instrument of torture.

He has tortured her for too long.

He places the knife on the counter. He tears off the lid from the tub of cream. Then he walks over to her, grabs her arm, and in one practised movement flings her to the floor. She hits her head on the corner of the granite island, and watches as the wire head shudders at the violence of her fall. The belt of her bathrobe has unravelled and her body is exposed. He's standing over her. She tries to move but every muscle has frozen. He lifts his leg and smashes his foot onto her left shoulder. The pain is astounding.

She looks up at him and, despite the agony – or is it because of it? – she talks and hears calmness in her own voice. 'Everything about you is disgusting.' She waits a second, gathering in the verbal slack, pulling it tighter. 'What was it like in prison?'

He smiles down at her. 'It's a place I won't be revisiting, if that's what you're hoping for. You know nothing, Jessica. You're pathetic. You're worse than me. Much worse. Have you ever stopped to think about that?'

She doesn't answer. Her words have dried, crumbled, like dust.

He kicks her in the ribs, and she hears the sickening crack of bone, feels it, her breath is taken, just as her words have been whipped away.

He carries on, his tone low and level, but the simmering fury lives inside his considered words. 'It's you who came over to me that day in the bar – *you came to me*. Don't forget that. And you knew. You knew about Juno. You knew, Jessica, that it was me on the boat with her.' He crouches down. 'You knew it wasn't Luke.' His hand finds her left breast, and then he begins to unzip his trousers. 'I'm going to fuck you now, just as I fucked your sister… and your…'

Lifting her head, managing to turn it slightly, she sees the wire head staring back at her. 'Who?' she whispers.

He doesn't answer. Just lifts both her arms over her head and pins them to the floor. With the movement of her whole shoulder girdle, the pain in her ribcage surges. If there's a broken rib this will surely make it puncture her lung.

Mason pushes down his trousers.

She rams her hips upwards, ignoring the pain, using every ounce of her not inconsiderable muscle power to try to move him, but to no avail. But in a slip of a moment he loosens his grip on her right arm and she punches him hard in the face, the crack of his nose as loud as the snap of her rib.

'You fucking bitch!'

She can almost see the red flashing behind his eyes. And then he jumps up with an agility that belies a fifty-five-year-old man, and he moves quickly to the kitchen counter and picks up the knife.

It takes her a second to register, but then she pushes herself off from the floor. As she does so, the weight she puts through her arms causes her to flop forward in pain. She's finding it harder to breathe. And in that moment of hesitation, he turns towards her, the knife held securely in his hand.

He's going to kill her.

Things have moved on too quickly, and in a way that she hadn't foreseen, or wanted to foresee. In one movement, ignoring the pain, holding onto the lower base of the wire head, she gets up. In standing she has a better chance.

He's coming towards her, knife held at waist level, his trousers halfway down his hips. And she wants to laugh, and she does. Utterly inappropriately, and for a second she thinks of Natalie's propensity to giggle at the wrong moment.

She's glad she can find humour in what she now realises will be the last moments of her life.

Smiling inside, too, that everything is recorded, everything on video.

He lunges towards her, and she waits, knowing the exact timing. All those sports meetings, the netball, the football, the fitness regime she's kept up, have taught her the valuable art of anticipation and rhythm.

Timing her move to perfection, she steps to one side. The wire protrusion on the head sits at the same level as his upper body. The wire spike enters cleanly the left side of his torso, hitting, with luck, she thinks, the upper part of his left lung. Hopefully his heart.

It takes a few seconds for the blood to erupt like red lava from the wound. She gasps with shock, more for the visual and audio, and inside her head she says, 'Thank you, Ms Head.'

She closes her eyes. She has no wish to see his face.

Finally, with the hurt inside her heart overshadowing the pain in her chest, she makes her way upstairs to retrieve her new phone, so that she can check the audio and visual settings.

The phone is sitting on the ledge of the bath.

He'd known. But he hadn't known she would win this. His arrogance is both chilling and breathtaking.

She picks up the phone and makes her way downstairs. In the hallway she starts to call 999, but then decides against it and instead picks up the landline from the hall table.

'My name is Jessica,' she says to the operator. 'Dr Jessica Keane. My husband has fallen onto a spike in the kitchen whilst trying to attack me. I think he's dead.' But then her legs give way underneath her. She sinks to the floor, the phone slipping from her hand.

'Hello, are you still there? Please answer, Jessica.'

She hears the words but she cannot speak.

Finally she picks up the phone and says, 'Raped me.'

'Your husband?'

'Raped my life.'

'I have a response car on the way now.'

The phone drops to the floor and she manages to stand. She looks down the hallway to the door of the kitchen. Her heart is racing at a speed she knows her body will be unable to maintain. She continues to stare at the door, expecting him to emerge from it. She sees his form. *Is that him?*

The dimly lit hallway darkens and she can't see him. She hears loud banging on the front door, so loud she thinks the new glass will break again. She screams. Her vision is blurred. Where's he gone? How can he still be alive? It's impossible. She's screaming. Screaming like she has wanted to scream all of her life.

There is the shattering of glass and then she hears the front door opening. She's on the floor again; she knows this because as she curls into the foetal position, she feels the warmth of the wooden floor on her cheek.

'Jess, what the hell is happening?'

She tries to focus. Is it Terence? He's broken the glass to get into the house. Mason will be so angry and she is so worried for her neighbour but is unable to do anything. Her eyes are still closed. She dare not open them. *Where is Mason?*

'Jess.'

She recognises the voice. The soft, almost indiscernible Irish accent.

Her eyes spring open. 'Connor... He's here. I think he's still alive.' She can hear herself panting.

'I heard you screaming. Is it your husband? Where is he?'

'Be careful, please...' She looks up, focusing on him. His hand is bleeding from punching through the glass. He's kneeling next to her. She's taking in his face, his features. The smell of him. So different from Mason.

'It's going to be okay...'

In the periphery of her vision she sees a shadow, a form. 'Connor!' she shouts in warning, but before he registers she sees the knife, which not that long before had been cutting mushrooms.

Connor jumps up. Blood is everywhere and she doesn't know if it's Mason's or Connor's, or her own. She knows nothing any more. The breath inside her lungs is disappearing and she envisages blood filling them.

Seconds before she closes her eyes, moments before the darkness of unconsciousness descends, she hears the noise of sirens, the impossibly bright flashing of blue lights, the ringing of her mobile, the sound of the landline. And just before she loses consciousness, an image of Juno and Hope, both on Raven Island, saturates her brain.

52

Teresa

As she was leaving, Teresa had left Natalie calling the police. Teresa is in her car now, the engine running, and is about to leave to drive over to Jessica's when her mobile rings. It's a withheld number and she picks up straight away, her heart thumping so hard she thinks it is going to burst from her chest. 'Teresa Harris speaking.'

'Mrs Harris, my name is DI Sarah Stanton—'

'Has my sister called you?' She is sure Natalie has already called, but this response feels so quick. An ominous feeling fills her.

'Mrs Harris,' the female detective is saying. 'There has been an incident at your sister's home. Jessica has been taken to hospital, the A and E at the Royal Free in London.'

Teresa feels as if she is going to pass out, and it's the very same feeling she had when she came home to the news that the person she had grown up with, and formed alongside inside their mother's belly, was dead. 'Is Jessica going to be all right? Please tell me what's happened.'

'We took your number from her mobile phone. She called you earlier today, is that right?'

'Yes, she did.' The police have Jessica's new phone. 'Please tell me what's happened. Is Jessica okay? Tell me.'

'It seems Jessica and her husband argued, and things escalated. The emergency services took a call from Jessica, and then soon afterwards a call came in from your sister's neighbour, reporting noise from the house. Simultaneously, we also got a call from a Mr Connor O'Leary who came to the property near to the time of the incident.' She pauses. 'We've also just received a call from Natalie Mitchell… who I believe is your other sister?'

'Yes, Natalie called the police.'

The detective carries on: 'The paramedics who came to the scene suspect that Jessica may well have a collapsed lung, as well as other injuries… I'm not a doctor so don't know the implications—'

Teresa is already getting out of the car, her phone wedged underneath her chin. 'Natalie will go to the hospital. I'll be at Jessica's house within an hour. I need to speak to you… Is Mason there? Have you arrested him?'

'I'll speak to you when you arrive,' the policewoman says.

Standing on Natalie's doorstep she disconnects. As she does so, Natalie opens the door. She looks awful.

'What's happened?' Natalie is saying. 'Jess—'

'She's been taken to the Royal Free. Call Oli and tell him that's where you'll be. I'm going over to the house now.' While she's talking, she's clicking on her phone, trying to access the app that, if Jessica managed to activate all the equipment, will show her exactly what has happened that night. But her fingers are shaking too much.

'Give the phone to me,' Natalie says.

She watches as her sister does what she cannot.

'Jess activated everything,' Natalie says, as she turns to go back inside.

343

What have we done?

In the hallway Natalie is grabbing her own phone. She calls Oli and then goes to get her coat. 'I'm going to the hospital. Did Mason…? Did he, has he…?'

'I don't know,' she replies. 'I think it's best I just go now. I haven't got time to look at the video, Nat. I need to get to the house. I'm meeting the detective who called me there.'

'What about Mason? Have they arrested him?' Natalie asks as she scrapes viciously at her scalp.

'Stop it, Nat,' Teresa says quietly. 'Call me when you get to the hospital? It's all going to be okay.' She really isn't sure if it *is* all going to be okay, and takes hold of her sister's arm with gentleness. She has to make sure Natalie knows. No ambiguities. She takes a breath. 'Mason and Dom were both sleeping with Hope… our sister. Libby told me.'

'I know, Teresa, you've told me this… I know.'

'I wanted to be sure you knew.' She smiles weakly. 'Libby also told me that Mason was utterly obsessed with Hope.'

So many emotions pass over Natalie's face. 'And Hope's death, Teresa?'

Knife-like jabs of pain penetrate throughout Teresa's entire body. Her twin sister's death has always been something she's never come to terms with; a question mark hovering from the moment she discovered how she had died. 'We'll talk later.'

Natalie inclines her head.

They leave the house together.

53

Teresa

Teresa arrives in Hampstead an hour later. The residential road has been cordoned off and the flashing blue police lights hurt her tired eyes as she pulls up next to the barrier. The detective she'd spoken to earlier had instructed Teresa to give her own name, together with the detective's – DI Sarah Stanton.

The uniformed police officer allows her straight through, although she has to park on the other side of the barriers. Before getting out of the car her mobile rings.

Natalie.

She answers immediately. 'Have you seen Jessica? How is she?'

'She's in theatre. Are you there?' Natalie replies.

'Just about to go in. Got to go, I'll call soon—'

'Someone else has been admitted too, Teresa,' Natalie says. 'His name is Connor O'Leary. Jess knows him through her job. Through the Grace case. He and Jess are friends—'

'Yes, I know about Connor, and yes I think they are friends… Is he okay?'

'A knife wound, that's all I've been told,' Natalie says.

'Look, I have to go. I'll be at the hospital as soon as I can be.'

'Okay.' And her sister disconnects.

Teresa gets out the car and makes her way to the front door. Such a beautiful house. Jessica's life. A life they haven't shared. Her quirky, clever and supremely odd sister, who she abandoned. She takes in the house again. A gorgeous and privileged prison, which Jessica shared with a psychopath.

I'm so sorry, Jess.

A policeman is covering up what is obviously a smashed pane of glass in the front door. Her heart is sinking inside her chest, plunging.

'My name is Teresa Harris. I'm Jessica's sister. I spoke to DI Stanton earlier.'

'You can't go inside, madam. I'll tell the guv you're here.'

Teresa nods and he disappears. A few minutes later a woman opens the door. 'Teresa Harris?'

'Yes.'

Gently, she takes Teresa's arm and leads her to a police car. 'We'll sit and talk in here.' She holds open the door and Teresa gets in, followed by the detective. 'I've had confirmation that Jessica is in theatre and is going to be okay, Mrs Harris.'

'Yes, I've spoken to my other sister, she's at the hospital now... and Connor O'Leary has been admitted too?'

'Yes, he has. He was conscious when we arrived at the scene. My colleague is currently questioning Jessica's neighbour to try and piece together what's happened tonight. But it seems that there's been an argument between your sister and her husband, resulting in an acci- dent... where her husband, Mason, sustained a serious injury... The neighbour has told us that he heard Jessica screaming and came outside to see what was happening, and was about to ring the doorbell, when Connor O'Leary turned up, heard the screaming too, and broke the glass to get into the house.'

'Oh my God.'

'Connor saved Jessica's life,' the detective says. 'I believe his injury is not life-threatening. He did manage to tell me the reason he turned up at Jessica's home so late. He wanted to give her good news in person regarding a trial verdict they were both waiting on.'

This must be linked to the Grace trial. The little girl who had been key in allowing Jessica to face her own painful truths.

Teresa nods in understanding. 'And Mason. Have you arrested him?'

The detective turns to her. 'Mrs Harris, Mason died on his way to hospital. We're unclear about the exact chain of events, as I've, obviously, been unable to talk to either Jessica or Connor—'

'I can help you, Inspector,' Teresa says quietly. 'Just over a week ago, Jessica came to my office and told me several things that I've not been aware of – my sister and I have been estranged for many years. But, she told me about her husband's violent behaviour to her—'

'And she didn't report this?'

She peers at the detective, who although looking tired, is so obviously alert. 'Jessica felt that marital rape wouldn't be taken seriously, and as a practising barrister, I can see why she would think that.'

'Tonight might not have happened, Mrs Harris, if Jessica had reported this.' DI Sarah Stanton looks her in the eye. 'Jessica could have left, found a safe place with either you, or your other sister.'

'She could, but she felt that wasn't the way forward.' She maintains eye contact with the detective. 'Jessica has been reporting quite a lot of burglaries in her neighbourhood recently. She had camera and audio equipment installed, and so you'll know exactly what's taken place tonight.'

The detective sighs heavily. 'This is a very dangerous game, Mrs Harris.'

'The cameras and audio are activated via Jessica's mobile.'

'We've found two mobile phones, Mrs Harris.'

'It's the Samsung, I believe.' She isn't sure whether to tell her she has access on hers. But she has done nothing wrong. 'I'm a joint app user and have access on my phone.' She pulls it out from her bag and activates the app. 'I haven't had time to look. I drove straight here.'

DI Stanton takes it, clicks it on, studies the information on the app quickly and turns to her. 'This might take a while – it's a multi-roomed house. It looks as if your sister put cameras in the bathroom too.'

'You never know where burglars are going to attempt a break-in. I've heard the bathroom is a favourite,' Teresa says.

The detective crosses one leg over the other in the cramped police car. 'Indeed.'

'There's a red light on the rooms where there's movement,' Teresa explains. 'They're the only rooms you need to look at. Please...' She takes the phone and studies it. 'Upstairs bathroom, kitchen and hallway.' She hands the policewoman her own ear buds.

Hunching forward in the car seat, the detective starts to watch the unfolding events in Jessica's home. Teresa sits back and stares out of the window. She cannot watch.

Not tonight. Whatever plan she, Jessica and Natalie had has paled into insignificance. But then she thinks of Matt, and of Juno, and a sense of purpose fills her again, overcoming the tiredness, the emptiness. She is absolutely confident that her resourceful sister will have got all that she needed for a new investigation to open up on Matt's case. Luke's case. She knows, because of what's happened tonight. Jessica has succeeded, but ice-like tendrils of regret are already clasping at her heart. She should never have agreed. Her decision was selfish; she so desperately wanted Matt exonerated... although then, and almost simultaneously, another thought takes hold. Jessica cannot heal until balance is restored, and for this to happen the truth needs to be released – to emancipate all three sisters.

They are sitting in the car for an hour as the detective watches and listens to everything. Finally she looks up, pulls out the ear buds and turns to Teresa. 'Are you Luke Harris's wife?'

She nods.

'And you haven't looked at this app, yet?'

'No, I told you,' Teresa says.

'You are Hope Keane's sister?'

'I am. Her twin sister.'

Something in the tapes has alerted the detective. She's absolutely certain that Sarah Stanton knows about Mason's relationship with Hope. Did Jessica already know about Hope and Mason, and hadn't told her? No, Jessica would have told her, she's so sure. *What a mess.*

'What about Hope, my sister?' she asks finally.

'I remember your twin sister's death, Mrs Harris... It would be helpful if you could accompany me to the station.'

She pretends to know nothing of what she suspects is on the visual and audio. 'Connected with what's happened here tonight?'

'Yes, but from listening and watching these, it would also seem that Mason may well have admitted to his involvement in the Juno Morrison case. The manslaughter charge for which, I believe, your husband served time in prison.'

'Yes, that's true.'

'Please stay in the car while I go and check in with my colleagues, Mrs Harris.' The detective shuffles to the edge of the car seat but appears to change her mind, swivelling around again. She turns to Teresa. 'Your stepfather, Dom Keane. He was having a relationship with your deceased sister, Hope, his seventeen-year-old stepdaughter?'

'It would seem so, yes.'

Sarah Stanton stares at her. 'In these recordings, it would also seem that Mason had also been in a sexual relationship with your sister, Hope, too.'

Teresa uses every ounce of her legal training to maintain a neutral expression. Mason *has* admitted to his involvement with Hope to Jessica. Like the early morning dawn light seeping in, a dark fold of suspicion unfurls within her. The accidental death of her vivacious and unruly but beautiful sister had always seemed the most unlikely of scenarios. Hope was so like Jessica, and not just in looks but athleticism too; the likelihood of Hope falling from the tree was so slim. The likelihood of suicide even slimmer. Eva had never got over her favourite daughter's death – because Hope had been her favourite daughter. If Eva had known Hope was in a sexual relationship with her husband, she would have been furious and they would all have known about it. No, Eva had not known about Dom, or Mason's relationship with Hope.

Teresa's head is throbbing, the background headache that she's been experiencing all week is intensifying. There is too much to take in, and too much that she didn't know until recently. And to bring Hope, her beloved twin, back into the land of accessible memories is just too much. She's buried Hope for so long, as have Natalie and Jessica. All three have, because none of them have ever come to terms with how their sister had died. She thinks of Jessica, who found the two bodies. Both at Raven Island.

The detective gets out of the car and leaves her in silence. Teresa taps the 'play' button.

She watches and she cries. That she has abandoned Jessica for so long will be something she will have to learn to live with, and she comprehends this before she has finished watching Connor smashing the window and opening the door from the inside. If he hadn't come, who knows what would have happened. It is Connor who strikes the lethal blow into Mason's heart, with the knife that Mason had been holding.

She wipes her tears away with her coat sleeve and then calls Natalie, who tells her that Jessica's come out of surgery. And she is alive. Connor is stable too. She calls her husband. He answers immediately.

'Luke.'

'It's Matt... you're upset... what's happened?' he says, love, concern and puzzlement lacing through his words.

'It's *Luke*, Luke. You *are* Luke again.'

And she tells him.

54

Teresa

It's two a.m. and Teresa had left the hospital, and a sleeping Jessica, an hour before. She's now sitting inside the police station in an interview room with DI Stanton and a uniformed policeman. She's been told that the invest-igating team have looked again at the video and audio footage.

There's no doubt in her mind that Juno's case will be reopened with this new evidence. It has all gone pretty much how they had planned, and hoped – apart from Mason's death. They had not planned that. They hadn't planned either on Mason's other revelation – his rela-tionship with Hope. And although she'd known about it, from Libby, she is still trying to come to terms with this information.

Teresa possesses mixed feeling about Libby. On the one hand she understands why the teacher hadn't gone to the police regarding her husband's alleged relation-ship with Hope – Libby had never known for certain and Mason never admitted it to her. It would have been very difficult, if not impossible, for Libby to have been in successful dialogue with the police concerning this. Hope was seventeen. Above the age of consent. Male police officers could have seen her allegations as those of a paranoid wife. But on the other hand, if Libby had spoken out and gone to the police, then lives would not have been ruined.

'Thank you for coming in, Mrs Harris,' the female detective in front of her is saying. 'We will be recording our interview.'

'Of course.'

DI Stanton clicks on the machine, giving the date, time and Teresa's name. She begins. 'My job today, Mrs Harris, is to piece together the chain of events at your sister's home tonight, although the images I've seen gives me a very good picture. When Jessica is well enough to talk, I'll be taking a statement from her too. However, because of the complexity and unusualness of this incident… and other implications arising from it' – she looks at Teresa – 'I was keen to get a statement from you as soon as was practicable. So again, thank you so much for coming in at such a late hour… and after such a traumatic evening.'

DI Stanton takes a sip of the coffee that's sitting in front of her. She looks absolutely knackered, but then Teresa is aware that she does too. She knows this because of the reflection that had stared back at her in the police station's ladies' toilets earlier. 'This must be very difficult for you,' the detective continues.

'It's fine. I don't think I'd have been sleeping much tonight anyway.'

DI Stanton smiles. 'I'm sure.' She coughs. 'We have a homicide, but it's clear from the visuals and audio, and also from Jessica's neighbour's statement, that Mr Connor O'Leary acted to protect both himself and Jessica. It is a very good thing he turned up when he did.'

'It really is,' Teresa says.

DI Stanton fixes her eyes on her. 'You previously mentioned that Jessica told you about a recent incident with her husband, where he attacked her... raped her. Did you discuss in depth with Jessica the implications of reporting this to the police, Mrs Harris?'

'What do you mean?'

'You mentioned when we talked earlier that you encouraged Jessica to install interior camera and audio equipment.'

'I did yes.'

'Was this suggestion made because of Jessica reporting to you about Mason's aggressive behaviour, which has been borne out from the video footage?'

'It was Jessica who suggested installing equipment, mainly because of the surge in attempted break-ins recently.'

'This "surge" is news to me.' The detective is not looking convinced.

'I thought it was a good idea... on many levels, so yes, I did encourage her when she came to see me in my office. We discussed it then. I agreed with her. It seemed a sensible thing to do.' She stares at DI Stanton.

'I've managed to speak on the phone briefly with Libby Thomas, Mason's ex-wife. She says that you contacted her very recently, asking about Mason.' She stares at Teresa. 'I'd imagine after hearing what Libby Thomas had to say about her husband, you may well have been alerted to the... potential of this evening?'

'His conviction was a long time ago,' Teresa replies. She is worried the detective may know about her visit to the policeman. Immediately, she thinks of Amanda and the coolness of dread threads through her for her friend.

The detective sighs. 'What I don't understand, in your capacity as a barrister, is why you didn't insist that Jessica reported Mason's earlier attack.' She pauses. 'That would have been the sensible, and professional, thing to do... don't you think?'

'I did, DI Stanton. Jessica decided to go against my advice.' She swallows as if gulping away her lie. But Sarah Stanton has not mentioned Amanda.

'Okay. I think I understand.' The detective pauses. 'We won't be pursuing charges in regards to Connor O'Leary. He clearly acted in self-defence.' DI Stanton places both elbows on the table. 'Mrs Harris, we will be investigating the recorded footage of this evening's events at your sister's home in more detail over the next few days.' Again, the detective stares at her with intent. 'And I will, personally, be following up the consequences of Mason's confession... regarding the death of Juno Morrison in 1991. As you know from our conversation earlier, I'm familiar with this case—'

'My husband was advised by his counsel to plead guilty to the involuntary manslaughter of Juno Morrison so as to minimise his sentence, Inspector.' Teresa is so desperate to put Luke's part across. 'Matt... Luke was, is, the love of my life. He lost his career, he lost his self-esteem. He thought he was going to lose me...'

The detective nods in sympathy, but Teresa does not underestimate the woman sitting opposite her. She is sure she suspects something but the detective, Teresa senses strongly, is already more on her side than not. 'Were you, or Jessica, or both of you, aware, recently aware, of Mason's involvement in Juno Morrison's death?'

She has anticipated this question. 'No, I wasn't. Jessica wasn't aware either.' Lying is so difficult for her and she can hear the higher pitch of her own voice. Always a dead giveaway.

The detective moves her chair close to the table. Leans forward. 'On a wider scale, how do you feel about all this, Mrs Harris? The emotional implications? I'm assuming neither you, nor Jessica, by observing her reaction in the footage, were aware of the relationship between your late sister and Mason?'

'No, we weren't aware. But this illustrates what an absolute bastard Mason was.'

'Okay... Was Jessica aware of Mason's previous criminal conviction?'

'No, she wasn't.'

Sarah Stanton leans over the table, looks at her watch and talks into the recording machine. 'Two thirty-five a.m. and pausing interview.' She notes the date too, and then turns to the policeman standing by the door, inclines her head. He leaves.

'Teresa... can I call you Teresa?'

'Of course.'

'Teresa,' she says. 'In 1991, it was Jessica's testimony that helped secure Luke Harris's arrest, together with her mother's testimony – your mother – Eva Keane. As well as your other sister, Natalie.'

'True,' Teresa says. 'Didn't look good, did it?'

The detective shakes her head. 'Your mother is dead and so is out of the equation, as is Mason now too.'

'True again.'

'If the case is reopened, Jessica and Natalie may well be called as witnesses. Both may well be investigated for perjuring themselves in court, Teresa.'

'They both told the truth as they saw it at the time.' She fixes her eyes on the detective's. She waits a few seconds.

And then tells her about Dom's suicide note – his confession regarding his relationship with his stepdaughter, and Mason's plan to give Juno the tablet that would in the end kill her, and how Mason, with Dom's knowledge, left Juno on the island to die.

The detective stands and paces the room. 'This will need to go on the record.'

'Yes.'

'Eva Keane kept the suicide note secret, that's what you are saying, Mrs Harris?'

'Yes.'

'I will need to see it.'

'My sister still has the note.'

'Good. And how long have you been aware that the note existed?'

'Only a few days,' she says, her voice strong and unequivocal. 'I believe the CPS won't pursue Jessica, or Natalie. It won't be deemed in the public interest.'

'You can't be sure,' the detective replies.

'No, I can't.'

The detective smiles, gets up, opens the door and sticks her head out. 'Please can you return to the room, Sergeant.'

He walks back in, attempting to stifle a yawn, and Sarah Stanton clicks on the recorder. 'Two thirty-nine a.m., resuming interview with Teresa Harris.' She pauses, gathers her thoughts. 'To recap and reiterate, Mrs Harris. Two weeks ago your sister told you that Mason forced her to have intercourse with him. He raped her.'

'Yes,' Teresa replies. 'She also said that up until that day their marriage was unconsummated.'

'Okay...' Sarah Stanton shuffles in her chair. She's uncomfortable. Teresa would be too if she was hearing

357

this statement from one of her own clients. 'How long have they been married?'

'Since 2002, so seventeen years.'

'Every marriage has its... nuances,' the detective says.

'They do... but as you've seen tonight, this marriage was not nuanced. Mason married Jessica because Jessica looked so similar to Hope... my deceased twin. That's what I think, that's what the recording suggests. Mason has controlled Jessica since the start of their marriage.' She goes on to tell her about how Jessica and he met up in the London cocktail bar, how she and Natalie believe he'd planned the meeting. How he visited Jessica so soon after her suicide attempt.

'This is all conjecture, Teresa, but I can see where you're going with this... So, Jessica told you, when she visited your office, that she was planning to install home video and recording equipment in her home, in the event that Mason displayed violence towards her again?'

'She had them installed because of the burglaries.'

DI Stanton gives her a tight smile. 'At the time of Jessica's visit to your office, was she concerned about your husband's, Luke Harris's arrest in 1991, and his subsequent conviction and prison sentence... and her husband, Mason's involvement... all these years later?'

'No, she didn't mention this.' Teresa swallows but holds firm. Jessica was concerned, it was why she had apologised about Luke in her office that day. It was why she told Teresa about Dom and Hope. But the detective cannot know this.

'Okay. So what we've seen on the visuals and audio – Jessica questioning Mason about Juno Morrison... this is all relatively new information, which prior to tonight, Jessica wasn't aware of?'

'Yes, I believe so. My sister had her problems when she was young, she's always been... different, but after my twin sister's death – it was Jessica who found Hope's body on Raven Island – she worsened. So when she found Juno too, I think she just shut down. I think that whatever happened connected to Juno's death, Jessica has had difficulty retrieving that information. I think there must have been an event recently that tripped her memory... Up until recently, Jessica and I have been estranged.' She looks at the detective. 'For obvious reasons.'

'When did you and Jessica... make up?'

'As I say, recently.'

'When, Mrs Harris?'

'The day she came to my office.'

'The day she told you not only about Mason raping her, but also that memories of the day that Juno Harris died were returning to her, and she suspected her husband's involvement?'

'No. Jessica did *not* mention anything about Mason's possible involvement in Juno's death on the day she visited me in my office.' It's imperative Teresa gets this point across. There can be no ambiguity. There can be no possibility that the police are able to pinpoint entrapment, or worse, premeditated murder.

'Are you absolutely certain?'

'I am absolutely certain, Inspector.'

DI Stanton represses what Teresa thinks is a frustrated shrug. 'Interview over at 3.04 a.m.' She clicks off the recorder. 'I suggest you go and get some sleep, Mrs Harris. Where are you staying?'

'At my other sister's home.'

Sarah Stanton nods. 'I'm going to get some shut-eye myself. And tomorrow I'll begin the process of reopening the Juno Morrison case.'

Teresa nods. 'Mason and Dom were responsible for Juno's death, Detective Inspector. I believe it would be pertinent to re-examine Juno's clothes and cross-match Mason's DNA.'

'Leave me to my job, Mrs Harris. I'll be in touch soon.'

Teresa stands. 'Jessica's been through enough.'

'Yes, it would seem so. And you have too. Good night, Mrs Harris.' She rakes her hands through her shoulder-length brown hair and turns to her. 'I'll also be looking into the details of your sister's death, as a matter of course.' She pauses, a thought occurring to her. 'Teresa, how would you describe the relationship between your late stepfather, Dom, and Mason?'

'They were in business together, as thick as thieves. But the reality was, Dom relied on my mother's money to survive, it propped up his business... and therefore Mason's business too. They were partners. Joint interest.'

'Do you think Dom was aware that Mason was having a relationship with Hope too?'

'I don't know, but I don't think so, no. Am I free to leave?' Teresa asks.

'Of course.'

Teresa makes her way outside, grateful for the freezing night air. She has no idea where this is going, and she isn't sure where DI Sarah Stanton will be going with it either. She is utterly exposed. Her career could be finished. But she acknowledges that she feels exactly the same as she did the night when she told Luke that she'd testify in court for him. She didn't care then that by doing so it might well ruin a career she hadn't yet started. And now, she does not care that Sarah Stanton might discover that everything that has happened tonight has been, more or less, her construction.

As she was then, today too, she's willing to give up everything for a person she loves.

Because she loves Jessica. So much. As she had loved Hope; Hope her elder sister by ten minutes. The sister who in many ways had held all the Keane sisters together. Wild, vibrant and mesmerising Hope. Mischievous, living-on-the-edge Hope. Clever Hope, whose IQ had been off the scale, a running joke between the twins. Juno had been so like Hope in personality, and the reason why Teresa had been unable to stomach her.

Suddenly, Teresa feels exhausted and sits down on the kerb outside the police station. She has no desire to think of Dom and Mason, but recognises that both men saw the vibrant spark of life in Hope, both wanting to take it for themselves. Hope had been a victim of two vile and opportunistic men.

She stares into the darkness of the night. It's becoming much clearer about what happened to Juno, but murkier about what really happened to her sister.

She feels the warm salty tears on her cheeks. They will never know now what really happened to Hope, but Mason was at Raven House the day Hope fell from the tree on Raven Island and died – and he was there without Libby. She delves into her memory banks of when she and Hope were both seventeen. Mason was around a lot without Libby. And yes, there had been a few times when she'd discovered that Hope had gone off in a motorboat with Mason, and it was always when Dom wasn't around. She'd never thought much of it, too busy with her A-level studies, as Hope should have been too; Teresa smiles at the thought of her twin never doing any work and always passing every exam. But now that she's aware of Hope's relationship with Mason, and with Dom, her twin sister's death is taking on an entirely different tone, although a tone that each one of the Keane sisters had felt from the beginning – a tone of doubt. Did Hope fall from the tree, or was she pushed?

It all ties together, but there is no way now to prove anything.

Oh Hope, my bad sister, my lovely bad sister. She will never know what was going on inside her sister's mind but she suspects that being the spirited girl she was, Hope might well have threatened to come clean to Eva about Dom, and perhaps even about Mason. She can't think about it.

She had stopped loving Eva many years ago, and loved her even less when she realised Eva had never shared Dom's suicide note, and his confession.

But, briefly, now, she feels for Eva. It was after Hope's death when Eva took the spiral road to self-destruction. It is another reason why she had not despised her mother as much as she was capable of doing.

She is glad that Mason is dead because if he were not, she would make it her mission in life to ensure that he wouldn't be alive for long. Connor O'Leary has done them all a favour, but he has also taken away the person who could well have had more knowledge surrounding her twin's last day in this world.

55

Two weeks later

Teresa

Teresa has been staying with Natalie for the past two weeks whilst Jessica's been in hospital.

Today is the day before Jessica's discharge, and the day she plans to return home. She and Natalie have tried their utmost to persuade Jessica to come to Natalie's to stay after leaving hospital, but she's flatly refused.

'I don't know why Jess doesn't stay with us,' Natalie is saying.

'She's going to be okay, stop worrying.' Teresa glances up and smiles as she carries on packing her suitcase, which is open on the bed in Natalie and Oli's spare room. 'Connor's been to see her more than we have. My guess is, he'll carry on going to see her when she's home.'

Natalie has her bottom wedged on the window sill. 'He likes her.'

'He does.' Teresa grins. 'A lot, I'd say.'

Natalie moves away from the window and sits on the bed. 'Jess's asked me if she can look through Eva's box of stuff. I took it over when I went over a few days ago to check her house is okay and fill up the cupboards.'

'Jessica asked for the box?' Teresa asks.

'Yes… I was surprised too.'

A kernel of disquiet plants itself in the pit of her stomach. 'Perhaps it would've been better not to have taken it, Nat?'

'I think it's some sort of closure for her. Jess just wants to "know" more about Eva.' Natalie lies down next to the suitcase, her head propped up with a pillow. 'Teresa…'

She looks up. 'Yes?'

'It's been good having you around, and Hope's adored it… despite the circumstances.' Natalie pulls at her arm. 'Sit down. We need to talk… we need to talk about Hope. Our sister. We've never talked about her. It was wrong we didn't.'

Teresa sits down beside her sister. 'Do you love her less because of her and Dom… and Mason?' she asks.

'Of course I don't.' Natalie scrutinises her features. 'You?'

'No. Hope was Hope. She and Juno were so similar…' She feels her voice trailing away.

'They were. I'm sure that's why I loved Juno so much.'

'And why I disliked her. I couldn't bear it. Hope was my antithesis, you know, my opposite. When she died, I felt like a piece of me died with her. I didn't even talk about her to Matt… Luke.'

'Oh, Teresa.' Natalie cuddles her and for a brief second Teresa wants to tell her sister her theory about the possible involvement of Mason in Hope's death. But no. No point. There is no evidence, and never will be.

'So is Matt "Matt", or is he Luke these days?' Natalie asks.

'He answers to either!'

Natalie's smile fades. 'I'm worried about where all this is going to go.'

'DI Stanton called me last night. Connor won't be facing charges, so that's one to tick off the list. The DNA results are back too.' She touches Nat's temple, where she sees the last vestiges of psoriasis. The flare-up has calmed down in the last few days. 'There's a match on Juno's clothes to Mason.' She holds Natalie's gaze, sees the tears forming like huge drops of rainwater in her eyes. 'It places him on the island, and so together with his confession to Jessica, this is enough.'

'Poor Juno…' Natalie sits up, and purposefully swings her legs over the bed and stands, as if making herself finally come to terms with what happened to her friend. 'Have you told Jess about this development?' she finishes.

'You're the first person I've told. Jess'll find out, though. DI Stanton will tell her — may well already have done so. I know she's interviewed Jessica in hospital several times — about what happened the night Mason was killed… and the day Juno died too.' She stands up and snaps her suitcase closed and pulls it off the bed. 'Mason is dead. It looks more than likely that Luke will be pardoned, Nat. It's over. Time to start planning Hope's graduation, I reckon.' She smiles at her younger sister. 'C'mon. Let's have a cup of tea before I leave.'

'Teresa?'

'What?'

'Hope, our sister Hope. Has it ever crossed your mind that her accident wasn't an accident, knowing what we now know about her relationship with Mason?'

'It was a tragic accident, Natalie. She fell out of the tree.'

'She was a brilliant tree climber.'

'The wind was strong that day. A storm.' Teresa needs to let this go, for now.

'What if she wasn't alone, just like Juno wasn't alone?' Natalie says.

'Hope was found with a broken back and neck sustained after falling from the top branch of the oak. That's how she died.'

Natalie's features are pleated in pain and anguish. No, her sister can't cope with this too: the mere hypothesis that Hope's death was not an accident.

Neither of her sisters would be able to cope with this.

More withheld secrets, and perhaps secrets that only exist in Teresa's own head, but sometimes that's the only way.

This is one of those sometimes.

56

Natalie

They had found out only a few days before Hope's graduation party that Luke was to be completely exonerated of any involvement in Juno's death.

Natalie is so glad that they got this news before Hope's celebration. Her family has congregated inside the house and she's sitting on the bottom step that leads to the garden, holding a photo of her, Jess, Teresa and Hope in her hand. The four Keane sisters.

Peering at it in the thin October sun, she acknowledges the incredible physical similarity between Jess and Hope, even when very young; and as Jess grew older, she looked even more like her older sister. And her own daughter resembles her two aunts so much. She tries to shake off the thought of why Mason married Jess. But why did Jess marry Mason? For the stability of a childhood that didn't exist? Mason had been around their household almost as long as Dom.

She gazes at the picture. How old would they have been in it? The twins, Hope and Teresa, look around twelve or thirteen. Were they all happy in this photo? She thinks they were. But then she remembers who took it. Dom. He'd always been so taken with Hope. She thinks back and remembers Eva commenting on his 'connection' with Hope; she remembers that Eva was pleased that her second, youthful husband had taken to her girls. Back then, Eva had been more of a mother. She had adored Hope, probably because Hope possessed many of Eva's own personality traits. She smiles wryly to herself. So ironic that she, Teresa and Jess loved Hope so much probably because she was so like Eva. She slips the photo into the back pocket of her jeans. *Oh, Hope.*

She brings herself to the present and surveys their garden. It's covered in a party-sized gazebo. Oli has switched on the heaters and done a last-minute check on the fridges, which hold the wine and beers. The caterers have dropped off the food and left. No waiter service today, no champagne buckets – only champagne for Hope's toast. She checks her watch. It's just before midday – a similar time all those years ago when Dom did his faux proud father speech. In many ways it's a full circle, but a consummately different circle. A new circle.

She gets up and plonks herself on the bench in front of the kitchen window and takes in a moment's peace, loving that she can't smell the river. Her mind travels to Juno, and the boat on the river. She had been unsure who she'd seen, and it had been so easy to say what Eva had instructed her to say. The paradox settles deep that it was not Dom on the boat, but Mason. Since knowing Mason again in adulthood, all the time he's been married to Jess, she hadn't liked him. But she had done nothing when he and Jess had got together, said nothing, not delved, left the situation unexamined.

She leans forward and takes in the scene before her. The garden and gazebo are empty – their guests aren't due for another hour. Unlike the Raven House party there won't be many 'oldies' here. Their home will be filled with Hope's friends – she has so many of them. Hope's so happy about today and has taken in her stride the events of the past few months, as she always does. *Hope, I love you so much.*

It's as if the Keane girls have been cleansed. If her daughter hadn't asked for a family reunion, would they all be where they are today? She doesn't think they would. Hope really is the catalyst.

Looking – squinting really, as she's left her glasses in the kitchen – beyond the gazebo to the end of the garden, she catches sight of a fluorescent green tartan and Juno's laughing and open face. Next to her is Hope, wearing the miniskirt and white T-shirt she had worn the day a young Jessica found her dead at the base of the oak on Raven Island. The scene in front of her now is welded in time. Juno is clutching a copy of *The Great Gatsby*, the book they'd been studying together; Hope, just standing, smiling, shrugging her shoulders in mild amusement, as she always did. Momentarily, darkness folds through her mind and as it does, Hope and Juno's image disappears too. Jess says she can do it – get rid of the blackness. And if Jess can, then so can she. If Luke can forgive her, and she knows he has, then the darkness will, one day, dissipate.

'Natalie, are you all right?'

Startled, she looks up. It's Mrs A. She's managed to navigate her way through the small French doors of their house with her Zimmer frame. She really is amazing. She's even brought her triple chocolate cake. She has no idea how she managed to make it in her nursing home. She must remember to call the manager and say thank you.

'Mrs A, what are you doing!' she says. 'You'll tumble if you're not careful.'

'I certainly won't be tumbling today, Natalie. I came to find you. Oli's waiting, we're all waiting. He's opening the champagne, doing the "proud father" speech inside, before the rest of the guests turn up.'

'Ah, sorry, I lost track of time.' She gets up from the bench.

The sun is strong for October, low too, and she squints. She looks for Juno and Hope but they are gone. Of course they were never there, only inside her mind.

But, as Jess says, inside the mind is such an important place.

Despite what Mrs A has said she doesn't look too steady and Natalie moves quickly to help her back inside to the kitchen, where everyone's waiting. Teresa and Luke, Jessica with Connor, Oli's parents who've come over from France, his sister, and Hope's best friend is here too. She makes sure Mrs A is sitting down before she goes and stands next to Oli. He pours the champagne.

They lift their glasses. 'To Hope, to her future, and to families,' he says.

She glances at Luke. They had a long chat weeks ago. He smiles and inclines his head, whilst at the same time wrapping his arm around Teresa. She smiles back, holding her glass in his direction.

57

Jessica

Jessica is sitting on Natalie's patio bench, huddled up in her winter coat. She takes a deep breath and flinches at the pain around her ribcage. It still hurts with the wrong movement, or just an ill-timed inhalation.

Earlier, inside the gazebo, she'd been sitting with Mrs A and had finally asked her about her relationship with Eva. A question she's wanted to ask since the day before she left for medical school, the day she took Dom to the jetty for a talk.

Why did you put up with her, Mrs A? She was always so rude to you.

I'd known Eva since she was a teenager. She was like the daughter I never had. And, like a mother, I forgave her everything.

She was Eva's daughter and perhaps a daughter should forgive her mother everything too.

But she will never forgive Eva.

She checks her watch. It's five p.m. Hope's party is still going strong, and she gets the feeling celebrations will be going on for a lot longer. She leans back, allowing the wave of pain in her chest to subside, and as she does so, Connor emerges from the gazebo's entrance.

'You okay?' he shouts to her. She can't hear him because of the music but she knows that is what he's saying.

Giving him a thumb-up, she smiles. She then points to the house indicating she's going inside. She holds up both hands, ten fingers – ten minutes. He nods, understanding what she means.

She and Connor have merged together so easily. He saved her life and is continuing to save it by just being with her. She has no desire to analyse why she loves him, and for the first time in her life she has no desire either to enter the inside of his head. She only wants to be.

She gets up and takes the few steps across Natalie's patio, back into the kitchen. She walks through to the lounge. It's so warm in there. Taking off her coat, she lowers herself onto the sofa.

She doesn't know how long she's been sitting there, and has half nodded off when she hears a voice and looks up.

'You okay, Jessica?'

'Luke,' she says. 'Yes, I'm fine. Just taking a breather.'

They have all aged, but somehow the aging process on Luke has jolted her. The guilt she feels of what she did to him will never abate, but she's learnt in the past weeks to not fight it, to allow the regret and sadness to roll over her. To live with it. Because it is the only way she is able to deal with it – and Luke has made it easy for her. She does not know from where his forgiveness comes, but she is teaching herself not to question, only accept.

'Think I'll take a breather too.' He sits on the armchair opposite.

'We're too old,' she says grinning.

His expression drops into solemnity and her breathing rate increases, feeling the thrum of pain in her right lung as she anticipates his words. She is ready, though. They need to talk. She needs to talk.

She finds his eyes. 'I'm sorry, Luke. I haven't said it and I should.'

'I haven't come inside to find you in the hope of getting an apology from you... I want to tell you something.'

She heaves herself up from the sofa and goes to kneel in front of him. 'I was there, Luke. At the bottom of the path. I heard you and Juno. I heard what you said to her.' She takes his hand. 'And because I did hear, it was why I thought it *was* you who took Juno to Raven Island. My thirteen-year-old brain led me to believe that, and when Eva told me to say it was you... it was so easy to do, and for other reasons too... I didn't want you to take Teresa away from us...' She hears her voice trail away. 'When I saw you and Teresa together in the cabin... what I saw was too much like when I saw Mason with Hope in the cabin. I don't know... you with Teresa was something I didn't want to acknowledge, just as I didn't want to acknowledge Mason and Hope... Dom and Hope. And all of it intermingled with me finding Hope on the island. Dead.' Taking her hand away from his, she strokes his cheek. 'I am so sorry.'

'I'm sorry too that you went through all of this, Jessica.' He finds her eyes. 'But I have to tell Teresa about Juno.'

'*No.* You do not. You were drunk. It was just a kiss. You've done your time, Luke. More than.' She stands. He's looking up at her. She offers him her hand. He takes it. 'C'mon, let's go back to your niece's graduation celebrations. She adores you. As we all do. This is the last Keane secret and we'll carry it together.'

It is not, though, the last Keane secret.

The last secret Jess will take to her grave. It is a secret that had been verified in Eva's diary. After bringing Eva's box home and reading the diaries that Natalie had only skimmed through, her eagle eye found an entry tucked away, almost written in code. Jessica's skin writhes still, weeks after discovering Eva's secret.

Eva had not tried hard enough to stop her seven-year-old daughter, her, Jessica, from taking the boat to the island that day and discovering her sister's body.

Again she vows to herself that she will never tell Teresa or Natalie.

To protect Hope and the future generations of Keane girls, she will tell no one.

The box and its contents were burnt weeks ago.

She and Luke walk outside together, and from the elevated patio they survey the graduation party on the lawn below.

Towards the end of the garden Juno's luminescent green tartan and Hope's mischievous smile disappear behind the back of the gazebo.

Thank you, Juno, for trying to help me.

Hope, I'm so sorry I didn't get to you sooner. I love you.

Epilogue

Then
Summer, 1986

Hope

Hope Keane glances at her watch as she gets into the motorboat. Everyone is out for the day: her sisters have gone shopping, Dom's at his office, and Eva left the house earlier to go and see her accountant, saying it was going to be a long session and to expect her back in the afternoon. And so Hope's arranged to meet Mason at Raven Island at 11.30, in an hour. She's going over earlier so she can have another go at climbing the big oak. She just *has* to get to that top branch – it's been eluding her for so long and today is the day.

It's the day too when she'll be telling Mason that the game is over. He thinks he's coming to the island for a morning of sex. It isn't going to happen, as much as she'd like it to be happening. She's going to tell him that she's going to come clean with Eva, about him, and about Dom. Dom has no idea she's having sex with Mason too, which could make it all much more complicated than she wants it to be. But she has to tell her mother, and for all sorts of reasons, but the main one being her younger sisters.

Eva needs to jettison Dom, and Mason. They are both shits.

The engine is running and she's ready to cast off. For a snip of a moment she worries, but it doesn't last long – that feeling never does with Hope. When she and Mason had started messing around it had been for a laugh, to see how far she could push it all. Because that's what Hope likes to do – push things. She likes sex too, a lot. Like Eva, according to Mason.

Your family is so fucked up, Hope, Mason had said, the last time he'd fucked her.

It had made her laugh, him saying that the moment before he came. It always took a while for Mason to come. He wasn't what he appeared, Mason. He'd told her in a flash of weakness that he and Libby weren't doing it at all. She'd figured that was why he found it so difficult to climax – unlike Dom – who came as soon as he entered her. She thinks it does something for Mason, knowing that he's shagging both her and her mother. Sometimes she thinks he wouldn't come at all if he didn't have that thought in the back of his mind. The daughter and the mother thing. But it's time to end it. Recently she's seen a different side to him, a side he hides from Dom and the Keane family. She wonders if Eva knows about this side.

Yes, she's seen a more violent Mason, and a few times now. It's begun to scare her. But everyone in the Keane family likes him, trusts him, apart from Teresa. But her twin is so bloody sensible and fussy about who she likes and dislikes. Sometimes Hope wonders if Teresa likes anyone. But Teresa's intuition is right about Mason. She smiles; she and Teresa are like the two faces of Janus. She bloody loves her sister though, loves all three of her sisters. Teresa would absolutely kill her if she found out about Dom and Mason. Yep, it's time to end it all. Come September and the start of the second year of her A-level courses, she needs to reinvent herself. Become more like Teresa, calm down a bit. Unlike Teresa, who's known what she wanted to be since talking almost, Hope has never known what she wanted to do when she *grew up*, not until the last few weeks. But now she does know and to attain the grades she needs to get into med school, she's going to have to knuckle down. No more arsing around being a bad girl. *The bad sister*, that's what Teresa calls her, but her twin always says the phrase with an indulgent smile.

She doesn't mean to hurt anyone, and the last person she wants to hurt is Eva – knowing she's her mother's favourite makes her feel ultra bad. She thinks back to the first time with Dom. They'd often go to Raven Island together; it was Dom who taught all the Keane girls to drive the motorboats, and he taught her to climb trees too. The first time had been the day when they'd been at the island sorting out the little log cabin and when he'd told her how to get to the top branch of the oak tree, which she still hasn't managed. She knew Dom liked her because of her tomboy tendencies; it was she who'd initiated it, if she's honest. And she might be many bad things but she's always honest – with herself, anyway. He'd brushed up against her and she'd felt his hardness. It all happened from there. Before she knew it they were on the mattress, him inside her. He came straight away. After that, they were both addicted. When did Mason happen? A few weeks later, although the first time with him wasn't in the cabin. That was in her bedroom. He'd come up to tell her lunch was ready. Libby was there that day too. It's probably what made it all so much more exciting. Mason knew she and Dom were a thing, because Mason knew everything about

Dom, and she suspected this turned him on even more. She and Mason never discussed it, but it was an unspoken agreement that Dom should not find out about her and Mason. And he hadn't. Obviously Eva shouldn't find out either.

Her screwing both men, though, is exhausting her. Not the fucking, but the secrecy.

With this thought she gets up, moves to the rear of the boat and casts off. Five minutes later she's at the island.

Half an hour after that, she's finally on the top branch of the tree, maybe sixty feet from the ground. And the calm summer morning seems to have changed in an instant.

The wind has gathered force and as if from nowhere the clouds have cluttered the sky. Dark clouds too. Ominous. As she looks down at her route back to solid land an unaccustomed feeling of fear wraps around her, as at the same time the leafy twigs on the branch nearest to her flog at her bare arm. The wind is strong.

She's achieved her aim of getting to the top branch, and now here she is beginning to wonder if she'll get down in one piece. She decides to wait for the micro-storm to die down. Mason'll be turning up soon. He's anal; he won't be late. He'll help her get down. She checks her watch. He's due in less than half an hour. Another blast of wind nearly unhooks her from her position; she's getting cold now too. How can the temperature have dropped so quickly? Bloody British weather.

She settles herself into the branch near the trunk and waits for Mason. And then the gushing rain starts. *Fucking* British weather.

Twenty minutes later and the wind is now brutal. She daren't budge from the spot. Where the fuck is Mason? She'll make a move. She turns around tentatively but as she does so another blast of air hits her and she loses her balance, and loses her grip too: she's falling. She grabs for the branch below and swings onto it, holding on for dear life.

Giving herself a minute to orientate herself, Hope pushes along the branch nearer to the tree trunk, stabilising her position, and looks upwards at the sky. God, it's pissing it down. She allows herself a grin. This is not how this morning was supposed to be. Anyway, at least she's nearer to the ground now. She looks across at the little cabin; the wind has ripped up one of the loose wooden boards of the tiny veranda, the one Dom said he's been meaning to fix for months.

Her line of vision moves to the left side of the building and she spots someone traipsing towards the small clearing, and her tree. Thank God. She really has frozen up here – both her skin and her ability to move; she just needs someone to talk her down. The person approaching is getting nearer, she realises, but because of the slanting rain she can't quite make out who it is. It must be Mason.

She peers down and she's about to shout to him.

But it is not Mason.

It's Eva.

Hope is completely disorientated and looks for Mason, who is surely with Eva, behind her. Her mother is supposed to be with her accountant and Eva can't drive a boat, and hates the water. Why has Eva come with Mason?

Her mother is about ten metres away from the tree and looking up at her. No Mason to be seen. He'd be more helpful in this situation, but just seeing her mum calms her and all thoughts of why she's there fall from her mind.

Her eyes dart away from Eva as she contemplates climbing down slowly – the wind has dropped now, and her confidence has come back. Although she is still a long way from solid ground. Eva is standing below her.

'Eva! So glad to see you. I'm stuck!' she shouts.

Eva's looking up, her arms folded, but she doesn't reply.

'Mum… what you doing here? I thought you were at the accountant's.'

'I could ask you the same question, Hope.'

'I came to climb the tree. Weather was gorgeous, then it changed.' And as if to reiterate her statement, another massive flow of turbulent air works its way across the island. She tightens her grip on the branch and leans forward, as if a few inches will make all the difference to Eva hearing her words. 'How did you get here?'

'On the motorboat.'

'You can't drive the boats…'

'I saw Mason at the jetty, Hope. I told him to fuck off home, back to his wife.'

Eva knows.

Despite shivering with cold, Hope feels sweat flooding her armpits, at the base of her spine and the palms of her hands. She tries to move her left hand and loses her balance, her right foot slipping. 'I need to get down, Mum.'

Eva tilts her head upwards a little more. 'I know about Dom. And Mason.' Her mother just looks at her. 'You little *slut*.'

Her foot slips again. 'I'm sorry,' she says, starting to feel a little desperate. 'I asked Mason to come here to tell him it's all over. Was going to tell Dom later too.' Again, she leans down and again the wind destabilises her. 'Mum, you have to get rid of Dom, he's no good for you, or us—'

'How *dare* you? How could you do this to me?'

'I'm sorry...' She can see Eva's face clearly now. She's never seen her mum look so angry, but then a flash of her own anger emerges. 'Like mother, like daughter, Eva? You cheated on Dad and he left us all, and now you've done the same to Dom.'

'You little shit, Hope.'

God, Eva really is mad with her. And the deep-seated angst that she really has done a terrible thing, and that she really is a bad girl, makes her forget her tenuous position forty feet above the ground. Simultaneously, and with this thought, a wave of wind hits the island and her tree, hard. She loses her grip.

The time it takes from branch to earth is an eternity.

The ground that breaks her fall also breaks her back.

It feels so long that she's been staring up at the sky, which is now totally clear of clouds. How odd. It's like the summer's day it had been when she'd climbed to the top branch a hundred million years ago. There's a raven flying high above, its black outline like an imprint against the impossibly blue sky. The bird is making its way towards her, wings flapping. Had Eva come to the island or had she imagined it? Was it Mason? Her eyes have closed and she feels something moving on her legs – her mother's hand or the bird, she isn't sure. Breath is eluding her, life is leaving her and all she can think about is her three sisters, especially Teresa, who has been by her side since before they were even born.

Teresa, Nat and Jess love her, but Eva does not and who, really, could blame her?

–

Eva touches her beloved daughter's leg. Moves the fabric of the impossibly short skirt so her upper thigh isn't exposed. Then she straightens up, turns and makes her way back to the motorboat, tears streaming down the flawed skin of her cheeks.

Acknowledgements

In many ways, and for various reasons, this book was both the easiest and hardest of novels to write. Ultimately, it is a story that encompasses female friendships, sisterhood, and truth, but as with many story ideas, although it began by taking one clear direction, it eventually found a different path. The end result is one of which I'm proud.

I suppose you could call this book my 'lockdown' novel, as it was written in the midst of that time, a period that I found very challenging. I like to think that those challenges added a layer of something special to the story. I hope so.

Thank you to my publisher, Canelo, my hardworking editor, Louise Cullen, and the rest of the publishing team, including my copy editor, Belinda. Again, as with *The Nurse*, the designer has knocked it out the park with the cover art.

A special mention too, to Leodora Darlington who in the early stages of the book's inception was so supportive.

My acknowledgements wouldn't be complete without mentioning my brilliant and incredibly patient agent, Camilla Shestopal. Thank you.

As usual, I owe big collective thank yous to my trusty beta readers: Emma Haughton, David Evans, Daniel Culver and Laura Wilkinson.

A special shout-out goes to Sarah (Essie) Fox who, in the midst of my writer angst, is always there for me and who, unfailingly, manages to say just the right thing, at just the right time.

I extend my gratitude, as always, to Paul Bacon, and Kam Chahal.

I couldn't have completed this story without the extensive help of HHJ Barbara Mensah who has been so giving of her time, and so generous with her advice.

A last nod of recognition goes to the River Thames that planted, so very firmly, the seed for this story idea.

As always, my gratitude to my family. You all rock.

JA